Overture

Overture

B.R. Storm

Copyright © 2020 by B.R. Storm

Revised Edition

Contents

	Acknowledgements	1
1.	Welcome Home	3
2.	Behind the Veil	25
3.	Examination of Mind	47
4.	Osmond Pyrrhal	61
5.	Introductory to Spells	85
6.	Hooch and Hypothesis	112
7.	Professor Goodall	140
8.	The Good Stuff	158
9.	Game Show for Secrecy	172
10.	Sun and Stars	187
11.	Survival of the Fittest	205
12.	With the Passage of Time	218
13.	Veil's Newest Inductee	235

14.	The Departure	*254*
15.	Foul Play and Fairies	*266*
16.	Alice, Where Art Thou?	*284*
17.	A Taste	*301*
18.	A Taste of Fear	*315*
19.	What Was and Is	*327*
20.	Under Threat of Determinism	*335*
21.	The Overture	*343*
22.	An Aftermath to Remember	*355*
23.	The Parting of Ways	*368*

ACKNOWLEDGEMENTS

To my most wonderful wife, Jessie. The production of this piece wasn't easy, as we faced many of life's uncertainties and various hardships. Your support through it all might be the only reason *The Infinity Series* ever got its start. Thank you for all that you are and for all that you had to put up with. I love you.

To my mother, for supporting an 11-year-old's dream since Day One. It took awhile, but at least we finally got one on the board.

Thank you, Julie Bradley of VeenaVieraVisuals. Your designs are amazing and I'm grateful to have you as a friend.

To Tim Marquitz of Dominion Editorial, for helping me evolve into something less of an amateur. I hope to work with you again soon.

To all other friends and family. Your support through this

entire adventure made all the stressful moments more bearable. No goal should be endured single-handed. Without support, an idol, and/or a drive to be more than what you are, how can you hope to be the next set of shoulders for those who would look up to you?

1

Welcome Home

The airplane screeched its way to a stop, and inevitability took charge for Collin. The flight from Minneapolis to Jacksonville was brutal. If you denied it, odds are you only did it for the pleasure of disagreeing with everything and everyone.

Yes, ladies and gentlemen, that was definitely one for the books, he thought, swinging his backpack onto his shoulders. He filed through the line of passengers and briefly smiled at the captain before stepping off. His expression fell flat after passing the man.

After all, it wasn't his fault for the half-a-dozen crying babies and toddlers, the overweight gentleman who snored uncomfortably as his gut overtook Collin's armrest, further cornering him into his window seat as a silent stream of flatulence gagged him between each bout of turbulence. Plus, the ride was entirely too cold, as they always were, despite having a long-sleeved shirt, a jacket, and jeans. Then his antique of an iPod decided to die prematurely, and he forgot his copy of *Salem's Lot* in Canada with his mom.

But to hell with it.

The flight was over, he was back home. He rolled the sleeves of his jacket to adjust for the July humidity of the Jacksonville heat when briefly transitioning from airplane to airport, then received a full-body slap from the oldest Floridian tradition of overcompensating with the A/C once inside.

Ignoring this, Collin pulled out his glasses, used more aesthetically than purposeful, and lengthened his stride. He turned on his iPhone and made sure to shoot a text saying he landed to his dad, who would be there to pick him up. Collin knew he would be sitting in some nearby parking lot, looking to save a few bucks instead of using the airport parking garage.

Lord knows the whiskey is more important, right?

He walked briskly from his gate to the exit, passing the entry restaurants, rocking chairs, grand piano, and plethora of people waiting to greet their loved ones. He soon passed the buffer zone and approached a strip composed of a ramp for the wheelchair-bound or luggage-draggers, half a staircase worth of steps, and an escalator equally small in height that you had to be the epitome of lazy to waste your time stepping on. He took the stairs. As he did, his phone vibrated in his hand.

Cool. Let me know when u have ur stuff, the alert said.

Collin didn't reply. He wondered if it made him a snob to think that short-cutting you, your, and you're was more for middle-school kids rather than middle-aged adults. Sure, it was convenient at times, but even with Collin turning eighteen in a few months, he could notice the attractiveness in people who text using proper grammar.

The walkway between baggage claim and security was the most appealing part of the airport, at least in Collin's opinion. The bright, white walls intermingled with windowpanes stacked above each other from the floor to the ceiling. The sunroof and metallic serpentine ornaments hanging above enhanced the natural lighting.

Unfortunately, the euphoric, down-to-earth stroll was brief, and he took the descending flight of steps toward baggage claim, wedged between a set of escalators. It was an enduring testament of the times to witness a head or two watch Collin in bemusement as he took the path of mild physical exertion, as opposed to being carried.

Throwing that moment into a mental folder titled *Why the World Hates Fat America*, he reached the bottom of the steps and strode over to his baggage terminal. There he paced back and forth for ten or so minutes before the buzzer announced it was time for everyone to grab their personal belongings. The crowd of families huddled close when the metal doors rose and the conveyor belt moved.

Over the last few years, Collin noticed a growing trend of people wrapping their suitcases in a common red and white tape, or strapping on some sort of flamboyant tassel to make them more noticeable along the assembly line of dark and bland colored carriers. However, last year it became *too* common of practice to the point where everyone had to check every tag to assure it was theirs.

Now people were picking up on the redundancy and started using distinctive suitcases instead. Occasionally, he'd witness full patterns of bright, motley flowers on a white background, Hello Kitty, zebra print, and the distinct black, gray, navy blue, and aqua blue camouflage. He figured in another year or two most people would pick up on this. Not him, though. If everyone moseyed on with the shifting trends, then over time keeping the same suitcase would work in his favor. At least that was the hypothesis.

His deep maroon suitcase with the ripped side-handle was escorted out from behind the wall in the order of ascending sizes. He lifted it off the belt and let his dad know he was heading outside to wait. Stepping past the automatic doors, Collin was greeted with ninety-degree heat and choking humidity, despite the setting sun. The goosebump-raising effect of the fading air conditioning paralleled that of a passionate affection for a lover fading into the remnants of an excruciatingly regretful parting of ways in the same amount of time it took to sneeze.

It got worse when the thick atmosphere fused with the puffs of cigarettes from other travelers waiting to be picked up. The station was setup with enough space for four cars to pass at a time. A median split the space in equal halves, dividing the crowd into those who had someone getting them and those who would be utilizing taxis.

The cacophony of sounds outside were as distracting as

they were inside. The purr of the engines of passing cars, the slamming of trunks and car doors, a handful of children playing in circles, the sliding open of the door behind Collin, the squawking of inland seagulls, and everyone talking. It was a concoction that seemed worse than it truly was due to an unruly day of flying. The sight of a child on a leash furthered his annoyance when he noticed the leash attached to a monkey-themed harness to seem more playful than neglectful on the parents' part.

Jesus, if people could hear my thoughts, they'd think I was the ritziest piece of shit.

He was fully aware he had the tendency to unintentionally rub people the wrong way. It had been a frequent debate in the back of his mind whether or not Collin would even like himself if he ever got a glimpse from the outside looking in. That didn't alter his belief that he might be the only person who saw society needing a little more sophistication and fewer armchair critics and easy fixes, but someone had to hold the fort down. If it made him an outcast here and there, then so be it.

If it made him seem like the most disgruntled teenager in all the land, then he would blare the older material of Panic! at the Disco, My Chemical Romance, and A Day to Remember until his ears bled. At least he had the decency to own his inability to change the world and keep his opinions more or less to himself. Before long, the glimmer of his dad's silver SUV caught his eye.

He stepped to the edge of the sidewalk to flag the vehicle

down. Jonathon Quinn braked at the curb before the speed bump that simultaneously served as a crosswalk into the parking garage, but didn't park. Collin swung open the back door, heaved his suitcase inside, slammed the door shut, and climbed into the front passenger seat.

"How was it?" his dad asked. He stole a brief, puffy glance at his son before using his sausage fingers to put the vehicle in Drive.

Collin knew the question was subtly directed toward the well-being of his ex-wife. Six years later and the man still used the divorce as a crutch to be a bitter, recliner-bound, alcoholic and the evermore victim. Even the pre-teen version of Collin could see his parents' marriage falling apart from a mile away. His dad was the kind of guy to always end his day with a rum and coke, even before Collin's time, but it was never an issue then. He never got belligerent, abusive, or overly frisky. It was simply something to take the edge off.

However, as how all drug abuses go, his dad's tolerance achieved a higher level of needs. It took a toll on their finances and love life as Collin's dad became the conductor of the denial train. He stopped working, using *overwhelming anxiety* as an excuse to tap into his social security funds prematurely and watch TV all day. It wasn't rocket science to see that Julia Quinn was pushed to her limits with trying to be supportive, so she moved to Canada after unsuccessfully trying to get Collin to come with her. Luckily, she got out when she did, because nowadays, in the short span of five hours, her now former husband developed the ability to go through nearly an entire handle. Collin learned to avoid it all by avoiding the man entirely.

But his mom wanted a new life, and did amazingly so in Toronto working as an editor for the *Tsubala* magazine publisher. The only reason Collin stayed in Florida was because his underdeveloped brain told the court during the custody battle his mom flew in for that he wanted to finish middle school and not leave his friends.

However, once he finished the eighth grade, most of his friends scattered in the winds of Jacksonville's nationally largest city limits. Afterwards, an internal struggle of being able to live with himself if he abandoned his father continued to anchor him to Florida. His mother wasn't too pleased. There were several tearful phone calls that went on for hours, but in the end, they came out with the closer relationship. That's when annual, and sometimes bi-annual, visits to Canada became a tradition.

"The trip was nothing unusual," Collin responded lamely. "Just the yearly routine of abusing Canada's healthcare with a dentist and eye appointment, then a bunch of sitting around doing nothing while Mom worked."

He usually informed his dad of his trip with disappointing connotations for the sole purpose of appeasing him. It was common practice that served as a win-win for him. He wouldn't have to deal with his dad being in a bitchy mood, and the honesty Collin shared with his mom about the matter kept their distant relationship sturdy enough that there weren't any more tearful phone calls.

His dad sniggered victoriously and didn't say another word for the duration of the ride. Instead, he increased the volume on the 80s radio station. After the day Collin had, the lack of human interaction was fine by him. He pulled out his cellphone as he witnessed his dad veering onto the highway. He had a list of friends to inform of his arrival.

One-by-one, he sent a text to Matt, Shawn, Tyler, Shannon, and Brittney. While he waited, he opened his email. He was set to get his SAT results tomorrow, but a part of him held onto the false hope of an early reveal during the waiting process. Those results would be his ticket away from home. What he would become from there lay the true mystery.

Collin had been commended several times on his mathematic ability, so fields like engineering or science weren't out of the question. He didn't feel tech savvy enough to consider a life in program coding or something of similar nature. Psychology and criminology sounded fun. Maybe he could study to become a detective. When he saw no email in his inbox, he checked the website to be equally disappointed.

His phone vibrated, but he ignored it. His right hand and phone were now tucked under his leg as he watched the billboard advertisements. Their journey was an otherwise mundane blur of passing facilities, vehicles, trees, and rubble.

Jacksonville was notorious for its endless construction projects. As soon as one project reached its halfway point another one started. Downtown was the worst. Collin sat on nearly two years' worth of driving experience, but there wasn't enough familiarity in the world to stop the heavy breathing and the steely tenseness he got when it came to riding through the heart of the city.

When his cellphone vibrated back-to-back with more replies, he withdrew the device and slid his thumb up the screen to activate Silence Mode before acknowledging the texts. He saw two identical texts welcoming him back and another suggesting getting their group together for a day. That wouldn't be a problem. Collin was the type of person who received his summer homework for AP English Literature and immediately space it out over a couple weeks so it was done early and with minimal stress. Plus, he was still young enough to reason not having a job, which left the remainder of his summer wide open.

He eventually texted his friends back and forth during the drive, while switching to Google searches of current events going on in the world, from conflicts in other countries, scientific progresses, and early hurricane activity in the Atlantic Ocean. He then checked his email again. Every day, multiple times a day, Collin obsessively sought the results of his SAT exam. He'd already compiled a list of schools for college. None of which worried him when it came to getting accepted. He had the grades, and his hours of volunteer work, in the form of tutoring math before and after school, broke triple digits. All that remained to seal the deal was his damn SAT score. True, he also took the ACT, and it served enough to place him above the eightieth percentile, but he wanted to be thorough.

He could stay local at the University of North Florida or keep it affordable at Florida State College at Jacksonville. Jacksonville University, albeit a private school, was *well* out of budget. There was the University of Florida out in Gainesville. It certainly had a good reputation as far as Florida schools go, but he wasn't after the atmosphere of football rivalry and parties. Then there was Flagler College. It was listed as a private school, but its tuition stood at tens of thousands of dollars cheaper than any other he saw. There were a few more options panned out, but he didn't have a final answer.

Not long after that, the car was pulling off onto the Old St. Augustine Road exit. Their awkward car ride would finally reach its conclusion. At the first set of traffic lights they stayed in the right-turn-only lane.

From there they rolled past the gas station, the Wendy's, the Winn-Dixie grocery store, and made the fourth available right turn into the junction with a Little Caesar's, a hair and nail salon, an Asian restaurant, and, of course, the liquor store. As small as the place was, it still had a drive-thru option his father favored, instead of the five-minute walk from their house. His doctors didn't warn the man about his weight for nothing.

"Seagram's Seven?" the Indian-American asked, when he opened drive-thru window and recognized Collin's dad.

"And a carton of Marlboro Gold," Mr. Quinn responded.

"Coke?"

"No."

Overture

Of all the types of places one could walk into and be recognized for ordering *the usual,* Collin got to be disappointed in his father for being publicly known for his drinking problem or, as the doctors would've put it, his alcohol dependency.

What a goddamn waste of a diagnosis, thought Collin.

Mr. Quinn paid in cash. For change, he stuck the bills in his wallet and pocketed the coins for when they got home. Next to the kitchen sink stood a large collection of coins inside a mason jar. Collin's dad hated having so many coins but never did anything with them.

One day, when the jar was nearly overflowing, Collin took the time to roll them. He figured it would be nice to have a little extra gas money from a source that was never going to be used otherwise, but as soon as he was done, his dad told him to leave the rolls on the counter and to not touch them.

Those coins would've sat there until the day your fat ass died, he had screamed internally.

Whatever. It was done and over with.

They pulled out from the liquor store and went to turn out from the same entry point they pulled into. When the oncoming traffic was spaced out sufficiently enough, the truck rolled forward in an arch directly into their neighborhood. A quick turn left onto Pathwood Way and their townhouse resided on the right.

Collin strapped on his backpack and heaved his trunk from the back of the SUV while his dad unlocked the front door. His dad walked into the house, pulled out a single pack of cigarettes, grabbed his lighter, and walked back outside as Collin edged around him. The distinct *smack, smack, smack* of the packet beat against his swollen beer gut as Collin lifted his suitcase up the two-part staircase past the kitchen and to the left.

His room stood at the nearest of the steps and to the right. Once inside, it was nice to see it cleaned the way he left it. The curtains were drawn shut, the bed made, the dresser at the foot of the bed remained dust-free for the two weeks he was gone. He imagined the worst thing to happen to his room *might* be a little ring of settled water around the toilet bowl. Coming home to a clean domain was more than anyone could ask. After that, he couldn't care less. He flung his backpack off his shoulder, laid the suitcase in the middle of the floor before flopping on his bed.

He melted into the chestnut-colored comforter. The events of that day gradually shoved their way to the back of his mind as his irritable mood slowly scrubbed clean. A knot he was unaware of in his chest loosened. All that remained was to feel sanitary.

After a good five minutes of laying still, he forced himself up and leaned over for the PlayStation controller and TV remote. He opened his video streaming account on Netflix and turned on the *How I Met Your Mother* sitcom for background noise. His own TV was only one of the major contributions to his ultimate Den of Introversion. Lord knows he had the type of introversion that could kill a college frat party if he put some elbow grease into it.

Starting from the bedroom door, any guests would see a small, but full bathroom to their immediate left, a bookcase next to the bathroom door stacked with your teenage classics of a tattered collection of *Harry Potter, The Inheritance Cycle, The Hunger Games,* and *A Series of Unfortunate Events.* Then he owned the more adult-oriented books, such as *The Lord of the Rings, A Song of Ice and Fire,* and a bunch of Stephen King novels. After that, there were the more timeless classics: *The Great Gatsby, East of Eden, The Alchemist,* a collection of *Sherlock Holmes, Huckleberry Finn, A Brave New World,* and a collection of Shakespeare's works.

That was just the tip of the iceberg. Of course, Collin also hadn't gotten around to reading every single book, but it was a goal of his to have at least four of the five shelves read during his senior year of high school, so long as he didn't miss his yearly revisiting of the *Harry Potter* novels.

After observing the bookshelf, Collin then owned a set of dumbbells adjustable between five pounds and ninety-five pounds. He then owned a workout chair that could incline and decline. He might not be the top athlete at school, but it didn't mean he wasn't rocking some above-average definition in his physique. An hour a few times a week was all it took.

He needed to make sure he ordered healthy meals when his dad took them out. Eating clean was next to impossible with their pantry of canned ravioli, macaroni and cheese, ramen noodles, canned cheese and crackers, breakfast pastries, and all other unhealthy foods to complement his dad's unhealthy lifestyle.

Finally, after the books and the workout equipment, Collin could add jigsaw puzzles, his laptop, and his PlayStation to his repertoire of reasons why the only need he had for leaving his bedroom was for food or occasional fresh air. He had no desire to spend his day doing nothing but watching TV from the moment his dad woke from eleven AM to midnight.

Collin checked his phone and saw Shannon sent him a text asking what he was up to. Included in her question was a winking emoticon.

About to hop in the shower. You? he wrote, matching her wink.

Shannon and he never surpassed foreplay, not to insinuate that either of them were virgins. They killed that delusion quickly. Truthfully, they never had much time during school. He was dead set on raising his weighted GPA of 4.4, and she held a position in the workforce and had a loving family that frequented constant functions. Their free times rarely overlapped. The only time they could get in the same room together was during classes or events with their friends

Same here. Be right back. Have fun, was the text he got back. Included was a picture she took, posed in front of a mirror in her bra and panties. Collin's pants flinched with arousal as he tossed his phone onto the bed.

He unzipped his luggage and pulled out Ziploc bags of toiletries and folded boxers, sweatpants, and socks.,The clothes tossed in disarray were fated for the dirty hamper. For no reason at all, he sporadically felt annoyed at himself for forgetting *Salem's Lot.*

There's bound to be a PDF online, he reasoned. It wasn't like his mom would refuse to mail it back to him. With a quick shake of his head he shifted his thoughts as his slacks grew tighter.

He took notice of the few streaks of purple that still stained the otherwise black sky as he entered the bathroom. Half a pace and there was the toilet. Turn ninety degrees to the left there was the wall-length mirror. Ninety degrees to the right was the bathtub.

He pulled the shower knob and twisted it towards the hot zone. As the water warmed, he stripped off his clothes and briefly observed his reflection. Running his fingers through his dark brown, fringed hair as he turned around, he slid back the curtain and started his shower.

His lower body was clothed by the time he finished. The final touches required his favorite charcoal gray jacket and a pair of running shoes he retrieved from the suitcase. Shannon hadn't said anything else as he pocketed his phone. That was fine.

Collin crept his door open and closed it quietly. Downstairs, his father was ranting to the TV about the "pussification of America," as he watched Fox News. It was awkward leaving his room in the evening. Collin felt more like a squatter than a resident of his own home, making going outside all the more rewarding. The brief trip toward the front door was the annoyance. He stepped lightly on the stairs. As he did, he noticed the inebriated overbite and glazed eyes shifting between the TV and himself.

Jesus, it's hardly been an hour.

"Where are you going?" his dad demanded.

No trace of a slur yet, believe it or not, but that tone never failed to bring his blood to a low boil. He was a prisoner, reprimanded for something that should've been nothing. The true annoyance was how his dad asked this every time Collin retrieved his keys from the kitchen counter. Literally. *Every. Single. Time.* The answer was always the same; it wasn't like he was going out partying in his sweats.

"Just a walk around the neighborhood."

His dad grunted and surrendered his attention back to the news.

Fuck you, too. Collin mentally rolled his eyes. He was so happy to only have one year left of high school, then he could be free of his environment and taste life away from feeling like a burden. This night, like every night, he couldn't help but wonder what his life could've been like if he moved with his mom. It was obviously too late to go back on his decision, but Christ how he begged for there to be more than this.

He locked the door behind him and stuck the keys in the opposite pocket of his cellphone. By now the sky was entirely black. The neighborhood was illuminated by streetlamps. Thankfully the heat was much milder and the air thinner.

He made a right at the first corner of his path. The area of townhouses he lived in, deemed *The Junction*, was a loop. There was an inner sidewalk with houses looped around a pond and an outer sidewalk with houses on the other side of Pathwood Way, Windtree Drive East, Windtree Drive South, and Shady Glen Drive.

Unknown to Collin as to why, but the only time he ever saw people outside was when the sun was set, and only when the police paid frequent visits to two houses caddy-cornered to each other. He didn't linger for an explanation. All he knew was he saw the red and blue blinking lights at least twice a week. Not tonight though.

An entire lap took roughly four minutes. By his second time around he noticed the neighborhood cats were nowhere to be found, and there were typically a *ton* of them. There was one house in particular where you would find about a dozen Occupying all the nooks and crannies of the property.

Maybe they're just sleeping early, he figured.

By the end of his fourth lap, he pulled out his phone to see that Shannon asked if he was free to hangout that Saturday.

As far as I know, he typed. *What'd you have in mind?*

He saw she was typing back right away, but got distracted by the fearsomely loud hiss of a cat ironically confirming their presence in the neighborhood. Looking around, he recalled how he'd been woken multiple nights by the shrieking of territorial squabbles. The hiss quieted, but quickly became a scream of pain he never heard. It got cut off midway.

Collin inched his next step forward. He was already approaching the halfway mark in the loop and figured he'd see it all the way through. The sudden dead silence of the night trailed chills down his spine and arms. His pace quickened. Coming around a bend, he noticed an object in the middle of the road that wasn't there his last four laps. The streetlamp ten paces away was out. Shattered actually. The faint light of the next lamp over was the single source of illumination from the only cul-de-sac in the community.

Edging around its shadows, Collin could've sworn he caught a glimpse of movement, but whoever it was must've been wearing dark clothing. The only giveaway was a sideways glance at what couldn't possibly be their face, but it's where the human face would've otherwise been. It was blurry, but there was no mistaking the elongated shape protruding nearly a foot long.

Collin shrunk back and bent over, hoping to stay out of sight. He hid behind the corner of a tall picket fence, trying to see through the gaps of wood. The person, or *whatever* the hell he saw, turned around for a distorted shot. The head bobbing in midair looked more like a skull.

A mask maybe? There was no way a human head could be disfigured that outwardly.

His throat tightened and his stomach burrowed deeper inside of himself. His adrenaline spiked to the point of trembling. Seeing this mysterious person and hearing the cat's cry in such a small window of a time caused Collin to make assumptions.

What in the actual fuck is wrong with people?

He stole a glance at the object in the road in front of him. A dark patch encircling the lump expanded. When he looked back a second later the person was gone. A few glances over his shoulders let him know he was safe from any horror movie clichés. He turned his back to the fence but continued crouching. The hairs on his arms raised as silence intensified. Time itself seemed to stop.

Seconds, or minutes, passed with each blink of an eye. The shaking wore off as he planned his way home. He could run back the way he came or he could go through the blackness to his left, through somebody's backyard, around the pond, and to his house. However, his sudden fear of the dark eliminated that idea. Instead, he peeked around the fence and saw the area remained deserted. A part of him still wanted to satisfy his curiosity with the unknown object.

He inched out slowly, eyes darting in every direction. It took a whole minute to cover four strides. His eyes were relatively adjusted to the dark by now. The outline of a head, mangled body, legs, and a tail were clear. Switching on the flashlight of his phone helped fill in the missing details.

It was a declaration of the desensitizing powers of gruesome TV shows and other media that Collin could stare at the desecrated animal swimming in a pool of its blood and be fine. It made more sense to be frightened by a confrontation with its killer. The fresh odor of iron attached itself to his nostrils and lingered on his tongue. Upon examination, the cat's head was crushed in with a clean cut from its throat to its belly. The rib cage had been cracked open. Most of the organs were either missing or had bite marks.

Collin's vision blurred as bile brewed in his stomach. He

stepped away. This wasn't the right time or place for someone to see him there, but before he could get any further, he was brought back into focus with a swift *click,* a short yelp, and a *thud* from the house in front of him. A woman ran into view of the kitchen window.

Shit, shit, shit.

He intended to turn left and run, but everything happened quicker than his body could register. A black blur rushed her and cracked her head on the wall hard enough for a stream of blood to splatter the window. The creature became still enough for Collin to recognize it wasn't some skull kid this time. It bent over the woman and took a bite or two out of her. It chewed sloppily and swallowed the flesh before catching sight of the blood on the window. It pressed its hands onto the glass, lapping it up like a dehydrated canine. Seven licks in and its and Collin's eyes locked.

Terror-stricken, Collin could actually feel the pigment of his skin growing pale as blood conglomerated to his organs. He mouth was as dry as sucking on a cotton ball as a chilled clamminess consumed him. Taking a bad step, his shoe slipped into the pool of cat's blood. That was all it took.

The creature in the window didn't break the window it was licking. Instead, it took the less noisy route and pelted out the front door. It was massive, easily seven feet tall. Maybe taller. From its head to its toes, its legs occupied about two-thirds of its height. Each of the five toes fanned out wider than a human's foot. Its arms hung lankily from its hunched shoulders, fingers extending three times the average person's. All four of its extremities were bone thin. The only hint of muscle tone was found in its quadriceps.

Its midsection was equally anorexic. Around the naval, the skin was stretched tight from starvation. There was a bony bump where the genitals would've been. The upper portion gave the creature a rounded V-shape. The rib cage sticking out had barreled arches. Its shoulders rolled forward.

The face was more rounded, also. The neck bent with a forward-head posture. Its beady eyes stared hungrily at Collin, shrunken into the skull. Nostrils were slits. The corners of its mouth extended past both eyes. Oversized canines made the rest of the teeth visible, protruding from the upper jaw to nearly the chin, or lack thereof. A string of drool hung from its mouth. It twitched every couple of seconds, struggling between striking instinctively and restraining.

Its skin was a decaying-gray and hairless, with periodic scar tissue depicting the mosaic of the beast's wild conquers. Collin detected the familiar scent of piss one could find when crossing paths with a homeless person.

Or musk? Fucking hell, I'm dead!

He wasn't a huntsman by any means, but he always heard of the raw musky scent having a rank, pungent odor. The concoction was nauseating, almost paralyzing. Although, the fear that gripped him may have been equally so. He would later assume it would be a good predator mechanism, but for now he couldn't even process a flight-or-fight response. Death was inevitable.

The creature took one step forward. A second step

forward. It bared its teeth and flared its nostrils. It was sniffing Collin head to toe. A low rumble emanated from its throat, but it never attacked him.

A second growl could be heard in the distance at the exact time Collin felt a magnetic pull on him. The force withdrew him backwards and sprawled onto the sidewalk before rendering him motionless. Stars appeared in his vision after his head collided with concrete.

"Don't move!" yelled an unknown man.

The source ran past him, accompanied by more strangers. How many more, he couldn't tell.

"You think it'd be easier to knock him out?" a second voice asked.

"*I* do. He's coming with us, one way or another," answered a third.

The third speaker stood over Collin. He couldn't make out a face. Hell, he couldn't make heads or tails of the situation. It was soon irrelevant, after being put under.

2

Behind the Veil

When he came to, he found himself strapped to a wooden office chair. His head too woozy to fully comprehend. It was like coming out of an anesthesia-induced sleep. Even weirder, there weren't any ropes or cords restraining his still body. Whatever bound him must be the same invisible force that earlier held him to the ground. The sensation was so familiar, his mind temporarily believed he was still in his neighborhood before the lag caught up.

Six desk lamps surrounded him, illuminating the tables on which they rested. Around him were walls of bookshelves stretching floor-to-ceiling. The age of their pages blended with the smell of…

Biscuits?

Collin sniffed earnestly. Not many things could top the scent of Pillsbury.

"Go get Ms. Glenda," a male whisper carried from the corner of the room.

Footsteps echoed off the wooden flooring. Collin's vision

grew lighter. An outlined figure leaned cross legged against one of the desks.

"Hey, hey, hey," the stranger said softly, kicking off and heading toward him. "You don't have to worry. You're restrained, but I promise you have nothing to worry about. Glenda will be here soon, and she'll clear it all up and you can be on your way."

He bent level with Collin, his green eyes genuine in the dim lighting. His thick, black hair covered his forehead. His pointed chin was pulled into a sympathetic smile.

"Where…" Collin grew nervous; his heartbeat growing quicker as a mental flash of the beast raced across his mind. "That thing…"

"Gone. It'll be explained shortly."

Sure enough, seconds later, a brisk pace clomped from the hallway.

"Give him room, give him room, Oscar," a stout woman entered the room.

The boy bent next to him, Oscar, got to his feet and resumed his position at the desk he was leaning against. A second boy came in from behind the woman Collin guessed was Glenda and stood next to Oscar. From their distance, and with the only lighting being from lamps, one could believe they were twins. They had similar black hair and stature, but the finer features were blurred.

As Glenda stood before Collin, he became fully conscious and could make out most of her features. She had a bit of a paunchy build filling out her maroon, batwing top and denim jeans. The age of her face suggested late forties with her prominent wrinkles and the firmness of her skin slightly loosed. Her wavy, dirty blonde hair hung an inch or two past her shoulders. Her bluish-gray eyes were unique. They told two stories. One involving a woman who loved her family more than life itself, with no limitations of blood relations, and a second story of a woman who would burn your whole world to the ground if you ever interfered with said family.

Her lips curled in a reassuring smile as she laid her right fist in front of Collin, grasping at air. She loosened her grip as she raised her hand, as if letting go of something. As she did, the unseen restraints around Collin lifted. He wiggled his left arm to be sure, but never left his seat.

"I'm sorry, Mr. Quinn," she said. "Can never hurt to have a little extra precaution with strangers in your home."

Awkward silence pursued. The second boy sniggered in the background. For a brief moment, Collin's head grew woozy once more, not as an effect of any sedative, but as a result of his brain struggling to make sense of this odd breakthrough in reality. He'd just been under the influence of something mystical and his confrontation with the monster was no easy feat to assimilate into his mental schema either. He was caught between the fleeting sensation of a dream and the crude realization he, and the majority of humanity, had been left in the dark about a lot of things.

"You probably have a good amount of questions?" Glenda asked.

"A few."

He didn't know where to begin. Acknowledging what happened was difficult. Asking what the hell was going on held the potential to confirm his insanity. Then again, he would have free reign to go psycho if these people were part of his delusions.

"What you did with your hands…" Collin trailed, but never finished his sentence. Magic would be an easier path than monsters. He was raised watching shows and reading books about it. Not that he hadn't about monsters, but magic seemed the lighter topic.

"Small spellcasting," Glenda said plainly. "Or binding spellcasting. There are different branches of casting: elemental, telematic, wayfaring, physical, medical, status, battle, and defensive for starters."

She took a step back and raised her hands. Her fingers bent uncomfortably in some finger-tutting performance. A spherical, marble paperweight flew into her left hand as a result. With her other hand, she continued her performance. The paperweight melted to the floor with no sign of heat. When every drop puddled onto the carpet, she cast something to make the liquid reform into its solid state and levitate back to its place on the desk. Oscar and the other boy gave a round of sarcastic applause, hoots, and hollers.

"Oh, hush, you two," she scorned. "The food is all done. Go finish setting the table, we'll be right there."

They both left obediently, clapping all the way down the hall.

"How did you…"

"A good amount of time, practice, and patience, unfortunately," she laughed sadly. "Nothing I would get your hopes up over."

Collin's hopes were already up. Recent transgressions past, he wondered if his down-to-earth blood and bones could manufacture such make-believe. Surely the dim lighting hid whatever gave off the special effects.

"Come on now. It's a little late, but some of our other members will be appreciative of a small meal when they're off duty."

Collin stayed in his seat until she stood waiting in the doorway. He gingerly got to his feet when she looked over her shoulder and gave him a scornful smirk.

"You don't have to eat if you don't want to, but we can't have you wandering around unsupervised. You either come with us or stay restrained in the chair."

"Right," Collin moved slowly toward her.

"Good." She continued walking.

With each step, the dreamlike sensation faded. When he stood in the same spot he last saw her, he gripped the doorframe and peeked into the hallway. There were four closed doors to the left and a bend at the end. To his right, he caught a quick glimpse of Glenda turning left near the door at the entryway into what he assumed was the dining room, or the kitchen. In both directions, the hall was lined with wall sconces. The walls were painted beige to complement the wood flooring only partially noticeable underneath the red and gold runner rug.

Collin could hear the sounds of clattering glassware and playful banter. Holding his breath to hear, his name soon became encompassed within the cocktail party effect, but nothing else was comprehensible. He quickly stepped out of the office to appear as though he were making an effort to join them for dinner. The last thing he needed in this bizarre situation was to anger the people who could melt stone at will.

Step by step, he got closer to the ornate front door. The material was a deep mahogany with four tempered panes of glass forming a circle, divided like a pie chart in math class. Reaching the edge of concealment from the dining room, Collin heard the lock on the brass doorknob click shut.

"Come on in here, darling. It's all right," said Glenda.

"Yeah. We don't bite," Oscar teased.

"Unless you ask us to, of course," the second guy chimed in.

"Clark!" Glenda barked with a soft swap of the wooden spoon in her hand before sinking it into a bowl of mashed potatoes.

Collin fought to keep the corners of his lips from curling into a smile while Oscar didn't bother holding back. It was apparent Glenda wasn't overly flustered by the comment. The two of them standing together with their mischievous grins gave the impression of a comedic duo who could make improvisation seem so thoroughly effortless. They no doubt gave Glenda a run for her money in the patience department.

"I'm sorry," said Glenda. "We haven't properly given our

introductions. My name is Glenda Goodall. These two are Oscar Blair," she pointed to the one who first spoke to Collin when he was under restraint, "and Clark McLachlan. And no, there's not a drop of relations between them, despite their appearances."

"That you know of," said Clark.

"After all, this is the South. We could very well share some cousins or brothers and sisters down the road," added Oscar.

Mrs. Goodall rolled her eyes and uncovered the biscuits from the cloth lining a wicker basket. Getting a better view of Clark and Oscar in the brighter room, Collin could see that, despite the reassurance of them not being related, it was only the small details distinguishing them apart. Clark had blue eyes, while Oscar had green. Clark had more of a bulb nose, while Oscar's was more refined. Clark's cheekbones were slightly higher and Oscar's jawline was mildly more pronounced. Hell, Clark's earlobes were detached, but Oscar's were joined. Otherwise, they shared the same height, same messy black hair covering most of their eyebrows, same thin frame, and even similar attire of jeans and a dark shirt.

"Or we could agree there's only a finite number of DNA combinations."

"Right!"

Mrs. Goodall gave a slight chuckle. Looking around the room, Collin noticed eight black, glass plates laid with paired silver cutlery and glasses, despite there only being four of them. Clark must've read Collin's mind when he noticed him taking stock.

"Taylor, Olivia, and Alice should be joining us pretty soon. They're putting the finishing touches on clean-up duty. The eighth dish is for Ms. Glenda's hubby."

"Sit wherever you'd like, dear," said Mrs. Goodall.

"Except at the heads of the table, or," Clark gestured to the left corner facing the back of the room, "that seat. Alice can get a little weird about that sort of thing."

Mrs. Goodall silently agree and sat at the head of the table closest to the entryway where Collin stood. He moved inside and chose the seat next to the forbidden corner. The dining table was a deep cherrywood extending roughly ten feet with clawfoots for legs. The boarder was ornately carved with no particular design, just swirls. The chairs shared a similar design. It looked brand new. Collin figured they either cared more about this table than any sane person or they kept it in perfect condition with maintenance by magic. Covering the length of the table was a black centerpiece mat with three candles spread out, five dangling wine glasses, and salt and pepper shakers on each end. Above it all hung a crystal chandelier and near the end of the table, opposite of Mrs. Goodall, was a window adjacent to another door leading into the kitchen. It was pitch black outside without a hint of a streetlamp.

Once tucked in, Collin saw dinner consisted of mashed potatoes, biscuits, collard greens, a garden salad, green beans, and two rotisserie chickens. Each still in the telltale black, plastic bottoms of the precooked Publix chickens. For drinks there were pitchers of water and sweet tea and a bottle of corked cabernet sauvignon. Clark and Oscar took their seats on each side of Mrs. Goodall and took turns pouring their selves water. Mrs. Goodall went for the wine.

"We won't worry about making you wait on ceremony," she said between sips. "Feel free to dig in. Sorry the chicken isn't home cooked. Things have been a little hectic lately."

Collin was hesitant to eat. If the chicken was the only thing not homemade, Mrs. Goodall did a damn good job with dinner, no matter how late it was. He looked to each of them for any sign of deceit.

Oscar, sitting on the other side of the table, took the task of assuring him it wasn't poisoned. He snagged a biscuit and took a theatrically large bite out of it before setting it on his plate. Clark took a large scoop of mashed potatoes and ripped off a chicken leg, chomping into it, and laying it atop the heap to save space. The obviousness of their performance was comedic to Collin. He followed suit with setting his plate. Not having a big taste for the Southern tradition of collards, but not wanting to be rude, he made sure he had a small portion of everything.

"I know what you're thinking," said Oscar, after a moment's silence of everyone building their plates. "We're not the most progressive bunch."

"We're probably the focal point of white, straight protagonism," added Clark. "But it gets more diverse the farther you branch out, sexually and ethnically. Promise."

"Especially in South Florida."

"Um, actually," Collin started shyly. "May I ask what time it is?"

Pulling his phone from his pocket, Clark informed him it was a quarter past nine. Seeing the phone did two things: it reminded Collin to pat the pockets of his sweatpants and jacket, only to find them empty, and caused Mrs. Goodall to jump to her feet exclaiming she'd forgotten something. She bustled out of the room and returned a minute later holding Collin's phone and keys.

"Sorry about that, dear," she apologized. "Just another precaution. We usually try to distance ourselves from outsiders as much as possible."

"Outsiders?"

"Outsiders of Veil," said Clark.

The clunk of Mrs. Goodall shoe jamming into Clark's shin was audible with a sharp look thrown his way.

"What? It won't matter anyways."

The two exchanged a look eluding an unsaid understanding between them. Mrs. Goodall's expression lightened from fury to a minor annoyance.

"What's Veil?" Collin asked.

A second awkward silence occurred within the same minute. Oscar stared at his plate and kept eating. He knew perfectly well Clark was the one who got the ball rolling on the topic. He wasn't going to risk upsetting Mrs. Goodall any further. Clark on the other hand kept staring motionless at his own plate, his eyes only moving to glance at Mrs. Goodall.

Mrs. Goodall must've been settling an internal debate with how much information to divulge.

"Veil –" she started to say, but before she could, the front door opened and the sound of two voices rung into the dining room. Three faces emerged.

Standing in the entryway, a surly, short-haired male, no more than five years Collin's senior, glanced into the room, saw Collin, glared, and trudged off. A girl entered into the room looking as happily exhausted as one could. Her face was tired, but her movement was graceful with each buoyant step and each swing of her hips. The first thing Collin noticed was the thin but curvy frame of her body. He became self-conscious about how he was wearing nothing but sweatpants and no shirt under his jacket. His seventeen-year-old hormones told him she was definitely fantasizable material, if he even survived this mysterious ordeal. Her face was similarly attractive. She had bright brown, California eyes to match her wavy blonde hair and olive skin. Her cute, softly perky nose sat above her natural, rosy-red lips. Either her makeup skills were on point or she had perfect cheekbones to accent her square face.

"How did it go, Olivia?" Mrs. Goodall asked the girl.

"Manageable," she replied, making herself at home to a seat next to Clark and piling a salad and a chicken breast onto her plate. "But it won't hurt to keep a watch over the area."

"I was wondering the same. Clark and Oscar, would you mind, since the others dealt with the containment?"

"Abtholuteyee," Oscar mumbled with a mouthful of biscuit.

"Thank you, and Liv," Mrs. Goodall noticing Olivia's eyes laying on Collin with a look as curiously penetrating as Clark's and Oscar's were mischievous, "this is Collin Quinn, our guest for the evening."

"The boy who came face to face with a wendigo and lived," Olivia said with a tone of exaggerated surprise.

Total bitch, Collin mentally established. She might be hot as all hell, but the immediate personality conflict had him rethinking his last assessment.

While this conversation was happening, a third person, another girl, stood stiffly in the doorway and stared at Collin uncomfortably sitting in the chair next to hers. She was scrawny. Her thin frame reminded him a lot of the track and field girls at his school, whose excessive participation of cardio left their body fat content low enough to the point of flat-chested emaciation. She had straight, brown hair styled in the long bob. Skeptical blue eyes stared at the floor as she strode around the table and pulled out her chair.

Collin was vaguely aware she may have settled herself in it a little more toward the corner of the table, rather than directly next to him. She didn't say a word. It was difficult to tell if she was cripplingly shy or if her level of introversion outweighed Collin's. Either way, based on Clark's warning of not occupying the seat she sat in, he figured she must be Alice.

"What's that?" Collin asked, turning his attention back to Olivia.

"A wendigo? The tall beasty thing?" she answered his questions with more questions. She eyed Mrs. Goodall. "Did you already do it?"

Mrs. Goodall shook her head. "I was under the impression Taylor would have some questions beforehand. I don't know why he left."

Olivia *mmm'd* before turning her attention back to Collin. "A wendigo is a creature created when a human eats another human's flesh."

"But they're usually found in the northern, cooler, more wooded areas," Oscar chimed in. "Which is what makes this situation a little out of the ordinary, and why Taylor was hellbent on bringing Collin."

Collin knew there was nothing ordinary about wendigos, but he hadn't expected that. His heart raced again with anxiety for being an outsider.

"'A little out of the ordinary?'" Clark grinned, turning to Collin. "Dude, it's the biggest off season since the Dirty Thirties. It's friggin' chaos out there. New York, Los Angeles, Vancouver, Toronto."

"Stop," interjected Mrs. Goodall the same second Collin perked up. The power of respect she held with each member in the room was unparalleled. She placed her fork and knife on each side of her plate and gave Collin a sympathetic look. "Veil is an organization officially established in the early 1700s to protect people from wicked things. Monsters and magic are real, but as the name suggests, we veil the truth from the general public. If everyone knew monsters walked the earth there would be mass panic, and if everyone knew magic was real, then everyone would be looking for magical fixes and demanding access to it. Even worse, we sometimes get members of Veil who decide to go their own way and cause trouble for us on top of everything else."

"How do you go unnoticed?" Collin asked. He broke eye contact long enough to watch a biscuit zoom out of its basket and onto Clark's plate.

"We don't," she answered. "Much like you, people are always in the wrong place at the wrong time, but Veil makes sure every member masters memory-altering spells even in their elementary courses. That way we don't leave behind any knowledgeable witnesses."

Collin's heart sunk halfway in his chest. As nervous as he was to be dragged into this world, he struck gold having his reality shattered with each spoken word. Flashes of the beast echoed in his mind. The hair on his arms stood. Shivers of fear and thrill entwined as they chilled his spine.

Would it be possible to leave this place with my memories intact? Did they make exceptions?

Joining them hadn't crossed his mind, but when he recognized that intricate fact, he knew exactly what Mrs. Goodall meant by the general public wanting magical fixes. Knowing all this was out in the world was terrifyingly seductive.

"So, when I leave…"

"Unfortunately," was all Mrs. Goodall needed to say as confirmation.

"Then why bring me here?"

"Totally Taylor's doing," smirked Olivia, flipping her hair over her shoulder. "Wendigos are ruthless. They smell a human, they eat the human. Zero middle ground."

Memories of the quick *click*, yelp, and *thud* were remembered. Mental images of the woman running and the blur of her killer moving indistinguishably fast flooded Collin's mind with the splattered blood. "But it didn't kill me," he said to no one.

"Bingo!"

"So, what? Does Taylor think he's a Variant?" asked Clark.

Olivia shrugged. "Might not find out though. You know how he gets –"

"When he doesn't get to be the one doing the interrogating?"

"When he isn't the one who kills the beasts?" continued Oscar.

"When he stubs his toe?"

"When his fingers get pruney?"

"When he breathes the wrong oxygen molecule?"

"Boys!" yelled Mrs. Goodall. Silence fell and she continued. "Despite what happened, I'm sure there's no reason to suggest he's a Variant. If I had known Collin was going to be sent here, I would've advised against it."

"Have fun telling him that," Oscar mumbled with a full mouth. "Thing's have been so off-kilter, he swears that seeing what we saw with Collin is another sign. Its hesitation in killing suggests that whatever is afoot may include our guest."

"Preposterous," Mrs. Goodall huffed.

Collin was dying to ask what a Variant was, but he no longer wanted the topic of discussion being centered on him.

"What about my dad?" he asked. "He'll notice I've been gone this long."

"We've already taken care of it," assured Olivia. She smiled before taking a mouthful of salad and talking ungracefully between chews. "He's…asleep in his chair…he won't…remember you…being out for so long." You could see the conservative lumps of food stored in her cheeks like a chipmunk between words, but her display felt blatantly purposeful.

The mental image of his dad asleep in his armchair was nothing new. If the clean-up crew were genuine, they would've made sure the television was left on, too. No matter, the longer Collin sat with them the more he didn't want to forget any this. This was the moment of a lifetime. A part of their world or not, to have this knowledge snatched away and be forced to seeing life once again as a forevermore monotony made him more terrified.

"What if…" He choked. Everyone stared at him in silence. They were clearly giving him the opportunity to finish. "What if…I…didn't…have my memory erased?"

The sympathy in Mrs. Goodall's expression turned to pity. This must not have been the first time she would have to break someone's heart with the inescapable fact of the matter.

Or the last, Collin figured.

"I'm afraid it's not permitted," she told him. "Veil is very strict on these things. We get these requests too often, and one of the first rules is to have all members be at least eighteen."

"I'm not that far away from eighteen," the words blurted at the slightest hint of a chance.

The inevitability of the situation was coming full front. Collin lowered his silverware and slowly inched toward his pants pocket for his keys. If only he could leave a trace of this moment before they wiped his memory, maybe it would conflict with the effects of the spell.

"I'm sorry, Collin," said Mrs. Goodall dismally. "I know this would've been easier if you hadn't been brought here."

Collin could hear a mousy *hmm* from his left. It sounded as though Alice was absentmindedly saying "told you so" to no one in particular. Glancing out the corner of his eyes, Collin was glad she was paying more attention to her dinner than to anything else, but as his fingers gingerly rubbed the teeth of his keys, he knew there would be no subtlety next to Oscar. Maybe if he could get away it would be easier to write himself a message on his phone.

"But," Mrs. Goodall continued, "as it happens, you won't be returning home tonight. I must agree that, given the atmosphere of things, it's too coincidental to follow regular procedure." Her furrowed brows eased sympathetically. She sighed deeply in acceptance.

"What're you thinking then?" Clark asked, his and Oscar's eyes widening.

Collin was confused with the direction of where this was leading. His heart skipped a nervous beat at the prospects of what the next words might be. It took a minute, but after what felt like much longer, Mrs. Goodall finally spoke.

"Ward up one of the rooms in the basement. I'll see if we can't get Paul to give him a look over tomorrow."

"Surely the basement is a bit much!" Clark said incredulously.

"It's *just* for tonight," Mrs. Goodall assured him calmly.

"Yeah, but the *basement?*"

She pursed her lips in doubt, but stood by her guns. As long as she served as the stewardess of the facility, she was determined to make sure no harm came to her people. No matter how slight the odds.

Oscar appeared to be just as flabbergasted by this news. He clearly wanted to argue, but understood the peculiarity of the situation. Everyone rose with Mrs. Goodall, save for Collin, who stood shortly after. Alice was hostile with her quick cast of a spell forcing his hands immobile by his sides. He couldn't even swing his arms as Alice guided him from behind as the others tread into the hallway.

"Everything will be okay, dear. No harm will come to you. It's only for a night. Please understand."

Collin knew he should understand. He nodded in agreement all the same, but it would've been nice to at least finish his meal.

They made a left at the end of the hallway. After passing a couple doors, the corridor split into two paths. They could either continue going straight or they could branch to the right. They kept straight. At the end of the hall was a solid metallic gray door. There weren't any bars or screen doors, but a plain style with sigils engraved ornately. None of which recognizable to Collin.

Oscar and Mrs. Goodall led the pack, with Clark and Olivia in the rear. Mrs. Goodall stepped forward and did a swift dance with her fingers that resulted in a clicking sound within the door. It swung forward effortlessly to grant them entry.

"Watch the steps, dear," she spoke quietly.

As he moved forward and into the doorway, the pitch black of the basement became illuminated by tiny incandescent orbs spaced ten feet apart on each side of the snow-white walls. The steps were steep, going several feet down. Once at the bottom, Collin discovered it to only be a landing descending further.

This must be at least twenty feet deep, he dazed in amazement.

Despite his surprise, his other mental faculties were undergoing a battle between how badly he wanted to trust these people and succumbing to the overall ominous foreboding that took hold the moment he heard he would be locked up in some basement. While the atmosphere wasn't entirely sinister, he couldn't help but be reminded of the cliché bright lights and walls that appeared in books and movies where people are usually forced to be unethical experiments.

He tried to slow his pace, but was nudged along. At the true bottom was a hallway with half a dozen doors per side. All were a matching metallic gray as the one leading them down here.

"Not to put a damper on your imprisonment," said Clark slightly, "but at least you weren't being put here four days ago. We had a werewolf here waiting for the moon cycle to end."

Mrs. Goodall turned on her heels and shot Clark a dirty look.

"What?" he asked innocently. "It's just a bit of light humor to ease the tension. While also being true."

That last part he said so quietly that the only person to hear him was Oscar.

"Better a werewolf than a lycan anyways," Oscar added.

"Zip it!" Mrs. Goodall hushed. "We don't need Collin freaked out any more than he already must be."

They walked halfway down the corridor before stopping. Mrs. Goodall did her hocus pocus to get the door open and everyone marched in single file. Like the entire basement, the room was lit by an orb manifesting upon their entry.

Inside, the walls matched the outside. A walled cubicle was built into the far end of the room to serve as the bathroom. A twin-sized cot sat on a four-pronged black, metallic bedframe in the corner adjacent with a change of white clothes awaiting the room's occupant. Other than that, it was bare.

Overture

There was no way around denying it was a prison cell. Collin turned around to face his ward and her guards.

Mrs. Goodall could feel his heart sink in his chest for him. The horror in his eyes for being locked away so inhumanely for something he didn't understand was torturous. He knew there was nothing to say to assure them he would rather go home at this point. They probably already knew. Over Mrs. Goodall's shoulder, Collin saw Clark and Oscar exchanging a significant look that translated into pity.

"Despite how this seems, is there anything I can get for you?" Mrs. Goodall asked.

"No, ma'am," he answered sullenly, eyes bouncing between her and the floor.

A warm hand touched his shoulder and broke the distortion in his sense of reality. Staring him dead in the eyes, Mrs. Goodall promised him once more everything was going to be okay.

"You should get some rest, dear. I'm sure you'll have more questions in the morning once we've sorted everything out. I believe Taylor may be right, that this isn't a coincidence. This is to ensure our safety as well as your own.

Collin nodded and his hostess nodded in understanding. The others turned toward the door. Clark and Oscar looked over their shoulders at him while Mrs. Goodall bustled them out, Alice shuffling in the rear. The door swung shut on command. Four clicks sealed it against any attempts to penetrate it, mechanically or magically. The air itself altered.

The cell became its own atmosphere, bearing menacingly on any occupant who dared challenge its security.

That night, he barely sleep at all. Not for lack of trying. The cot was surprisingly comfortable in spite of the mattress's thin design. Instead, Collin spent the last couple of hours before sunrise trying to make sense of it all. The words *magic* and *monsters* echoed relentlessly across his thoughts.

The comfort of the bed eventually took hold of him. His mind was plagued with so many questions, he never got the chance to evaluate how tuckered out he was.

3

Examination of Mind

A rattling on the door woke him a couple hours later. The sound jump-started his heart rate in parallel with the sensation of falling in a dream. The quick jolt and the unfamiliarity of where he was placed him back in bed at his dad's house for a split second. One look at the opposite wall told him otherwise. He shifted to see the door to his prison cell swing open.

"Yo, Ms. Glenda said to see if you wanted to come up for breakfast," said Olivia through smacked bacon, a half-eaten strip in one hand with the other hand tucked beneath her breasts. She had changed from her gallivanting attire into a snug and revealing pink camisole and pink booty shorts.

Collin stared at her blankly. His sense of time may have been out the window, but he could still tell from the heaviness of his eyes that the time lapse between going to sleep and waking up was too short to be talking about breakfast.

Olivia cocked an eyebrow at his lack of a response. Collin blinked, gently shook his head, and tried using groggy body language to suggest he was staring out of fatigue rather than at her chest.

"Sure," he finally said.

"I'll leave the door open then. Can you find the kitchen from here?" she asked.

He could. It shouldn't be too difficult to backtrack their steps from the night before. That was good enough for her. Olivia stuck the rest of the bacon in her mouth and walked away.

"The boys are already out, so you're stuck with Ms. Glenda and Alice for dining companions," she hollered matter-of-factly.

With nothing else to wear except for yesterday's attire, he trailed after her. Once he left the room, the door slammed shut, locking him out. Luckily, he remembered to snag his keys and phone beforehand. His phone hadn't received a single bar of service since he'd been brought down.

Even if he didn't know his way back to the kitchen, the unmistakable wafting scent of bacon and pancakes lured him in the right direction. He was astounded by how hungry he was now the previous night's adrenaline fizzled out. The stage of uncomfortable stomach growling had been skipped and went straight to a tight pull of his navel.

Turning the corner, he saw Mrs. Goodall at the head of the table with her back to him and Alice sitting in her usual spot. Both were more properly dressed for the day. Olivia must've returned to her room.

"Collin!" yelped Mrs. Goodall happily, leaping from her

seat. "Good. Good. I'm glad you came to join us. Please, sit anywhere you'd like."

With Alice already seated, and remembering how reluctant she was to sit next to him, Collin chose the seat to the left of where Mrs. Goodall sat. As soon as he was situated, she gave an introductory on his variety of options.

"We have eggs in several different forms. Bacon, turkey bacon, sausage. Muffins, toast, grits, pancakes, fruit," she gestured to platters of colorfully organized foods "You name it. For drinks, we have coffee, water, milk, juice, and sweet tea."

The display was utterly astonishing and she had the genuine Southern hospitality to ask if it was okay for *him*?

"This is great. Did you make all this this morning?" Collin asked in disbelief.

Mrs. Goodall smiled sweetly at him. "It's not much of a fuss when you have magic to help."

He supposed not. It seemed embarrassingly obvious that magic had more practical uses than merely being used on paperweights. Still, it was nice to see she was at least acting like last night's tension had been alleviated.

"Oh, well, thank you. It looks great," he said bashfully.

"Well, tuck in. It might be cold, though. I can heat it up."

"No. That's okay. Please," he urged, not wanting to be a burden.

She resituated herself in her seat and took a sip from her coffee. Collin stood to reach for some of the plates. He dug a large spoon into a heap of scrambled eggs, pulled a few strips of turkey bacon, and half a plate of fruit to start. He was also eyeing the pancakes, but there were only two left and he didn't want to be the stranger who finished them off if someone else wanted any.

By the looks of it, over half the food was already gone. Clark, Oscar, Taylor, and Olivia must've already had their share, but he didn't want to risk being on Alice's bad side. He was sure Mrs. Goodall would insist he eat them out of courtesy. He settled for a piece of wheat toast. Next to the platter of the now cold toast, there was butter, peanut butter, strawberry and blueberry marmalade, and honey. He kept it plain. He poured himself a cup of coffee from a large French press and mixed in some milk before finally eating.

Even lukewarm, everything tasted extraordinary. Either Mrs. Goodall was a natural with cooking or cooking with casting added extra flavoring to food.

"I don't want to worry you," Mrs. Goodall spoke cautiously, after Collin shoveled down half his plate, "but we have someone stopping by shortly to give you a sort of..." she paused and bit her bottom lip worrisomely, "look over."

"How so?" he inquired stiffly.

"Just to see if there's anything peculiar about you involving last night."

"Because I wasn't killed on the spot?"

"Precisely," Alice chimed in. She was giving Collin a cold, calculating look. "We don't typically come across people as lucky as you to still be alive."

"Alice, that's not necessary," said Mrs. Goodall.

"Sorry, Ms. Glenda." She withdrew under the authority of her guardian.

Mrs. Goodall turned her attention back to Collin. He could tell by the way she continued to wring the mug in her hands that she was choosing her words carefully and kindly.

"Paul is our specialist when it comes to mental examinations. He has somewhat of a proclivity for going into people's minds and finding any...odd details."

Collin swelled with apprehension. There were a lot of *odd* details tucked away in his memory. None of which he was particularly keen on allowing other people to dig through.

"Ah," he said in a tone making his displeasure hard to miss.

"It's completely harmless, and Paul is very professional with keeping personal experiences confidential. And when it's all over we can send you back home without the slightest recollection of us and under sort of a witness protection to make sure your neighborhood is safe."

The idea of mental probing occurring with or without his approval made him slightly squeamish. What made it worse was that he wasn't ready to forget any of this. The peak novelty of his exposure to this society was running its course and he was warming up to the companionship of these strangers, despite their brief exposure. In his sluggish wake, he came to realize he was no longer the big fish in a little pond of peers. He was the phytoplankton in a sea of nothing but blue whales. He was a misplaced jigsaw piece in an irrelevant picture.

What moved him more was comprehending how these people possessed a set of characteristics that made him want to strive to be part of their world, or maybe *be* them entirely. Well, maybe not Taylor, and Alice and Olivia were still a bit of wildcards, but the other three seemed to at least be interested in him without making him feel like an experimental outlier.

"I'll do it," he said calmly, as if he had the choice to not participate. "When will he be here?"

Mrs. Goodall beamed at him and furtively exhaled a sigh of relief. She looked at her watch. "In about a half hour, if you'd like to finish breakfast and wash up beforehand."

Collin liked to keep his showers for the evening to wash away the grime of the day, but he did still need to wash out the copiously pubescent amount of oil in his hair. Plus, after all the excitement, he soon decided it might be best to shower twice that day.

"Alice," she switched her attention, "would you mind putting a fresh pair of clothes in the bathroom for him?"

Alice gave a slight look of indignation. She was still clearly skeptical about leaving him unsupervised by anyone other than herself.

"We'll be fine," Mrs. Goodall assured.

Alice hesitated but stood slowly, as if any sudden movements might set Collin off like a rabid animal. She moved equally rigidly around the table.

"Thank you."

"Yes, ma'am," Alice whispered.

When she was out of sight, Collin proceeded to finish his breakfast with a little more fervor. He couldn't say what inspired his serene and momentous revelation, but he was overcome with the desire to prove himself, and started by mustering a little bravery in the face of the unknown. If they were willing to promise a harmless act of mentally meddling for his monograph, then he was willing to oblige them. Was it an ideal way of how he thought this day was going to go? Definitely not, but he was clinging more and more to the possibility of this opening a whole new door for him. There was one concern, however, lingering overhead from the night before.

"What happened with my dad?" he inquired, despite his distaste for the man from a life now meaningless.

Mrs. Goodall looked away from the far wall, her coffee still clutched in both hands. "We put his mind under a kind of stupor, similar to what you were in the night of the wendigo. He'll be able to go about his day like any other, but he'll have a hard time retaining or reacting to anything that happens."

Collin nodded along.

"Then, once everything is settled, we'll go ahead and block his memory of your time out of the house and replace it with something else.

"That's assuming he even wakes up before we're done."

"That would make things easier, yes."

His breakfast was finished by the time Alice returned. By then he was able to show himself to the bathroom, right after the study. Inside, he found a towel, a washcloth, and a neatly folded pair of plain, white, long-sleeve shirt and matching scrub pants, as well as a pair of socks and boxer briefs stacked on the marble countertop extended from the sink. Next to them was a small bottle of Dove shampoo, a bar of Irish Springs soap, a factory sealed toothbrush, and a travel sized tube of toothpaste.

Collin grabbed the towel, washcloth, and soap, and hung them over the top of the glass encasing of the walk-in shower. He stripped naked and moseyed inside. When he examined the mechanics of the shower, he was relieved. Typically, whenever he used a shower that wasn't his own, there was no universal method for turning on the water. More often than not, it took more time adjusting the water temperature than actually getting clean. This time around, all it took was a simple turning of the lever upward into the hot zone.

The water flowed instantly heated. There was no buffer between cold and hot. Steam accompanied the spewing fluid drenching him. He lathered his hair and rinsed it. Two minutes later, he was rolling the bar of soap within the washcloth until suds poked thoroughly through.

***

Rushed and ready, he stepped out from the bathroom slowly. He glanced left and right and saw no sign of life in the hallway, but could hear the faintest conversation back in the kitchen. One muffled voice he recognized as Mrs. Goodall. So, he headed there.

Sitting to her right was a bespectacled man with a slightly

hunched posture. He had a pallid complexion with dishwater hair. Overlooking his sunken face, he looked at Collin with the friendliest of grins.

"Ah, Paul, this is Mr. Collin Quinn," Mrs. Goodall introduced.

She climbed to her feet and gave Collin a strange side hug.

Were they familiar enough to be giving those?

Paul also stood but went to shake his hand instead.

"Collin, this is Mr. Paul Ganley. He'll be the one making sure nothing in your life has tagged you for further danger."

"Hi," Collin said, accepting Mr. Ganley's hand.

"Hello, Mr. Quinn. How are you?"

"I-I'm fine," he said uncertainly. "You?"

"I'm good! Thank you for asking."

Collin noticed he spoke with such zealous euphoria. The corners of his lips stretched far enough back to reveal each of his yellowing teeth. His smiling eyes showed the settling of Crow's Feet.

"I know all of this must be scary, but, if you'd like, I'm ready to pull the bandage off quick and painlessly."

He gestured to the chair to the left of Mrs. Goodall. Collin obliged him shakily. Between them was an empty bronze bowl, no bigger than a cereal bowl. He rested his hands in his lap.

"Excellent!" said Paul. "Now, if you don't mind, I need you to stare at this bowl, here, and before you know it, this will all be over."

Collin stared at the bowl. Through the corners of his eyes,

he could see Paul performing a finger-tut from across the table. Once he finished, the bowl was no longer empty. A spark ignited into a tiny flame that grew slowly, burning copper green. It was like watching a seedling grow into its designated plant the way it started so small. As it expanded, licks of flame branched from its base until it was completed, sustained by nothing. Collin was instantly entranced by the spectacle. His pupils dilated and his muscles relaxed. There was nothing he could do to fight the mesmerizing pull. Once snared, he didn't simply lose track of time, he forgot the concept of time wholly.

It would be an hour later before he came out of his mental slumber and about as bad as coming off a rollercoaster with a full stomach. Mental images scanned across his retinas like an old-timey jukebox flipping through its albums.

His first memory ever was of having surgery for his eardrums. He could see himself sitting in a car seat, bawling his eyes out while his father shouted at his mom to shut him up. The simple passing of vehicles on the road produced a sound comparable to nails on a chalkboard now, only exemplified.

He was forced to relive the time when he pissed himself on the neighbor's trampoline while the five of them were laying on their bellies laughing. He tried to pass it off on the least popular of them, but he recalled the expression everyone shared when they knew he was lying, repulsive child who failed to accomplish proper potty-training at five years old.

He was forced to re-watch as the boys across the street

offered to pay a six-year-old version of himself twenty-five dollars for his Gameboy game, but only paid with twenty-five cents. He didn't have the backbone to tell them no, and he never told anyone else about it either.

The family that moved in after them was no better. He could remember the negligence the single mother had for her own children. Buried deeper still within his subconscious was the time spent with her alone as his babysitter. Not that his pre-teen mind fully grasped the extent of her perversion. Nor did Collin realize how the things he underwent under her care were moments he should've alerted other adults.

The more prominent memories he had were of her son, and of helping him win the affection of child-like passions for the girl he also carried the flame for, only to have her reject him after hers and neighbor boy's schoolyard crush faded. Then there was the incident back on the other neighbor's trampoline.

"Don't ever touch me," the boy from across the street had said, as they played trampoline-tag.

Collin didn't pay much stock to the warning. He tagged him again. Next thing he knew, he was shoved off, landing flat on his back on the hard ground as the boy leapt off after him, wringing his hands around his neck. He tried hiding it from his mother, but she saw the reminiscent red hand marks after she forced him into a bath.

Not a year later, that same neighborhood boy had the majority of the students on the bus giving a tumultuous round of laughter at Collin's embarrassment. He was called a loser and chubby, and several others let it be known how they wished he would leave their bus.

Less than a year after that, he was sitting in the principal's office for hitting his school crush at the time, Summer, with a rock. She tossed them at him first, after all. He thought she was simply being playful, so he threw them back. Not hard. Although, in hindsight, his overhand shots versus her underhand throws differed significantly in momentum. That same day, he was grounded from friends and toys, and set on all fours, bare-assed as that iconic leather belt welted crimson, blotchy trails on his skin to last a couple days.

Then he was fourteen. His parents divorced. Most of his friends were now scattered across the vastness of Jacksonville. He remembered catching the attention of one, Jacqueline Lamb. She was two years older than him and convinced him to forfeit his virginity to her one January morning on her birthday. It was Christmas break, but her parents still had to work, so it was convenient to have the house to themselves after biking around. Come to find out, she only sought him out with the goal of ruining him, because a friend of hers had her eye on him. His heartbreak was the result of some bullshit middle school squabble.

The next few years were easier. His dad lost his touch as a *responsible* parent. He became a lazy asshole who blamed all his problems on his divorce and self-proclaimed anxiety. Collin had no problem maneuvering around all this, waiting until sixteen to start finessing his abilities of seduction after the whole Jacqueline situation. Of course, when it came to his sex life his father couldn't care less. It was his healthier lifestyle of eating fruits and vegetables and working out which caused his dad to learn a whole new vocabulary for the sole purpose of criticizing his habits.

"Fuck him!" he wanted to scream so badly.

What good was a dad who only recognized a playboy jock as the only son worth having?

He should've gone to Canada.

Not all of his experiences were bad. He relived trips to Disney and riding Space Mountain. His first time there, he thought the shooting stars on the ceiling were for effect. Come to find out they were participants on the ride. There was the Christmas leading to his parents' divorce. For his sake, they were determined to make it the most festive one yet. Which it was, but it was also the last one before all superseding Christmases became too forced. There was time spent with friends, Shannon, Matt, Shawn, Brittney, and Tyler. A long line of A's on each report card flashed across too, along with scenes of him desecrating school textbooks with highlighters, but never getting reprimanded for it.

He was nearly back to the present and he could see as clear as day the bared teeth of the wendigo as its natural instincts begged to rip him limb-from-limb for dinner. He caught a brief glimpse of the figure in the elongated skull mask before the copper flame extinguished. Collin was freed.

It took a brief second for Collin to transition his attention to where he was. A lump had manifested in his throat during his time in captivity. Patches of moisture chilled his cheeks.

The stinging of his eyes told him he'd been crying. Withheld tears still occupied the bottom of his vision. He wiped them away as surreptitiously as possible.

"I'm sorry to put you through that," Paul said softly. "Thank you for sharing that with me."

"Yeah," Collin whispered.

He was choked on latent remnants of his past. Memories he didn't realize he still had burned a hole of sadness in his chest.

"I'm so sorry," said Mrs. Goodall. "Any bad feelings, I promise, will pass. I have a few bars of chocolate if you think it might help."

While Collin was sure a heap of chocolate couldn't hurt with his overwhelming spur of emotions, he was still far too full from breakfast to consider eating again. On the contrary, he wondered if he might vomit it all out from sheer emotional trauma. He shook his head in response.

"Collin, do you know who the person in the horse skull mask is?" Paul asked.

4

Osmond Pyrrhal

"A sick individual," he muttered.

Paul gave a *hmm*. Judging by the way he was pondering his inquiry, Collin questioned if he knew anything about the strange person. When he asked Mrs. Goodall about any updates around the city involving anyone wearing a horse skull, she denied knowing any such information with quizzical disgust. Paul gave another *hmm*.

It turned out Paul didn't want to contact some council *just* because of the horse masked person, or because Collin was a danger to himself or to others, *or* because Collin might've had some strange connection to their supernatural world he was unaware about. Instead, he wanted to contact this council because, in his words, Collin "was someone of extraordinarily promising potential." Mrs. Goodall was as flabbergasted as Collin. If he hadn't been sorrowfully induced, he might have swelled with pride.

"He is too young!" Mrs. Goodall argued without hesitation.

"Mr. Quinn has a birthday coming up in October when he'll be of age. Do you not, Collin?"

Collin did. The gleam in the pale man's gray eyes twinkled with intrigue as he fiddled with his glasses. Whatever he saw in Collin's life set him on a determined path. This made Collin half-excited and half-nervous. There was hope after all.

"It doesn't matter!" Mrs. Goodall's voice rose with an almost frantic tone, quavering adamantly. "The Council would never agree to inducting seventeen-year-olds off the street and enlisting them into Veil. They—" Glenda composed herself with a deep exhale.

"Collin," she said with tame exasperation, "would you mind waiting in the study for us?"

He gave no reply, but made his way out into the hall. He could've sworn he spotted a patch of black clothing and brown hair turn out of sight as he swiveled around the doorway. The distance of the hallway was stretched enough to easily have been mistaken. Regardless, the study seemed an interesting place to kill time.

He'd been inside before, but only in the daytime could one truly appreciate its magnificence. It looked about the size of a football field with bookshelves occupying every inch of wall. The height of them required a sliding ladder he found in the back. In the far-right corner was a loft leading to more books. Half a dozen desks filled the room, each with their own hutch, lamp, and printer. Their wood was espresso brown with a strip of black leather across the work surface. Two desks extended the right side of the study, three extended the left side, and one sat along the far wall. An undraped, nearly wall-sized window brightened the room without any electrical assistance.

Collin's nostrils filled with a medley of antiques, an abundance of sophisticated literature, and…

Dust polish?

It was heaven. Did he ever think he could afford a room like this in his future dream house? No, but that didn't stop him from doing just that: dreaming.

Taking a left, he thumbed through the ancient collection of books. Most appeared leather-bound. Any appearing newer were hardback, but not a single paperback edition was to be found. His selection was at random. Collin scooted out *The History of Spells in the European Sovereigns* by Elizabeth Aewin and pushed it back in place. He repeated this long enough to become cognizant of the thousands of books being organized alphabetically by authors' last name. There was *The Rise and Fall of Persian Spellcasters* by Elaheh Ahura, *Transition of the Order of Origin: 1900s* by Jonathon Campbell, paired with its 1800s and 2000s edition, *Guide to Gwisins* by Min Jung Chen, *Modern Potions 8th Edition* by Jerry Daggs, and on and on.

The sadness that drowned him moments ago drifted back to the depths of his memories, but the images still plagued his inner vision. How he ever managed to not let his life fall apart he'd never know. Did he get lucky and have all the horrors of his past occur in a spread-out sequence? He felt like a prime candidate for Freud's psychoanalytical theories on defense mechanisms. He choked on a swallow and forced his mind clean. Surely the library was more interesting than any baggage he carried.

There were self-help books about harnessing spellcasting via breathing exercises. Books on housecleaning spells. Books on tracking the púca of Ireland and killing them in the event of receiving bad fortune. There was a five-volume set on William Wrights' *Elementary Spells, Intermediate Spells,* and *Advanced Spells.* Collin even came across whole textbooks dedicated to wars throughout history when magicians changed the tide incognito as well as textbooks about wars between *only* magicians unbeknownst to conventional society.

"Looks more impressive than the reads actually are."

Collin turned around to see Olivia hanging on the doorframe. She had changed out of her pajamas and was snug inside a pair of jeans and a black t-shirt she must've known accented her features all too well. Admittedly, his jump was so embarrassing it was practically mandatory for his cheeks to glow red. There was no way she couldn't have noticed, but she paid no mind either way.

"Ms. Glenda shoo'd me from the kitchen and soundproofed the damn thing, so I assume they're talking about you."

He remained silent. She was right in her assumption, but he didn't like to admit being the topic of discussion.

"So, how'd it go?" she asked.

"The thing?" he asked to clarify. He felt stupid for being vague, but Olivia understood.

"With Mr. Ganley, yes."

"It was…" he trailed off.

There was nothing nice to say about it. True, some moments were of pure joy and drive in his past, even some of his present, but the majority of it was pain and humiliation.

"Shitty?" she finished for him.

He nodded in return. She grinned grimly and pushed herself off the doorframe.

"It's that way for everyone. You can't expect to get into Veil without a tale to tell, but there's little chance you'll get in on Ms. Glenda's watch."

"The man said I had good potential."

Olivia stared at him with amusement. She almost looked like she was fighting off a smirk the way her expression contorted in a weird angle. It even looked as though pity were peeking through a façade. Collin was growing tired of everyone's pitying stares.

"It's uncommon to ever see exceptions made for members of Veil, especially with the age restriction, and you're only seventeen."

"How do y'all known so much about me?" Collin asked.

The term *so much* might've been a stretch when only referring to the fact they knew his name and age. He considered it a fair question nonetheless.

"We had your phone the night we found you. We unlocked it and found everything we needed to know. Plus, it's our job. We may joke and find fun in what we can, but we still dabble in serious shit."

Collin's shock must've betrayed his expression. No good

could come from snooping through his phone. He had pictures, videos, and texts he'd rather keep private. Thank god he only used private mode on the web browser when it came to his night habits.

"Relax, you're safe." She winked.

Not feeling too assured and quick to change the subject, he asked "What's the council that Mrs. Goodall and Paul were talking about?"

She paused to find the right words to explain. As he waited, he redirected his attention to the bookshelves and backtracked through the alphabet, only paying half-attention to the titles.

"Imagine Veil as a community, okay? Veil has its government, and the inner circle of the government, like the president, Senate, etcetera, is what's known as the Council of Spell. They govern America."

"So, people in Veil are governed like the wizarding world and the Ministry of Magic?" Collin referenced *Harry Potter*.

"If you're a nerd, sure, but we don't go by witches and wizards. Too much stigma after all the witch-hunts, and we don't all go by magicians either. We're not a party trick."

"So then, what do you—"

"Hello!" boomed a man's voice from out in the hall, cutting off their discussion.

Olivia perked up at the sound of the voice and smiled. She left without another word.

"Hello!" she greeted loudly, with a sudden curtly swap of her tone. "What took you so long?!"

Collin dashed to the doorway to bend an ear to this new voice.

"Hello, Olivia," the voice said cheerfully, sending deep vibrations through the air. "I'll explain everything, just round everyone up for a moment."

"Taylor, Clark, and Oscar are out, and Ms. Glenda is having a meeting with Paul."

"Ganley?"

Collin crept his head around to get a look at the new inhabitant, but ended up stepping entirely out into the hallway. He noticed immediately how well the voice fit. This stranger was undoubtedly over six feet tall with a thickly toned build sticking out from under his brown three-piece suit he wore. His physique lessened around his facial features, placing him somewhere in his fifties. A mane of salt and pepper hair hung around his head. A thin, kempt beard connected from his sideburns, covering his cheeks, chin, and upper lip. A deep scar lashed across his left cheek.

"Yup," said Olivia.

But before the man turned to the kitchen, his gaze traced over Olivia's shoulder and landed on Collin.

"Hello," he greeted, with a deep softness that mimicked the coaxing of a small animal. "Who're you?"

Olivia didn't fill in for him. Instead, she shot him a casual look that forced him to introduce himself.

"Collin," he stammered with every effort to extend his voice.

The man looked at Olivia to confirm he heard correctly. Collin could see their mouths move, but heard nothing.

"C'mon over here, Collin."

As Collin slowly moved forward, the stranger saved him some time and strode toward him. Each of the man's steps were firm and confident, covering approximately three-quarters of their space apart. His hand outstretched to greet this newcomer in his house.

"Osmond Pyrrhal," he said as they shook hands. "You must've met my wife then, Glenda. What brings you around these parts?"

"Collin, here, is a civilian who came across a wendigo and managed not to die. So he's staying with us while we try to find out why," said Olivia. She hung behind Osmond, never standing directly beside him.

"What about protocol?" Osmond never took his eyes off Collin.

"We're in the process of following them."

Osmond's eyes expanded in surprise. He cocked his head minutely to the side as if it enhanced his examination skill. When their eyes met, Collin got the uncomfortable sensation that Mr. Pyrrhal's intense gaze was piercing into his mind. At their current distance, the color of Mr. Pyrrhal's eye were a deep and calm shade of twinkling blue that exposed a nurturing in the man's personality. They were instantaneously ascertained to be the same color as the Jacksonville ocean water past the coast, once you got past the murky repercussions of general littering. They were the burdened eyes of experience one earned when paired hand-in-hand with life's many inexplicable calamities.

"So, you're a bit of a troublemaker, hey?" he asked Collin. No tone of actual accusation resonated. It was more a question meant to be paired with a grin and a nudge on the side.

"Accidentally, I guess," said Collin.

An inkling of mirth shone through Mr. Pyrrhal's attentive look. "Accidents do happen, I suppose."

"Not according to Taylor," Olivia chimed in, almost bitterly.

The man turned to face her. Collin could tell he was all too familiar with Taylor's idiosyncrasies the way his face morphed oxymoronically. The corners of his lips curved crookedly into a half-smile, but his eyes drooped in an almost sorrowful guise.

"We can't blame someone for being cautious," he said instructively. "Taylor may be quick on the trigger, but I have faith in his intentions."

Olivia appeared to be tottering on a more brutal retort, but suppressed it in present company. "I'm sure. Just wish he wasn't PMS'ing all the time. Sorry," she added when she saw Mr. Pyrrhal looking disapprovingly at her, but her tone sounded unencumbered by her sycophantic demeanor.

Mr. Pyrrhal gave no further notice to her slight, letting the matter slide as he returned to his guest. "I suppose we ought to check in on my Glenda and Mr. Ganley then?"

Collin shrugged.

His emotions were torn with the suggestion. On one hand, he had the right to know what the two were discussing in private, seeing as it was him that they were discussing in the first place. On the other hand, however, he was worried about the possible rejection he would receive, being forced to forget everything and return to the mundane world of college, taxes, family, all leading to an inevitable death by old age.

Or car accident, blood heating at the reminder of god-awful drivers who didn't know how to use a goddamn blinker. *It is Jacksonville after all.*

But all the same, his biggest fear was disappointment. He didn't want to be disappointed by getting his hopes up for nothing and he didn't want to disappoint these people by coming off poorly in any sort of way.

Olivia let Mr. Pyrrhal walk past her, preferring to follow. Collin trailed after her. Mr. Pyrrhal wiggled his fingers and they heard a soft *click* of the door unlocking.

"And I'm telling you, he won't find joy out in his world. He'll want this opportuni—" came the faint sound of Paul's voice before Mrs. Goodall cut him off.

"Olivia, I told you to—!"

She looked at the door and gasped.

"Oz!" she cried, and leapt from her seat.

They embraced as though they hadn't seen each other for quite some time, and, gathering from everyone's reaction to his presence, Collin deduced they hadn't. The tenderness they shared was unique. The delay in their hug made Collin throw a side glance at Olivia, who met his gaze, and wondered if she mimicked his sense of intrusiveness on their reunion. The thought was immediately wiped, however, when Mrs. Goodall leaned back and swiped Mr. Pyrrhal in a back and forth frenzy with her left hand, her right arm still wrapped around his waist. It was almost funny to watch a woman shorter than Collin smacking a man as large as her husband.

"Osmond. Pyrrhal. Where. Have. You. Been?!" Every word paused between hits until she ceased and let him go. "It's been nearly a week! You haven't returned *any* of my messages, texts, calls! I was about a day away from notifying the Council. What case could possibly be so bad that you have to go AWOL for?"

"Glenda, darling, you know I wouldn't disappear on you like that," Mr. Pyrrhal switched to a gingerly approach.

"I know you like to carelessly get wrapped up in your work!" she scorned.

"Well…yes, you're right. I'm sorry, darling. But I promise this time was different. There's something going on in this city that's very unusual, but I can't pick up a trail. Whatever it is, it's clever."

Mrs. Goodall's glaring eyes softened only a little. Her hesitation on a retort allotted enough silence to remind her there were others in the room with them. She conceded with the slouch of her shoulders.

"Fine, fine," she said with lingeringly strained agitation. "Come in, come in. We can catch up on it shortly. Your timing couldn't be better. Maybe you can talk some sense into Paul. Olivia, would you please give us a moment? Collin would you please wait just outside the door?"

"Yes, ma'am," Olivia said.

"Of course," said Collin.

Together they turned to face the hall. Olivia bid him good luck and disappeared to her room near the end of the hall, while Collin chose to obey and not wander this time. The scooting of chairs and whispers on the other side of the wall became muffled before becoming entirely silent. He assumed a soundproofing spell was reestablished for his benefit.

Either way, he chose to sit on the floor, cross-legged. Everything was still so new it made everything that was happening appear in fast motion, becoming difficult to digest.

And what did Paul mean when he said 'He won't find joy out in his world. He'll want this opportunity?'

That was a bit of a presumptuous thing to assume, but, then again, had he not been recently thinking the same? Who the hell would refuse to learn magic anyway? He would absolutely accept the opportunity, because he found no happiness in the idea of going to college, finding a career, and living that apple pie life. What if he raised his hypothetical kids unintentionally like his father did him? He'd have to worry about financial stability, the possibility of his spouse having an affair, among many more of life's unpredictable situations. No thanks. He wasn't *that* naïve in his youth.

What all had Paul seen in his memories? Did he only see the things Collin saw? Did he see more?

God knows there's certainly more to see. What if he saw everything from birth to now?

Surely the best objective judge of character was the person who knew someone's entire life from the outside. Collin knew he was biased. After all, it was his life, his own experiences, and his own opinions.

Did Paul see Collin's willingness to join them attributed to his love of fictitious adventures, especially his love of J.K. Rowling's works? Collin hoped so, but an empty pit in his stomach knew otherwise. If they shared even a fraction of the sorrow Collin felt during his examination, Paul would know he was bordering on anhedonia, keeping to himself, his books, his studies, his close-knit group of friends, while all-the-while watching the pantomime of life drift by with no care of taking part.

Sure, he liked to kick back and let loose now and again after a long week of classes, but what teenager didn't? However, as he considered his behavior from Paul's perspective, he supposed his extreme level of introversion provided a subliminal purpose. After all the shit he endured at an age younger than any child should have to undergo, he turned out alright. He was among the top of his class. He wasn't a danger to himself or others. Collin considered himself to be a promising contribution to society after he managed to finish with all his post-secondary education.

But even now?

He couldn't see why not. Would he decline if they offered him a spot in Veil? No! Yet, if they didn't, they would undoubtedly make sure every memory of them and this place were extracted from his mind. After that, he would simply continue on continuing on. God, he hated self-reflection. Talking his way into acknowledging a void in his life only upset him.

The door to the dining room finally opened after an hour of dwelling in the hall. The *click* of the doorknob made him jump as easily as Olivia's voice in the study had.

"Collin, would you join us?" Mrs. Goodall requested in a nearly inaudible whisper.

"Of course," he answered in a voice equally soft.

She held the door open for him and resealed it behind him. Mr. Pyrrhal had already lifted a chair to the head of the table his wife sat on, leaving the chair to their left free, as it had been for breakfast. Once everyone was situated, Mr. Ganley led the discussion.

"Mr. Quinn, I would like to start by saying that I believe you might like to be a part of Veil, and that you have the potential to be an *outstanding* asset to the community."

As he spoke, Collin could see the flecks of sheer abhorrence mixed in with Glenda's more outwardly annoyed expression. She looked about ready to pummel the man to no end for even suggesting it, yet she bit her tongue until he was finished.

"I haven't revealed what you shared with me, but, if you'd like to join us, I may need your consent for further persuading."

"And I say that if we go ahead and start recruiting minors

then we may as well start setting up posts during Career Day at schools, or in the malls, or outside movie theaters," said Mrs. Goodall sardonically.

"Glenda, dear –"

"Don't 'Glenda, dear' me, Oz!" she snapped. "You know it's wrong."

"I know picking up every other teen on the street who's had it rough is a matter that's out of the question, but I also know the council may see someone who's seventeen, turning eighteen in three months, with a predisposition toward our abilities on the magnitude Paul claims, as a gray area. We agreed to get Collin's answer with no promise of the Council's ultimate decision."

His voice was calm as he sat back in his chair, arms outstretched on the table with his fingers interlocked. In the battle of for-and-against, Osmond Pyrrhal was proving himself to be the mediator for both sides. Any old TV show or book told Collin that Mr. Pyrrhal would pay later for not having his wife's back one hundred percent.

"Fine," was her succinct submission. The muscles in her jaw flexed to display a pair of firmly gritted teeth behind her pursed lips.

There was a brief period of silence that allotted anyone a chance to have an outburst or a side note interjected. When none was had, Mr. Pyrrhal pressed forward.

"What you need to understand, Collin, is that this isn't a life most members choose freely. More often than not it's a last resort to cope with whatever's going on in that person's life, and that's *only* if they have the misfortune of crossing paths with a Veil member. This isn't some game or great adventure novel where being a part of Veil means you get to be endowed with great honor and happily-ever-afters. It's a dark and uncertain life of constant vigilance and training and paranoia about what the next day holds.

"Paul has informed us you have a very clever mind and a dedication to succeed beyond the average person, and you could put that towards *anything*. You could be a lawyer or a doctor, or maybe even the President if you wanted to. You could be well-paid and acknowledged for being the master of any other field than this one. You're going into your senior year of high school. You have your whole future ahead of you. Any doubts you may have about that, or any piqued interest you have about us just because we can do magic, will fade with time. That's a natural part of life."

Collin was listening politely, but in the back of his mind, he couldn't help but roll his eyes internally the second Mr. Pyrrhal started speaking in clichés. Based on his first impression, he enjoyed this man. Hell, that this man was willing to sit him down and try to give him life advice already made him a better father-figure than his own. However, that didn't mean he was going to let his daddy issues fog his opinions of this unknown man.

"What's your story?" Collin asked.

Mr. Pyrrhal looked taken aback. He clearly hadn't been anticipating this.

"I'm sorry?" he asked.

Overture

"You said people don't usually join except as a last resort to cope." As the words came out of his mouth, he regretted them. They sounded insensitive and dug into entirely too personal of matters. "If you don't mind me asking, of course," Collin added, trying to save his mistake.

Mr. Pyrrhal didn't seem to mind the curiosity. He diverted his gaze away from Collin long enough to lock eyes with Mrs. Goodall. She pondered the confession for a moment before giving her husband the faintest look of approval. Osmond stopped to consider where he would begin their tale before he finally said "Okay. Have you ever heard of changelings?"

"Like…shapeshifters?"

"No," Mr. Pyrrhal shook his head and ran a hand through his black mane. "Changelings are more of a creature from Irish lore. They're a type of fairy creature whose infants require human milk."

Collin confirmed he understood what was said.

"Twenty-four years ago, aft-after Glenda and I got married in Plant City, we were due for a pair of twins, a boy and a girl. We agreed he could take my last name, and we'd give our daughter Glenda's maiden name, in honor of her grandfather."

He paused to clear his throat in an effort to keep it under control. Traces of moisture already lined the bottom of Mrs. Goodall's eyes.

"Lily and John were born on April twenty-sixth, alive and healthy, and screaming bloody murder the day we brought them home. They were the most colicky poor souls I'd ever met, but by the third day Lily grew out of it. Being the naïve, first-time parents we were, we hoped maybe she would start her role as an influential sibling early, but at times it seemed like John only picked up the slack for her when it came to making noise.

"The older they got, the more divided their personalities became. He became a trouble-making, toddler hellion most parents look forward to having until they actually have them, and Lily remained quiet and played with her toys by herself and clung to Glenda and me like white on rice."

He paused again to clear his throat. The silences between his momentary lapses cut the air like daggers by how pronounced they were. The atmosphere screamed about the importance of what Mr. Pyrrhal had to say. Collin took that moment to take a quick gaze at the room's other occupants. Mr. Ganley was looking at his lap, dedicated to keeping his mouth shut, and Mrs. Goodall had only eyes for her husband as she gripped his hand tightly and tenderly.

"She didn't really get along with the other girls her age," Osmond continued. "She was very brilliant with school though, but not a big participator. We took her to doctors and psychiatrists, and no one had effective answers other than she had a predisposition for being introverted. We were given practice exercises to get her to be more social and talk more, but they didn't prove much.

"The year the kids turned nine was the year we joined Veil. Johnny was still a pain in our ass, but, in hindsight, we spent so much time trying to help our Lily not be so isolated that sometimes we failed to give him the extra attention he also needed. He wasn't a bad kid by any means. He still ate his vegetables and helped with the weekly chores, but he developed a jealousy we were only just starting to pick up on. He picked on her, refused to share his toys and games, even pushed her down or swung a tiny fist a time or two. We tried to tell to him why we were punishing him and explain how it was his job as a brother to look out for her, but he didn't want to hear it.

"August thirteenth we had finished dinner. Glenda and I were in the kitchen cleaning and discussing how we were gonna make ends meet that month with Lily's therapy bills, and the kids were off washing for bed."

A faint cry resonated on Mrs. Goodall's throat, but never escaped. Mr. Pyrrhal placed his other hand on top of hers for comfort.

"What we didn't hear," he said, "was Johnny going into her room while she was changing in her PJs. To this day we have no idea why, but we did hear a scream. We ran to her room and found Johnny on the floor with Lily bent over him. She had these eyeless sockets and a few extra rows of razor teeth that shouldn't be humanly possible, and the blood of her brother smeared across her cheeks. Her appearance returned to normal and she went about her business while Johnny was dying at her feet. In the short span of him screaming and us getting there, she had bit him on the arm, the face, and twice on the neck. She nicked his jugular enough times that he was dead before the ambulance could get there.

"We didn't know what to do. Glenda rode in the ambulance and I stayed there to keep an eye on her and answer questions from the police. Of course, the truth was too far-fetched for them, but before they could arrest me for suspected murder, a woman, Eleanor Merriweather, from Veil intervened. The cops were sent home and I gave my recounting to her. Apparently, they caught wind of what happened and sent a couple other members to the hospital to clean up the tracks.

"After they brought Glenda home and bound Lily, they told us what she was. If we hadn't seen what she did to Johnny we wouldn't have believed her. They proved it with a little fire. She changed back into the monster as the fire made contact with her skin. Delirious and confused, we still tried to save her, but were forced to watch her shriek and burn to death. We were then told that our Lily had been swapped out for that *thing*. We…"

He stopped to clear his throat again, but his voice was too shaky by now to bother trying to hide his discomfort from reliving the pain. A tear swelled and rolled down his face.

"We had our baby girl for only three days before she was taken from us without us even knowing it. We were told changelings usually dispose of human young to reshape and replace them so they can grow strong on human milk. Even though she'd been gone for years, we lost both of our children that night. There was no coming back from that.

We were given a little time to let the pain lessen, but we were offered a choice to forget everything that'd happened or to join Veil and help protect families from ever having to suffer the way we did. Forgetting the pain seemed like a much simpler option, but we were able to utilize that pain and put it toward a cause worth dying for. And that's…how we came to be here."

"I-I'm sorry," Collin whispered, breaking eye contact to notice the glistening streams now trailing Mrs. Goodall's face.

Mr. Ganley finally looked up, but still didn't say anything. The jubilation Collin initially felt radiating from this man bled out with the tale.

"Thank you, but I want you to realize that I'm telling you this to help you understand how every day in this business can be just as horrific. Monsters are real, and people need protecting, and more often than not the only way a spellcaster gets out of Veil is from dying on the job. And you *will* be forfeiting everything. Your family and friends, school records, medical records, past library cards, social security number, social media. *Everyone* who knows you will forget you. Every *trace* of you will be erased. That's not something most people are willing to forfeit."

Collin knew Mr. Pyrrhal meant well, but he wasn't most people, and as terrible as his and Glenda's story was, he knew this moment was more of a calling to be a hero. He was being given the chance to save people from legitimate evil. It was as opportune as any of your classic, run-of-the-mill books and movies, where the protagonist got to stare his or her fate dead in the eyes and rise to the occasion.

His decision had already been made in the hall, and everything he'd heard since merely locked his intentions in place. He might miss his mom and it would be a shame to not find out how he and Shannon ended up, but the college parties, internships, and working endless shifts at some restaurant to help pay off student loans couldn't ensnare his interest.

While moving on and experiencing life's million whims and joys and heartbreaks might be some people's definition of what it means to live life to the fullest, it simply wasn't Collin's. He didn't want to be a part of the ebbs and flows of humanity's daily routines. He didn't want to be stuck in 9-to-5 traffic jams and worrying about shithead roommates or job security. In the real world, horrible things happened with or without monsters, for no reason at all except that some cosmic entity loved to get its rocks off on countless people's misfortunes. Before locking in his answer, one curiosity still needed satisfying in the back of his head.

"Ms. Glenda, may I use my phone to look something up?" he asked. His cell still hadn't received any signal.

The adults exchanged glances, not sure what to think of such an odd request. She took his phone and performed a snappy spell before returning it.

"Thank you," he said confidently.

He noticed he had a few messages from his friends, but

ignored them. He went straight for his email and opened the link to the SAT score released that day. Once he was logged in and read his score and percentile rank, his chest swelled with pride. He'd scored a 1440. With 1600 being the maximum, he saw how his percentile put him in the top five percent of all his fellow test-takers. That locked in the majority of all options for college, but now that the option was there it didn't seem to matter.

Making the mistake of staying behind wasn't one he'd be repeating. He foolishly stayed in Jacksonville, not following his mother, and wound up living miserably. Yes, he was a good student, possessed decent looks, had good friends, and much more many would be envious of, but it somehow wasn't enough. That lurking shadow of a home where his father resided overcast the hopeful light of the young and ambitious. He locked the phone and handed it back to Mrs. Goodall. She took it, no questions asked, and Collin felt at perfect ease. Knowing he'd spent months waiting for results he no longer cared about felt satisfying, and now…

Now I'm gonna become a goddamn *spellcaster.*

"I appreciate everything you've told and warned me about," said Collin, "but this is an opportunity I can't pass up. I may still be an ignorant kid, but this is a calling in my eyes. If the Council will accept me and teach me how to defend others in more need than myself, I would love nothing more than to join Veil."

Mrs. Goodall sniffed sadly but agreed all the same. Osmond nodded, but with a slight upward curve on the right side of his mouth. Paul Ganley had a glimmer of victory sparkling brightly in his eyes and a wide, close-lipped grin.

"I'll contact Ian Botnick right now," he said, standing from his seat and vacating the house.

5

Introductory to Spells

It took nearly an entire week before anyone received even the slightest scrap of news from the Council. Paul Ganley had departed immediately upon Collin's acceptance of applying to be a part of their community. Mrs. Goodall expressed her displeasure inexorably, but she did so in a way that never made Collin feel like it was his fault. She said things like: "What's next, if we're just going to induct children," or, "Poor kid, having magic thrown under his nose and being expected not to be interested." She couldn't stress enough how gruesome their job could truly be, but at the same time Collin realized Mrs. Goodall's motherly nature spared her from sparing him no detail.

Mr. Pyrrhal did what he could to keep Glenda's mind off the matter, to no avail, so he spent the majority of his efforts apologizing to Collin. That didn't mean Collin wasn't warned several times to not take the situation lightly, and that a spellcaster's greatest attributes were his or hers observational skills and reflexive reactions. After a while, it all meshed together as typical parenting speeches about precaution.

Collin didn't mind it. In fact, their affectionate caring filled a hole in his heart that felt neglected for some time. He also hoped the others would be pleased to see him. He was willing to place a heavy bet Taylor wouldn't be, but he was pretty confident about Clark and Oscar. Olivia and Alice were hard to read, but he didn't get bad vibes from them.

That same day, after Mr. Ganley left, Mrs. Goodall went into the office and grabbed a piece of paper. Collin watched her write a short message, fold it, write Taylor DeWitt, and then make a *snap* with her ring finger and thumb with the note held between her index and middle fingers. Her exhortation to return home burst into green flames and extinguished immediately. The letter dematerialized without a trace. Ten minutes later, the three boys returned through the front door, as opposed to using portals into the study.

As much as Collin could guess, and much to his chagrin, Taylor wasn't thrilled to see him. At first he seemed content, entering the house with a bored and almost daydream-like expression, but as soon as he walked into view of Collin, his eyes narrowed and adopted a mutinous glower, proof enough of his unabated, unprovoked contempt. He was prepared to storm off at the mere sight of him if Osmond hadn't come into view. Collin almost wished he had left. The previous night, when he got in their way with the wendigo, sure, anyone could get annoyed with the added complication to their job.

But what's his excuse now? Is he so opposed to outsiders? Surely, he was an outsider at some point, too.

Overture

While Collin tried to remain understanding, he was irritable with the boy who was always angry with him. Where the inner conflict laid was with Collin wanting everyone to like him. Pleasing everyone was a feat more fit for the gods, but surely seven people couldn't be too damn difficult. Mrs. Goodall may never give her wholehearted blessing to his megrim decision, but he still wondered if his feral dedication to prove himself may still earn her affirmation.

When the three boys recognized that Osmond returned home, a silent, raw veneration overpowered the atmosphere. Only a fool would argue against Osmond Pyrrhal doubling as a father figure with all the hugs given eagerly. Even though Taylor's affection softened a little with the turn of his attention, he remained silent. On the other hand, Osmond's mysterious disappearance had Clark and Oscar clamoring for answers for what he'd been up to. Apparently, this was the conversation starter Mr. Pyrrhal had been hoping for, because he called for a family meeting with promise to answer their questions. Alice's sly apparition was so unnervingly silent and well maneuvered that Collin barely noticed she was mingled with the crowd.

Glenda Goodall didn't take her place at the head of the table nearest the hallway door. Instead, she headed for the kitchen to prepare lunch, while her husband sat opposite of her usual chair. The others took their determined places. The only spot remaining for Collin was the one between

Alice and Clark. Olivia sat directly opposite him and Taylor occupied the seat to Osmond's left.

The air became galvanized with anticipation and excitement. Osmond was well aware, his silence tantamount with the glee parents possessed watching their children attack Christmas wrapping paper with great fervor. He took a moment to observe everyone around the table with a smile. It became apparent to Collin that this man shared enough love for them all as suitably substituted children. This struck him as a little odd, since everyone appeared to be in their early twenties, but he paused to be cognizant of the fact he wasn't a parent. He'd most likely remain ignorant to that level of unconditional love unless the time came.

"It's not really a great adventure story," he finally said, his deep voice sending faint vibrations through the wooden table. "I never even left Jacksonville. I got carried away with a case."

A contemptuous, "Hmmph," emanated in the background from Mrs. Goodall.

"What were you hunting?" Oscar asked.

The interest of the others was mildly peeked, although Alice and Taylor showed the least amount of care beyond the straightening of their heads and the squaring of their shoulders.

"Well," Mr. Pyrrhal pondered. "A lot of things, I suppose. I was sent out more to follow leads, you see. Lately there's been a lot of talk of necrotics, vampires, werewolves, and knee-high tarantulas running around the city."

"Necrotics is our word for zombies," Oscar swiftly cut in after looking at the confused expression on Collin's face. "Sounds more serious."

"Ah, yes," said Mr. Pyrrhal. "Well anyway, for the last few days, I've just been burning the midnight oil, trying to minimize the mayhem."

"Then why couldn't we come with you?" asked Clark.

"I know, I know," Mr. Pyrrhal chuckled. "But it was best this way. I did find a werewolf or two, but that was it. I couldn't track much else, so I met with the branches in San Marco, Springfield, Deerwood, Beaches, and Arlington, and they all say the same thing: there's been a lot of sightings with the general public, but no actual manifestations."

Collin was surprised to hear Mr. Pyrrhal listing off a handful of the different neighborhood regions of Jacksonville. Knowing how entwined Veil was within his city actively excited him. He was able to decide they must've been staying in the Mandarin branch, if there were other Veil outposts throughout the community.

"So that's it?" asked Clark.

"That's it. A dull goose chase. Nothing we think y'all couldn't handle but, from what I hear, I'm glad y'all stayed here." He eyed Collin with a welcoming smile.

Collin squirmed diffidently and could feel his face developing the early stages of the deep red shade of embarrassment. Nobody laughed, and that Collin was grateful for. Clark and Oscar were the only ones to grin along. Olivia sort of did. She gave a half-smile coupled with a pair of piercing eyes expressing the sum of their parts, saying "Look what we dragged in." Afterwards, the almost-twins went into a rendition about how they came across Collin.

By the time they concluded, Mrs. Goodall finished her preparations and volunteered Olivia and Oscar to help with migrating food from the kitchen to the table. In the short time it took for Mr. Pyrrhal to inform everyone of his insipid adventure, and for Clark and Oscar to give their tale, Mrs. Goodall managed to put together a platter of half a dozen peanut butter sandwiches, grilled cheeses, and turkey sandwiches. There were also heaping vegetable platters, cheese boards, and a boiler-sized pot of French onion soup, along with pitchers of water and sweet tea.

"I'm so sorry, Collin," she said apologetically. "I should've asked. Do you have any allergies I should know about?"

Collin shook his head. "No, ma'am. This all looks great."

The nonchalant devouring of Mrs. Goodall's lunch was spent mostly in silence. Every now and again someone would ask a question related to news circulating the nation. Apparently, a banshee had been harassing a camping crew out in Colorado, and a poltergeist had taken the task upon itself to creep the suburbs of Beverly Hills.

"I saw somewhere in *The Spellbinder* that an entire small town disappeared? Is that right?" Taylor asked Osmond intelligibly.

"It's being looked into," Osmond said tersely, dipping his turkey sandwich into his soup before ripping the sodden section with his incisors.

After all the food was eaten and every dish cleaned, Mrs. Goodall gave Collin a brief tour as she guided him to the room he would be staying until further notice, not in the basement. Clark, Oscar, Alice, and Olivia tagged along since they were headed in that direction.

From the dining room they made a right turn down the hall. On the left were the study and the bathroom Collin was already familiar with. Between the two, the first door on the right was Oscar's bedroom, built right beside Clark's, whose bedroom door was directly across from the bathroom. They took pleasure in describing their methods to disintegrate a portion of the wall between their rooms so they could share one large room.

"It's a fun reminder of the days back in college," said Oscar.

"It works pretty well," Clark added. "We'll put up an illusion spell over the gap, like the whole sock-on-the-doorknob analogy, whenever one needs a little privacy."

Mrs. Goodall shot them a sharp look from the front of the pack, causing them both to stare in opposite directions in a not-so-casual way. Olivia gave an audible "Ugh" and a roll of her eyes. Collin grinned so wide it took all his self-control to fight back the laughter swelling behind his teeth.

At the end of the hallway, Olivia's room was found on the right as well. From there, she departed from the group as they veered left. Around the bend, and on the right, was Alice's room, who also splintered off.

Directly across from her room was a closet door. Mrs. Goodall warned him about it having started out as a typical closet back when the house was erected in 1817, but that, over the course of more than two centuries, it had been magicked time and time again to be bigger on the inside. However, as previous architectural spellcasters died out, the stockpile of spells faded with their owners, and, as it turned out, casting a spell was far more circumstantial than Collin gave it credit for. The room would expand and cave in and expand and cave it.

There was no telling what state the closet would be in each time someone were to open the door. Its dimensions could alter over the span of a second, an hour, a day, a week, and the only cure to it would be to either tear down the room entirely or spend an ungodly amount of time reversing centuries worth of work. The ultimate decision was that it wasn't worth the time undoing, and wiping it off the face of the earth would result in the loss of several historical relics.

Continuing on, Collin recognized the metallic door leading into the basement all too well. Looking back on it now, there was nothing about his experience worth holding against Mrs. Goodall. The integrity of Veil and all its well-kept secrets would be attenuated if a parade of gimme-gimme beggars and ill-wishers were granted entry on demand.

"You might not associate that door with anything good," said Mrs. Goodall, "but with the proper spell, there're stairs that lead to more floors than the one. Like our training room, for example."

"Training room?"

"Yes, dear. Safe space to learn spells, sparring, a gym, and such."

He was sold with that news. With magic, monsters, a room of impossible junk, and alternating staircases, he momentarily became absentminded about the seriousness of the darkness prowling the world and started living in a miniaturized cutout of *Harry Potter*. He fan-boyed to the core, fantasizing about the possibility of chocolate frogs and flying broomsticks.

His daydream was short-lived, however, as they ventured to the right and his bedroom was pointed out to him as the first door on the left. Clark and Oscar seized the opportunity to make their departure from the tour to go upstairs, claiming they wanted to experiment with a spell involving conjuring rashes. Mrs. Goodall surveyed them suspiciously, but let them go all the same.

A second spare bedroom was directly across the hall. Further along was Glenda's and Osmond's master bedroom, directly across from Taylor's room.

"Would you like to see your room? Or we could see the rest of the house?" Mrs. Goodall asked.

It was a tricky question. Collin most certainly wanted to see the rest of the house, but if he wasn't permitted to go anywhere else until further notice from the Council, he figured he was in no rush. Plus, the emotional rollercoaster of the day's events still lingered on his conscience.

"I might just get acquainted with the room for now. I'm still kinda tired. "

"That's all right. That's all right. Let me know if there's anything I can do for you. Or feel free to ask anyone else. I'm sure they'll be able to help."

She stood by, watching Collin adjourn himself to his anointed bedroom. Closing the door behind him, he found the light switch to be a dimmer switch. He pushed it inward, hearing the *click* of it being turned on. Not a single source of light was observed, but the room lit with even distribution. Collin tested the dimmer a couple of times in awe of the lack of a light fixture.

The room itself was massive. Perhaps it wasn't as long as the dining room, but it sure as hell compensated with twice the width. In the far-left corner, an ornate, four-poster king-sized bed lay facing the doorway, the wood of the bedframe a dark, varnished walnut. Collin made his way across the sea of beige carpet and stiffly climbed on top of the mattress. There was relief to find the level of firmness would suffice in reducing his tossing-and-turning habit.

Facing the bed was an empty bookshelf consisting of two three-feet-wide shelves joined in the center with a third shelf half the width designed to be adapted for the corner. All three segments stood over six feet tall with six shelves. On the opposite corner of the room sat an L-shaped desk similar to the ones in the study, hutch and all. It even came equipped with a rolling office chair. Opposite of that was a wide dresser, underneath a double-pane window, with wide drawers.

Next to the dresser, Collin inspected a door going to

his personal, white-tiled bathroom. In it was a black, marble, basin sink, a white ceramic toilet with buttons on the tank, depending on whether he took a shit or not, and a walk-in shower comparably smaller than the public bathroom. He was mesmerized.

If this was a spare bedroom, did the others have rooms of equal or greater size? God only knew how massive the master bedroom must be.

He found his way back to his bed and laid down to evaluate the accumulation of events. As he did, he was instantly sedated with exhaustion. The strength allotted by his few hours of sleep now burned fumes. At first, he only succumbed to the weight of his eyelids. His thoughts in the façade of semi-darkness were all he needed at the moment.

***

He was graced with a couple more undisturbed hours. By the time dinner rolled around, he found his stomach still full from lunch. His absence was understood, yet the heavy pangs of guilt toward his hostess throbbed.

The duration of the week was spent similarly. The reaping of his consequences caught up to him on a psychological level, and distance from people was his only known method of coping through it. Not to say he was regretting his decision by any means, but the concept of eliminating seventeen years of his past wasn't a decision even he could move on from overnight.

What helped was that, on the second day, Mrs. Goodall allowed him to borrow *Elementary Spells, Volume One* to study early, but only with the vow he wouldn't attempt any spells without supervision. It was a promise that bought immediate remorse after flipping to the first page.

While he'd been forewarned about the peculiarities of casting, what he read reached a whole new level of expectations. As it turned out, the power of spells relied on a combination of miscellaneous occurrences. The easiest to judge included moon rotations, seasons, weather, one's terrain, and sometimes planetary positions. The last was less crucial in casting posture, except per ninety-degree increments, and especially during an alignment of the solar system. During those rare periods, magic apparently experienced a complete blackout.

What proved even more shocking was how a person's sex could alter one's casting. The differences in feminine and masculine formation of spells were slight, but could make all the difference in the world when paired with the proper genitalia. For this reason, Collin wasn't surprised when the table of contents divided the area of actual spells to the first six hundred twenty-eight pages for males, the next six hundred twenty-eight pages for females, and the third section for hermaphrodites and transgenders. The text had clearly been updated to become more extensive on these two conditions.

By the end of his second day in the Mandarin outpost, Collin had ingested over a hundred pages of introductory material that, for the most part, seemed dully outdated. Its purpose served as a textbook, and, while his bread and butter was academics, it didn't seem necessary to ramble on for thirteen pages about the author's misogynistic opinions of his time on how he believed women would never truly harness the willpower necessary to cast.

Alice sure as hell seems like she's damn capable.

The notation on hermaphrodites and transgenders shouldn't have been worth looking over, knowing for damn sure William Wrights must've prepared for a field day on the topic, yet Collin powered through it. Learning about the general train of thought in a far past era was the equivalent to learning history, in his opinion, and he wasn't going to be another sensitive-minded American who got offended by every little great divide. Nevertheless, it wasn't information worth retaining.

The only other bit of actual theory read was how *Elementary Spells* was a necessity in mastering if any reader possessed the intention to advance further. Most of the intermediate day-to-day spells were built on the choreography and theory of basic spells. Even something as simple as starting a fire from a distance required an in-depth knowledge of how to ignite air, project, and expand a spark.

The third and fourth day had been dedicated to finger exercises. This included stretching, bending, and shaping in some of the most supernatural and excruciating ways. There was the common spreading of the fingers, shaking them, and wiggling them, but that was child's play. One of the first lessons expected even the youngest students to be able to rest the tip of each finger on the proximal interphalangeal joint of each adjacent finger without aid of the other hand.

That meant pinky finger stacked on ring finger, stacked on middle, stacked on index, and backwards. This required a bit of sideway twisting more painful than thought possible when building off the pinky finger from the bottom.

One particular stretching exercise amused him. He brought his hands together and used his middle fingers to lock in his ring fingers, the tips of which served as eyes, the tips of his middle fingers forced together triangularly as the upper jaw, and his thumbs facing upward, side-by-side as the lower jaw. With his pinkies interlocked for stability, he saw the head of a snake.

He continued to practice into the fifth day, submitting that, until the flexibility of his fingers alone could outdo the full-body skill-set of a contortionist's, he'd be at it for some time. For now, though, he was content on learning to fundamentals. His promise to Mrs. Goodall to abstain from using spells took a masochistic turn. Each spell was detailed with their origins, description of outcomes, and theory behind the purpose of the movement of each distal, middle, and proximal phalange, and even a couple metacarpals. There were written instructions for each hand movement, in addition to picture diagrams.

As it turned out, the most fundamental spell in all of a spellcaster's career was to summon a white noise, tingling sensation to the tip of the index finger. In its description, the author wrote how it should match the pins and needles sensation one got when a limb goes to sleep. Mundane and as seemingly useless as it might be, Collin still embedded every word to memory as best he could.

There were copious amounts of magic still to learn. One could learn to summon a single spark from each finger, temporarily change the hue of different limbs to any shade, and project the sense of touch on distant objects. This didn't include gripping and moving said objects, just touching them. There were also lessons on how to create light from nothing, create heat and cold, and creating a small breeze. The list went on.

It mostly seemed like childish stuff, extremely microcosmical in the vastness of one's environment, until he reconsidered the author's mention of mastering these spells before expanding upon them. Collin supposed *Elementary Spells* could be comparable to being given the bricks needed to build with, instead of being given the whole damn house. God only knew how deep the other four volumes of the series delved into.

In the stillness of that same night, Clark and Oscar were the first ones to invade his space with a knock on the door. He had been sitting in bed in his now redundantly white outfit after taking his shower for the day. His vision was mildly blurred from the subsequent days of solid reading. According to them, Mrs. Goodall had requested everyone to not bother him while he was getting adjusted to the potential prospects of calling, what they deemed Mandarin Mansion, home.

"But we figured that was stupid, and you've had enough time to yourself, so we came to see how your studies were going," Clark half-whispered, aware they were in the room next to Glenda's and Osmond's, and sneaking around at night wasn't forbidden, but it was frowned upon.

"Would've done it sooner," said Oscar, "but we figured if we did what she asked for a few days, it'd seem less suspicious when we finally did pop in on you."

"Ah," Collin said sheepishly.

"So?" Clark and Oscar asked in unison, with the obvious trailing off of their tone that inquired about his progress.

"It's not bad," Collin replied. "I've read up on a lot of the spells already."

"Have you tried any yet?" Oscar asked.

Swelled excitement fluttered in Collin's chest at the mere mention of him doing magic. In his excitement was a mixture of foreboding for something he hadn't even done, like driving with a cop behind you, paranoid of being pulled over when all the traffic laws have been obeyed.

"Ms. Glenda made me promise not to."

"Nah," said Oscar, with furrowed brows and a jaunty wave of his hand telling him 'don't listen to that old crow.' "There are some spells you definitely shouldn't try without guidance, but there's no need for such a verboten request." Toward the end of his sentence, he adopted a formal, southern gentlemanly voice. "I think you can manage a few sparks without anything destructively flammable around."

Oscar hopped onto the foot of the bed cross-legged. Clark, however, stretched out his arm and an open hand toward the office chair. It zoomed toward him without any finger-bending.

"Howwww...did you do that without moving your fingers?" Collin asked.

"*Advanced Spells*," he said, tapping his nose and taking a seat. "No spoilers. Now let's not leave you behind on these serendipitous times. Let's see what you're made of. Do this."

He held his right hand up straight and instructed Collin to do the same. Collin did the same, mirroring ever step before recognizing the motions as the spell used to summon sparks in a single finger. Right hands straight up, they each bent their index finger and squared off with the base of the finger. They fanned out the pinky and the thumb with the middle and ring fingers still bound together. Next, the tip of the thumb met the ring finger half way, near the center of the palm. The middle finger crossed to lay on top of the ring finger, and the pinky was brought down to be tucked on the fleshy area of the thumb. Then, in one swift motion, they snapped their thumbs on each's ring finger simultaneously with bringing the index finger back up.

If done rapidly and smoothly enough, the energy of the snap would transfer to the index finger and a few sparks would briefly fly out of it. For Clark, this was so. For Collin, not so much.

If he hadn't already been working on his finger stretches, he would've been beleaguered by his immediate failure. If he hadn't watched in awe at how the spell worked so effortlessly for Clark, he would've been left groping myopically for reasons why, beyond the simple explanation that practice makes perfect, things went differently for him. His sudden disappointment in himself was pinpointed back to a dire need to impress everyone in the house.

That's not too unreasonable, is it? he asked himself, but soon switched his thinking. *You're being stupid. I'm sure they weren't master spellcasters by their first casting. Technically, firing off sparks is a chapter three spell.*

"No worries," said Clark. "We'll hang around until you get it."

That warmed Collin. There weren't many moments when his brief bouts of panic would kick in at the slightest breeze, but when they did, God help him. He took a deep, frustrated breath and nodded before his second attempt, followed by a third and fourth attempt, and a fifth, sixth, and seventh. By the eighth try, his hand, already sore from his exercises, cramped worse.

Nonetheless, the pain forced him into a state of stubborn resolution to see the task through. In his mind, determination manifested into the neurotransmitters enhancing his ceaseless doggedness. It wasn't the first time he'd felt this way. This experience typically arose when solving puzzles or difficult math problems, or taking on secret bosses in video games significantly harder to beat than any storyline opponent.

It's all about will. You have to truly mean it. You have to dig into your guts and soul and past, present, and future, and you have to truly fucking mean it.

And he sure as shit meant it. He dedicated the next few

seconds to accumulating purpose from pain. As he snapped his thumb on his ring finger, while it came in simultaneous contact with his index finger, a single spark shot out.

"Hey!" Clark exclaimed softly. "You got something."

"Not much, but something," Collin said with controlled excitement, his chest giving two good heaves.

"But it's a start," Oscar encouraged. "Get the hang of the motion and remember the feeling of it. It gets easier if you can recreate your expectations for each cast."

Collin tried it again. Nothing. He tried a second time and another spark came out. The duo stayed for a few more minutes to give him pointers: Do stretches relentlessly, force his willpower into his spells, imagine the effects as they're anticipated, and so on.

"Not everyone can do spellwork, but theoretically anyone should be able to," Oscar quietly informed. "A lot of the motions are obscure enough and require a bunch of well-rehearsed hand sequences, that spells are difficult to stumble upon, and even if someone does, it still doesn't mean they're eligible. Magic requires sort of an innate bit of you. It *is* a bit of you. It's something you can almost feel, and it requires dedication and painful amounts of self-control."

"And you don't have to be a genius to do it," Clark added. "It's more cliché these days than ever, but children can typically tap into it pretty easily, but, again, the motions are what trip them. Plus, it's considered too unethical to raise children to do spells, unless your parents are already certified spellcasters. There are a few families out there, like the Brackens or the Claridges. As you get older, though, brains become more of a prerequisite, *especially* with the Generation Z shitheads and younger."

"Generation Z?" Collin asked.

"Yeah. Gen Z, the iGeneration, the Post-Millennials. The underage assholes that make millennials look like the hardest workers of this century."

"Ah," Collin chuckled.

"Yeah, Clark and I tried to teach a few kids a trick or two…With the full intent of making them forget," he paused to emphasize. "But there comes an age when they can't comprehend instructions unless it's shown to them in a video on a tablet. *Seriously!* You thought *our* generation was bad…"

Not long after, the almost-twins left with a brotherly slap on the shoulder and vehemently whispered exclamations about not letting anyone know about how they had experimented with teaching pre-teens spellwork, and took their leave. They crossed the distance between Collin's room and theirs like shadows until they were safely stationed. The hour struck passed midnight before Collin finally drifted off.

On his sixth day in Mandarin Mansion, the two boys didn't openly approach him around Mrs. Goodall, but shared the occasional wink if they ever passed each other. Collin continued to practice the spell for summoning sparks in privacy, but only the one spell. He still felt guilty for breaking his promise and worried it could raise suspicion on

Overture

his pledge to remain abstinent from casting before even becoming a hypothetical honorary member of Veil.

Nevertheless, he was damn sure going to master that single spell. You couldn't give someone the key to heaven and expect them to say "Nah, I'm good." He still studied the theory, origin, and sequence of other spells from Wrights' textbook, but his time was allocated more for those tempting sparks. Only when his hands seized with cramps did he stop, but that wasn't until briefly before dinner.

By then, he was okay with calling it a day. By then he could perform the spell with his eyes closed and hands behind his back, and could keep the combusted air particles around for nearly the duration of an average sparkler. He went to bed with a grin of satisfaction etched on his sleeping face, not knowing the next day was going to be one of the best days he'd remember until the day he died.

***

His day started after Mr. Pyrrhal left Mandarin Mansion early to help the members at the Arlington division with a missing-persons case developed the previous evening. He took Alice with him, Collin found out, when he went to join the others for breakfast at six-thirty. There were the usual wide array of meats, carbs, fruits, yogurts, drinks, and condiments. Collin deduced this to be the usual buffet based on the past week's assortment. He took his place at the middle of the table, on the left-hand side, and dished up a plateful of items. He put a few squirts of ketchup on his eggs and a splash of milk in his coffee, but saved the syrup for when we was ready for his pancakes.

Olivia and Oscar appeared to be deep in conversation, but Collin could see Oscar peeking stealthily past Olivia's perched elbow and raised arm angled into her temple. He was conjuring a spell for complicating Taylor's absentminded attempts to get food in his mouth while reading a newspaper titled *The Spellbinder*. The viscosity of his grits became so soupy it was practically repelled by the spoon. Collin saw out the corner of his eyes Clark adding fuel to the flame under the table with one hand and a piece of toast in the other. Whenever Taylor achieved a successful scoop, Clark made the substance spill over at the last second.

"Goddammit, will you stop!" he bellowed more fervently than what seemed warranted.

Olivia, who'd been trying with all her might to keep a straight face throughout the ploy, burst into gasping laughter. It would later be revealed they'd been messing with him all morning with making his eggs too rubbery to spear, giving his syrup an immiscible nature with his pancakes, and making his fruit mold prematurely.

Mrs. Goodall looked up from her own newspaper with full intentions of putting an end to it there and now before a green flame combusted from nowhere next to her plate. In its suddenly unburned place was a letter. She gave a deep pause of concern after scanning the front and vacated her seat. She pressed on around the bend of the table and handed the letter to Collin.

"I don't know if this is something I want to read, dear," she said with a voice flooded with enough somber to horde the attention of the entire room.

Collin's heart leapt to his throat as he took the letter. It was addressed to Mrs. Glenda Goodall and Mr. Osmond Pyrrhal of the Jacksonville, Florida, Mandarin Branch. Its return address was simply scrawled, in a calligraphic font, *The Council of Spell*. The pause of anticipation grasped at Collin much as it did Mrs. Goodall. In his hand was the answer to his future. He would either carry on with his training in magic or he would be exiled from the society permanently for sure.

"Go ahead," Clark urged.

Collin hastened to tear at the seam of the envelope before noticing a wax seal to make things simpler. Lined inside the red wax was an emblem he didn't recognize, and no doubt shouldn't recognize. In the center was a solid vertical line. Running through the line was a wavy figure he associated with wavelengths from a physics class he took. On the top-left side, the wave curved outward and back around to approach the line, passing through the center. It curved down and reflected the pattern toward the bottom-right of the symbol. From the tips of the waves that never touched the polar ends of the center line, there was a second curvature. On the left side, moving down, and on the right side curving upwards before stopping without touching the vertical bar again. At the end of the left outer curve was a line going slightly up, in parallel, with the center bar, while the end of the right curvature paralleled downward. Collin's closest comparison was of two incomplete scythes swirling clockwise.

He broke the seal and lifted the flap. Sliding the business printed paper out and unfolding it, he read aloud:

Mr. Osmond Pyrrhal & Mrs. Glenda Goodall,
It has recently been brought to our attention about the case of a one Mr. Collin Quinn from Paul Ganley, Head of the U.S. Examination Department of Veil. As you know, most applicants under the age of 18 are denied and returned to their previous or most adaptable standard of living. Mr. Ganley, however, has provided insight to Mr. Quinn's peculiarity. It has also been brought to our attention that Mr. Quinn has a coming-of-age birthday set to take place in less than three months, on the 28th day of October. With this date being within 90 days, we have elected to take the timing of Mr. Ganley's proclamation with serious consideration.
That being said, while we do not typically condone personnel to undergo induction into Veil at a technically young age, we cannot ignore exceptionalism, and provide a counteroffer in light of our current predicament: Mr. Collin Quinn may enroll as an honorary member of Veil, but will not be granted the title of Spellcaster until a legal adult. For the initiation to commence, a signature is required on the Terms and Agreement attached for the inductee AND the guardian of the Veil, Mandarin Branch, located in Jacksonville, Florida, U.S. of America. Until Mr. Quinn's birthday,

he is required to approach his studies as normal, but is banned from partaking in field work.

After the attached form is signed, you agree to personally educate and protect your student from mortal peril until Mr. Quinn has achieved acceptable marks on his examinations in his novice course. We wish you luck on your endeavors and hold great esteem in your teachings.

Sincerely,
Eleanor Merriweather
Head Councilwoman of the Council of Spell

Collin rubbed his thumb and index finger on the packet of papers and noticed two other separate pages. One sheet was the Terms and Agreement form for him to sign and the other was for Mrs. Goodall to sign. The font was squint-small, but as ornately detailed as any other run of the mill "Click 'I Agree'" documents.

"Don't worry about reading it," said Clark, as if reading Collin's thoughts.

"Yeah, it's just your common liability waiver," added Oscar. "If you get hurt, it's your own fault."

"Your friends and family, and anyone who could potentially pick you out of a lineup, will be forced to forget everything about you, so don't go looking for them," bantered Clark.

"If you lose an eye due to poor spellmanship, you're not allowed to sue."

"If you die due to poor spellmanship, you're not allowed to haunt. You know…the whole works."

Collin was sure they were right, but he still felt obligated to at least glance it over, at least until he saw Mrs. Goodall agreeing solemnly. The formality of the faction compared to average, mundane society was annoyingly businesslike, but he wasn't going to give it any more consideration. Mrs. Goodall summoned a pen from the study to whiz airborne through the hallway and into the kitchen, clicked the tip open, signed her form, and handed the pen to him. He watched as she snapped her thumb and ring finger to ignite the paper.

"Am I able to send it myself?" he asked.

"Yes," he could hear the forced positivity in her voice. "The form is already embedded with the tracer, so nothing special has to be done. Once it's sent, it'll go directly back to its author."

So, Collin imprinted his signature onto the sheet and stuck it so one side of its border hid between his middle and index finger. When he rubbed his thumb against the two, there was no trace of it in his sense of touch. He snapped his thumb and ring finger and observed the Terms and Agreement form burst into the familiar green flames, no heat.

Two seconds after the flame dissipated, a second letter singed into existence. This one indicated it belonged to Collin. No one made a motion for it to be read to the group. Collin was glad, for this letter was significantly shorter than the first, and so generically to the point he wondered if all acceptance letters said the same:

Mr. Collin Quinn,

We are pleased to announce your acceptance into Veil, a community dedicated to the safety of the people. While we are sure you have come to be aware of the existence of magic, we hope you are also aware that being a member of Veil requires a strenuous course of spellwork, history, physical education in combat, and potion making.

As I am sure you have been informed that, since you are still considered underage, you will not be granted the title of Spellcaster until your 18th birthday. As I am sure you have also been informed, you will be expected to complete an examination to graduate from your novice rank into more intermediate coursework. This exam will take place exactly six months after your birthday, on April 28th. We recommend you begin your studies as soon as possible. We are placing you in the care of Mr. Osmond Pyrrhal and Mrs. Goodall. Congratulations!

Wishing you luck,
Eleanor Merriweather
Head Councilwoman of the Council of Spell

And their seven became eight.

6

Hooch and Hypothesis

No studying occurred that day, but there was a build-your-own-taco bar for dinner. Collin never saw his favorite food given so many options. Mrs. Goodall had laid out monstrous plates of different tortillas, meats, cheeses, and veggies, to be complimented with salsa, sour cream, taco sauce, and guacamole. It was heaven.

Osmond was sent the news of Collin's acceptance right away, but he and Alice didn't return until the sun was setting and dinner was almost completed. Beforehand, the day mainly consisted of putting together a schedule to outline the upcoming days. Mrs. Goodall would be teaching the history of spellcasting as far back as the Ancient Egyptians. It would be Olivia who would be in charge of teaching him spells related to elemental, wayfaring, and telematic spells. Alice, although only considered an intermediate spellcaster in the eyes of the Council, possessed a knack for battle and defensive magic, and would be passing on her knowledge to him during Wednesdays. Clark and Oscar, even in the classroom, would still come paired on Thursdays. Their specialty being status magic, they were set to teach what all three of them humorously agreed to, in gaming terms, as buffs and debuffs. That is, enhancing attributes to items and people and reducing similar traits.

The worst news was Taylor being assigned to educate Collin in physical combat, already the least of his desired lessons. With Osmond as the head of the division, he wasn't expected to be around much, but his wife insisted she'd find something for him to contribute.

Each weekday would be dedicated to its own field, starting, to Collin's secret dismay, with history. He didn't want his path to becoming a spellcaster to begin by learning about their past. He wanted to cast ASAP. Instead, tomorrow, Monday morning, he was instructed to be in the study at six-thirty in the morning. Each class would take five hours out of his day.

Once all the details were ironed out, Collin was given the rest of the day to work on finger exercises, with great assurance he'd need to get them good and limber by Tuesday with Olivia. An additional perk was that he was promised to be taken clothes shopping after class, so he didn't have to keep wearing the repetitive, white long-sleeved shirt and scrub pants.

After dinner, and after the layered devil's food cake, divided and covered by fudge frosting and dark chocolate dipped strawberries, he retired to his bedroom and washed. Dead set on getting a good night's rest before his first *real* day, he was tucked under his comforter with eyes closed and peaceful, rhythmic breathing by nine-thirty.

It almost annoyed him, then, when he was awoken from his slumber only two hours later. A glaring, baby blue globe of light burned past his eyelids and went straight for the corneas. When Collin sat, the oddity sank into the carpet and glowed rhythmically in the darkness. He was hesitant only momentarily, making sure he wasn't dreaming with a biting pinch to his bicep. Throwing caution to the wind, he pelted out from under his bedsheets and landed softly on the floor.

As his feet landed near the glowing dot, he noticed it move about a foot forward toward the door. He stepped in its direction and it moved again. A quick conclusion decided it was leading him out of his room, but whether or not this was something to be trusted hadn't quite been discerned. The concern dissipated as quickly as it materialized. The likelihood of something dangerous trailing him outside of such a heavily warded home seemed foolish. Nevertheless, he threw on his white uniform and allowed his curiosity to see how far this light would guide him.

He crept to the door and watched the glowing light slip underneath. Slowly, he twisted the knob of his bedroom door with exaggerated control so as to avoid the *clicking* of the latch bolt. The door was soundlessly swung open. The dim orbs of light that typically occupied the hallways in the late evening were extinguished and the only illumination came from Collin's escort. Dead silence buzzed ominously as he sucked in his breath and held it unknowingly. Another step. Another.

The light guided him to the right, to the end of the hall, to the left. Along the way, he scarcely made out the silhouette of Alice's bedroom door and the closet Clark and Oscar once dorkily dubbed the *chaos-et*. The lack of life chilled Collin like a young child stumbling to find the bathroom in mortal terror of darkness, forced to maneuver through the vast void of existence to return to bed. He himself regressed to that inevitable stage between each step, pondering the possibility of each move toward the light being his last altogether.

In this new world, it couldn't be too far-fetched to be true, right?

But he followed through the motions, his mind and body divided.

Past Alice's room, he turned right and came to Olivia's door. All throughout the remaining hallway, silence ensued. Only a couple of times did he realize he was choking on withheld air only to repeat the mistake. His heartbeat thudded in his eardrums with quickening pace as the trail lengthened. Despite the age of the house, it was a pure, uncut miracle that not a single floorboard creaked. This feature was most likely attributable to magical upkeep.

Not much further, the lighted path did something unexpected. It didn't motion to lead Collin to the front door, but instead angled itself to the left and underneath Clark's door. Puzzled and unexpected, Collin involuntarily jumped in fright as the door to Clark's bedroom swung open with Clark standing in the doorway. The light from inside the room didn't flood the hallway as one would expect from the natural phenomenon. In fact, there was nothing natural about what Collin was seeing. No noise was emitted from the bedroom either, yet there Clark was, waving him in while his lips formed the words *come on, come on.*

Looking past, Collin saw Olivia and Oscar seated on the edge of Clark's king-sized bed, next to an espresso black, horizontal bookcase, engaged in conversation. The attire for the two boys was nearly business casual. They each wore a pair of jeans with brown leather belts sticking from underneath their matching charcoal gray dress shirts laid with vests over top and black ties to complement. Olivia was dawned in a ruby red dress with matching lipstick, her blonde hair styled in curls. A little show-boaty, but attractive nonetheless.

Collin followed Clark's gesture. As soon as he broke the threshold of the doorway he was bombarded with a temporary sensory overload. Clark was welcoming him with a pat on the shoulder while Olivia and Oscar glanced at him before resuming their discussion. The music in the background was unmistakably *Fly Me to the Moon* by Frank Sinatra. The lyrics serenaded an immediate hunger for classy cocktails and pinstriped suits.

The bedroom was enormous, to the point where even Collin knew Clark and Oscar must've done much more than open a section of the wall between rooms. The carpet had been torn up and hardwood flooring laid polished in its place. The walls were expanded nearly twice the size of Collin's and the ceiling was raised several feet higher than all the rooms throughout the entire house, save perhaps the study.

The door was symmetrically center with the dimensions of the room. On the right, Collin saw the reconstruction between the rooms. There wasn't a mere hole in the wall, but an actual door carved into a makeshift wall. Not just any door either. It wrought the vivid memory of the Doors of Durin in the first of the *The Lord of the Rings* trilogy, the ones leading into the Mines of Moria. The fine, silver inlay with the two pillars and the two trees on the inside of the arch wrapped around them. Clark and Oscar must've put some genuine effort into this to go so far as to include the elvishly "C" in the top left corner, the "N" in the top right, and the "P" at the foot of the trees. They even included, going bottom-up, a single star, a hammer and anvil emblem, a crown with seven stars, and the elvish writing within the arch of the two pillars that, according the books, said "Speak, friend, and enter." There was more, but he couldn't recall it all.

"Caught your eye, heh?" Clark noticed, wrapping an arm around Collin's neck, and redirecting his attention toward the bar stationed to the right of the door. "It's fully functional too. Look."

Clark shouted "Mellon" at the entrance and the flush doors swung outward. Collin was speechless. He knew the pair were the humorous occupants of the house, but never imagined them being about to use magic to indulge in the iconic pleasures of pop culture.

"It's all nice and well," said Clark, "but tonight is cause for other celebrations."

He waved at the table in front of them. There must've been nearly one hundred shots laid out. Left to right, rows and rows of libations were organized by the classic ROYGBIV of the visible spectrum. Some had a crown of fire on their surface. Some sparked of their own accord. Others fumed tendrils of smoke that wrapped around their own glasses. Many were layered, most were blended or straight. A few bubbled forevermore like peroxide on a cut, while a select few appeared iced over, mucky, or like the activated contents of glow sticks.

"We might consider ourselves hunters-slash-students by day…and by night, but that doesn't mean we can't be rowdy party animals off duty, c'mon. There's too many too explain. You can choose what's most appealing or I can point out the top rated, but I recommend starting with the non-magical ones until you're warmed up."

"Top rated will be fine," Collin said. His cheeks flush with embarrassment for his nature of clamming up during social events around new people. While he'd spent a fair amount of time seeing these people on a daily basis, he hadn't officially consented to considering them anything more than acquaintances. The dynamic duo being the only two possible exceptions, but he still didn't *know* them.

"Okay, so we first have straight shots of absinthe for the black liquorice lovers," Clark spoke like a wine store employee offering free samples with a slight backstory to each variety. He pointed to a cluster of acid green shot glasses. "We then have the Wolf Bite," he pointed to the shots next to the absinthe. These were layered like a reverse traffic light with green on top and red on the bottom. "It includes, absinthe, Midori, pineapple juice, grenadine, and lemon-lime soda." He next pointed to a set of red shots. "Next is what is apparently called Dream of the Red Chamber. It's sure to get you wherever you need to go. This is more of a catch-up drink, *only* if every single person in the room is already several drinks ahead of you."

"Which we are!" Olivia shouted over at them with a paired giggle, her speech a tipsy slur.

Collin and Clark looked over at them with teeth-bearing grins, before turning back to the plethora of libations. "In it, there's cherry liqueur, blood orange liqueur, blood orange tea, Alchermes, and the one and only baijiu," Clark continued. "Then there's the personal favorite of quite a few sorority delights from my time at UF…Yes, I was a frat man in the boat shoes, pink shorts, and a polo, but I was never frat tool enough to cock my hat backwards, rest my sunglasses on said hat, and proceed to bitch about how bright the sun was, but I digress. This concoction is the crown jewel Pink Panty Dropper. Mr. P.P.D., himself."

Next to the baijiu shots were significantly more pink draughts. Based on the color and sweet aroma Collin's undivided attention detected, he could already guess the flavor of this one.

"It's beer, tequila, pink lemonade from concentrate, and

good ol' Everclear. Not the poor seventy-five percent grain alcohol Florida can only sell, but the actual 190 proof we make trips to Georgia for, and there's no shame in dudes drinking it also. It's practically candy. No burn, but it'll kick your ass.

"I may as well also warn you that all of these are spiked with a little pure grain alcohol to give them that extra boost, but they're still drinkable. Oscar and I are still trying to perfect our own pure grain alcohol as easy to put down as water, but you can't rush perfection."

Clark's gait and the social eccentricity he thrusted around himself, mixed with the lively and classy atmosphere of the room inspired Collin to want to take part. The feeling made him uncomfortable. He'd only been drunk around his friends from high school, but it thrilled him all the same. He wasn't sure how much older they were compared to him, but that didn't mean they couldn't take up the mantle as symbolic older siblings. He would have to trust them at some point, so might as well take part in a little team-building.

He hesitantly snagged a shot of the Pink Panty Dropper. A quick kickback of the head and it slid down the hatch. Instantly, he knew Clark had been correct in his description. It was almost as sweet as drinking pure lemonade. How, with beer and tequila, he had no clue, but their recipe worked. He clutched another and slammed it back.

"One more, just for luck?" Clark coaxed, a gleam of victory twinkling in his bright blue eyes.

Collin knew he shouldn't. If the concoction was as strong

as advertised, he'd be on his ass in the first hour. Peer pressure could be a righteous bitch at times, though, and he yearned for their approval. He cocked back a third.

"I'll need a minute," he insisted.

"No problem, Grasshopper," Clark laughed. "We'll get you going professional soon enough."

Clark snagged four shots, two per hand, and they turned for Oscar and Olivia. Doing so, Collin was able to finally observe the rest of the room. Hanging from the wall by the foot of the bed was a massive curved TV. The entertainment center below had a few gaming consoles. Collin was willing to make an educated guess there would be several other consoles inside the cabinets. At the actual foot of the bed were two dark, leather recliners. Underneath them, the wooden floor looked to be adjustable.

On the opposite wall from all the drinks, their bookshelf was nearly full of videos games and movies. Alice stood in front of it, perusing through the selection.

"Hey! Alice is here," Collin said, not holding back his surprise.

"Yeah," Clark chuckled. "Don't let her fool you too hard. She may portray her typical tenebrous nature in any other setting, but we can occasionally get her out of her shell," and he lankily took one of the shots in a single gulp without spilling the second in that same hand. "Taylor shouldn't be too much longer either."

"Taylor?" Again, Collin's lack of restraint on his surprise

failed him. Only this time his surprise was mingled with a hint of discontent.

"Sure. Never misses a function."

Clark clearly picked up on Collin's tone, but he didn't rub his nose in it. Instead, he wanted to set the record straight in an amicable manner. "Don't worry too much about him. He's a lot like Alice in that they're a bit misleading."

"How so?" their pace slowed as they neared Oscar and Olivia.

"Well…He likes to play the strict one, but as the somewhat unspoken leader of us tweenies, and you and Alice, he cares a great deal about our safety."

"Ah," said Collin softly enough to have his voice muffled by the music. He was quick to change the conversation in fear of giving off his unyielding distasteful impression of Taylor. "If he's the leader, then who's everyone else?"

Clark laughed and took another shot.

"Ms. Glenda and Osmond are the obvious foster parents. Oscar and me are only here for the comic relief. Alice is our brains and the true powerhouse of spellcasting—"

"And I'm the hot piece of ass!" Olivia interjected with a fist in the air and a slight glaze in her eyes.

Clark and Oscar cheered, and they and Olivia toasted this declaration with another helping of shots. Euphoria welled inside Collin's chest at the same time. The sensation got him excited. Maybe that was the alcohol. While he didn't consider himself as cripplingly shy as he did Alice, he knew he had a knack for confining himself to his thoughts and his own personal ambitions. When he drank, however, he was livelier.

A reverse Jekyll and Hyde, except the only antidote for alcohol is rest and water, and the effects aren't eventually permanent. Jesus, he wasn't kidding about the alcohol!

The ball of joy in his chest migrated north. The sides of his face tingled before the overall numbing localized in his lips. His brain played tug-of-war with the idea of getting another shot and waiting it out. While he was inexperienced with holding his liquor, his logic dominated at the last second with refraining from taking another dive at the adult beverages.

"So, Collin," Clark left a quick pause to allot the opportunity for everyone to hear *Feeling Good* by Michael Bublé now playing, "how does it feel to be the youngest member of Veil in, what, a few good decades?"

"*Honorary* member," Olivia corrected with a playful sneer.

"*Honorary* member. My apologies," Clark adjusted, more for Olivia this time than Collin.

"I suppose I should eat my words though," Olivia admitted. "I did tell you the odds would be slim with getting in without being an adult and having a horror story of your own." Her enunciations of the letter *s* were progressively elongating.

Collin didn't know what to say except shrug in ignorance of how he should feel other than ecstatic for breaching into the world of magic. The concept of monsters becoming glossed over with each day.

"Nah. It's not the first time exceptions have been made, and I doubt it'll be the last," Clark replied.

"Definitely not," Oscar added. "There's *way* too much going on right now. If it stays this way, I wouldn't be surprised if they lowered the age limit for new recruits."

Collin understood they were delving into a topic of politics of their people, and he was okay with staying on the sidelines of the discussion, but his soon-to-be-swimming brain had already diminished a healthy portion of his inhibitions.

"What's going on?" he asked.

"I'm sorry?" Oscar said.

"What's going on that's way too much?"

Both Oscar and Olivia opened their mouth to answer, but Clark stepped in to silence them with his empty hand raised and a shake of his head.

"It's nothing of importance right now. I'm sure it'll get settled before too long. Tonight is about celebrating you," and in a haste to distract them from the conversation, he changed the subject. "I could've sworn you were a Variant, the way you survived that wendigo."

There that word was again. They mentioned Variants before, but never elaborated on.

"What's a Variant?" he asked, taking the bait to swap topics.

"Ah yes," Clark uttered lyrically.

He set his shot glasses down on an unoccupied nightstand, the three empty ones segregated from his fourth. With two vibrant claps, the lighting of the entire room dimmed, only to be sourced by a string of lights without origin emanating along the crevice between wall and ceiling. Perfect mood-setting ambiance.

"Story time!" Olivia squealed, her hand stretched out to summon a shot from the variety on the table.

Clark held out his hand to Oscar as if requesting a dance. "Would you care to do the honors?"

Oscar waved him off, taking a leaf out of Olivia's book and using a spell to force another round into his hand. "I surely would," he said through wetted lips. "Gather round, ye olde jackanapes," he joked, "for 'tis time to tell ye the tale of *The Healer and the Fool*."

Collin glanced around to see Alice looking in their direction as she passed toward the table. Clark and Olivia laughed with knowledgeable anticipation. If Collin's intuitiveness was accurate, and this was to be Oscar's origin story, it was difficult to decipher on whether or not it was a matter to be taken more seriously. After all, Glenda's and Osmond's was a goddamned tragedy. Here, another person's story was being pawned off as a renaissance reenactment. He laughed all the same. He was on his way to a robust level of tipsy with people who cared enough to at least invite him to their late-night shenanigans. Even Alice joined in on Olivia's right once she picked a couple of her poisons.

Collin was strangely aware of her posture, but was doing his best not to be obvious with his observations. He wasn't sure how many more drinks she was ahead of him, if she even was. The two shots in her hand could've been her first two drinks of the night, but it didn't feel likely. She wasn't as chic as Olivia in her barefoot attire of jeans and a black t-shirt with a posterior, anatomical view of a bumblebee facing upward, wings spanning over her breasts, but she also didn't seem as tense as she usually did. Her shoulders were more relaxed and her back showed signs of minute insouciance. No other feature was out of the ordinary for what Collin was accustomed too, but the overall effect made her seem, for lack of a sober-minded assessment, lovely.

"You mind if I grab another drink first?" Collin asked. The tingling in his face achieved its peak and he knew soon would be the joyous numbing of the vestibule within his inner ear.

"I'd be insulted if you didn't," Oscar returned, his Cheshire grin beaming dapperly as he ran a hand through his messy black hair.

Turning around to make way for the table of shots made it apparent his balance was already impaired. He wasn't stumbling, but he figured he'd be better off with only grabbing one drink, and, for God's sake, no P.P.D.s.

As Collin reached his destination, he heard the others cheering. When he turned to see what the commotion was about, he saw Taylor had arrived.

"What the hell took so long?" he heard Olivia bark.

Whatever Taylor's response was, it was drowned out by the racket Clark, Oscar, and Olivia were making. Collin's euphoria diminished slightly, but hadn't abated enough to make him want to remain distanced from the group. Clark did vouch for Taylor, and he admired Clark enough take his words into consideration. Snagging a frosted, neon blue shot, he rushed back to rejoin the circle they formed, where the others were informing Taylor that Oscar was about to share his story about Variants for Collin.

"'Twas the age before shootouts were frequent plagues 'pon the nation, and our young hero, of the ripe age of two and ten, sat in school learning about the wonders of mathematics," Oscar flamboyantly recited. "The merry folk of Room 108, and the rest of the school as a matter of fact, were unbeknownst to the terror to strike them with thunderous rat-tat-tats. Our door was wretched open. The teacher, the first to fall ill to the parade of lead that penetrated her sweet bosom and glowing face that won many-a pubescent hearts, whether lads or ladies.

"Door locked behind, the students began to fall to the metallic rain. One such fool was given the grace to be revived twice only to fall mortally wounded each time, for our young hero had a special gift that even he barely knew about. His parents called him special, for a time or two this hero was able to heal sick pets with sheer will of mind and touch, and heal simpler cuts and bruises, and so we shall call him Healer.

"Back to our young fool hiding behind a thick table with many-a students, chocked full of superhero movies and believed him the savior of Room 108. With courage mustered, he stood to vanquish this villain, but was lethally wounded on the spot. He collapsed with grim prospects as the Healer leapt for him from behind the table. The might of his abilities still a mystery, he was shocked to find the bullet removed from this fool's body and his wound pieced together once more.

"But the fool didn't stop there. No sir! For his resurrection was prophetic. Here 'twas the god-sent hero, touched by the hand of destiny and possessed by the ghost of raw ignorance. Knowing all would play to the young fool's favor, he did not learn from his mistake and snuck out the side of the table, where he was shot in the shoulder. Well the Healer could still grab his shoe and so he revived the idiot once more, and wouldn't ye know it the shooter 'twas now barren of ammo."

At this point, Oscar paused to take another drink. There was a glaze over his eyes that now matched Olivia's. Collin looked around to see everyone's face. Taylor and Alice were the only straight-faced members of the audience. Taylor already summoned an acid green and a black, bubbling drink to his hands and consumed them both. Collin drank his own and was caught off guard by the searing trail of ice as it flowed down his esophagus and chilled his stomach. The illusion of his insides dropping below freezing didn't stop there. His initial and subsequent gasps exhaled clouds of frozen breath. Everyone but Taylor and Alice laughed, but even they cracked a smile beyond all odds.

"Suppose that wasn't the worst one you could've tried, but shots of Ice are usually supposed to be paired with Fire," Clark laughed.

He jogged past Collin and returned with a shot glass of lava red liquid with a short flame atop. Collin tried to grab for it, but was stopped when it became obvious he wouldn't be able to hold the drink without spilling it in his trembling hands. The icy feeling seeped into his circulatory system. It was astonishing how many arteries, capillaries, and veins one human could have without even realizing it. His skin was going pale, his lips and fingernails blue. Each abundance of air was a struggle to get in and out without a sharp scraping along his throat and lungs like knives. Clark fed him the second shot. It took an equal amount of time for Fire to cancel the effects as it did for Ice to cause them.

"You should try them in reverse next time," Taylor said in his solemn voice.

"You should do it now!" Olivia suggested with unnecessarily high exuberance. "It almost makes you feel like you're on fire."

"Maybe next time," Collin choked, still bent over, finding peace in the familiar quality of warm soup belly.

He straightened in time to catch Alice's eyes. His drunk goggles found her grin most charming. A grin was returned and she looked away. Not with rejecting intentions, but merely because Oscar was preparing to take the stage again to finish his tale of *The Healer and the Fool* as everyone's amusement was coming to a head. A *John Mayer* tune played through the bouts of settling chuckles. The nostalgia of hearing such a song kindled a youthful spark in Collin's chest before his dizzily encumbered vision limited his range of thinking.

Five shots, he counted in disappointment. *Five shots and I'm about as drunk as I've ever been.*

Standing straight was a hassle. Either he or the ground they stood on, he couldn't apply common sense, was wobbling so viciously that he was astonished to look to his left and see Alice swiftly manage to maneuver over to him. Turning his head forced his eyes to roll in their sockets as a wave of numbness travelled from his brain to the base of his neck.

"Just try to stand still," she spoke in his ear. "I'll try to keep you up."

Her words were incoherent to Collin, but her message was somehow translatable. He tried blinking his eyes to focus his ears. Perceptibly, the outcome proved useless, but his level of inebriation left him so fucked up that logic was as abstract as the enumerable hypotheses of life after death.

Oscar eventually did finish his story. It was almost completed anyways. Collin swayed to the oration like it was a slow song at a concert. His concentration was razor-like, except that he was only fooling himself. The fragments he was able to surmise from the telling was that Oscar was the Healer who could heal people and animals on touch with no magical background. He was born with the gift, making him a Variant. There were people who could perform unique pieces of magic as second-naturedly as eating and breathing. Oscar's revival of a student multiple times didn't go unnoticed and the spreading gossip put him on Veil's radar. His gift offered him a full ride into Veil, but only when he would become of age. However, he apparently resisted and chose the normal route of college before allowing his curiosities to overtake him between multiple invitations. Each rejection required a memory wipe.

Somewhere in the conclusion of the story were three more shots pushed on Collin. Half of the first was slopped onto his shirt and the floor, and therefore didn't count. Of the other two, the latter was a Jäger Bomb. All three, naturally, were mixed with a bit of pure grain alcohol. Needless to say, it sealed the deal on anymore drinking for that night.

The more seasoned members of Veil spent the next half hour asking Collin ceaseless questions about his life. Where he went to school? Status of his parents? Previous future academic plans and occupational dreams? Even more outlandish questions such as his favorite color, favorite cartoon to grow up with, the age he received his first kiss, and much more. Some bordered on uncomfortable, such as when and where he lost his virginity and how old he was when he first discovered the joys of masturbation. Between questions and answers, Collin was caught in more than one instance of singing horrendously along with whatever song played in the background. There was Panic! at the Disco's *Death of a Bachelor*, Jack Johnson's *Banana Pancakes,* and significantly more Frank Sinatra.

An unperceivable amount of time afterwards stole Collin's ability to sit or stand with his eyes opened or closed without his impaired balance invoking periods of nausea. Only when the others decided he'd had enough did Clark approach him with one more concoction. Collin tried to shove the offer away through shut eyes, slurring feeble streams of *nnnoooo*. They tried insisting through hysterical laughter that it would help him, and by the end of the argument it boiled down to Clark and Olivia forcing the drink upon him.

Throughout the duration of the night he went from timid to casual to outgoing to obnoxious to nauseous, and now, for a brief moment, his drunken insanity perceived the manhandling as bullying. He was suddenly misinterpreting their intentions and becoming scared and angry, but only for a second.

"Wwhat wasss that?" he asked after swallowing.

He saw Alice taking a shot of whatever it was too.

"It'll help with the hangover," Clark grinned. His enunciations were dragging as well.

Collin was suddenly, miraculously, able to understand what was said in the thirty seconds the elixir sat in his stomach.

"We would never sssend you off to your firrrst class with Ms. Glenda plassstered out your mind."

Collin's heart sank, but he was contrarily happy to know he could scrutinize on the emotions of sadness and remorse for his actions. In a few short hours, he was to be meeting Mrs. Goodall in the study for his first history lesson, yet he spent his first night drinking to the cusp of utter mortification. While he was sure he acted silly, he prayed to whatever higher power that he didn't make an absolute fool of himself in front of these people he hoped to call friends. He was incredibly grateful not to have vomited.

"So no hangover?" he asked.

"Ssshouldn't," Clark replied. "Potion making may be out-da-ted, but sssome is still worth knowing."

"I'll get him to his room," Alice swiftly stepped in uncharacteristically. "Make sure he gets there without waking Ms. Glenda and Oz."

Olivia perked up like a dog's ears hearing something in the distance. A devilish smirk spread across her face.

"Oh, don't be gross," Alice snapped through burning cheeks, knowing full and well what that look was alluding to.

Olivia feigned hurtfulness with a playful swipe of her hand like a paw and a "me-ow." She proceeded to engage Taylor in conversation with a sly side-glance at Alice, her smirk still prominent. Even Collin's sauced and sobering mind was pleased at the prospect of being escorted to his room by a pretty girl. Imagination even got the best of him for a second or two, when he noticed a twitch against the seam of his pants. It was a fantasy requiring an immediate distraction to avoid the risk of pitching tent in front of everyone in sweats.

Collin gradually got to his feet. The acid trail withheld in his throat during his fits of nausea were now dissipating. His dizziness was still present, but less prominent. There was no denying he was still inept in the art of linearly putting one foot in front of the other. Alice put one hand on his lower back and the other on his left shoulder as she guided him toward the door.

"Goodnight, sweetums!" Clark hollered.

"And good luck tomorrow!" Oscar added.

"To the nnnewest *honorary* member of Veil!" Olivia cheered as an excuse to take another shot.

Darkness and silence engulfed the pair after they crossed the threshold of the door.

"Don't move until I move you," Alice whispered.

Collin's eyes didn't adjust to the darkness quick enough for him to see she was creating a spell to ensure their silence. They swam through the abyss all the way through the extended hallway. Alice's hand on one of his shoulders guided him until they were both safe from detection in Collin's bedroom.

"Thanks," he said.

The two of them alone made him nervous. He wiped his sweaty palms on his pants and motioned to go sit on his bed while she continued to stand in front of the door.

"Uh huh," she regained some of her stiff personality as Collin regained more of his sobriety. "Did you enjoy your initiation?"

"Initiation?" Collin leaned back until his upper body was flat on the comforter.

"Oscar was here first. He and Clark started the tradition of getting all newcomers drunk and harassing them with questions. Even people who *were* here, but were assigned somewhere else. It's their way of testing out compatibility."

"Ah," Collin acknowledged. "Well…did I pass?"

From the corner of his eye, Collin saw her standing stock still, but giving his room a good look-over. He was a little self-conscious with how bland it was compared to something as fun as Clark's and Oscar's domain.

"With them, I'm sure," she answered. "But the rest of us are more here for our own education, on top of preparing you."

Collin sat up with piqued curiosity. Judging from her tone, he assumed she wasn't there to top the night off with any saucy interest, but she did appear to hold some amount of investment in him.

"You seem like a good candidate, and a little less..." she bent her head in the direction of Clark's and Oscar's ongoing party. "Not to say they're bad people. I like them. I just want more people who are..." This time she was showing signs of struggling for the right word, but Collin suspected what it was she was trying to say.

"Familiar?" he suggested

"Yes." Quick enthusiasm sparked then flickered in her voice. "And in the short amount of time you spent in our world you showed a determination to *stay* a part of it that rarely anyone shows. I want to observe what might come of it."

"Thank...you?" Collin said, unsure if she was praising him or referring to him as a means of experimental amusement, or both. She didn't notice his befuddlement either way.

"And now you're actually a part of us," she continued. "So I figured it might help to give you some advice while you go through the beginning phase."

"Okay."

Collin pulled himself toward the head of the bed into a

cross-legged position. It was effortful not to show her what he could do already. Hesitantly, she proceeded to take a seat at the foot of the bed, one leg bent over the sheets, the other still slung over the side.

"I was planning on giving you a chance to work ahead of the curve. So for the time being, focus mostly on studying the forms for different circumstances, stretch daily, and practice tirelessly. By the time you hit the advanced classes, you'll be expected to conduct your own hunt."

"For a monster," Collin said, more as a statement than a question.

Luckily his mind cleared enough to comprehend what was being told. Whatever potion Clark forced him to drink was a godsend.

"Yes. Not everyone chooses the hunter occupation, but the intensity of the creature will be the benchmark for how you'll be judged as a member of Veil. Especially in the higher ranks."

"Huh," was all Collin could say.

He wasn't even aware of what kind of beasts roamed the nation outside of wendigos, werewolves, and lycans. It was highly appreciated what she was doing to forewarn him, but simultaneously it frustrated him to be reminded of how his inexperience temporarily made him an outcast.

"You'll learn a lot about that sort of thing with time," she said, as if reading his thoughts.

"Do they have you prepare during intermediate classes?" he asked.

Alice shook her head. "No. The others here are all advanced spellcasters and they're preparing to do their…dissertation, if you will."

"And so, you're working to get ahead of the curve?"

She nodded. He noticed her cheeks growing rosy once again. Surely, he'd never met anyone in his life who embarrassed so frequently and so easily. It almost made him feel like his social insecurities trumped even the most confident of introverts. Oh, but how endearing it was. She may be nineteen, but the age wasn't a horrendous discrepancy.

"Do you have any projects in the works?" Collin asked.

Again, she nodded. "Do you remember what Osmond was telling us about his week around the city?"

"Yeah."

"Well," she pulled her slung leg up and went cross-legged like Collin, "I went with him this morning to help investigate a missing person, but we didn't find anything."

She must not have known he already knew this. Even if she did he was getting the impression this was all part of a spiel she'd been dying to talk to someone about. Her shyness oddly melted to reveal spunk and passion. There was a fire in her eyes he doubted would've sparked if they hadn't already been softened by a couple drinks, elixir or not.

"I think the missing person and Osmond's previous search are related. I think we're dealing with a shapeshifter. All the cases that we *do* know about involve only sightings of necrotics and what not, but they all seem to be related to *scary* stuff."

"So," Collin interjected quickly, "not all monsters are scary?"

"No," Alice replied with a tone sharp enough to convince him he didn't know the sum of two and two. "There's the caladrius, the raiju, the peryton, fairies, the list goes on. The fact that only frightening sightings have been reported by regular people is a little uncommon, especially when the sightings are things people tend to *fear*."

"And you think it's a shapeshifter. So, you think it's a shapeshifter that takes the shape of what people fear?"

"Yes!" she exclaimed, and immediately cupped a hand to her mouth and staring bug-eyed at the door. "Shit. *Usually* the rooms here are soundproofed. I'm sure nobody would hear us from the reverse, but yes."

"So, like a boggart from *Harry Potter*?"

Collin knew his suggestion hinted that this must not be the most difficult monster hunt in the history, especially when it was something J.K. Rowling's characters could counter in a single classroom session, but that was his nerd showing. Figuring it best, he kept further opinions on the matter to himself. A zealous Alice could be more dangerous than an angry Alice.

"Jesus, no!" she said irascibly, leaping to her feet and pacing back and forth. "Think Pennywise from *IT*, except you don't have to *believe* just to be preyed on. They aren't as divinely as Pennywise either. We call them timoras, not the Scots' glamours." At that point, it seemed she was having a conversation more with herself than Collin. "But they're rare. *Extremely* rare. Extremely powerful and clever, too. A timora hasn't been documented since the early 1800s. God only knows what this could mean if it *is* one."

Alice used firm hand gestures and flailed her arms in the air so uncharacteristically. Collin had no input. He was simply going to let her self-debate run its course as her volume fluctuated between energetic thrusts and inaudibility.

"The amount of missing people should be a lot more than it is, or at least what we know, but, if it's trying to stay undetected in a busy city, it may be having a hard time collecting victims." Her voice dropped below Collin's detectability for a distinct period of time before returning with vigor. "*But*, if it stays hungry long enough, it's possible it might get careless and go on a feeding frenzy. Sorry."

She recognized how her eccentricity got the better of her, and resumed her usual, apprehensive nature. She made motion for the door with the clear tenacity settling some sort of unfinished business. Stopping, she had one last request to make.

"Please don't tell anyone about what I told you. Good luck tomorrow," and she left.

Silently, Collin agreed. Slightly disappointed at the lack of romance in the air, but understanding all the same. He prepared for bed with impenetrable anticipation.

7

Professor Goodall

The others weren't joking about the elixir. Collin would have to remember to repay them for saving his life on his first day of...

Spellcaster School of Goddamn Sorcery, he laughed to himself as he silenced the alarm clock on his nightstand.

But it was true. Not only was he headache free and relinquished from the horrors of vomiting, but he couldn't recollect ever waking in better spirits, even with only a few short hours' worth of sleep. He was all hustle and bustle, cleaned, dressed, and raring to go by five-fifty.

He vacated his room and power-walked to the dining room to find Mrs. Goodall and her husband sitting next to each other sharing a mug of coffee.

"Good morning, dear," Mrs. Goodall greeted in an unnecessarily quieted tone. "Sorry the usual array isn't ready, but I'm sure everyone can fend for themselves on Mondays. Can I fix you anything before we begin?"

No, no, that's okay," Collin assured her with a polite smile. Surely, she did enough for the entire household. He didn't want to deprive her of a most certainly deserved break. "I can take care of it."

"Do you know where everything is?" She raised an eyebrow.

"Mmm. Not really. No."

"Oh, c'mon, dear," and she ushered him into the kitchen.

Along the far wall, from left to right, Collin observed a dishwasher, a double-bowl sink, a microwave sitting on granite countertops built above white-painted cabinets, and a stainless-steel double-door refrigerator with a bottom drawer serving as the freezer. All along the opposite wall, to his right, were cabinets and drawers above and below, filled to capacity with dinnerware, plastic ware, and an abundance of appliances for any food-based occasion. On the wall to the far right, farther from the door was a massive six-burner stove with two separate ovens. To the left of it was the pantry. The walls were all a light shade of gray and the flooring was almost diner-like with a black and white checker pattern.

"I usually change the style at least once a year, but with everything going on I haven't found the time," Mrs. Goodall said with no elaboration of what exactly was going on in her world. Their world now.

The dimensions of the kitchen were those of a multi-million-dollar household, and so, as most likely every other room in the house, was assumed to be expanded by magical means. In the middle of the room was an island designed with the entire surface being one large cutting board, save the border, as it was matching granite. There was a set of knives on top, and drawers full of tools for just about any task.

Mrs. Goodall gave him the tour of where to find everything he would need before giving him free reign to roam the pantry and fridge. The coffee pot was already half-full. That saved him one trip.

"Don't be shy to leave any dishes you use in the sink. I'll take care of them."

Collin thanked her and she left. When he looked into the pantry, he saw how it too had been altered to be bigger on the inside. There were eight shelves and it took a stepladder to retrieve anything from the top three. Each was arranged so excruciatingly satisfying that victims of obsessive-compulsive personality disorder might believe they were looking into the pantry of God.

The top shelf was grains. There were militia amounts of breads, cereals, oatmeal, pastas, rice, and such. The shelf below was stocked with canned goods ranging from acceptable to downright unappetizing. Next, there were standard sauces, and then sauces that went beyond kitchen commonality. The fourth rack was all the baking necessities one could dream of, all the way down to unopened yeast packets and molasses.

While in awe he might've been, Collin merely took a quick notice of the endless spices and seasonings, various produce, such as potatoes and sweet potatoes, and wines. Wines most of all, seeing as how two shelves were dedicated to red and whites.

Overture

Collin climbed aboard the stepladder and retrieved a loaf of whole wheat bread. Excited as he was, his anticipation left him on nerves and therefore lessened his appetite. Toast would do. Perhaps peanut butter toast. He snagged a jar of creamy Peter Pan and made his way to the toaster situated roughly center of the countertop on the side of the kitchen with the door. While the slices were getting heated, he dashed to the refrigerator and found it patterned as nicely as the pantry: a row dedicated to beverages, one for dairy products, one for meats. Drawers wouldn't cut it. There were shelves for the gentler produce, one for vegetables and the other for fruits. The cubbies on the inside of each door contained previously opened jars and uncorked wine bottles.

He pulled out a bottle of grape juice, rushed back to the toaster to find a glass to fill. He then pulled out a knife and proactively smothered one side of the blade with peanut butter all in the amount of time it took for the toast to pop up at a perfect golden brown.

Once his breakfast was prepared and all his ingredients returned, he scorned himself for forgetting to pour himself some coffee. With the annoying sense of being rushed, the grape juice was chugged with all the addicted determination of needing caffeine in his system to survive the many hours of history lesson, magical or not.

"Will I need any school supplies?" he asked, finally joining Mrs. Goodall and Mr. Pyrrhal.

"Just paper and pencil, if you choose to take notes, and

we have plenty of that. Otherwise, you'll only need the books we'll be going over, and we have plenty of those, too."

If I have the books, then I don't need the class, Collin reckoned, but reasoned that if it were that easy, there'd be no need for an education system. That was, provided every student were motivated enough to read the damn thing.

Mrs. Goodall excused herself from the room, leaving her cup of coffee behind for her husband. She informed him she still had a few things to get together and bade him good luck. It was an odd gesture from Collin's point of view. Mrs. Goodall, after all, was going to be his professor in addition to his guardian. The duality of the paradigm was an unfamiliar one, and being wished good luck from the same person who would serve as his academic observer summoned a mildly conflicting atmosphere. All the same, he thanked her and worked on finishing his breakfast.

From the corner of his eyes he could see Mr. Pyrrhal going back and forth between reading his newspaper and examining him. It wasn't an overall unsettling feeling. There was almost a comfort in his gaze. From the few interactions they shared, Osmond proved himself a better male role model Collin could ever recall crossing paths with. He was always kind and gentle and open to sparing a moment to listen to any problems, or assist with tasks as simple as cleaning the dishes or putting books away in the library without an ounce of spellwork. Where work was needed, he was first to volunteer without any questions asked. He was classic in the sense that he brought home the bacon.

Not that there was any bacon needed to bring home, unless bacon was metaphorical for keeping his friends, family, and community safe. This may also have entailed pouring his wife a healthy glass of wine at the end of the day with one hand, while passing on his wisdom to the younger members of their household with the other. If there was ever a temper on this man, he hid it well with decades of experience, and was always patient when it came to teaching daily tasks or spellwork.

"How're you feeling?" Osmond asked in his booming voice.

"Nervous," Collin answered meekly through sips of coffee.

Osmond chuckled lightly at this. "You don't need to be. If Paul was accurate in his assessment, and he rarely misses a beat, I believe you're up for the task."

"Hope so."

"Usually spells are a topic people find too interesting a subject to slack on. So, with the right dedication, it should come naturally before too long, especially if my suspicious are right and you may have already experimented yourself?"

Collin was shocked before realizing it was pointless to be. His first instinct was to live with the off-topic truth that he'd been practicing his hand stretches daily, but Osmond raised a hand to wave off his need for an explanation.

"I've spent enough time with Clark and Oscar to know they're deviousness wanders a great distance outside of Glenda's precautions," he amused. "They did the same with Alice and Olivia, but I doubt Taylor. He was always…different. More a strict and nose-to-the-grind kinda guy."

Mr. Pyrrhal broke off from talking. His expression morphed into reminiscence of simpler times. It was the look Collin associated with adults who promised he would look back on his high school days and genuinely miss it. That currently seemed impossible. However, he knew most people weren't in the position he was with Veil.

"Anyways," Osmond said, regaining himself, "don't stress too much. Glenda wouldn't give you anything you can't handle and history is typically a less significant portion of any of your graduating exams. Study it, but focus more on your spellwork."

"Thank you."

Nothing more was needed to be said. With his food gone, his mug of coffee was placed in the kitchen sink, and his trek to the study stepped rhythmically with each eager heartbeat thumping. He made a quick venture to the bathroom to stall any urinary discomfort during his lessons before doubling back to the makeshift classroom.

The study was lit brighter than a fully risen sun could typically suffice. The desks were scooted closer to the bookshelves to provide more room in the center. A wide, mobile whiteboard, a teacher's desk, and a student's desk for Collin had been migrated in for the two of them.

Day one.

He sat nervously, hands wringing under his desk. Mrs.

Overture

Goodall was there waiting with a stack of five books. Collin made out the top two to be identical.

"You ready?" Glenda asked.

Collin gave a weak "Yes."

Mrs. Goodall twiddled and twirled her fingers briskly with the undeniable motions of a spell. The top book of her stack of five lifted and separated itself from the others, and the others levitated in front of Collin before resting neatly on his desk, spines aligned.

"These books are going to be your material for your first standardized exam in April. The Council was nice enough to give you three extra months to study and practice, so I think you'll be fine."

There was a note of impersonal professionalism when she spoke. It didn't help Collin with her division of guardian and educator, but at the same time his own mannerism molded into his well-rehearsed scholarly idiosyncrasies. His back was straight, his hands now entwined on his desk, his face serious, but mingled with a glimmer of curiosity he mastered as a mask meant more for the pleasure of teachers' who taught subjects he deemed simple enough to teach himself at home. This time it was genuine curiosity. While history wasn't his most sought-after subject, his observation of the books in front of him lessened his distaste.

He saw the familiar title of *The History of Spells in the European Sovereigns* by Elizabeth Aewin from when he was perusing through the study a week ago. There was also *Veil: The Overture* by Charles Solomon, *Alchemy Throughout the*

Ages by Rowena McConnell, and *The American Movement* by Jeremy Littler. Judging these books by their covers, his new historical texts weren't too displeasing.

"You're not going to need to read them all from cover to cover," Mrs. Goodall continued. "Aewin and Solomon, most definitely, but there are points in *Alchemy Throughout the Ages* and *The American Movement* that we'll stop and worry about when you're an intermediate spellcaster."

If, Collin thought.

"We are, however, going to start with *The History of Spells* first. It's typically the second least enjoyed book, so hopefully the next two will get a little more appreciation."

Collin laid the designated text aside from the remaining three. Flipping through it, there were over four hundred pages. Base on his experiences in Advanced Placement classes in high school, this page-count was on par. Content depending, Collin could breeze through these books in his spare time somewhere in the span of two or three weeks, let alone nine.

"Do you have any questions before we dive in?" she asked.

"Yes, ma'am. Is it safe to highlight when reading?"

Mrs. Goodall was taken aback. It was clearly a question she hadn't anticipated. Whether it was one she didn't hear often enough to be inoculated again, or one that simply mortified her, Collin was unbeknownst.

"For learning the history of things, I think so. Removing graffiti isn't impossible, but for your other lessons I recommend learning the application of the material, instead of only memorizing."

"Of course," Collin said bashfully.

"Alright then!" Mrs. Goodall half-shouted with summoned enthusiasm to get her class underway. She cast one spell that materialized an inch-tall stack of loose leaf, one black pen, one blue pen, one mechanical pencil, an eraser, and spare graphite sticks. A second spell was conjured with no apparent outcome except when she began talking. "Today, we'll start easy, with a touch on philosophy. Debating the very beginning tends to be a good jumping-on point." The whiteboard scrawled the key words and phrases she spoke without any writing utensils. "So, without further ado…where do spells come from? What is the source that makes magic a reality?"

Collin perked up at this. The question plagued him for the longest time outside the bona fide proof of its legitimate existence. Magic words and swishes of wands always seemed too simplistic, yet here he was.

"Much like the differing between religions, the belief in magic's source has also created a history of factions among spellcasters. Luckily for us, Veil, as a majority, has learned to set aside their differences, same way a Catholic and Islam can spend a peaceful day with each other if they wanted to. The foundation for the popular beliefs of magic's origin divides into religion-based, metaphysical-based, biological, and nihilistic. If you want to give nihilism its own category, or sub-categorize it under religion, is a completely different debate."

Collin dived relentlessly into his note-taking. Pacing was rough. Sometimes he'd be able to copy everything from the whiteboard. If there was enough time between Mrs. Goodall's pauses to jot a few mental notes onto paper, he would. God, how he hoped their intro was the only fast-paced session. Otherwise, he'd have to resort to one-to-two-word notes and that was hardly worth jotting.

"In the religious belief, people tend to believe magic is a gift from God. Whether their god, your god, or a new god entirely, we will only dub this entity as the God of Magic. *That* particular road has led to countless new faiths throughout Veil. The ferocity of new branches showing up has died down, but its peak can be pinpointed in the early-to-mid 1500s, running roughly in tune with Martin Luther's Ninety-Five Theses in 1517 and the rise of Lutheranism. There will be entire chapters dedicated to each topic," she paused to say, noticing the intense pace of Collin's scribbling and the subtle rise and fall of his crestfallen countenance each time the whiteboard cleared what he was copying before finishing.

"Ah," Collin said sheepishly, but still didn't cease on his notes.

"The metaphysical branch," Mrs. Goodall resumed a little more drawn out, "is full of people who believe our reality runs parallel to another, and, while the foundation of our reality is mundane and magic-free, this other reality is nothing *but* pure magic. Somewhere along the line, our worlds touched and a piece of magic was transferred to us. Whether or not anything from our world was transferred to this magical realm is unknown since we don't have a shred of evidence this parallel world even exists.

"The biological belief in magic is founded on the idea that people are born with magic in their blood. This branch has had the most progress in its discoveries since the mid-90s. Even though there's no specific gene to determine if someone will be a spellcaster or not, scientists managed to find sequences to suggest that one's magical potential can be placed on a spectrum. The order of certain every day genes, and even junk DNA, plays a part in the bigger picture of spells.

"Even more, there's strong correlative studies showing magic being passed down through families of spellcasters, but since correlation doesn't imply causation, there's a non-inheritable faction of the biological approach that suggests most, if not all, people are born with the capability to tap into spellcasting. These two groups share the idea that some people are more promising than others, but it's been acknowledged that some people could have the genes, knowledge, determination, and every finger motion to the tee, yet still not produce even the most basic spells. That's when psychologists like to establish the nature versus nurture debate. Calvin Littler is the current leading psychologist to study the environmental factors that may determine someone's ability to cast. You doing okay so far?"

"Yes, ma'am," Collin flipped over his first ever page of notes on magical history. Her initial description of the natural aspect to magic's origin seemed straightforward, but her last explanation left him confused and in need of research to clear the matter up.

"Alright, lastly, we have the nihilistic approach to the mystery of magic. This is the simplest approach to believing where magic comes from. The nihilists believe magic is simply a part of the world. There is no source magic flows from, or higher powers, or capacities embedded in our DNA. Magic is as commonplace as all life. Just as different organisms utilize oxygen differently, so do to people's ability to tap into magic. Like we have the white man and the black man, or the woman and man, we have spellcasters and the non-magic folk. There is no rhyme or reason or ultimate point to it or how we even came across it. It's an unfair, unequally allocated fact of life. Spells were here before man, and they'll continue to exist when we're gone."

Collin laid these options before himself. He was never the type to be religiously-inclined, and he didn't see a top-to-bottom alteration in his beliefs happening anytime soon just because magic was now a part of his life. The metaphysical branch was his second favorite choice. The concept of a world made of pure magic, or, hell, even half magic, would have to be the modern-day equivalent of spending a weekend at the Willy Wonka factory.

While his nature of observations and calculations appealed most to the idea that one's inclination for spellcasting was measurable in the genome, Collin foresaw genocidal implications in the wrong hands. The term eugenics had an ominous ring in his ear.

Thank God for AP Psych.

The same ring coincided with the mental image of a real-life reenactment of *Harry Potter*'s Magic is Might movement.

Thank God for J.K. Rowling.

Collin raised his hand in the air to get Glenda's attention, an act bred from twelve years of expectations of being an obedient student as far back as kindergarten. His attempt was superfluous considering they were the only two there.

"Yes?" Mrs. Goodall asked.

"Does Veil offer anything like a DNA sample kit?"

He was self-conscious about the question the second the words were out, but she confirmed there was a company that patented an at-home service of the sort under a decade ago.

"Nevertheless, digging to the root of why magic is what it is, be it a gift from the gods, from another world, an inheritable trait, simply a fact of life, or none of the above is a futile search. One could look at gods as the source and expand to wonder where *they* came from. One could look at the parallel magic realm and where *it* came from, and so on and so forth with genes and life as a whole.

"Now, if you'll go ahead and open your first book to page eight, we can move forward with history's earliest records of spellcasting."

***

The rest of the class became like every other. Mrs. Goodall

stood at the front of their arrangement and paced around her desk while giving an in-depth lecture on the emergence of magic during the Old Kingdom epoch of Ancient Egypt and beyond.

Every hour and a half they'd take a quick break to give each other a chance to stretch their legs. By eleven-thirty they concluded their lecture with promise of hopefully beating any traffic into the Town Center shopping area to *finally* get him some new clothes, and perhaps some décor for his room, after lunch.

His homework was to read the entire first chapter and take notes. In his head, Collin scoffed at the idea of stopping with the first chapter. There was some disappoint in his first day of class, however, and that was with only getting to see small bits of spellwork.

But tomorrow will be significantly different. He imagined what tomorrow would be like with Olivia as his instructor.

Once everyone ate, the pair stepped outside. Glenda kept one hand on Collin's shoulder as they crossed the threshold of the house to protect him from their security enchantments. The trail leading from the front door to the wrought iron property fence was inlaid with black cobblestone that proceeded linearly with the center of the path being the exception. In the middle, the stone inlay was constructed circularly, and in the center of that was a waist-high marble pedestal holding an unsullied, golden sundial shaped like a broken gyroscope with an arrow shooting through the center. A band of metal underneath the arrow had the numbers one through twelve engraved in Roman numerals.

The health of the lawn displayed an evenly cut sea of emerald green, blossoming orange and apple trees, and boxed topiaries establishing the inner membrane of the fenced yard. Flowers of all sorts tastefully complemented the livelihood of the face of the two-story house with their potting underneath the shuttered window sills and the border of the construct. On the front door was the same double-scythed emblem with the center vertical bar branded on his envelope from Eleanor Merriweather.

Collin was in utter awe. Even more so once they passed the iron fence and an illusionment spell materialized. Looking back, Mandarin Mansion was now the shithole he recalled driving by from time to time. He knew exactly where they were, and it wasn't too far from where he used to live. This was the kind of place even a homeless squatter or a heroin addict wouldn't deem good enough to lay low in. The yard was barren with nothing but literal tumbleweeds and dead branches. The sea of green now a patchy artwork of black soil and brown grass. A crack in the foundation of concrete that wasn't there two seconds ago was more a fissure. Its enormity extended to the house itself, where the damage separated a portion of the building from the whole. Windows bore holes with jagged glass for its borders. The rotted roof was nearly caved in, and any minuscule pressure put atop it may finish the job. At least the door remained intact.

"Impressive?" asked Mrs. Goodall.

Collin nodded in silent agreement.

"It's a live illusion too," she said. "It looks like it deteriorates with the passage of time. It may be destroyed by next hurricane season."

"Hasn't anyone crossed the fence and seen it's fake?"

"Less often than before, but this plot of land is warded with so many alarms that we've had no problem catching trespassers and altering their memory, like if you entered or exited the premises without an escort, it would trigger about a dozen spells."

"Even though I'm in Veil now?" Collin asked with a little more indignation than he intended.

"At least until your birthday. New recruits go through a sort of ceremony for their induction and the location they'll be stationed at. It involves a small bit of blood magic so the spells that guard each outpost will recognize you. Whatever exceptions the Council made to let you in at *seventeen*," her voice now betrayed her concealed indignation, "I assume there are *some* traditions they'd rather uphold than others."

"Ah," Collin replied tersely.

Glenda must've realized her unabated dissatisfaction of the Council's decision may have shied Collin off, because her demeanor quickly transformed back to the gentle version of the selflessly caring woman she was.

"I'm sorry," she said softly. "I don't hold you to any negative opinions. I know your heart is in the right place when you agreed to join."

"It's okay."

He followed her to an aging maroon Impala that would escort them to Town Center. The Avenues Mall would've served just as nice, but now it was more like a sacred place for past memories to be best left un-impugned.

Mrs. Goodall revved the engine and made her way from Loretto Road to Old Saint Augustine Road, onto I-295 South. She had been correct in her assumption that it was early enough to dodge the traffic getting there. Unfortunately, they wouldn't be so lucky on the way back. Going north on I-295 was a nightmare between four and seven o'clock with its torturous stop-and-go flow and Type A personalities eager to cut you off with mere inches between cars, but none of that could bother him today.

8

The Good Stuff

The following morning had a groggier start than the previous. When Collin returned to Mandarin Mansion and scarfed down dinner, he headed directly to Alice in request of any sort of spell or potion that might enhance his wakefulness, and perhaps even his attention span.

He had a strong intuition Clark or Oscar could've easily fulfilled his request, and with great interest. Nevertheless, the inkling of doubt in his mind stressed them perceiving him as an overeager nerd. He hoped to be able to hold a subtle high-school-cool repertoire with his other peers. It was Alice's late-night confiding about her attempts to preemptively complete a successful solo hunt as an intermediate student that gave him the courage to ask for assistance in getting ahead at the beginner-level. Which she did.

The brew wasn't exactly a secretive one, but she gave him a glass, amber vial with a rubber dropper and the instructions of only taking two drops every six hours, never exceeding six drops a day, and never using the potion for more than three days in a row. Seemed simple enough with a hot cup of laced green tea to get one through a vigorous study session. Of course, nothing was ever as simple.

The shakes and the nausea were the only two side effects he suffered through, but their duration was only twenty minutes. Twenty positively vicious minutes. Even with *The History of Spells* textbook laid flat on his desk, Collin was confident his eyes would vibrate out of their sockets. The tea didn't stay in his system for long either. Nor did dinner, unfortunately. Collin was on the cusp of suspecting Alice of having it out for him, until it all stopped, and all he was left with was a pure, ethereal focus.

He was high, there was no denying that, yet his enlightened sense of cognitive abilities allowed him to believe nothing within the vicinity was beyond his comprehension. Whenever he looked at something, he was able to observe it with an unadulterated fixation. His other senses also enhanced. Where there were sounds to be heard, he could practically calculate the constructive and destructive interferences contributing to the noise or cancel it out entirely with undivided attention. The taste of vomit imprinted on his tongue consisted of flavors he could pinpoint as far back as lunch. All this and more, and he chose to spend his evening studying history.

Reading and highlighting were easy. Deciding to take notes while reading and highlighting hardly complicated the matter. He was the epitome of implacable. By the end of it all, it was two in the morning and he'd managed to summarize half the book in twenty succinct pages. Only one dose was consumed. He was pretty sure that if he sacrificed his willpower for divine wakefulness right off the bat, it would harbor problems later.

Besides, he was grateful to have gotten *some* sleep, since next morning was a relatively rough one. The potion only left him feeling as though he'd missed a few more hours of rest than was the norm for him, but there was no definable crash. Nothing an extra cup or two of coffee couldn't fix, and he made sure to bring one with him to class with Olivia.

To get to the room she designated required an escort, seeing as how Collin had yet to explore the upstairs region. Mrs. Goodall was nowhere to be found that morning. According to Mr. Pyrrhal, she unyieldingly insisted on taking her husband's place in a meeting between the heads of the Jacksonville divisions so he could rest. So, with a full belly and coffee in hand, Osmond led the way to the metallic door.

"You'll have to know this to get to the rest of your classes," he said, instructing Collin to add a new spell to his repertoire.

Osmond only needed one hand for the task. It turned out to be a much simpler task than when Glenda opened the path for the basement. He held his right hand almost like a gun with his thumb, index, and middle fingers for the barrel. He twisted his elbow distally so his hand turned in the same direction. Remaining planted, he raised his hand and twisted his elbow back to its original location. The door swung ajar to reveal a spiral staircase equipped with a handrail and all.

"Now you." Mr. Pyrrhal shut the door and gestured for Collin to take the wheel.

Collin copied his motions flawlessly and watched in delight as the staircase came back into view.

"Excellent!" Mr. Pyrrhal congratulated. "Now, if I'm not mistaken, Olivia has a preference for the third room on the left. Good luck."

It was fair to debate the staircase was as high as the basement was low, judging by the burning in Collin's quads and a small trickle of sweat effusing from the middle of his back. It wasn't likely to be noticed now he was clad in a pair of new jeans and an undershirt, concealed by the black button-down emblazoned with a lion emblem on the left of his chest.

Once on top, there were five rooms in total, three on the left and two on the right. The hallway was wide enough to allow seven or eight people to walk side-by-side. All doors were shut, save the one Osmond recommended checking for Olivia. Peeking around was out of the question, at least until after class.

Once at the far end of the hallway, Collin peered through the entry and saw Olivia sitting at the front desk with her fingers intertwined with expectancy. The room was similar to the study in that there was a teacher's desk, but this time there were two student desks set beside each other. The entirety of the room in all was bland. Dull white walls and a single square window at the far end of the room was as electrifying as it got.

As she stood, he saw she wore a dark brown, pencil skirt and a white blouse tucked under the waist that wore tight with enough bust to accentuate her breasts. Her hair was fashioned in a bun, and Collin was growing increasingly self-conscious about her being the hormonal center to his inexperienced fantasies.

"Hi," she said, but the intonation and startlement with which she used made it obvious he might be the first person she'd ever taught.

"Hey," he said just as quickly, hoping to implement the proper body language to insinuate he was only there under the statute of Veil.

When he himself was aware his *too cool for school* bit fizzled out in the first fifteen seconds, Olivia offered him a smirk in exchange for his blush. All things considered, she was nice enough to pity him and let that awkward moment pass.

"How was yesterday with Ms. Glenda?" she asked.

"It was good. Just spent last night studying."

"Well don't stress about history too much."

"So I've heard." Collin took a seat in a desk identical to the one he sat in yesterday.

Olivia ambled her way to him, book tucked under her arm.

"You already have this, don't you?" she asked, showing him a copy of *Elementary Spells*.

He'd received a copy the previous day.

"I-In my room." He felt stupid for not bringing it.

"That's fine," and she laid it on his desk. "There's enough of these things laying around the house."

Sure enough, she leaned under her desk and withdrew another copy from a cabinet. Instead of simply opening the book, she conjured something to make the inanimate object flip to their first spell. Collin's textbook followed suit. Observing its resting spot, his excitement wavered to see it was *the* first spell the book offered.

"I know Clark said you've been successful in making sparks," Olivia said candidly, "and I know it's a couple dozen of spells deep, *and* I know that giving your fingers white noise is dull as dirt, but it's where I was instructed to start."

"I understand."

"Alright then. It's my job to teach you the background of each spell, the motions for them, and the different stipulations necessary to give each spell traction. If you have the book, you shouldn't need to take notes. It's all there."

"Okay," and they began.

For the next few hours, it became apparent that learning spells and casting them were so exhaustingly different from each that Collin was eager to inaccurately consider them antithetical. Theory and application were two sides to the same coin, but that didn't make one any more fun than the other. With enough time to sit and study, he was a goddamn all-star with memorization, and with hands-on experience he could become the source of envy with all his previous friends, but this was something else.

Immediate remorse flooded him when he realize it wasn't going to be as simple as when Clark and Oscar taught him to cast sparks. He knew spellcasting required specific circumstances, and Olivia was moderately thorough enough in explaining and demonstrating them. Although, after the first few spells, it was obvious even she was losing interest in the redundancy. The hand positions were only altered so slightly that she informed him that he clearly got the gist, and from there on out they would cast the most generic form, whether it was more or less powerful than it could be. Collin was happy to oblige if it meant learning quicker.

"You'll be expected to know them inside and out for my tests and for the Council's examinations," she informed.

Otherwise, they managed to learn how to numb one finger at a time before numbing the whole hand. Projecting the same sleeping sensation to other areas of the body or onto others was a completely different set of lessons. They also ventured into cooling and heating each finger separately, and then together in the same manner. With the thinnest manageable sewing needle, they conducted a spell that wobbled the object only a sliver, but didn't shift it wholly. Lastly, they worked on levitating a tiny sticky note. Less baffling when given an explanation, Collin found out levitating objects had different sets of hand motions based on size, and, with unparalleled obviousness, lighter objects required less energy to get traction on the magical field.

Despite the bookwork of it all, he'd come around to not being entirely displeased. His homework for the week was to study the wide variety of circumstances for each of the five spells and work on mastering them. Olivia highly deterred from working ahead, emphasizing, for the hundredth time, the vitality of being able to utilize a spell to its maximum capability. *Especially* in any sort of fight against creatures that aren't meant to be trifled with.

By eleven-thirty, Collin stepped into the wide hallway to find three more doors were opened for his inspection. Across the hall was the gym he heard about. It was by no means a letdown. There were cable machines, bench racks, dumbbells weighing from five pounds to one hundred, squat racks, machines for individual muscle groups, treadmills, bikes, step climbers, and even a stretching station. The whole floor was lined with rubber tiles and mirrors lined the wall of the dumbbell racks to the far right as well as the cable machines dead ahead of him.

The room next door was more of an arena. If Collin had to guess, he would say it was where he would be spending the majority of his classes with Taylor during physical training, unless they were supposed to spend five hours in the gym. In which case, he hoped they had spells to extinguish lactic acid buildup and tiredness altogether.

The next room, next door to Olivia's classroom was nearly identical to the one he'd spent all morning in. The biggest exception was a single table in the center of the room, instead of desks, and a pile of books someone had been studying previously. At a closer glance, Collin saw the titles *Historical Beasts, The Truths and Falses of Downfalls, Encyclopedia of Shapeshifters,* and *Nocturnal Nuisances.*

Alice, he assumed, but considered it probable that she wasn't the only person with motives to research this type of material. According to Alice, Taylor, Clark, Oscar, and

Olivia were all preparing for their practicum in hunting creatures to graduate from being advanced-level spellcasters.

When back in his room, Collin withdrew his copy of *Elementary Spells* from his desk and opened it to the material Olivia and he covered. He understood her reasoning for only focusing on what they discussed, even more so considering it took him over two hours to get most of the finger-numbing spell accurately. His hands already cramped as was. To help, he spent a half hour afterwards doing the text's finger stretches in order to ease into the second spell of creating warmth in his digits.

Practicing with his left hand proved the hardest. The ineptitude of its coordination made it equally frustrating when he couldn't tell if he was doing the spells incorrectly or if the mandatory hand adjustments per cyclical situations were too far on the low end of the spectrum to even show. Nevertheless, when he was performing a spell properly, he knew it. His mental expectations adamantly willing magic out of him brought about a new wind of purpose with each cast.

He suddenly knew what Paul Ganley meant when he said he wouldn't be satisfied in the mundaneness of his old world. By all the gods, he was learning how to raze centuries-worth of physicists' works with a few wiggles, albeit painful wiggles, of his fingers. He also understood now how not many people could stumble across magic based on the complexity and precision of each subsequent movement. Fuck his old life, and fuck what he said about not using

Alice's brew consecutively. He was determined to be the best damn spellcaster Veil ever had.

***

By Wednesday, Collin was slightly drowsier than even the previous morning, but his routine was falling into place. He quickly got his breakfast. A heap of scrambled eggs was shaped into a messy sandwich with tomatoes and sriracha. Two cups of coffee became the default, one for now and one for class.

When he arrived upstairs, this time in the room he found the books in yesterday, he found it empty. He stepped inside to wait, but was almost buffeted to the ground when Alice bustled in behind him.

Jesus, I didn't even hear her behind me, but he was forgiving.

Her silence and swiftness weren't to be challenged. He considered the possibility that Alice frequently functioned under a number of stealth spells the way she always made abnormal apparitions.

"Sorry," she sputtered, turning her usual shade of blushing red.

"It's okay," he promised, his own cheeks getting warm.

"It's not," she palmed her forehead.

He only grinned. Her eyes spoke remorse, and Collin caught himself finding her as charming as he had when inebriated Sunday night. It was no mystery she and Olivia were night and day. Paraded sex appeal being one of the key characteristics, but not the only one. Alice at least possessed the alluring shy and humbleness. Funny how those two typically came paired with even the mildly awkward. She was also extremely clever, silently ambitious, and now somewhat of a klutz in situations not requiring a fight. Alice was someone whom he believed he could trust and be friends with on a different plane than the almost-twins. He reveled in that thought.

God only knew how Shannon would react if her memory were intact enough to see this. At times, her jealousy could be a force to be reckoned with. That got him daydreaming about what it would be like to win Alice's affection and watch them in a duel for his love, but that fantasy was immature and short-lived.

New life, new me.

They walked together to the elongated table. There weren't any desks today.

"Are you okay sitting like this?" she asked, waving a finger at the two chairs beside each other.

"Of course."

Once they were situated and facing each other with their chairs pulled out, Alice thumbed through her tagged pages, back straightened, shoulders tucked, legs crossed primly, and stopped at the first tab. Collin held out his own edition to turn to the designated page, noticing it pertained to counterspells.

"Eisenhower's Counters were designed to be more of a program within the learning program," Alice informed. "They start as basic as minimizing a spell's potential damage to rebounding spells tenfold and become a lot harder to grasp than your average casting fire or pulling something toward you."

That wasn't good news. Collin was overall pleased with his two days of progress, and he knew *eventually* everything would become more difficult, but he hadn't imagined an escalation during his first week.

"What makes them different?" he asked.

Alice squirmed a little, but her response was effortless.

"Eisenhower's Counters requires that the spellcaster not only focus on his or her will to manifest the effects, but to also remain sharp on the external environment, anticipating the timing, the angle, and momentum of impact of oncoming attacks."

Christ, more circumstances to add to the circumstances.

He went to skim through the page when he saw Alice recited her response directly from the text without breaking eye contact for a second. A pang of envy for her innate gifts left an acid-reflux-like burning against his sternum.

"So how are we gonna practice exactly?" he inquired. "Are you gonna throw stuff at me to block?"

"That's exactly what I'm going to do." Collin grew excited. "But first we have to make sure you know the hand movements, the theory, and the different forms of the spell. Then, if I think you've got the hang of it, we can touch on the theory of the differences between jinxes, hexes, and curses at the end."

But there wouldn't be time. The theory and application behind Eisenhower's Counters, proved to be unbelievably complex. Alice promised him it always seemed that way at first, but that it would become second nature before long.

It took the entire first two and a half hours to cover background information before they would end of practicing the spell for the remainder of class, after their ten-minute break to stretch their legs. The upside of counterspells was they were designed to be quickly executed and by no means difficult to perform, but by the time eleven o'clock rolled around, he stepped out from the room covered in minor scorch marks.

If those aren't supposed to be difficult, then I might be out of my league.

There was no damage worth concern. According to Alice, the flames she shot at him were so minor that a properly performed counter would've extinguished them wholly, if he hadn't failed at every attempt. The author of *Elementary Spells* wasn't joking about the need to simultaneously utilize willpower and calculations to effectively cast defensive magic. Collin was so wrapped up in trying to get the spell right, he lost all track of any intimate curiosities he held about Alice. If anything, he was substantially self-conscious about the pressure of being a good student in front someone who he knew could likely outperform the others, despite her rank.

She even warmed up to him slightly, without the assistance of libations. At one point, Alice made blatant attempts to prudently catch him off guard with her baby flames. While a few times were obvious enough to still fail at countering, others still caused Collin to sillily dodge like a person

Overture

frantically avoiding a bee. Once, he even fell over and got to listen to his mentor laugh at his humiliation.

He made a promise to himself to practice these spells without the concentration serum. For some reason it seemed more necessary to become skilled at these spells without performance-enhancing brews. Or, at least, that's what he convinced himself to believe, denying his hoping it would please Alice to know he took her lessons more serious than Mrs. Goodall's or Olivia's.

9

Game Show for Secrecy

Dinner got skipped that night for the sole purpose of studying, with immediate regret upon waking. As he was quick to find out by Osmond at the dining table, magic also came at a bodily cost when sapping energy.

"Some spells are designed with self-sustaining features. For example, the spell for levitating small objects you recently learned requires constant input to keep it going, but there's a more advanced spell you'll learn later on that only requires a single cast and the object will remain there. It's mostly for decorative purposes, but a more complicated spell to cast all the same, and therefore more energy needed."

Collin promptly acknowledged he understood as he guzzled his Greek yogurt and toast. As he ate, he watched Mr. Pyrrhal return to his newspaper. The heading on the front page read *Rabies Goes Airborne, Not Infectious for People*. He had an overwhelming desire to read the article, but had already lost too much time devouring a portion of his breakfast before even leaving the kitchen. He made a mental note to look into the matter as he cleaned and bustled down the hall.

At the metallic door, he made the almost-gun gesture, bent his elbow out, raised his hand, tucked his elbow back in, and waited for the passage upstairs to become available. At the top, he saw the room he had class with Olivia in laid ajar. On the wall was a green neon sign in the shape of an arrow reading *This Way for Education,* like the smartasses Clark and Oscar were. Collin smiled brightly nonetheless. Inside, Oscar was stationed at the teacher's desk, feet propped up as he leaned back. Clark wasn't there.

"Almost late," Oscar cheered. "Almost proud."

"What?" Collin asked, confused.

"Just joshin'. Clark should be here soon, he's in the gym talking with Taylor."

"Working out before class?"

Oscar slid his feet off the table and grasped the book next to him.

"No, no. He wanted to go over a case that came up. Some talk about a potential poltergeist a couple blocks over. Small-fry stuff. You already have one of these, right?" he asked, waving what looked like *Elementary Spells.*

"Shit!" Collin exclaimed. He'd been in such a hurry to get food in him and make it to class in time, he forgot the textbook on his dresser for the second time that week. "I can go run and get it."

"Now I'm proud!" Oscar laughed. "Leavin' behind your class material and all, but no. Trust me, we have plenty." He withdrew a copy of the text without breaking eye contact. "Too many, in fact."

Collin was obliged to believe him at that point based on everyone's manifestation of multiply copies. He still felt guilty about not bringing his own, despite the gleeful smile on Oscar's face.

"Sorry I'm late," Clark said, strutting in behind them with no expression of being sorry at all. "Where were we?"

"Just starting, actually," answered Oscar.

"Ah, well, yes. Suppose I should've taken longer, huh?"

"Not too late."

Clark shrugged and smooshed his face into a look that said "What does it matter to me?" Collin's head kept twisting back and forth to follow their classic banter.

"Well, if it's all the same to you, I guess we oughta get to the important details of Collin's first lesson."

"So we should!" Clark looked genuinely surprised and threw a finger in the air as if to exclaim "Eureka!" as he dashed to the front of the room with his inseparable buddy. "I think a good jumping on point would be to ask our Mr. Quinn when he developed the hots for a one Ms. Pottle."

"Who?" Collin asked.

He had no idea who they were talking about, but he did have an inkling. If it was who he thought they were eluding to, he was prepared to deny it and spend the next few days trying to figure out how they were able to detect what even he was unsure about. Surely, he had been subtle enough during class. He'd certainly been too busy to make any such suspicious exchanges elsewhere. A part of Collin hoped they were referring to Olivia so he could deny them with indubitable honesty.

"Alice, of course," Oscar replied. "C'mon, you were eyeing her a little too hard at our little Sunday soiree."

"Not to mention your occasional passes in the hall when you come out of your cave."

"I don't…think of her like that…though," Collin fought to sound convincing.

"You think of her like something," Clark said, "but I'm sure she's equally oblivious to how you're looking at her as you are."

Collin was at a loss for words and it must've showed. He was here to learn, not to be harassed.

"It's not a bad thing," Clark assured.

"Yeah, you're both quiet, ambitious people. You have loads to bond over. Just be smooth."

This was misery, humiliating. Collin knew they were only teasing him, but he could feel his cheeks burn regardless. He'd barely been in Mandarin Mansion long enough to warrant being the center of any inner-circle gossip.

"Don't sweat it. Your secret is safe with us," Oscar winked. "Now, shall we get into the lesson?"

Still embarrassed, Collin didn't even respond, but walked to his desk and sat, while the other two meandered to the front. All the while he couldn't help but ponder…

Alice Pottle.

It had a ring to it. At least, in his opinion, but she was

older anyways, even if it was just a year. Surely, his attraction was more Romeo and Juilet-esque: a quick burn with no actual substance. They'd only just met. It was ridiculous to think they could form a relationship meaningful enough to stand the test of time, right? They were members of Veil after all.

He shook his head to focus on the current situation and opened his text when he was instructed to go to page seventy-eight. *Schliemann's Swift* the title read.

"We're gonna let Day One focus on buffs and debuffs with getting objects to move faster or slower," Oscar informed. "But it's *extremely* important that this specific spell isn't cast onto any living thing."

"Why?"

"There's something in the mechanics of the spell that only makes it safe for inanimate objects," said Clark. "It flat out wouldn't work anyways. There are spells for speeding up living things, but they require a little more energy and a different form of casting that isn't introduced until Intermediate Level."

"That's whyyyyy..." Oscar reached underneath the desk and produced a black shoe box that had seen better days, "we have a bunch of objects for you to practice on."

He removed the lid and flipped the contents onto the desk. There was a marble, a wind-up duck toy, a slingshot, a quarter, and a few other miscellaneous items. Collin looked at the junk and skimmed more over the material in the book before him.

Overture

"I don't suppose we'll be going over history and circumstances first?" he asked.

"What a keen student you are," Clark teased. "And yes, you will be forced to suffer through the hardships of actual learning before we get to the fun stuff, but that's why…Oscar! Lights!"

Oscar snapped his fingers and the room went dim. A spotlight appeared over a vacated spot as Clark pulled back an invisible curtain and rolled out a game-show-styled wheel. Oscar must've been doing the spellwork for their bit.

"Fucking Christ," Collin whispered with sheer bewilderment.

There was no way for him to detect the wheel had ever been there.

Were they able to materialize it from nothingness?

"We're gonna make a game out of it. We're sure you're sick of sitting there taking notes, so every time you get a right answer from a question on the wheel, we'll teach you the fingerwork for Schliemann's mumbo jumbo in pieces. We'll start practicing the spell on items once we're done with the wheel. Sound good?"

Collin chuckled a "yeah," and the lights turned back on. Reading the wheel, there were approximately two dozen segments with repetitive subjects like *History in the Making, What to do, When to do it, Do's and Don'ts, Cast that Spell,* and *Life or Death.*

"Then the rules will be that we won't have a timer," said Oscar, "since you don't actually know any of this stuff just yet. So, you're free to take as long as you need to answer all the questions on the wheel—"

"Even if it takes the whole five hours?" Collin interrupted.

"The longer it takes you, our smitten little kitten, the less time you'll be able to do real spellwork. Doing actual magic is your incentive."

"That's a fair incentive."

"*But* for every question you get wrong on your *second* try, we'll create different ways to let others know about you and Alice, with Olivia being our..." Oscar locked eyes with Clark to ponder something they considered reasonable. They shared a significant look, raised their eyebrows, and nodded their heads in collaboration. "...fourth option."

"Olivia?" Collin asked with a hint of uncertainty.

The idea of the entire household knowing of an attraction he was still unsure was worth having was unsettling enough. He'd had plenty of experience with gossipy bitches in high school, not necessarily that he considered Olivia a bitch. However, the number of occupants in Mandarin Mansion wasn't exactly three thousand and growing. The two would-be brothers grinned an ear-to-ear devilish grin.

"He doesn't know," Clark said sadistically.

"Should we tell?" Oscar suggested.

"Should we let him risk finding out on his own?"

"Maybe we should."

"Maybe we should," Clark repeated in an almost inaudible whisper.

The banter sent chills down Collins spine. He couldn't

recall seeing the two act so ominously. "Don't be dicks," he said in a feeble, almost irritable manner. He didn't mean it angrily, despite the spark of annoyance from their threat. For Collin, it was a sign of growing camaraderie to be able to cuss at friends and not let them take it so damn offensively. Simultaneously, Clark and Oscar eased off their creepy playfulness and resumed their cheery delights.

"We're just playing," Clark said with a slap on Collin's back.

"Sort of. We'll still tell Olivia," said Oscar.

"But we can make her the seventh option, since this is your first time."

"That does sound fair."

"Oh, totally, but she'll still make sure everyone from here to New York knows, because that's the kinda girl she is."

"But we love her."

"One of a kind."

"That ass."

"Mmm!"

"Hey!" Collin actually did let out some of his aggravation now.

Clark and Oscar shared another meaningful look and made their way back to the lesson at hand. Oscar sat at the teacher's desk, while Clark moseyed back to the wheel.

"There's also a positive to this though," Clark assured. "For every question you get right on your first or second try, we'll cross out an option on the list of ways to tell people…" at this, Oscar displayed a piece of loose-leaf paper numbered to twenty-four, "going from the bottom and working our way up."

"Y'all are assholes."

"We're motivators," Oscar laughed.

"Plus, remember you have the entire morning to make sure you find the right answers in the book."

There was a begrudging groan of acceptance on Collin's behalf. It's not like he was going to narc on them. He did still operate under the peer-pressure of wanting to fit in with everyone he was now living with, and he couldn't deny their methods were, indeed, motivating. Although, he could just as easily not answer any questions, and therefore wouldn't get any wrong, but sitting around for five hours could grow dull.

Before they started, the duo eased off him to make sure he knew it was all meant to be fun and games. Collin did know, but it didn't stop him from thinking how exploiting his underdeveloped attraction for Alice was a low blow.

"Aaaaalright then, ladies and gentlemen!" Oscar's voice went almost baritone. "It's time to *spin…that…wheel!*"

Clark transferred his bodyweight into spinning the wheel. The iconic *click, click, click, click, click* in rapid succession reenacted the inescapable association of *Wheel of Fortune*, except there was no promise of monetary gain or fancy vacations. This was a battle to save face.

There was a grand total of six rotations before it finally stopped on *History in the Making*. Collin's fingers each held a different page with keen anticipation. If nothing else, at least the last week and a half of skimming through his textbook gave him a proactive knowledge to the layout of each topic dedicated to each spell. Clark detached the slice the ticker landed on and cleared his throat.

"What year did Lawrence Schliemann develop the theory behind enhancing the speed of inanimate objects? What year did he begin to develop the spell? And what year did he finally complete it?"

If Collin wasn't frustrated beforehand, he certainly was now.

Twenty-four questions now had the potential to become seventy-two?!

"Good and easy," said Oscar. "Feel free to answer any time after the question has been asked."

Collin obliged and flipped rapidly through the chapter. It wasn't necessary to go deep, since usually the history of a spell was the initial segment to each passage. Oscar wasn't joking either. The answers to each question were simple to narrow down in a matter of a couple minutes considering, in a sea of letters, the years were written in numbers and easy to pick out.

"He developed the theory in 1877, began developing the spell the same year, but didn't perfect it until 1879," he answered.

A circumambient *ding–ding* told him he got the question right. As much as Collin wanted to inquire about the spellwork it might've taken to embed that sound into their game, he bit his tongue.

"Correct!" Oscar shouted. Together, the two taught Collin the hand position to start off Schliemann's Swift.

"Now, Clark, if you'd be so kind?"

"But of course," and the rapid *tick, tick, tick* ensued.

Twenty-three more to go, Collin repeated again and again in his head. Even though the circumstances of the game boiled his blood, he couldn't help but acknowledge the competitiveness of his nerdy, straight-A student persona riding on the heat of being timed to save his own ass. The ticker stopped at *When to do it.*

"*When to do it!*" Clark reiterated. "With these, we're going to give you a specific form of Schliemann's Swift, and you're going to have to be able to work backwards to deduce the appropriate timespan to cast it. Okay?"

Collin nodded with immediate regret. By timespan, did he mean on a twenty-four-hour clock or on a 365-day cycle? Whatever.

What's a little challenge to spice the fun?

"If I told you this spell needed to be done with the ring finger entwined with the middle portion of the middle finger and the thumb bent slightly inward, which season am I talking about? And what weather pattern and moon cycle would require a choppy cast?"

"A choppy motion is during a waning moon while there's overcast," Collin responded reflexively.

That got a pleasurable "oooo" from the judges. How Collin could even recall that information from the textbook was beyond him. What good came from complaining about a good thing? The rest was all Greek without any active searching.

Answering was almost easy after a little skimming through each seasonal footnote under the chapter dedicated to hand positions. Turns out twisting the ring finger around the middle of the middle finger and having an inward bent thumb was mandatory to conduct during the autumn months.

Clark and Oscar's game show for secrecy barely lasted two hours. In the end, Collin missed three out of twenty-four, but his instructors merely reminded him they were motivators. Their threats to unleash his underwhelming attraction for Alice Pottle had been entirely empty.

"You can't screw a bro like that," said Oscar.

"I mean, you could," said Clark.

"But that'd be pretty fucked up."

"Without a doubt."

The three of them did take a short break after the game to procure snacks, otherwise the class lasted another two hours before ending early. As it happened, Schliemann's Swift was incredibly easy. Once he could feel the spell warming and scrambling to latch onto something in the physical plane, they practiced on the tools from the shoebox. With the penny, his teachers magicked it to raise on its side and spin at will. It was Collin's duty to speed it up. They practiced with stacking Schliemann's Swift to make the coin rotate faster and faster. They even pressured Collin to keep the penny moving as they countered it with the occasional slowing spell.

The wind-up duck toy was also a stacking simulation to test accurate speediness. They demonstrated their ability to get the object to briskly pace its way from one end of the room to the other in the same time it would take any one of them to power walk. For Collin it wasn't so. His performance wasn't overall insufficient. The penny trials helped, but he was only able to get the duck across the room with three winds.

By ten-thirty, they anointed him adept and bid him the rest of the day to focus on his other homework, but, as much as he wanted to, he wanted to be able to step outside and get some fresh air. He was fearful of falling into his typical routine of going straight to his room for the remainder of the day with his nose in a book and his fingers cramped. He needed additional stimuli to keep him going.

"Do you not know about the sun room?" Clark inquired, waving Oscar away to meet up shortly.

They were on the ground floor already.

"Nnno?" Collin said with questioning intones.

Was he supposed to know about it? Nobody made even a mention of it in the two weeks he'd nearly been there.

"Well c'mon then."

They turned on the spot to face the metallic door that sealed behind them in eerie silence.

"It's insanely easy," Clark informed. "It's gonna be the exact motion you use to go to the second floor, only instead of keeping your pointer and middle finger together, you're gonna use your pointer, middle, and ring finger. The number of fingers equals the number of floors you're going up or down."

"Is there a fourth floor?"

"There is, but it's enchanted to only let the heads of branches in. It's only used when communities are in a state of emergency, and that hasn't happened since the Cold War. There's probably an inch thick of dust covering the damn place. But anyways…"

Clark demonstrated the spell and the door swung open once more. The same staircase stood rising.

"And I don't suppose there's a copy of *Elementary* there too?" Collin half-kidded, but dominantly expected to receive the sly grin and slow nod his friend currently gave him. "Perfect." He gave an unenthusiastic thumbs up.

"You gonna be at lunch?" Clark asked.

"I should. I'll get situated first. We've still got, what, over an hour?"

"Sounds good," and Clark walked off to find Oscar.

It was good enough to be left at. Collin rotated with the balls of his feet planted and began his escalation. He truly believed he may have underestimated his physical condition. Where his quads burned with the conquering of a single flight of stairs, his other major leg muscles were shrieking with defiance by the time he conquered the second flight. There was no way he climbed a mere two floors worth. He was distraught with the idea of having to do this every time he would want to be in the sun room, but conflictingly pleased with the concept of having rippling legs in no time at all. Of course, that would all depend on whether or not he found this room to be study-worthy as he laid his hand on the door and pulled.

10

Sun and Stars

And goddamn was he pleased. Judging from the outside of the house, he suspected there wasn't a single crevasse in this facility that hadn't been tampered with magic. The dimensions of the sun room must've matched the entire first floor square inch by square inch in all its colossal beauty.

The ceiling stood perhaps thirteen feet high with the walls and roof being a collective of square, glass panes arched like a transparent greenhouse. A cobblestone pathway led out from the doorway to the center of the room where he observed a granite waterfall fountain nearly touching the ceiling. The trickling of water gifted his ears from several yards away. Encircling the waterfall were classic park benches of metal legs and armrests and wooden seats.

It's a freakin' miniature park squeezed into a house, he thought in amazement.

Before the waterfall, Collin saw a cobblestone trail branch off into different compartments. All around him greenery invaded his nostrils with overwhelming floral aromatics. To his right was a vegetable, fruit, and herb garden blossoming fruitfully. The reddest tomatoes, peppers, and strawberries grew next to the healthiest heads of lettuce, stalks of broccoli, and watermelons. Stalks of corn grew next to cocktail trees. Raspberry and blueberry bushes trailed half the length of the room. Beside them wafted the peacefully blended scent of green onions, basil, rosemary, garlic, and a hint of peppermint. Nothing could ever bring a man more to earth than the overwhelming sensation to dig his hands in this nutritiously thin, yet impossibly sustainable soil.

Magic prevails again. He was curious of the impossible roots.

To his left, the rocky road lead to a patch of emerald green grass. Closer to the center of the room was a life-sized bronze statue, bordering on cliché, of Guido Reni's depiction of the archangel Michael defeating Lucifer. Michael's wings were expanded with a sword raised high and facing downward in his right hand, preparing to plunge it into the flesh of his fallen angelic kin beneath his left foot. They left no details out, from the bulging arms, shoulders, and back muscles of Satan, to Michael's tiny and erect right nipple.

The closer Collin approached the statue, the louder some cosmic ambiance radiated from the display. Nothing overpowering, but strong enough to allow one to cancel out their own thoughts and find peace in emptiness. The others may call this place the sun room, but Collin was prepared to dub it a modern-day Eden, and his exploring was far from over.

Advancing toward the fountain, the borders of both sides of the room transitioned into being encompassed with a thick variety of flowers far exceeding the exterior plantation of the house. From roses, to tulips, to orchids, to chrysanthemums and sunflowers, there was a plethora whose names escaped Collin. Their arrangement was based on the color spectrum, with white daisies and roses on one end and black calla lilies and dahlias on the other.

At the base of the waterfall was a pond collecting and recycling water that smelled familiarly of ocean water. A thin buildup of seafoam formed as conglomerations of bubbles split from the main group and ultimately burst into memories. The clear blue water revealed sparkling coins of gold and silver, but years of knowing not to steal money from other people's well-wishes granted him the ability to resist the temptation of being in the presence of readily available gold.

Encircling the tower of running water, he saw nothing but gray, speckled stone, and in the back lay the flawless engraving of the double scythed emblem of Veil. Its symbolism escaped him, but he was without a doubt there'd be an explanation in a book somewhere in the study room. Assuming there wasn't one already in the textbook he was reading for Mrs. Goodall.

Past it all was a field of grass to lay in or a few more benches to sit on. Dead center was a blue and green marble globe resting on a silver pedestal. The continents were outlined in black. Behind it were two sets of large telescopes farthest away, against the glass wall. Several paces later, Collin was drawn to the statue of the world by the beckoning of white lights spread across its glossy surface. Staring at North

America, there were bright pinpoints all over, especially New York. In Florida, he noticed a good amount in Jacksonville, Tallahassee, and Miami, but still none compared to the plethora in the city that never sleeps. Practically the entire state was blanketed in light. Expanding his gaze, he saw spots of red as well.

"They're locations of different outposts," a voice spoke from his right. Alice's voice.

"H-hey," he responded with sheepish surprise.

The serenity of the natural ambiance gave him the assumption the room was empty. He made a mental note to not let himself make that mistake twice.

"Outposts," he stated to nobody before redirecting to Alice. "So like Mandarin Mansion?"

"And the Arlington, San Marco, and Beaches outposts, among others."

"Each have their own light?" Collin asked with rhetorical expectations.

He could see the area around Jacksonville speckled with bits of whiteness.

"Yes."

"And the red lights?"

"Closed branches. They were either no longer needed, relocated, or demolished."

The white-to-red ratio won by a landslide. What was more impressive was how widely established Veil was. There were so many divisions, it was next to impossible to believe anyone from the mundane world could get by without experiencing at least one confrontation with the supernatural in their life. The least Veil-populated states were Montana, Vermont, Wyoming, Alaska, and the Dakotas. In those areas, Collin recognized a more balanced number of three or four of both colors.

"And if an area is about one-to-one?" he asked.

"Could mean something, could mean nothing," Alice sighed. "If you're talking about the less populated states, odds are the locations were closed due to lessened activity, or re-established if there were a resurgence. Every quarter the globes get updated to help keep track of additions and removals of lights. There's only so many memos people can keep up with if a location were to go red without being informed."

"Well that's cool," then, to break free of the awkward silence that proceeded, he asked, "So how's the research going?"

Her demeanor stiffened a little at the mention.

"You haven't told anyone, have you?" she demanded. "I've put a lot of work into this, and I don't need anyone telling me to abandon it."

"No, no," Collin hastily assured. "I was just making awkward small talk."

His heart caught in his throat as his cheeks grew warm. Alice did something he hadn't expected: she smiled. Not a friendly, in-passing smile that asked you how your day was, but of apologetic embarrassment. Her perfectly straight teeth gleamed as her eyes bowed to show remorse for jumping to conclusions.

"Sorry," she said, turning several shades darker than Collin.

Her right hand bolted to her shoulder-length hair, where she found comfort in running her fingers through her scalp before dropping back to her side. Collin almost translated it as impatience, but he saw through it. He was well aware they shared some social disabilities and gave her an easy-out to vacate the moment.

"I won't hold you up, or I can go if you need the silence?"

"No, that's okay." Her words came out quick enough to be confused as one word. She had to pause before continuing in order to get a grip on her vocals. "I was on my way to lunch anyways."

"Oh. Cool. I was gonna head that way after I checked everything out for studying."

"It's a good place," Alice smiled again and walked past him.

She turned to wish him good luck and made her way to the door. For a moment, he was relieved their brief encounter was over with, but she turned at the door once more.

"And the research is going good!" she shouted from the far end.

No response was necessary. He grinned to show understanding, but, given as she was eclipsed by the waterfall, he realized it was an inadequate response.

Exploring was limited beyond what he'd already seen. He could've easily gone to lunch, but wanted to give him and Alice space for fear of giving off the impression he might've

Overture

been following her. Instead, he flipped open his book to Eisenhower's Counter. The stiffness in his fingers felt almost calcified. A good portion of his lunch break would have to be spent stretching them out. If he didn't advance on his flexibility soon, he feared the requirements of future spells might lap him on his capabilities.

Twenty minutes later, he did just that. He bent and twisted his phalanges to their searing limit under the table, switching hands as he gorged on a couple of tuna wraps with a side of hummus and assorted veggies. Everyone palavered about the events of their day with no drastic news emanating. The only two people not there were Osmond and Taylor. Alice's twitching gaze at their empty seats displayed subtle discomfort at their absence.

Back in the sun room, Collin's calves now Jell-O, he spent several hours practicing the counterspell for Alice's class. Once the standard hand motions were perfected, he worked on mastering the minuscule alterations for varying circumstances, as well as practiced them while moving at a brisk pace throughout the garden.

Once satisfied with Eisenhower's Counter, he temporarily broke his moral about taking from the fountain. A gold coin from the salt water would have to suffice until he finished performing the spells he covered with Olivia.

The best part about revisiting previous spells was the familiarity. He was no means a master spellcaster, but after dozens of executions his hands moved in effortless sync. Afterwards he would compose a spell as if he were a woman, a transsexual, a hermaphrodite, or a transgender for the daytime, for dusk, for nighttime, for dawn. He cast for summer, spring, fall, and winter, for full moons, for new moons, and on and on. His pointer finger had to aim up, down, touch the base of his middle finger, the tip of his middle finger, and then his knuckle had to touch an adjacent knuckle without coming into contact with any other surface. His hands and arms burned with satisfaction. The caloric contents of lunch were ousted in each bead of sweat and every muscle fiber soaking in lactic acid, but he was going to prove himself.

By the time six o'clock rolled around, that golden coin was his bitch. Collin managed to teach himself how to transfer heat and coldness from his hands to objects. He could make it float no problem, and even found the spell necessary to make it flip around. This was a spell he implemented for Schliemann's Swift, once he magicked it to stand and spin on the flat seat of one of the park benches.

Collin was disheveled, but he earned the right to parade it into the dining room for dinner with a full table. Alice matched his untidiness. For a short-lived moment he recognized a twinge of competitive jealousy blended with a shared pride of mutual suffering.

"How was it?" Clark asked.

"Perfect," Collin grinned, scanning the room and noticing Osmond wasn't there again, but Taylor was.

"Have you seriously been up there all day?" Oscar inquired with a look for astonished disgust.

Overture

"Oscar!" Mrs. Goodall exclaimed. "It wasn't too long ago when you were just as eager to study as Collin is."

Mrs. Goodall had been laying out a large bowl of foil-wrapped baked potatoes to complete what Collin considered an otherwise Southern Thanksgiving meal, black-eyed peas and collards included.

"True," Oscar admitted, a pitcher of sweet tea in hand, "but I can't recall spending entire days studying, except around exam time."

Clark seconded that. "It's almost like we have another Alice in the house."

Collin locked eyes in horror at the obvious attempt to make hint of the pair. Clark winked as they each noticed the implication dissolve unnoticed by everyone except Oscar, who eyed them behind his raised beverage.

"It would be refreshing to have a few genuine scholars in this household," Mrs. Goodall motherly scorned. "You two just make sure he's well informed by the time the Council examines him."

"Nah, he's got plenty of time. He'll be fine," Oscar promised.

"Probably be halfway through Intermediate by the time the bigwigs come around," Clark added, and everyone but Taylor, Alice, and Collin chuckled. Although, Collin did smile at the idea.

When Collin stole a glance over his shoulder, Alice shared a weak smile bearing him confidence. When he did the same with Taylor though, his hopefulness was exchanged for an inexplicably lowered sense of self-worth. Even this far into becoming a member of their household, this guy was adamant about shunning Collin, and for what reason? Everyone else vouched for him, despite cautioning how Taylor was slow to warm whenever it came to new people.

"You should've seen him when Olivia and Alice came around," Oscar had told him last weekend. "The guy was ready to rip out his own damn kidneys to keep anyone from taking any empty space here. Just keep doing what you're doing and he'll come around."

While that wasn't exactly the most encouraging of postulations, Collin understood some people could be beyond reason in their narrow-minded stubbornness. He'd had plenty of years growing up with his simple-minded father to gain a little patience in that department, but, even near the end of two weeks in Mandarin Mansion, he was susceptible to feeling downtrodden whenever Taylor delivered his repugnant glower so deliberately.

That same look haunted Collin through the duration of the evening. Further words of encouragement he received from the family, he decided to test calling them, granted him the motivation to keep on studying. His spell practice was a little stiff, so instead he studied his history notes while simultaneously doing finger stretches. By this point he was able to perfectly stack the tip of each finger onto the base of each consecutive finger, forwards and backwards, without manipulating them with the other hand. He also twisted and twirled and tangled his phalanges in odd motions never imagined plausible. It was almost as if he could disjoint them, but still command them.

The surrealism of it all didn't sink in until well past lights-out. The recognition of where Collin was and what he was doing suddenly seemed like nothing more than a dream. Perhaps it was his tired body and blurred eyes, but the subtle sensation of distortion from reality was bordering on enlightening. After all, he was only another boring human, destined to define his entire life's accomplishments from the A's he received on school exams and develop tunnel vision narrower than his dad's for nothing but academics, only to achieve nothing less than average in the field of application.

Now he was bending the very laws of physics? Holes were being poked in the foundation of what was always believed to be the ticking away of the social clock. And what gave him the right? What made him special enough to be privileged to stand next to the greatest defenders of blissful ignorance and divine knowledge? Simply being in the right place at the right time? No, that felt too easy of an explanation.

Something in that precise moment of sitting at his desk brought him to the mindset of the doctrine of determinism. He could smell the hands of fate molding him with purpose and hear the clock striking away at the eventual alignment of some cosmic puzzle revealing the bigger picture.

Sadly, as with all grand moments of insight, Collin only got a few brief minutes of mystic relief before the moment faded and the here-and-now dragged him back to the task at hand. He examined his notes on the Salem Witch Trials, during the period when spellcasters had forced their way into hiding. During the months of July, August, and September of 1692 the citizens went berserk with paranoia and accusations of people in possession of witchcraft. They executed over a dozen people in the settlement of Salem, Massachusetts, and accused over two hundred. Apparently, that was nothing. Collin was shocked to find this historical event spanned as far back as the fourteenth century when tens of thousands of people were killed. Of course, the witchcraft fad being one directed at *witches*, it was mostly woman who were hung or set aflame.

However, the book explained much more on the perspective of spellcasters, which intrigued Collin the most. Usually, whenever there's a conflict, the only side of the story one hears is the victor's. Now he better understood the tale worth knowing than the singularly simplistic fact that people in earlier times were more driven by fear of damnation than actual logic.

But magic was less guarded then. Maybe people had a reason to spark this movement.

They didn't. It all eventually boiled down to fear of damnation and the seductive powers of almighty Satan. What had happened was a famished farmer was forced to sit and watch as his crop died little by little without bearing any fruit. They obviously had no prior knowledge of plant diseases or pesticides during that period, and blamed so many unfortunate and foul events on God's punishment. So, Veil's righteous martyr, Victor Ludwig, a travelling man in possession of magic by sheer accident, aided the man.

He breathed new life into the farmer's plantation, and as a consequence he was condemned to die of asphyxiation, choking on the fumes of burning wood before the flames could consume him. The tragedy was in him not knowing how to cast a fireproofing spell. The good news of it was he was able to pass along what he did know of the mystic arts. He, alongside a few others, were deemed the fathers and mothers of the magical escalation. Nobody really acknowledged the Egyptians. Magic wasn't as up and coming then.

There wasn't much information on how spellcasters survived such a critical period when they were being hunted without enough spells under their belts to protect them. They did eventually form groups over the hundreds of years and expanded on their followers. Eventually, there was a division between those who wanted to take their place above the magicless humans and those who wanted to blend in. Obviously, the less tyrannical side won, or else Veil's secrets would be public, but that was the extent of it. He wanted to know more, and there was a footnote to guide him: *Gutting the Global Witch Trials,* written by Madeline Pudeaux.

Nothing could explain why, but something compelled Collin to snag that book that instant. Mayhap Mrs. Goodall would perceive his additional knowledge of the subject as true scholarly material, since convincing her to be proud of his decision to join Veil was still a challenge. Not that he didn't think she *wasn't* getting cozy with the idea, but a little could go a long way.

He flipped through the table of contents of *Elementary Spells* to locate a series of silencing charms. It took another ten minutes to find one and the overall premise wasn't too promising. It was exactly what he needed in terms of quieting the collision of two objects, his feet and the floor for example, but, much like what Osmond had told him, it was a one-and-done spell, not a self-sustaining one.

The spell wasn't a complicated one, and he practiced it several times on a pen he suspended a couple feet from his wooden desk before releasing. Once he managed it, he practiced on a book.

Having to perform the charm for every step he took would be annoying. Worth it? One could only hope. It was enough to make him want to abandon it until morning. God only knew the teasing comments Clark and Oscar would manufacture if he were caught. Alice did say rooms were typically soundproof.

Is all this precaution even necessary? Could the house be warded once everyone went to bed?

He hadn't been informed about any enforced curfews, nor had he bothered to ask about it. He was able to creep over to Clark and Oscar's room from their welcome party for him though so, surely, he'd be safe. In the end, Collin said to hell with it and flipped his bedroom light off while cracking open his door. With only his socks on his feet, it should help. He wasn't going to conduct the silencing spell until it was time to creep past Alice's, Olivia's, Clark's, and Oscar's rooms.

With any luck, he wouldn't need it at all. Despite the age of Mandarin Mansion, the floorboards beneath the hallway runner were sturdy enough not to creak under his weight. He still used precaution around the corner, past the mismanaged closet. His throat clench with apprehension at the unsuspected swinging open of the bathroom door. Frantically, Collin doubled back as quietly as possible, unsure if he succeeded. He couldn't make out who it was, but the lack of approaching feet gave him enough security to peak around the corner to no one.

Why would anyone need to use the community bathroom if each bedroom had their own? Collin wondered.

The terror of his own curiosity drew him forward. Had the suspect been Clark or Oscar that would've been the end of it. Collin proceeded with enough caution to make out the faint silhouette of someone standing in the entry to the study. Whispers were heard between stifled breaths, but hardly audible.

"—expect me to ignore the signs, sir," Taylor's voice hissed. "There's too much going on between the disappearances of outposts, the unusual migrations and behaviors of the creatures out there. And I still don't trust –"

"I understand your skepticism, but that doesn't mean we can throw around accusations without facts. Sometimes coincidences can be just that."

The voice was Osmond Pyrrhal's, calm and perceptive

as always. Collin's blood drained as he eavesdropped. His breathes grew shallow until they ultimately stopped before an intake was mandatory.

"What we need to focus on for the time being is what's going on in Jacksonville," Osmond spoke. "Things are getting worse. The number of murders and disappearances are climbing exponentially. The Council is trying to keep it only among the heads of each branch, but they can only keep it swept under the rug for so long, unless it gets handled soon."

"And what if everything I've talked to you about is a part of what's going on here?" Taylor demanded. The sound of his tone bore a bitter impatience that, strangely enough, still sounded respectful to the head of the house.

"*If* Collin were involved with the danger at hand, and that's a big *if*," Osmond emphasized, "there's no way he would know. Ganley searched his memories thoroughly, and the only thing questionable about him is the person in the skull mask."

Collin's fingers grew numb as mild symptoms of trepidation sank into his nervous system. It was difficult to piece together what they were saying without being there from the start of the discussion. He couldn't assess whether they were talking about the chaos Veil was facing or if they were discussing the creature Alice previously led on about. Either way, Taylor seemed determined to pin it on him? But how? Collin never asked to get involved with the monsters of Jacksonville. What happened was a coincidental matter of…

Overture

Being at the right place at the right time, he considered. *Could coincidence be more than just a coincidence?*

It had to be. Never in Collin's life had he any experience with the supernatural. His gray life had now been given color. He'd literally sat in his room and pondered this topic not too long ago, but Taylor was persistent with the idea of there being a bigger picture.

"I've searched that neighborhood high and low, multiple times, and couldn't find a trace of anything."

"And you think that trace came with him?"

"It's a possibility. No matter how improbable, it's still probable."

"I think you've given this *too* much thought. You're resistant to anyone who becomes inducted."

Collin translated a sharp pause to become a retort before being cut off.

"*And*," Mr. Pyrrhal said sternly, yet still fatherly, "I sympathize with your reasoning. Glenda and myself swore we would protect what you went through, but we also believe you have a tendency to let your past and your anger fog your judgement. You are *very* talented, Taylor, and a natural leader, born to do great things for this world, but never for a minute think you're going to achieve them alone. The foundation of Veil was built on the belief that *we,* as a *community*, will protect the innocent from the darkness. Not one singular individual. Now, we've spent enough time on this subject. You need your rest for your lesson in the morning."

A reluctant pause ensued.

"Yes, Sir," Taylor finally spoke.

"Thank you. And I want to hear that were fair on –"

On what, Collin didn't get to find out. As soon as Taylor gave his affirmation, his footsteps could be heard echoing down the hall with impatience. Collin tiptoed swiftly through the corridor, knowing he and Taylor shared the same path to get to their separate bedroom. With any luck, Osmond's comment must've distracted Taylor, since Collin managed to make it safely around the corner.

Once inside his room, the door safely shut, Collin fumbled his way through dark and into his bed, heart prepared to beat out of his chest. Piecing together what he heard was a difficult task. The only topic he could focus on was how it sounded as though Taylor believed him to be tied to something evil.

11

Survival of the Fittest

The night came and went without a lick of sleep. How the hell was one supposed to close their eyes knowing someone sleeping mere yards away was keen on believing something monstrous enshrouded you? Collin was awake, fed, and advised to wear more flexible clothing. Wondering where the hell he was going to get tight-fitted attire at the ass crack of dawn, Mrs. Goodall delivered a pair of hand-me-downs tucked away in the abyss of the confounded closet.

The long-sleeved portion was all black. Judging by the snapping of the material when Collin stretched it out from his skin and let go, it was unmistakably spandex. The pants were black too, but were significantly less conforming around his body.

He trudged sluggishly up the stairs, nervousness and frustration meshing into a forbidden fury.

How the fuck am I supposed to face this guy and act like everything is hunky-dory?

The *only* good news about today was that it was Friday. He would soon have the entire weekend to master his weeks' worth of lessons in the sun room, and then inevitably begin studying ahead of the curriculum.

On the second floor, Taylor stood leaning against the wall at the farthest door on the right. His expression was outwardly as pissy as Collin felt inwardly.

To the gym, he remembered that Taylor was in charge of teaching him combat. *Not that anything bad would* ever *come from that.*

Taylor was basically given the license to abuse Collin and call it a learning experience. Now Collin was fit. His years of wanting to stay healthy and never become his father proved motivation enough to never steer from his goal, but hand-to-hand, hand-to-feet, hand-to-magic, or whatever else, were areas where his expertise drew a blank.

"C'mon," Taylor ordered exasperatedly. "We're testing your strength before anything else."

Easy enough. Lifting weights and jogging would be a cinch, until the possibility of doing it for five hours sparked a bout of unease. Collin was accustomed to accomplishing an hour-long session, maybe an hour-and-a-half. Anything more would be considered overworking. At least that's how he was informed.

Too worried to be amazed all over again with the gym setup, Collin was mentally exhausting himself trying to stay casual and force his eyes not to narrow into a glare. Realistically, he was more scared than angry. While it was infuriating to be unprovokedly accused of something, it was preferred to everyone keeping a watchful eye over him for any suspicious or dark activity. Like Osmond said, Mr. Ganley searched his brain high and low and found zilch. Instead, today was a day to muster his will and transform his anger and fear into a need to prove himself a viable asset to Veil.

Together they spent the first half hour testing the limits of Collin's flexibility with simple exercises, like bending to touch the floor, holding a squatting position as low as possible with feet flat and their arms held out, stretching the chest with each hand held by the other behind the back, and so on.

Once they were loosened, they went into testing cardio, but this was no simple matter of jogging or rolling around on an elliptical. Between circuits of jogging, cycling, burpees, heavy rope training, and going a few rounds with a punching bag, Taylor proceeded to observe Collin fail at tossing a large tire consistently to the other side of the room and back. Hell, he didn't even make it all the way to one side a single time. Taylor's training had his ass beat by the time he was thrusting thick, weighty ropes up and down into the shape of calculable wavelengths.

Collin barely lasted past a half hour before he was forced to endure Taylor's unbearable sneer. What he wouldn't do to be a master spellcaster and incinerate Taylor on the spot.

"You better show more potential than that if you expect to stay with us," his teacher jeered.

Hunched over, Collin's chest clinched with rage and humiliation under physical and emotional strain. There was no response worth throwing back. He wanted so badly to usurp Taylor's fitness and outperform him with every step. The unrealistic standard to which he was being held to was additionally disheartening. Denying that all his peers could physically outdo him would be foolish. They'd been there much longer. They've passed their exams to become intermediate and advanced spellcasters, but the mental image of scrawny Alice lugging that massive tire around the room without breaking a sweat was almost laughable. Especially considering she held the air of a woman who prioritized brains over brawn.

"Five-minute break." Taylor moseyed over to a machine designed for chest flyes.

Collin heaved like he'd been revoked the ability to inhale. He was determined to never take the influx of oxygen to his lungs for granted again. There was fit, and then there was *fit*. Once, there was a time when he thought he was a prime specimen as far as above average went. Now there wasn't a doubt in his mind Taylor was prepared to lead him to literal death and laugh with a sadistic grin.

He shut his eyes and slowed his inhales and exhales to gradually reduce his heart rate to a tolerable pace but, by the time his heart reached that point, it was back to the grind.

He sat at the fly machine while Taylor stood observing him with arms crossed. His above-it-all attitude was becoming an ever-more bitter pill for Collin to choke on.

"Let's see what you can do?" Taylor instructed.

Collin straightened his back, tightened his core, and stretched his arms out until they were far enough back to grip the handles. The resistant hindrance stopped him dead in his tracks. There was no anticipation to buffer the blow. Usually trial runs started low. Pride and labored self-control allowed Collin to refrain from glancing behind himself to see which level of weights Taylor was a big enough dick to start him out on. He didn't drop the weight just yet. Instead, he gripped his seat with his thighs and thrusted his bodyweight into the motion to hopefully bring his arms together.

He didn't accomplish a single rep, but he did manage to bring his arms closer together by roughly three-quarters of the distance. The looks of disdain and quieted snide remarks from the solo peanut gallery were ignored with great effort.

How the hell am I supposed to get through today without snapping?

Yet he did. They tested more of the chest before each other major muscle group. Each time he was given too heavy of weights, and every time he felt like a pathetic string bean. Afterwards, they focused on stretching again to enhance flexibility. By the time it was their final hour, every muscle fiber in Collin's body was screaming in agony. Inside the gym was an installed drinking fountain to satiate his thirst between workouts, but his thirst was nothing compared to how much pain he was in. The cherry on top was knowing Taylor was going to milk every minute of their time *teaching*.

Taylor led him to the door connected to the room adjacent to the one they were in. Inside was a large black matted hexagon ring Collin correctly assumed was for sparing.

"It's also for magical duels. When you're finally in good enough shape, we'll hold classes in here."

Asshole.

"For now, I'm going to test your combat level."

"They're nonexistent," Collin admitted.

What use was holding onto pride and determination when he knew damn well his instructor was maliciously waiting to degrade them?

"Then I'll show you what I expect from you by the time the Council has you examined."

They walked into the padded hexagon. Collin more so limped. The buildup of post-workout fatigue set in far too quickly. With any luck, he might be able to raise his arms halfway in defense of whatever barrage of assaults were to come his way. Taylor stood on the far end of the arena and turned to face his student.

"I want you to try to hit me."

Collin was shocked for only a second before acknowledging he was being provoked. It was the perfect excuse to attack someone and call it self-defense, but the fantasy of landing a fist in his face was vivid and longing.

"Okay," Collin remarked.

He'd try, with full expectations of not succeeding. He figured Taylor was expecting a direct blow, so he shook off his sore legs and approached with a plan to fake a swing. The dance off initiated with the crossing of each combatant's legs as they paced in a circle. This was the basic movement Collin saw in any fight, theatrical or athletic, but suddenly he felt silly. Was he seriously going to offer himself to getting a whooping? He wanted to stop, but didn't. Internally, he reasoned there'd be no hope of progressing as a spellcaster if he didn't handle this professionally.

They circled the ring a time and a half before he decided Taylor wasn't going to give him an opening, and the sear in each calf with every side step refused to grant him more tolerable time to stall. He shuffled closer, closer, leapt to the left, but lunged forward and redirected to the right with balled fist.

Something as meager as a contemplation was paltry with Taylor. He had Collin gripped by the wrist of the raised hand and twisted it downward while his lower body flung off the ground. Gravity did the rest. Upon landing, he twisted Collin's whole arm until his body escaped his control. His body did a somersault to prevent his joints from being spun to the point of snapping, and he collided with his back on the floor.

"Again." Taylor released him.

Getting to his feet was a struggle. Laying still for ten seconds was all the time needed for the aches to instill their tendrils of fatigue deeper into his muscle fibers. He didn't budge until Taylor had to repeat himself with exuberant annoyance.

Collin rolled onto his stomach and forced himself up one limb at a time. By the time he was back on his feet and getting ready to follow through with a defensive stance, Taylor already crossed the distance that separated them. He dipped low and swept his opponent's feet out from underneath him and landed a blow to his gut before Collin even had time to make contact with the floor for the second time.

"Goddamn it!" Collin bellowed out his own aggravation.

"Until you learn, you better get used to it. In this class you need to learn to fight like your life depends on it, because I can guarantee you it will."

He was stepping back and gauging Collin's behavior rather than enacting the cliché circling of the prey. Did he honestly expect him to withstand an hour of this?

Or maybe it's a test? He suggested to himself. *It would make sense. He hates me, sure, the feeling's fucking mutual, but it could also be about testing the ability to take a hit and keeping getting up?*

It wasn't his favorite thought, but it wasn't an impossible one either. With searing determination, Collin suffered through the stiffness of his body and tried rapidly to calm his heartbeat and replenish the wind that was knocked out of him. In the process of standing, Taylor closed the distance between them again with a blink of the eye and bashed him swiftly to the ground.

Collin was catching on though. He stalled long enough for Taylor to gain some distance before staggering to an almost-standing position. Once approached, he launched himself to the left to miss another fist, but staggered too much to secure a firm landing, resulting in finding himself back on his hands and knees.

Overture

"It's a start," Taylor mumbled.

Prick.

Hit after hit, there was no escaping the buffeting attacks. The skill levels were incomparable. The only option was to let the skin toughen and eventually decipher Taylor's patterns of motion, which were considerably more difficult to dodge. Taylor was a trained warrior, on the cusp of graduating, and this was Collin's first day of combat training. Getting beaten and bruised was practically in the job description. A hazing ritual if you will.

Collin's rage wasn't subsiding. Nothing could withhold the fact that the same person who was knocking him over was the same one trying to raise suspicion of him in everyone else. Or, at least, in Mr. Pyrrhal. Making a hasty generalization could actually hurt his image further than what might already be tarnished.

By the end of class, the battle marks painted onto Collin's mural of a survivor's face included a black eye, bloodied lip, and a few puffy scuffs around the cheeks. Beneath his clothes were about a dozen more splotches of black and blue discolorations. Some on his back, stomach, arms, and legs. He was instructed to see Mrs. Goodall, who managed to put him right as rain with a menthol-smelling salve and a couple spells. The bruises dissipated and his muscle soreness lessened, but failed to be alleviated completely.

"I'm sorry you went through that," she whispered tenderly, the hint of tears being fought back from the corners of her eyes.

"So that *is* training?"

"Unfortunately. Osmond and I had to endure it too. Veil isn't a fairy tale adventure of defeating evil. Especially for those who choose the life of a hunter. It's a never-ending horror movie. It's gory and unfair, and once you've joined the only way out is with your memory erased or to die in the line of duty."

This time a couple of tears did fall.

"I'm not scared of what needs to be done," Collin lied.

Deep down, he could feel his intestines twisting in nervous knots at the recollection of the wendigo. He knew the brutality of it all, Mr. Pyrrhal and Mrs. Goodall warned him of the dangers lurking in the dark, but it didn't alter the gravity of his self-made fate. He faced the reality of it every single day he remembered the spraying of that woman's blood against the window pane. For some reason, it was the beating he'd received from Taylor that helped bring everything into focus.

"I'll do better," he promised more to himself than to Ms. Glenda.

She grabbed his shoulder. A forced smile spread on his lips as a smaller tear trickled its way into the thin crevasse of her nose. "I know you will. Just don't let your time with Taylor fool you into thinking he's a relentless bully. He's very…*determined* with his duty for our society. He would much rather *everyone* be kept to code, and is *very* skeptical of newcomers. It may take a lot to impress him, but it's worth it to pull it off."

Overture

Collin understood. The patter of his heart grew subtly more frantic at the idea of being in the same room with him. He almost consulted her about the conversation he overheard between Taylor and her husband, but decided against it. He could stew on it for a while longer. In the event she was unaware, there was no sense in worrying her further.

The remainder of the day was for resting. For the sake of providing his body the nourishment necessary to grow, he attended dinner, but he couldn't deny coming off as distant. His mind wasn't there. Over the hours, he progressively found his attitude more and more negative toward his own capabilities. He seemed fine on spellwork. Plus, he'd have the whole weekend to sharpen his abilities and study circumstances, especially for Alice's lesson.

He paused his train of thoughts to remember he still had a few doses of Alice's amber vial of energy and all the good it would serve him the following day. His stomach doubled over with disappointment when he returned to his self-doubt. His instinct said to talk to Alice about it. Surely, she had some input that could put him to ease, but his male pride conflicted with carrying through the actions.

Wandering back to his room afterwards turned out not to be in isolation. Clark and Oscar tag teamed him around the bend with routine bouts of tomfoolery.

"Had a rough day, eh?" Oscar inspected as he sidled up on Collin's right.

"Course he did. Friday morning with the Taylor-nator?

That's enough to ruin anyone's day," answered Clark on his left. "The sad truth is that it's just the way he is."

"Luckily for us," Oscar gestured at him and his companion, "Taylor was the third to join our soirée of younglings, but that doesn't stop him from being a royal thorn up our ass when it comes to staying on top of everything."

"The moral of the story is we're here to help."

As much as Collin wanted to be alone, he enjoyed their presence more than anything that moment. Even more than with the idea of speaking to Alice. She may have the feminine might to put his mind to ease, but she could never match brotherly comfort. The almost-twins softened a frightened clutch in his chest by letting him know he wasn't alone.

"Help how?' Collin inquired.

"Help ease the transition of having Taylor DeWitt as your commanding officer," Oscar offered.

"We usually start our weekend exercises early in the morning if we can. You're welcome to tag along."

"We can give you our usual workouts and make some sparring time so you don't have to keep coming out bloodied and bruised."

Oscar was at the ready to respond to Collin's quizzical look about how they knew he'd gotten roughened so brutally.

"He trained Olivia and Alice."

"No holding back," added Clark. "He's an absolute Nazi when it comes to getting people in shape."

Their talking was silenced by a deeply exaggerated clearing of the throat. All three of them peered over their shoulders to see Taylor standing four feet away. While the sight of him drained the color from Collin's face with nervousness, the almost-twins remained unperturbed.

"Atten-tion!" Clark bellowed, and he and Oscar separated themselves from Collin and stood with their legs together, backs straight, and their shoulders squared.

Taylor walked past without a second glance. Meanwhile, the trio were cracking at the seams to hold back their laughter until he disappeared behind the sound of his door shutting. They collected themselves after a few minutes of letting loose.

"Anyways," Clark started. "We're sure your first week may have seemed overwhelming. Maybe it hasn't."

"But either way," Oscar continued, "we feel it's fair to warn you that it'll only get harder—"

"That's what she said," Clark mumbled.

"—and we wanna help give you the advantage."

"We did the same for Alice, you know. Before long though, she outpaced us."

"I see a bright future in that one," said Oscar.

"The brightest, mate. So, you in?"

They stopped at Collin's door. He was almost humiliated they even had to ask. He agreed with resounding gratitude and his entire foul mood and self-doubt melted away with the promise of one helluva productive weekend.

12

With the Passage of Time

That's how the weeks flew by for Collin Quinn. The remnants of his past life sloughed off him with surprising ease. He had Monday with Mrs. Goodall, Tuesday with Olivia, Wednesday with Alice, Thursday with Clark and Oscar, Friday with Taylor, and Saturday and Sunday he spent perfecting his weekly lessons, reviewing notes, and spellcastings from previous weeks, as well as reading ahead in his textbooks.

Spread throughout the week, he kept to a strict workout schedule Clark and Oscar gifted him with that first Saturday. Each day was dedicated to a different major muscle. These consisted of chest, back, arms, shoulders, and abs, followed by a day solely for cardio and stretching. Only one day was for rest, but they allotted it a good day to work on sparring per request. Taylor shockingly showed leniency when he allowed Collin to implement his workout routine into class time, provided they spent extra time on combat.

It wasn't until August's uproar of natural disasters that Mandarin Mansion truly became his home. With it, a key component of being a budding member of Veil became an embedded aspect of his self-identity.

Hurricane season started between the months of June and November, and, from recent observations, the bulk of approaching disasters bombarded the east coast around August. According to the caretakers of the Mandarin branch, they and the other divisions assisted with damage control as best they could. Turned out, the majority of their duty was to clear out any unwanted migrating organisms without being detected.

This year was a busy one in particular. Collin had seen it once before, the back-to-back barrage of Category Twos, Threes, and Fours, but it wasn't too often of an occurrence and they were never as powerful by the time they reached Jacksonville. This year was a consecutive collision of three storms measured at nothing less intense than Category Threes. Two of which were Fours, with howling gusts of one hundred thirty-something miles per hour. The eye of one storm had gotten closer than anyone anticipated.

For the beaches, floods typically expanded far past the usual 3rd Street, a mere three blocks inland. This year, the waters waded in nearly an entire mile inland, not including the areas forced underwater by the torrential downpour of the storms.

Mandarin Mansion wasn't located in an evacuation zone, and was far enough from the ocean and the Saint John's River running vertically through the center of the city, but the areas directly lining the river still required attention. Whenever free, the other branches banded together to assist the more damaged regions. A few groups even travelled south to cities such as Saint Augustine, which took damage beyond repair with such an outdated and sensitive drain system.

Collin would never forget when the warnings came. As per usually, the citizens were in a state of hysteria. Whenever a state of emergency was broadcasted, gas would sell out quickly, canned foods would be wiped off the shelves, and hordes of people hunting water would stand in line for hours for a few bottles. The prices for large sheets of plywood became inflated. Batteries, flashlights, candles, and first aid kits would be on backorder, and the higher the Category, the fiercer the state of mass hysteria. Some people would evacuate, but a good amount would stay, deeming it good barbecue weather as they ignited their grills in poorly-vented garages.

It was apparently tradition for the occupants of Mandarin Mansion to camp out in the sun room and watch the city become blanketed in darkness. The view from above was impossibly heightened to overlook the dangers invading their city like a foreign parasite leaching onto its host. As a family, impatient and distant Taylor included, they laid out comforters to picnic on and silenced the waterfall fountain to listen to the raging winds bend trees in half and ripping off business signs.

Off yonder, they heard the zapping of power lines as transformers burst visibly like fireworks. The wind shook the windowpanes, but never threatened them. The entire facility was so heavily warded not even a point-blank shot with a shotgun could compromise the integrity of the glass.

They all spent the evening chatting, snacking, and playing some type of game based on the art of illusion. The concept wasn't complex to grasp, but Collin's current gamut of spells left him at too high a disadvantage to play. The scope of the game was to take any old random object from a boxset of over one hundred items and layer it with a maximum of twenty phantasms. The goal of the deceiver was to obscure the object beyond recognition without changing the object itself. The participant whose turn it was only had ten spells to peel away each illusion until the object was revealed.

Even Alice took time out of her studying to play, and trumped them all. It got to the point where everyone, Osmond and Glenda included, designated Alice the illusion creator to test everyone else's skills at banishing concealments.

In between games, Oz, as Collin came to referencing him as, would treat the glass that surrounded them like a TV. He would pause the whooshing and whipping they saw outside to rewind and slow the flashes of lightening streak across the sky before resuming the live feed.

The hurricanes did put a delay on Collin's lessons. Members of their household were ceaselessly running to and fro their assignments of ridding the city of potentially dangerous beasts to the point where classes became entire days of self-teaching sessions with assigned spells. By the time the third hurricane nicked Jacksonville, however, Collin was granted permission to tag along on a job.

"Most likely it won't be anything serious," said Mr. Oz. "A couple of selkies, maybe a finfolk or two. The only real difference is the selkie's romantic nature; they're both kidnapping shapeshifters. If we're lucky, we'll only have to deal with some vodyanoys."

Collin shook his head to let Oz know he had no clue what he was talking about.

"Ah, they're weird algae-covered, overweight frog men with long, green hair, beards, scales, and a fish tail. Notorious for drownings. They're amphibious bastards, but not nearly as worrisome as each-uisge or yacuruna."

"Or a hydra," Clark added.

"Clark!" Mrs. Goodall yelled from the kitchen as they prepared to embark the following morning the third hurricane vacated city limits.

"Hydra?" asked Collin, making sure he understood. He had no idea what on Earth an each-uisge or a yacuruna was, but by the gods if he wasn't familiar with a hydra. Disney's Hercules, Marvel's infamously villainous syndicate, or your plain-Jane Greek mythology, sure, but to hear it aloud like a casual conversation was mind-boggling. "Like cut off one head and two shall take its place, hydra?"

"Sea hydras haven't been spotted since 1917," Alice muttered in passing, her nose deep in her studies with her examination only two days away.

"But they *exist*?"

"*Did* exist," Osmond spoke uncertainly. "A sea full of hydras would be difficult to go unnoticed. They're massive and ravenously indiscreet, and Veil's watchlist goes well beyond land."

And sure enough, as they tread the flooded community of Jacksonville, the worst they ever encountered were shapeshifting finfolk, with their human-esque appearance, but slimy skin with patches of scales, gills along the neck, a wide, fish-like mouth, and largely reflective black eyes. Among land, it crept on two legs, but, when the gang managed to find it, it attempted to escape swiftly with its transfigured mermaid's tail sending ferocious ripples through the water.

On their adventure, Collin met several other magical settlers of Jacksonville. Shane Johnson, head of the San Marco division and his colleague Tabatha from the Springfield region. What an abnormally active area that was, according to hers and one of her apprentice's, Tom Gallo's, retelling. Olivia displayed close association with Tom. There were a few others, but introductions were so sudden before getting straight to work that most were omitted from long-term memory.

Watching master spellcasters in action was such a treat. The creatures were slain or scattered off so efficiently and with minimum bystanders. Whenever something exciting did occur it was over before the moment could be savored. It did, however, raise a moral alarm to witness the slaughtering of such…

Could they be considered animals?

His curiosity was satiated when the division of beasts was explained. According to Tom and Olivia, the beasts kept from the general public are those which possess magic of their own. The ones typically exterminated are the ones reliably inclined to cause harm to others or expose their world.

"Very black and white material," Olivia claimed. "Not all creatures are bad, so not all need to be killed, but some are given limitations to abide by."

When their seasonal duties slowed in September, Mrs. Goodall insisted they pursue the curriculum, despite Collin's eagerness to work ahead with his history lessons. "Repetition is the mother of learning," turned out to be her favorite quote whenever discussing coursework. By now, they were nearing the end of the second textbook. In his spare time, Collin was nearing the middle of the third, with the assistance of what Alice called the draught of diligence.

Paul Ganley swung by a couple times to ensure he was progressing as swimmingly as he vouched for. As far as spellwork went, some, such as Ms. Glenda, Oz, Olivia, and the dynamic duo, believed his impressively improving abilities were a sign of innate dexterity. Naturally, only Alice and Taylor were aware of the mind-numbing hours dedicated to the craft. Countless times, Collin found himself bumping into one or the other in the sun room. They usually kept their distance from each other, but, at least, Alice grew comfortable enough not to shy away at his appearance.

Collin had achieved much in Olivia's class of

miscellaneous spells, from undoing locks, to summoning objects, to stunning small creatures, mostly bugs and rodents, with temporary paralysis, and turning appliances and fixtures off and on from a distance. They'd covered significantly more, but they're real focus was on the long-awaited memory charms.

With the volume of bystanders and victims spellcasters were likely to encounter, the memory charm was the bread and butter of any public encounter with the mythical and monstrous. Collin hoped Alice would be the one to teach him this material. Her mastery work was one to marvel over after all. As luck would have it, Alice accompanied him to class. Based on how she informed him, memory spells had to be taught with supervision at all times in the event that something went detrimentally wrong and needed correcting.

Alice and Olivia were so contrasting in mannerisms and style to the point of almost being silly. Alice was too prim and proper with fully erected posture. She only taught by the book and directed with her experiences conducting spells. Frequent side eyes were thrown at Olivia who was telling him to go with the flow and that whatever happened would happen. Collin was suspicious of the fact that, while the laid-back persona may be a dominant trait in Olivia's repertoire, she might've been magnifying it for the sole purpose of agitating her partner.

The first makings of altering another's consciousness wasn't overly complicated. There weren't any requirements for locating specific memories or even different regions of the brain. The introductory concept of wiping someone's recollections was centered on a full-scale blackout, at least temporarily. That's why first-year students weren't allowed to conduct any task that required public display. A self-sustaining spell, irreversible even by another spellcaster, would need more powerful magic. However, while the spell may be temporary for first-years, there have been minor catastrophes with improper form. Hence Alice being there. She was talented enough to reverse anything needing tampering with.

They'd spent a couple weeks fine-tuning the choreography of the charm, and they would spend weeks more of it on each of its conditions, making sure the hazard of the spell was kept in check. The first couple sessions were duds. As the time continued to fly by in Mandarin Mansion, it became a cinch. Before long, they were practicing eliminating more elongated spans of time.

His time with Alice was proving fruitful as well. He could slow attacks, develop fragile barriers between him and assailants able to withstand a single hit, and manifest a wall that froze projectiles with enough duration to escape impact. Battle magic still proved the most difficult for him, especially without taking the draught of diligence, but he was promised once he learned to implement the mechanics of different spells into one and create combinations with an intimate knowledge of the arts, the subject would come much simpler.

Lessons with Clark and Oscar became mildly more

professional in terms of their teaching style. They moved on from speeding things up to slowing them, to confounding enemies, and creating small confinements as traps. He learned how to create the ringing nuisance of tinnitus, how to briefly blind someone, and how to sustain himself in midair with each jump. This last skill was limited via altitude and would only allow its user to levitate eight feet in the air. He then learned to enhance his hearing, effectuate night vision, and to better silence his steps from the spell he originally meant to use the night he overheard Osmond and Taylor.

After roughly two weeks since his first class with Taylor, Collin had spent too much time dwelling over the idea of there being something wicked about himself. He sought books on human possessions and monsters taking on human form. He even considered the possibility of something happening to himself in the past and having his consciousness cleared. He eventually cracked and confided with Alice. She assisted him with his research at times, albeit at a toll of tolerating her overeager desire to track the timora she believed to be terrorizing Jacksonville on the down low.

According to her, the other factions of Jacksonville, including theirs, had no idea what they were dealing with, while she was growing more and more confident by the day. It was found uncanny, and Collin suggested someone be informed, but Alice was adamant on keeping silent. Opportunities like this for advanced spellcasters, which she recently became, were entirely too rare.

"And, so help me god," she warned, "if you tell anyone, I will burn you to the ground!"

"Okay, okay, geez," Collin swore. "I just thought it would be safer to keep it off the streets. Isn't that what Veil is all about?"

"I've been keeping an ear out for the missing person's reports and sightings, and its activity has dropped to a minimum-to-non-existent. If it were on a rampage, maybe I'd agree."

"Is it possible the thing is feeding on the unrecorded population?" Collin suggested.

Judging by the feint glimmer of guilt in her expression and her inability to maintain eye contact, he figured she'd already considered his point. Nevertheless, she remained persistent with sticking to her research so as to know everything about timoras for when she confronted the one roaming their city. The biggest problem was that lore on such ancient creatures remained ridiculously scarce. She'd exhausted all her sources in their provided library and needed to rely on outside literature.

Collin possessed a moral duty to inform Oz, Ms. Glenda, and the people he was comfortable enough to consider friends. They deserved the same respect if they were willing to treat him as much as a sibling or be his confidant, but he couldn't bring himself to reveal Alice's secret.

The only person who refused to budge an inch was Taylor.

Overture

He was still nothing more than a drill sergeant as far as their acquaintanceship went. He even lacked the common decency to apologize whenever they bumped shoulders in the hall, although it might've been Collin's fault. Late at nights, Collin found himself crossing paths with the asshole in the sun room or in the study more and more, now he was comfortable enough to wander without fear of a curfew.

So long as he was being a productive student and ready for his lessons in the morning, his nighttime strolls were nobody's concern, but he still couldn't shake the feeling of something being misplaced. This was especially so when he spied Taylor multiple times on the second-level platform of the study. This was where most of the sketchy and forbidden magic was conveniently separated for research purposes for advanced spellcasters or special cases, according to Ms. Glenda.

Nevertheless, Collin learned how to conform his suspicions and loathing for Taylor into the fuel for his fire when it came time to train. Before long, and with the more patient aid of Clark and Oscar, his improvement was no longer negligible. Despite the fact he still didn't stand a chance against his instructor, his performance with dodging and blocking was effective enough to keep Taylor working a little more. A couple of times, Collin had grown proficient enough with pivoting both feet, ducking, and utilizing his forearms as deterrents from oncoming blows, that he found himself able to plant a palm-heel strike into his opponent's collar bone. Watching Taylor stagger brought brief satisfaction to calm the beast before he proceeded to get pummeled. The regrettable awe that sculpted his face was instantaneously steeled over, so if his teacher was impressed, he stubbornly wouldn't admit it.

When it came to enhancing his physique, he'd never been more amazed at his own transformation. His idea of being fit and Veil's idea of being fit were worlds apart. Being thin with noticeable abs was a small-fry, high school ideal. In eight weeks, he noticed his chest swell dramatically, his back widen, his arms and legs thicken, and his shoulders become more rounded. The first two weeks of muscle soreness were the worst to endure, but he was allowed a potion to reduce the duration of fatigue. Between the energy drain from spellcasting and the unbelievable exhaustion from working out, his capacity for food evolved insatiably.

"When you're…starting out…it's important," Oscar explained during a session on a stationary bike. "You gotta be…in your prime…if you wanna make it…to the top. I've seen…a lot of older members…who've let themselves go…once they graduated completely. And honestly…there aren't many…beasts out there…you can take on…with hand-to-hand combat. It's really…only mandatory…to loosen you up…and learn how to move. It's mixing it…with magic…that's the…trickier part."

Another important tip Collin learned was to find a perfect balance with weight lifting. Working hard for a formidable figure apparently hadn't always proven itself necessary. For other members, they've gotten addicted to staying fit to the point of practically becoming professional bodybuilders.

"It's too much bulk," Clark discussed during arm curls. "You lose all that flexibility, and you're so weighed down that you can't run at peak performance, so you rely *too* heavily on spells."

And while Collin didn't disagree, he knew he was far from achieving such a threat. He added a few extra minutes to his daily stretches nonetheless.

He managed to go about town only when accompanied by other members of their household so they could cloak him under the precautionary spells implanted in their home to prevent unwanted company. His birthday couldn't arrive soon enough. By then, some small blood ritual would be performed, granting him access to nearly any Veil safe house in the world, minor stipulations included.

When Alice passed her examination with flying colors, she became equal with Olivia, Clark, Oscar, and Taylor. However, and this satisfied Collin's perplexing wonder, she chose to undergo the half of her curriculum requiring her to accomplish a solo hunt *first*.

The only reason the others were so accompanying with serving as Collin's professors was because they all chose, and succeeded in, the book-learning segment of being an advanced spellcaster. As it turned out, being considered advanced meant taking on a dominating role of independent studies. In other words, the Department of Magical Education gave you all the materials needed to know, and you were required to master them in a six-month period. If you passed, then you'd be given six months to prove yourself with a victorious hunt and a report to go along with it.

However, each six-month period was interchangeable. So, naturally, most people, such as everyone *but* Alice, chose to get the most out of their education before applying it to fieldwork.

Alice wasn't most people, and it was her outlier peculiarity that eventually made Collin openly admit to himself that his attraction for her went beyond hormonal engorgement. Her overall appearance developed a glimmer with his adoration. She was nerdy and cool in his eyes. She was characteristically determined to the bones. If she had a goal in mind, she would accomplish it. Not that she had to go about it solo.

Collin offered his help to her with research whenever he could, but she consistently declined. Finding the timora was her project. It was her way of letting every spellcaster around the globe know she was a force to be reckoned with. The real anomaly, though, was how off the radar the monster suddenly became.

Reports of fearsome sightings in the conventional world slowed, but never stopped. There was no pattern to accurately located it either. One day it would be in the south of Jacksonville, the next the west, north, beaches, etcetera. This told Alice it was smart to never stay in one place at a time, which was nothing she hadn't already learned from the minute history of the species. Their archaic rarity only added to their complexity, and, on top of it all, *every* single source felt the need to point out the deviously violent nature of timoras.

There were plenty of abandoned areas in Jacksonville, but Collin wanted to laugh at the unusual similarity to Stephen King's *IT*, with the possibility the timora might be lurking in the sewers. Whenever he tried making any suggestions to Alice, he was silenced before saying "Do you think –" She wanted zero help, and with each passing day she was growing more and more frantic, fearful someone may catch the trail and put an end to all her hard work. The fact that nobody else *had* caught on was nothing shy of a miracle, but the rest of their makeshift family started inquiring about her progress, as if Collin's inquiries weren't pestering enough. He could tell. God only knew how she felt about everyone else piling on their plethora of questions.

By the end of September, Alice acknowledged there simply wasn't enough literature dedicated to her would-be prey. Worried, Collin's additional attention to her led him to discover she was now taking her work to the streets. Every other night she snuck out. Instead of creaking open the front door, it was sheer accidental to come across her exiting via the study through a tear she created that served as a portal.

Whenever he approached her the following morning, she furthered to apply more threats to his life and bribed him with extra study time and draughts of diligence. He assured her he'd keep her secret, but not without hinting his concern for her safety. That was the only time he came across her leaving. She'd most likely confined her portal productions to her bedroom.

Unless he was underestimating all the research he'd done, every time timoras became the topic of discussion, all Collin could imagine was a spitting image of Stephen King's Pennywise. Not the original from 1990, but the remake. Not that he doubted the 1990 *IT* was terrifying in its time, but the newer edition had the technology and less television regulations to amp up the horror.

Alice's progressively frowzy demeanor was a concern he silenced time and time again for his own sake. Admitting his emotions could cause problems in the household.

Don't dip your pen in company ink, he reminded himself.

Compiling onto the subject of Collin's concerns was the onset of October, and, with it, his birthday. Which meant, with the quick-paced passing of time, Mr. Collin Quinn had an inauguration to prepare for.

13

Veil's Newest Inductee

No matter how hard they could've tried, Jonathon and Julia Quinn would never have been able to compete with the birthday celebration awaiting their son's coming of age. Collin knew it was a big day for him, huge. Becoming eighteen was big even in normal society, where he could now purchase scratch-off tickets. Not too long ago he would've been able to buy a pack of cigarettes. Now you had to be twenty-one. Not that he'd smoke them, or have much use for American currency anymore, but he could simply because it was his given right to piss away money on the useless things he couldn't yesterday.

His birthday fell on a Wednesday, which was slightly unfortunate. That would mean he wouldn't get to spend the morning with Alice since he was *gifted* with cancelled classes for the rest of the week. Which, if nothing else, spared him a Friday with Taylor. They figured with all the extra time Collin put into studying as an underage, honorary member of Veil, he technically wasn't falling behind on anything since he still had the traditional six months from today to study for his exit exam.

Even with the rest of the week off, his body was too accustomed to his morning routine to grant him the ability to sleep in, proving beneficial for him. He found Mrs. Goodall, Mr. Pyrrhal, Clark, Oscar, and Alice all seated around the table as he trailed his way into the dining room at six in the morning.

Waiting for me?

In unison, they broke out in *Happy Birthday.* His cheeks grew warm with humility and love for everyone surrounding him. As they sang, Collin noticed the unbearable exhaustion on Alice's face as she mumbled the lyrics.

She must've been out last night, he pondered. *Did she even have time to sleep?*

He wasn't about to pummel her with questions now. It made his heart swell knowing she took the time to participate. Furthermore, it fueled his hopeful fantasy that it was a display of affection she had for him to not be asleep.

Blanketing the table was one of Mrs. Goodall's classic banquets. The most eye-drawing was the massive tray of regular, whole wheat, chocolate chip, and blueberry pancakes. Each stack of a dozen pancakes was impaled with ever-burning sparklers and calligraphed whipped cream into the collective message *Happy. 18th. Birthday. Collin.* Surrounding the display was the usual array of buffet-styled breakfast foods and beverages.

"Thank you," Collin said, shakily with surprise and a secret detest for that song, but appreciative all the same. "It looks like you outdid yourself again, Ms. Glenda."

"Oh not at all, dear, not at all. Come, come," and Ms. Glenda gestured him to his seat between Alice and Clark. "Get a nice and cozy start to your big day."

The greatest gift he could've ever received was the disappearance of Glenda's mildly bitter tone at the prospects of him joining Veil. It pleased him to believe all his hard work at being a formidable apprentice may have finally dissuaded her opinion of him joining their organization. Did that mean he believed for a second she wouldn't prefer him to go on living a normal life? Not a chance, but her warming up to his decision was still satisfying all the same.

"Which pancakes you want?" Oscar asked from across the table.

"One of each, if that's alright?" he replied.

He asked it more out of politeness and humbleness at this point. They were no longer strangers from whom he truly needed permission as far as meals were concerned. He knew their response would be in the affirmative, and with his metabolism exceeding record peaks, he wasn't shy to throw down when it came to indulging in such a mountain of food. It would be rude to all of Ms. Glenda's hard work after all.

"Absolutely, it is!" Osmond's voice boomed throughout every crevice of the room. Collin noticed the stubbly cheeks of the man.

Was his night as equally long as Alice's?

That wonder forced him to involuntarily sneak a glance at

her. Up close he saw the early signs of bags developing under her slightly reddening eyes.

"Did you get any sleep?" he whispered out of earshot after he'd piled on the pancakes, scrambled eggs, and turkey bacon.

She simply shook her head and went about building a conservative plate of her own. The subject was left at that. He was aware bringing attention to her was the last thing she wanted.

Breakfast was joyous enough to get Collin through the day with the most festive mood. Less than an hour after they'd started, Olivia joined in on the well-wishes and gave her own rendition of Marilyn Munroe's *Happy Birthday*, "Mr. President" and all. The rest of the room laughed along and applauded. To his surprise, months of exposure to her off-the-charts sexuality no longer conjured his primal urges. He found the whole display amusing more than arousing.

Taylor slid through the front door as breakfast tapered off. He wanted to provide a report to someone named Shane Johnson before the day progressed. Across his face was the expression of someone less detestable, almost...*amiable?*

Must've gotten a talking to to be nice today, Collin considered, but his sub-thoughts had a more negative approach. *Or he got some news displeasing enough to only make someone like him seem happy.*

But, weirdly enough, he trusted them. All of them. There was no way not to. He'd already gotten this far in his teachings. Why waste anyone's time like that?

Overture

Once the meal was finished, Osmond ordered everyone to do whatever they needed to do to be presentable in front of the Council of Spell within the hour.

"This early?" Collin asked.

"Oh, yes," Osmond told. "The Council's been busy nonstop these days. Inaugurations aren't necessarily on their list of priorities, unfortunately, but don't worry about it too much, son. We'll be in and out of the courthouse in thirty minutes, forty-five max."

"Are we driving?"

"God, no," Osmond chuckled. "We'll create a tear there. Less stress."

Didn't he know it! Weekday morning commutes headed downtown were a nightmare. They were as bad as the evening rush hour, if not worse. A more pressing concern was what he was going to wear that served formal enough for his first encounter with the Council of Spell, but the answer awaited him on his door.

Hooked to the knob were black slacks, a matching jacket, and a tie to go with a royal blue dress shirt. Pinned to it was a note:

First impressions last a lifetime, and I know you don't own a suit. Figured the blue would match your eyes. Don't worry about it fitting. Just put it on and it'll take care of the rest.
Happy birthday! Best of luck,
Ms. Glenda.

Collin was in unutterable awe. A suit. His first ever suit. He almost dashed back to the kitchen to profess his gratitude, but knew they were on a tight schedule. However, she was correct about the suit. As soon as he slid into the pants, shirt, and jacket, the fabrics tailored themselves around his body until they hung custom fitted. He moved quickly afterwards. They were on the clock for his induction, and the less interruptions with the Council's personal schedule the better.

Once everyone was cleaned, dapper, and spritzed with fragrance, the entire crew gathered in the study with Oz at the lead. He waved his fingers elaborately with choreographed motions until ripples waved in the air like the elusive fumes of evaporated gasoline. Fingers dug into the mysterious nowhere that served as a shortcut to their destination. Through the haze on the other side was a room of bright walls and Grecian pillars planted into a reflectively polished marble floor. Voices from half a dozen people echoed like a plummeting pebble *clank clanking* the circumference of a stone well. They crossed the threshold in an orderly fashion. First went Osmond, then Mrs. Goodall ushered Collin next, followed by Alice, Olivia, Clark, Oscar, Taylor, and finally herself. Everything came into vivid focus with an eight-inch step over the line dividing the possible from the incomprehensible.

Only twice in his entire Floridian residence could Collin recall laying his eyes on the Duval County Courthouse. He supposed he should count himself lucky. Its infrastructure, however, was impressive enough to make him wish he could cross paths with it more often.

Its entrance mimicked elements of a Greek temple, minus panes of glass occupying the gaps past the first row of pillars. To the left and right and behind the entry, but never rising higher, was a flat, red-roofed foundation extending half a block. Directly behind the Grecian entrance was a near-identical copy with multiplied dimensions laid on top of the foundation, and nestled between a left- and right-wing, flat, red-roofed extension built on top of the building. In short, it resembled a small-scaled built atop a large-scaled version of the same construct.

"We're now several floors below ground. No one from conventional society has access to this area," said Osmond, approaching two security officers. "Don't even know it exists, actually."

The windows surrounding them begged to differ, but Collin was told they were there for effect. Natural lighting still reminded workers they had lives outside their lawful dungeon.

The guards, one tanned male and one dark-skinned female, were clad in black uniforms fitted to each's body like a glove to prevent any impediments in movements. On their right shoulders bore Veil's emblem of the opposite scythes linked by the vertical bar. On their hips were matching Billy clubs and .40 caliber handguns.

"I thought magic rendered those useless," Collin whispered over his shoulder to Clark.

"If they hadn't been improved, maybe."

"They're enhanced?" He was astonished he could still find himself surprised that magic surfaced even in the relics of his old world.

"Good morning, Mr. Pyrrhal!" greeted the male security guard with a slight bow and an extended hand. "How're you now?"

"All's as well as can be," Osmond's deep voice echoed in the great expanse of the room they stood in. He accepted the handshake. "How about you, Harold? Jenny?"

The lady shrugged and the man tilted his head in a defeated sort of gesture.

"Just another day, I suppose," replied Harold. "But they did increase security today with the Council in town for a hot minute. They said they'd be here for you?"

"For our newest inductee, actually. Mr. Collin Quinn."

Osmond turned toward Collin and the officers followed his gaze. Collin became embarrassed when noticing the avid interest the man took in his presence. The loosened collagen in his face told a tale one too common in Jacksonville about a sun-kissed man and the slim, salty waves. Minor sunspots sung with affirmation, but the graying of the man's shoulder-length hair helped Collin believe he was at least aging comfortably. Jenny, in contrast, gave him an empty stare from her dark brown eyes that almost looked to breed suspicion.

An occupational hazard, I'm sure.

She was considerably younger than her counterpart. Still

Overture

young enough to possess a sense of constant vigilance. Vigilance being a trait Collin was taught couldn't be exercised enough these days, although still for reasons not fully known.

"Mr. Quinn! Yes!" Harold exclaimed. "Happy birthday, young man."

"Thank you," Collin said graciously, inquisitive as to how many other people were aware of his existence.

"Mr. Pyrrhal, do you all have your IDs on you? Standard routine," said Harold.

"Of course, of course."

Osmond dug into the inner pocket of his suit and the others followed suit. Alice pulled out a thin, black card from a pocket she fashioned in the skirt of her charcoal gray dress suit. Mrs. Goodall withdrew hers from the purse strapped across her body, and Olivia from her bra. She ignored the look of disapproval from Mrs. Goodall with blatant imprudence.

"Perfect. Perfect. Perfect," Harold mumbled with each clearance.

By the time he reached Collin, he pinned a visitor's pass on his chest and waved him through. On it was his name and the words *visits remaining: 1*.

"They're very particular about not letting non-Veil members in," said Oscar.

"Yeah, if you're not inaugurated by your second visit, they'll wipe your memory and never consider a third chance," Clark supplemented.

"So, I still get another chance if today doesn't go well?"

"You won't need it, dear," Mrs. Goodall butt in. "That's only for when they do a quick test of someone's proclivity for spellcasting, which you'll have no problem passing at this point. I wouldn't be surprised if they didn't bother testing you at all, since Paul's been making visits."

It eased his rapid onset of anxiety by a sliver. Still knowing the Council could be displeased by him was unsettling.

"The inauguration is in seventeen minutes. I reckon you know the way, Mr. Pyrrhal?" Jenny asked flatly.

"Yes, ma'am, I do," and he herded his flock into an impossible rotunda.

"How, in *the* hell, if we're underground?"

"Magic, mate," Oscar told, brushing past him.

In the center of the circular room, every nook and cranny were violently bewitched. The floor they tread on alone made his heart flutter with uncertainty in its stability. The void below was like walking on glass, and the space underneath was the infinite celestial landscape of their night sky untarnished by the city lights of urban pollution. Somewhere along the constellations was their emblem growing brighter than the North Star.

He was warned not to focus on it too much and how it tended to make first-timers dizzy or even sick. So, he focused his attention elsewhere. The dome above that wasn't architecturally possible was sustained by the combined strength of more Grecian pillars, but less plain. They were sculpted with vines and flowers and bees. Cherubs were engraved to encircle each monolithic support, stone rippled with the ribbons they strewn.

The dome bore a renaissance mural with a golden backdrop. It painted a story of growth and victory. It recapped the burning of spellcasters hundreds of years ago at the hands of simple village folk. The mural transitioned into the establishment of communities, a mighty war between kin, and then, standing in the center of opposing sides stood a man and woman garnishing black cloaks bearing the sigil of Veil. Afterwards Collin noticed it rotate into black-cloaked members passing a book down to a younger generation to symbolize the inheritance of their knowledge and tempering the next wave of neophytes.

Their strides had too brisk a pace to observe the entire story. Their path veered slightly to the left where seven doors lay in semicircle from Harold's and Jenny's checkpoint. Each was color coded. From left to right lay bright red, white, a radiant gold, charcoal gray, sparkling silver, black, and cobalt blue. Each door was stationed with its own guard. They passed through the golden door with a tip-of-the-hat salute to its overseer and a polite greeting.

Inside was nothing like the outside. The hallway was nothing but nonindustrial granite cobblestones, illuminated by sourceless balls of radiance lining the ceiling. Despite the dungeon-like vibe, Collin still found it warm.

"This is one of the oldest rooms in all the country," Oz informed. "Anyone who's ever enlisted comes through here. No matter the location."

"We all did," Olivia spoke, being either surprisingly silent this entire trip or surprisingly unheard.

At the end of the passage lay a classic chamber door of wood and wrought iron and a knocker that echoed loudly with each *clank–clank* of metal on metal to announce their arrival. The door swung willingly inward, exposing the crew to its inhabitants.

The décor of the room was still in tune with the archaic hallway. The walls were constructed from heaps of granite, although somewhat more refined. The ceremonious room lay largely circular enough to accommodate two semi-circular jury boxes to the left and right facing center. They were divided by a red carpet leading to a singular, dark brown podium standing on a thin platform. From there, the carpet rolled further to what Collin compared to a courtroom judge's bench, but widened to quarter at least, he tallied, a dozen black-cloaked bodies. The judge's bench extended six feet from the ground. Built into the base was an enchanted fireplace. Behind the bench were two arched windows glowing a saturated blue.

Seated in the right jury's box were two individuals. One with a laptop at the ready, and the second was none other than Paul Ganley, the prober of his memories. The stranger's fingers moved wildly as the family approached, but that wasn't Collin's focus. The lighting of the room misconstrued Ganley's expression to be either glee, insanity, or gave the faintest malicious glint flashing across his eyes and smile.

Overture

Why on Earth would it be anything like that, he scorned the skeptic in him.

"Welcome, Osmond and family," echoed a woman's half-disinterested voice, "and welcome, Mr. Quinn. If you will please approach the podium while the rest get seated."

It was a command, not a question, and Collin's heart pitter-pattered anxiously as his support group separated from him somberly. Not without an encouraging pat on the shoulder from Mr. Pyrrhal and Clark first. Each step afterward proved difficult. Everyone was seated before he reached his destination.

He'd spent months as a resident of the Mandarin branch and was learning, and *retaining*, all his studies with worthy praise. If they asked him to change an object to red, he could. Or, better yet, he could bend light from the vibrant windows and ignite a candle. It was more intermediate level, but he'd skimmed over the spell and had a passable understanding behind the theory of fusing basic spells. He almost considered the possibility of being able to burn the Council alive with the raging fire below them. However, the closer he got, the more he realized the flailing flame didn't behave exothermically. Nor did it portray the traits of an endothermic flame. It was merely decoration.

"Mr. Collin Seguin Quinn," the same woman's voice rang out from the center of the Council's bench, "my name is Eleanor Merriweather. I am Head Councilwoman for the Council of Spell."

The top bitch of the United States, in all her glory, thought Collin.

He cut his thoughts short to pay attention and hopefully shudder off the creep of trepidation across his skin.

"You are here, on your eighteenth birthday, to be sworn in as an official member of Veil, is that correct?"

"Yes, ma'am," Collin answered softly, almost hoarsely.

He cleared his throat and repeated himself, utilizing forced confidence. His first impression of his inauguration felt more like a trial. The evenness of her voice gave him the impression she didn't want to be there, or that exhaustion owned her from all the responsibilities she possessed.

Unfortunately, the dimness of the room prevented extracting exact details about her expression. What it did grant was the deduction she was an older woman, if not by the aged rasp of her voice, then by the withering silhouette of her body and light gray hair wrapped into a librarian bun.

The rest of the council was equally difficult to observe, but from what he gathered, they were an eclectic bunch. To her left was a man as old as dirt, with paper-thin hair and a pair of bifocals. He sat there twiddling his thumbs with no visible interest to be there. The man on her right, however, was the exact opposite. He was the only person in the room whom Collin could make out almost as clearly as if they were inches apart under a cloudlessly scorching sky. Each strand of golden hair glowed with magnificent contrast to the blue hue of the room, his brilliant blue eyes matching. He had a strong, stubble-free jaw and a piercing gaze of utmost interest. Instead of fiddling, he leaned forward, fingers locked, elbows spread. Collin would later learn this man was a Nephilim.

Spreading out to the other members of the organization, Collin was limited to relying on the blurred features making them stand out. One woman, next to the inhumanly illuminated man, possessed hot pink hair to her shoulders and an abnormally large hooked nose. The bespectacled gentleman beside her had flaming red hair.

Come to realize, they all possessed distinctive hair. One lady had blue, while another had green. One had a normal head of jet black, a second silver. The only two people who seemed normal were Merriweather and her ancient companion.

Christ, it's like I stepped into an anime show, he chuckled mentally.

"One of our advisors, Ganley, has vehemently informed us you are an invaluable asset in terms of dedication and moral compass," Merriweather pursued, "and your current guardians tell us you truly do display a knack for spellwork."

Collin's cheeks grew warm. He wasn't too sure about the moral compass part, but it was still nice to receive recognition for the last few months.

"And so, now that you are officially of age, we are willing to accept your request to join us, *but...*" she paused for dramatic effect, "it is our duty to make sure you are aware and appreciative of the fact that being a member of Veil is not as simple as using magic as a means of personal gain within conventional society.

"We are the guardians of common sanity, the division between order and chaos in respect to what the outside world can and can't comprehend. They can read about the fantasy world and watch it cinematically, glorifying it as a means of adventure and fulfillment, but what they never tell you is the cost. Are you, Collin Quinn, prepared to forfeit your life among the conventional world for the sake of opposing the darkness that dwells this earth, the great ancient evil Veil has sworn to keep at bay, knowing full well it may cost you your life?"

Eleanor paused to give him a long appraising look.

That's what it was right?

By the sound of her austere tone, what else could it have been? The effort made to decipher her expression delayed his response.

"I am."

"And you are prepared to submit to the lessons our society has established to ensure all members are well-equipped for what awaits us in the supernatural, and accept that it is forbidden to conduct your own investigation until it is mandated as a curriculum staple?"

"I am."

"Very well," Merriweather gave a curt nod to a mysterious figure unseen behind the stand. "Unfortunately, we must keep this quicker than our traditional preferences. There is much to manage these days, and only so many hours in a day to do so."

A robed figure stepped out, face hooded over, and approached Collin with an obsidian box clutched in gloved hands. The container was laid before him on the podium. One of the gloves was removed to reveal a grotesquely withered and blackened hand, fingernails almost an inch long and discolored. With the pointer finger extended, the mummified person scraped a nail across the top of the case and a white line glowed equatorially. The top of the box was removed, revealing a gemstone with the power to summon greed in even the humblest of hearts. It was a perfectly spherical blue goldstone, mimicking the starry night sky and large enough to wrap both hands around and still not conceal its entire surface.

"You are required to fulfill a blood oath," Merriweather informed.

Her voice was growing flatter with each sentence and quicker in pace.

"This will grant you access to all designated Veil facilities, as well as bind you to the magical network. It serves as an enhancer of spells. It connects each of us to the heart of magic. It binds us to a contract pledging ourselves as responsible users and defenders against the darkness."

Collin's eyes were so glued to the orb he didn't notice the hooded figure withdraw a knife embedded with enchanted engravings, its handle a sheen obsidian.

"Take the blade, Mr. Quinn, and provide the stone with a sample of your blood."

Hearing his name snapped him out of reverence. Hearing the instructions frightened him a smidge. It was stupid to be frightened by the concept though. Blood would surely be a routine experience, and he did just swear he'd be willing to make the oath. There would be zero redemption from chickening out now.

Taking the weapon in his right hand, he drew the blade to the base of his left pointer finger and hesitated. He'd never purposefully had to cut himself. Not that he expected any surprises from the process. There were plenty of people from his past school who endured the self-infliction like a daily ritual. That was high school. Did that make them braver than him, or more desperate? If it were desperation, he could probably match tic for tac with his desire to escape the gloom of his dull past. He relinquished his fear and slid the sharp object into his palm.

The skin broke as the blade rubbed diagonally. Blood welled and poured over, a shallow pool of dark, rich red. His body tensed as he stifled a gasp. He fought to keep his hand steady as he lowered it to the cool surface of the mesmerizing stone.

Vibrations penetrated his body the instant his blood made contact with the stone. Reverberations could be heard, not from his eardrums, but from inside himself. A song hummed from his toes to his brain. He could feel it serenading every inch, from his mind, his stomach, his spleen, fingernails, even his penis. It was nirvana, like a post-massage when left on the table to bask in the sensual relaxation.

Every angry and bitter fiber of his humanity became docile, eager to welcome the magic flowing in his veins, embrace it, make love to in. Everything and everyone around him vanquished into meaninglessness. This was his apotheosis. He was everything and nothing, divine and damned. He was balance. Only when the stone was plucked from underneath him was he forced back into the torment of existence.

"What was that?" he inquired brusquely, forgetting his tamed manners in the presence of the Council.

They paid no mind to it.

"That was your induction, Mr. Quinn," Merriweather's voice echoed off the dungeon wall. "The stone may not accept everyone, but it's accepted you. Welcome to Veil."

14

The Departure

"Does touching the stone make an *actual* contract?" Collin asked.

They were finishing up another celebratory meal, and Mr. Pyrrhal managed to convince his wife to bring forth a few bottles of wine. Ignoring the underage laws, he wanted to make a toast.

"Not so much a contract as an introduction," Olivia replied.

"Huh?"

"Imagine it like being introduced to a dog," Clark explained to Collin's right. "Touching the induction stone is equivalent to letting a dog sniff you, except it's magic and not a dog. If it likes you, you get all tingly, and if it doesn't you get bitten."

"Define *bitten*."

"Dead," Oscar said plainly.

"Hey!" Mrs. Goodall cut in, but it was too late.

To Collin's surprise, he wasn't actually surprised from this news. He barely even knew if he should take it seriously or not. If it weren't for the sharp glare the two received from Mrs. Goodall, it most likely would've passed as a joke.

"And...how often do people die from it?" he asked.

"It's very rare," Mrs. Goodall said quickly. "*Incredibly rare.* It's unlikely to even get to see the stone without certainty of passing."

It was clear she didn't want to give Clark or Oscar the opportunity to say anything. The abrupt change from angry to worried actually strangely annoyed Collin.

"And nobody felt the need to tell me I might die?"

He reached for the mashed potatoes with his left hand, the same hand the decrepit individual rubbed a thin layer of salve on after the ceremony. The wound healed without a trace. The tone in Collin's voice fought to sound casual rather than demanding.

"Nobody here," Oz spoke up for his wife, and Collin couldn't help but notice the subtle glower on Taylor's face, "doubted that magic would accept you. You've proven yourself admirably without even touching the stone. Now we get the pleasure of watching you progress so much faster."

He had a point there. Ever since they'd gotten home, after a few snide remarks on the impudence of the Council and their out-of-the-ordinary briefness of the entire ordeal, it was clear the angelic effects of the orb had lessened, but never fully subsided. He tested out a few spells in his bedroom and was pleased to find they bordered on effortlessness. Draught of diligence was practically irrelevant now his spellcasting could grab traction in reality easier than chained tires on a four-wheel drive pickup truck.

After dinner, Oscar slipped him a note alerting him to another soiree in their bedroom that night around eleven. *Suit mandatory*, he'd written. Never in his life had he had cause to dress formal twice in one day.

Perhaps with a quick nap first?

Wine's first impression appeared to be mildly hypnotic. So, he slept, and slept hard, and by the time his alarm went off he still had an hour to fix his immediate bedhead and dress. Trudging to the bathroom to spruce up, the weight of waking was gravitational. Napping had the annoying aftereffect of making him more tired.

Maybe the draught won't be as irrelevant as I thought, he considered, taking a single drop straight on his tongue.

There wasn't any flashing light to guide his way now he was familiar enough to creep through the hallway. He knocked, but there was no echo. The door swung open and he cross the threshold into Clark's and Oscar's bachelor pad.

"Hey, it's the new kid!" Olivia shouted from the bed.

"Hey!" Collin shouted back, prolonging the pronunciation of the vowel.

He immediately rerouted right and moseyed over to the table of shots. It was pertinent to avoid too many being pushed on him this time around, sobering elixirs or not. Then again, he did have the entire rest of the week off.

No!

It wasn't about the time off and letting loose. It was a

matter of not letting loose too much and making a silly ass of himself again. He stuck with one PPD for now.

Returning to the group, the only person not present, and not surprisingly, was Alice. Everyone else, Taylor included, dressed in dapper fashion. Olivia wore a new, blinding white, backless dress, Clark and Oscar in a pair of matching three-piece, pin-striped suits, and Taylor with the classic, black suit, white shirt, black tie arrangement.

Fellowship of the Ring played soundlessly on the TV. Collin was delighted by the recurring theme of dim lighting and classical and swing music wafting melodically all around.

It ended up being a great night for team morale. They laughed and joked, even played beer pong. What was different about the frat favorite in this world was the mandatory use of spells to launch the pong ball into cups. Clark and Olivia paired into teams while Collin and Oscar formed the opposing side. Taylor observed from the sidelines with his signature scoffs and eye-rolls, but when Collin and Oscar lost, mostly on account of Collin's inexperience with trajectories, Taylor stepped in and stole the championship solo.

Next, the almost-twins pulled out their long-handled tobacco pipes and puffed shapes into the air, giving them ridiculous stories of utter nonsense. There was the god-sent meteor fated to give the world a fresh start, a cat surviving on its eighth life and in search of a good luck amulet, and the immortal man who died before his time.

Naturally, the two reenacted the Bilbo-Gandalf smoking

scene, where Clark blew a large smoke ring and Oscar puffed out billowing tendrils of gray air molded into a ship that sailed through Clark's ring. After an hour of laughter and a couple more shots, Collin concluded Alice wouldn't be making an appearance.

Collin hoped she would, he'd even been actively seeking her every ten minutes or so. Undoubtedly, she was spending another night hunting her target. Instead, he saw this as an opportunity to question his friends for their opinions.

"I dunno what's gotten into her," Clark sighed with a portrayal stating they clearly did know.

"Or hasn't gotten *into* her," Olivia teased.

"Ooo, sassy," Clark and her bantered. "We can't go judging like that. She's just…enthusiastic. Like our Collin!"

"To Collin!" Oscar roared, and everyone raised a toast and shouted in unison, Taylor too, minus the yelling.

Collin blushed and looked around the room. It wasn't the direction he'd planned for the conversation. After everyone's shots were kicked back, a floating metal platter served them more.

"You can't blame Alice for wanting to focus on her course, especially now she's an advanced-level spellcaster," Taylor defended.

"Of course not," said Clark, "but it's not like we don't already know she's gonna outperform every single one of us. Even probably you. What does she have to top? A catoblepas?"

"Yeah, all our solo ops reports were done last month. We're

waiting for the official due date to hand them in. It's not a hard task, but you can guarantee she'll make it one," said Olivia.

Tonight was definitely not the night to drink heavily for Collin. To hell with making an ass of himself, sloppily blurting Alice's secret was his number one concern. He was happy to be the only one in the know, despite the information being dangerous in nature.

"Alice is ambitious enough to go the extra mile," Taylor conceded. "We could use more members like her the way things are going."

"What things?" Collin cut in, much to Taylor's annoyance, and Olivia's, her mouth wide with rebuttal. "All I hear is that Veil is facing problems left and right, but there's never any detail."

The four of them exchanged conspiratorial looks. He could see the debate each of them weighed among one another. The questions were decipherable enough. *Should we tell him? Do you think he's ready? What are we even permitted to say?* It was strange to find a topic even Clark and Oscar were hesitant to divulge on.

"I am an official member now, y'know?" Collin reminded them, and in response, he got a sigh of resignation from the almost-twins.

"Shot first," Clark bartered.

Collin obliged and retrieved another from the platter. He took a gamble on an acid-green libation, but it was only sour apple. Afterwards, it was Taylor who led the conversation.

"More and more, we're noticing other Veil personnel going missing, sometimes entire factions. The number of innocent casualties has also been increasing, so it puts more stress on keeping our world from being detected."

"Then, to top it all off," Oscar started, "A lot of the creatures out and about have been roaming outside of their natural patterns, like we told you you're first night. Woodland creatures in the arctic. Arctic creatures chillin' on the beach. Nocturnals hunting during the day, and breeding is off the charts!"

"Veil had a grip on everything just a year ago," Taylor added. "There was balance between the good and the bad, and gradually the scales have been tipping, and the harder we try, the more things seem to be in disarray."

"Hell," Clark said, coughing down another drink, "Oz said earlier today one of the other safe houses is thinking all the strange sightings people have been having might actually be tied to a timora. Can you believe that? Right here in our city! I don't know if you've ever seen –"

"What?!" Collin cut off a little too enthusiastically.

His heart went from zero to one hundred with panic, but he did his best to play it off as curiosity. It was time to find a way to wrap up quick to warn Alice. If she found out someone was onto her project, it would send her into a frenzy.

But it's dangerous, he argued from within. *Maybe she shouldn't know. She could use all the help she could get.*

"A timora. A shapeshifter that plays off people's fears. They're supposed to be extinct."

"No, no, I know." Collin now fought to play things more casual. "I glanced at them in a book." It wasn't technically a lie. "There's supposed to be incredibly powerful , right?"

"Monumentally," Clark supplied.

Collin already tuned them out. He could fake sick, say he had stuff to do tomorrow, or maybe say he was simply tired. They didn't have to know he'd taken a dab of Diligence. On the other side of the coin, though, Alice probably already summoned a tear off the premises. Staying and enjoying himself was proving a probable option, but his heart told him the right decision.

"Hey, could y'all give me a minute? I think I forgot something in my bedroom," Collin lied.

He gulped his drink in good favor and they beckoned him to return soon. There was no way he could enjoy his time without knowing if Alice was unreachable. If she wasn't, she deserved to know someone was on the trail, but a part of him worried this news could send her into a frenzy.

He scampered to her door as soft as a whisper and knocked firmly, yet without echo. When there was no response, he knocked sturdier still. More nothingness.

"Shit," he whispered under his breath.

He headed for his bedroom, weighing the possibility of finding a spell for sending messages scattered in his textbook.

When he cleared the bend, however, he found Alice already waiting for him, finger pressed to her lips as a preventative measure against startlement. She pointed to his door and he got the hint. The second the door shut behind them, he burst into warning.

"People are catching on about the…the…the…*thing*!" he bellowed.

"I heard," she appeared absentminded.

The calm in her voice was unwonted, coming from the same girl who once got herself in an exuberant conversation with herself out of sheer passion over her own ambitions.

"But what're you gonna do if someone finds it before you?"

"That won't happen. I'm close."

Collin proceeded to protest, but the same finger Alice pressed to her lips for silence was now pressed to his for the same effect. Despite the frowziness of her nature lately, he couldn't help but detect the scent of cherries on her skin as his stomach simultaneously clenched nervously. It was one of the rare times they'd come into direct contact, but it felt strangely intimate how much her touch left its mark on his skin. He became self-conscious about whether or not his breath reeked of alcohol. He didn't have much time to worry. Without warning, Alice removed her finger and pressed her lips against his.

"What're you—" he started to ask as they kissed, but she shushed him and he obeyed.

Maybe it was the liquor bringing out the emotional in him, but he was suddenly frightened by the velocity of her actions.

They never held any discussions of affectionate investment for one another, let alone held hands. Hell, Collin wasn't even aware if she possessed any interest in him.

Maybe she'd been drinking alone, his voice echoed unconvincingly in his mind. *This isn't like her.*

She was authoritative, yet seemingly demure about her assertion as she initiated the steps toward his bed. Collin found it arousing as she guiding his hands to her hips and led him backwards. The waistband of his slacks grew tighter when one of her hands hooked around his neck and the other rested on his chest for that extra push.

The taste of her lips was equally intoxicating as the subtle scent of cherries also emanated from her breath. He raised one hand to run his fingers through her silky, brunette hair. The lack of resistance was too surreal for him, like perhaps he never woke from his nap and this was all a cruel dream.

If that's all it is, then let it be.

His chest tightened with excitement. Sure, it'd been a little while since he'd been involved with anyone like this, but for that dry spell to be broken by Alice was about as lucky as winning the lottery, or being accepted by the ritual stone of Veil.

As soon as they bumped into the bed, Alice shook off his coat and let it fall to the floor. Collin kicked off his shoes and socks. Alice gestured to jettison him on top, but he took the lead this time. He gripped her and switched their positions so he could wrap one arm under her butt and lift her onto his mattress. She released a gasp of pleasure and surprise and positioned herself flat. Upon her, Collin lowered his chest onto hers and tucked an arm under her lower back as they continued to exchange passionate whispers.

Before long, her cold, fearing hands ripped his dress shirt out from under his pants and planted themselves on his warm stomach, grazing the ridges of the muscles still in development. He decided to follow her lead. With his free hand, he crept along the hem of her shirt until his fingers came in contact with her smooth complexion, but he ventured further with a wave of huge confidence. His touch burnt a slow trail into her skin as he traced his way to the center of her torso and to her small breasts where she shivered.

The hands on his stomach were removed and used instead to hectically maneuver the buttons free from his shirt. He intuitively removed his own hands to help. Once bare, it was time for Alice's shirt to go.

Fair was fair.

She sat up to reveal the lacy, pale blue bra underneath, which she proceeded to unclasp herself. Their languid foreplay, short lived, augmented with a mutual need to have each other now. It was an unspoken law translated as preordained.

Softened eyes locked as they each removed their pants, a condom retrieved from her pocket beforehand. Chilly nervousness heated to a feint sheen of sweat blossoming from ecstatic heartbeats. All that remained were the undergarments, but everything so far was perfect. Alice was a

Overture

work of art. The type most people would never expect from scrawny, nerdy stereotypes such as themselves.

From her toes to her face, you could tell she treated her toned figure like a temple. She was the epitome of balance in mind and body, and Collin could've sworn he fell in love that night. With the whole package of intelligence and primal magnetism, his heart usurped full control of the wheel from his hormones.

Her hand took his and proceeded to shift it downward until he came in contact with the warmth between her thighs. She was instructing him to remove the final article of clothing. He obliged. There was no need to rush. He slid her panties gently free and ran a hand through her mound. She moaned and smiled those glowing, perfect teeth, but not another word was spoken. Swiftness ensued as his boxers were tugged off and her doe eyes urged him to conduct the inevitable. Again, he obliged, and their bodies danced in rhythm to the enchanting moans they shared in unison until the sweet release of climax.

***

Nobody was sent to check on Collin for the remainder of the night. Nobody would've been able to get ahold of him even if they did. Alice granted him zero time to speak about *them*, and it broke her own heart with necessary insolence. Come morning, Mandarin Mansion would find itself one member short.

15

Foul Play and Fairies

Nobody was aware in the beginning. Alice's absence was chalked up to her studying or finally catching trail of something. However, after an entire day of her absenteeism, and the lack of her presence at the following breakfast, questions arose. Even Collin was clueless. He couldn't deny it stung to awake to an empty bed, but, then again, Ambitious Alice wasn't exactly one to waste time. Her eagerness toward him could've told him that much if he'd focused more on the elusive details of that night, rather than the meager fact that they had sex. Clark, Oscar, and Olivia threw an accusation or two for not coming back, but he merely lied and claimed he passed out. Which wasn't entirely a lie, for all they needed to know.

Curiosity evolved to worry, and worry bled dry until there was nothing left but fear. Mrs. Goodall and Mr. Pyrrhal tried to send her letter after letter, but she'd warded herself against outside communication and the paper burnt to ashes in their hands. By the third day, Halloween, with no word, they'd sent a formal missing person's notice to each of the

Jacksonville safe houses and to Veil headquarters in New York.

One of the quietest members of their household was Taylor. While Collin had been pulled aside by everyone, especially Clark and Oscar, to see if he had any information to divulge about Alice, he was the only one who lurked predatorily in the corner with anticipation. For what, Collin wondered on several occasions, but he never considered the extreme Taylor would take it after that third day's breakfast.

The entire family agreed to spend the day actively trying to find her. Creating tears to locations was easy. They were fixed points requiring perfunctory spellwork. Locator spells were slightly more complicated with objects when it came to pinpointing an item which more than one exists. Finding people was a whole other story. People changed, their locations changed, and it was next to impossible when someone as skilled as Alice warded herself against being found magically.

"Why would she leave?" Mrs. Goodall begged from no one in particular, on the verge of tears.

It mercilessly ripped Collin's heart from his chest to have a pretty good idea why she would leave, but to still not tell anyone. When she swore no one was going to find the timora before she did, he had no idea she already planned to leave to track the damned thing. Alice was worn out and depleted as it was. God only knew the condition she might've been in now.

On his way to his bedroom from breakfast, he was

forcefully slung inside at the slightest crack of his door. Whipping around, he saw Taylor standing before him. The bedroom door slipped shut on its own accord to leave them uninterrupted in their soundproof confinement.

"Where is she?" he asked coldly.

He scrutinized Collin with rueful distaste strong enough to evoke fear. Collin intended on feigning ignorance, but found his lips form words he hadn't planned on saying. He shut his mouth quickly, but it failed to go unnoticed.

"You can't lie. I spiked your coffee."

A chair zoomed across the floor and knock Collin out at the knees. His arms were lifted to the chair's and became bound with enchantments.

"What?!" Collin bellowed with disbelieving indignation for such unexpectedly unctuous behavior.

Taylor brushed off the agitation with a derisive grimace. The kindling of skepticism Collin was familiar with since the night he overheard Taylor and Osmond appeared to combust into a conflagration of hatred.

"While most people think potions are outdated, I find them useful for more subtle tasks, such as interrogation. Everything had been going as good as could be until you came along. Oz and Ms. Glenda aren't too fond of my suspicions, and I was foolish enough to let my guard down, but I believe you've been an ill omen ever since that wendigo didn't kill you. Now, Veil is falling at an accelerated rate and Alice goes missing the same night we get robbed."

"Robbed?"

Overture

Speaking only earned him a sharp stab in each shoulder from invisible needles his miscreant teacher conjured. The sting dug deeper and deeper until he was satisfied with their settlement.

"You're not asking the questions. Where is Alice?" he asked.

The bitterness in his voice bordered on the overture of madness. Collin couldn't tell if he should be infuriated for being the lucky victor of this man's cynicism or immaturely jealous of the level of concern he showed for Alice. Taylor's pious dedication toward their family was appreciable, but it was a dismal discovery to still not fall under that category.

The pins and needles dug deeper and spread like cancer with each moment's hesitation. The magic burned a trail all along his arms, into his gut, and down his legs. It felt like deep scratches across his back, but those situated more as discomfort than tortuous pain. If Taylor wanted an honest answer, he would get one. Collin was determined to piss him off in the process.

"I don't know," he said through gritted teeth.

It clearly wasn't the answer he'd expected, but he didn't allow his displeasure to resume torturing on false pretense.

"Did you have anything to do with her disappearance?"

Goddamn idiot!

"No," he answered.

"Then what is she doing?"

His question summoned an innocuous force to Collin's throat. He had the answer, but he didn't want to share it. He delayed as long as possible, his frantic eyes a dead giveaway. The sharp prickle rose to the level of razors grazing the top layer of flesh and digging deeper. Biting his tongue was futile. After a second, a scream exhumed its way to his lips, words formed involuntarily, offered with grim resignation.

"She's hunting the timora," he rasped.

It didn't stop there. The instant the truth perfused from his mouth, there was nothing to intercede excessive knowledge from trickling out.

"She's been studying it for months, hoping it'd keep a low enough profile until she could hunt it for her project."

All pains diminished. The magicked bindings around his wrists loosened. The embodiment of wrath faded to an eerie placid nature.

"Why didn't you tell anyone?" Taylor asked somberly, his crestfallen eyes now annoyingly pitiful.

In his own split second of fury, he dispensed a bolt of magic across the room at Collin's dresser. It exploded into innumerable splinters and tufts of fabric. A haze of sawdust swirled into the air they breathed before it tickled their nostrils on its way back out. It was an act even he must've deemed uncalled for as he snapped his fingers to repair everything back to their original form.

What the hell *was that?* he reflected on both, Taylor's rapid change of mood and his second exposure to magic performed without a series of hand movements.

"You should've told someone."

"I wanted to."

"But?"

"But she forbade me from doing so, and I like her."

That last part was another side effect of not being able to stop the truth, and it made his ears and cheeks turn hopefully not too red, but he supposed he could've unwillingly forfeited more secrets. Hearing those words made Taylor look scornfully at him like a scolding parent lecturing their child on how they should've known better.

"The Jacksonville heads of houses were already creating a group to take care of it!" Taylor exclaimed, showing effort to keep his temper under control. "We have people…" He paused to compose himself more professionally. "We have people coming from out of town to help take care of it. These things aren't meant to be taken on alone. They're insanely smart, extremely difficult to locate, and even harder to kill, even for Alice. Goddamn it! She doesn't even have her advanced spells under wrap!"

The dresser was blasted and repaired again. It was unknown as to whether or not Collin should be scared or guilty, or both. Taylor's alterations in attitude were abruptly discordant.

"We don't have much time," Taylor muttered more to himself. "Everyone is going to be looking for her."

"She won't be happy if we do," Collin added lightly, which warranted a snappy retort.

"I don't give a rat's ass!" Taylor enunciated each word with bitter weight. "The five of us are going to form our own search group."

It was an idea provoking no consideration. After all, Collin had been progressively feeling guiltier and guiltier for letting her carry out such a mission the way she did, not that he believed he could've stopped her even if he tried. Besides, Collin couldn't get in too much trouble for spilling the beans, right? Even Glenda and Osmond had no idea. At least she got three full days for a head start.

If she even gets to finish it.

A worse thought entered his head that needed squishing immediately.

If she's even still alive.

"We have *zero* time to waste," Taylor commanded. "Get ready. I'll inform the others and convince Oz and Ms. Glenda we'll be better off covering more ground separately."

Collin signaled that he understood, but was almost lashed at for not moving fast enough. He bustled at a pace spurred by the motivation of adrenaline. Taylor stopped at the door to survey him pensively. He could be seen from the corner of Collin's eyes, but he didn't dare pause to ask what it might've been about. The door shut.

His teeth could stand to miss a brush session and his hair recently became short enough to skip a molding. He merely slipped on his clothes and ran for it. He could hear their guardians considering Taylor's suggestion as he turned the corner down the main hall. There wasn't a chance to make it to the dining room, however. A hand gripped him around the cuff of his arm and yanked him into the study. Clark had a finger pressed to his lips as Collin glimpsed to see he was joined by Oscar and Olivia.

"Taylor said to wait here," Clark whispered. "Didn't tell us much else."

"Alice is hunting the timora," Collin informed, the relief melted away the fear he held for being responsible for her secret these last few months.

"How do *you* know?" Olivia contested accusatorily.

He gave them the summarized version of his times spent with Alice, neglecting to inform them about their most recent night. Truth serum or not, he could still fight the toppled floodgate of information to some extent. Taylor manifested toward the end of his tale to cut him off and tell them Oz and Ms. Glenda signed off on their quest with one stipulation: that they keep Collin safe at all cost. While the four of them may almost be fully graduated spellcasters, he still had a long way to go.

"Where should we start?" Oscar asked seriously.

"Losco Park?" Olivia suggested.

"Mandarin Park?" added Clark.

"She likes Riverside," Oscar said matter-of-factly.

Taylor's eyes were closed in concentration as he said "I've already recommended Riverside to Oz and Glenda. It's usually more crowded. I doubt she'll leave a trail there. Losco might be the best place. It draws in less people and has those secluded trails."

Collin listened intently on the way they conversed

over their knowledge of their missing friend. His missing girlfriend? What were they exactly?

Now's not the time, he scorned himself. *You were an emotionally comforting booty call.*

When nobody spoke, Taylor got to work. The ripples in the air waved the imminent tear in reality that would bridge their way out the house.

"Any wagers on the number of witnesses?" Clark added.

Oscar dug in the pockets of his jeans and pulled out a twenty. With currency's needlessness to Veil members, their money served more as betting trophies.

"I'll wager one morning jogger."

"Focus," Taylor reprimanded.

Olivia mouthed "A gentlemen's agreement" as Taylor dug his fingers into the tear to part their way open. Olivia insisted on going first to scope the area. Taylor scowled at their foolery, but took second nonetheless.

Single file, they strutted out into a patch of largely grown trees, branches jutting out low, wide, and sturdy enough to seat visitors. Before them was the main area of the park, with an empty soccer field constructed on the border of Losco Park. Near them stood a small, beat up brick men's, women's, and family bathroom. A children's playground lay engulfed by a sea of wood chips, a green, tin-roofed gazebo, and a pond filled with murky water composed most of the park. Behind them, leading into a forestry, were the trails Taylor mentioned.

Overture

"Nailed it," Oscar jived, pointing to a dumbstruck woman gawking at them frightfully in her jogging outfit.

"Hold on." Clark halted to examine the entire perimeter.

Taylor was already ambling over to the woman to erase what she'd seen. Everyone else was making sure they hadn't been caught by anyone else.

"Commissioner?" Oscar nudged.

"Oscar wins this round," Olivia stated, and Clark swore loudly as he pulled two ten dollar bills from his own pockets.

"Are you done dicking around?" asked Taylor, trudging back with his signature look of annoyance.

"Yes," Clark said gloomily.

"What now, oh Captain, my Captain?" asked Oscar.

Apparently even serious situations were sanctioned with impenetrable humor from the two. Collin didn't overly mind, but perhaps when Alice's safety required the conglomeration of Veil members other than themselves, then a time and place could be taken into consideration.

Taylor pointed toward the trails and they moved as one.

That first step into the light of the freshly risen sun both worried and exhilarated Collin. As a novice magician, this was his first true step toward potential danger, but also his first true step toward something larger than his self. He witnessed the synchrony the four operated on with each stride, with each swing of the arm, and each person gazing keenly in their own designated direction. Their fingers wiggled to remain warmed and ready for any spurred need. He longed to be how they were. A couple years would be required of him to be as they were now.

"This is almost three miles worth of searching. Are you sure she'd leave us a trail in there?" Olivia asked.

Without breaking vigilance, Taylor commented, "As reckless as she might've been leaving us, she's not a reckless person. She knows she bit off something more than she might be able to chew. If she's smart about this, she wouldn't leave us without a clue as to where she'd be or what might've happened to her. Whether it's in these bushes is beyond me."

Past the pond, where civilians were laying in the grass or sailing their electric toy boats, they reached a gate and a bulletin displaying a map of the red, white, and pale blue segments of the trail's extensions. Olivia was right about the total distance tallying to nearly three miles.

Would Alice have left them a blatant sign to follow, or will we have to scrutinize every inch?

Collin worried it might take them all day to search. They could easily spend all this time and come out with nothing to show. He wanted to express this concern, but figured he'd leave it to them. If they knew her enough to know this was one of her favorite spots, they must know her enough to know what to look for.

As their trek began, Collin couldn't help but let his imagination escape him as he envisioned this being the border of J.K. Rowling's Forbidden Forest, but disappointingly less magical. He'd been here before with groups of schoolmates and there was never anything particularly entertaining, unless you counted the occasional whiff of marijuana or condom wrapper. That was about as spellbinding as it got. He did, however, have a new set of eyes. Maybe there was a lot he missed.

At the earliest divergence in the trail, they agreed to divide. Clark, Oscar, and Olivia would go left and take the longest path. Having more people would compensate for having more ground to cover. Much to Collin's dismay, that left him and Taylor to scour the path to the right. Before they parted, Olivia conjured a spell for herself and Taylor that left a matching scar in their forearms.

"Whoever finds anything can touch it with any simple magic and the other person will feel it," she explained to Collin. "Easily reversible too."

He was amused by the brilliant simplicity of it, but didn't deem it pertinent to dawdle on the concept's parallelism to a certain fantasy world. Taylor beckoned him along, but not as crudely as he usually would've in his attempts to save time and stay focused.

Won't fix what you did to me.

When they were out of earshot of the other group, he said something that caught Collin off guard.

"I'm sorry about earlier," Taylor said with firm, reluctant leniency. "I don't expect you to be forgiving about it, nor would I expect anyone else to be if they were to find out, but these people took me in when I was ready to end my own life. I would do anything to protect them, and I—"

"Don't trust me. You made that clear."

It was clear where his bitterness was coming from, but he wasn't sure where his bravado did. Did he feel safe knowing the others weren't too far, or had his rage with this guy, not much older than himself, hit a whole new height of honest carelessness. Either way, he didn't hold his tongue there.

"I also heard you and Oz in the study a few months back about not letting me join."

Taylor didn't pause. He didn't show any sign of hearing him, but after a moment he eventually spoke up.

"And I still want to know if you've had anything to do with the suspicious things that've been occurring since we found you."

The mistrust was a nuisance, but Collin ignored any resistance against the last few drops of the truth serum in his system. He was torn between continuing his efforts to get on Taylor's good side and telling him to kindly eat his ass. He chose not to saying anything.

Their venture carried out in silence for the next five minutes. A jogging couple passed by, but paid them no mind. Taylor even bewitched their shoes to restrict the sound of crunching gravel, right up until the quiet awkwardness spilled over. Despite every bruise and degrading comment, it was Collin who sought out some sort of affirmation in their manhunt.

"You know what we're looking for?" he asked.

At first, Taylor didn't respond. His attention buzzed in all directions, from the trail to the trees, to the tracks and the bushes. Not a rustle bypassed his notice. "Not particularly," he finally said. "*If* she left something behind for us to follow, it wouldn't be too obvious for anyone to find."

"It looks too plain to me, so I'm guessing she did a good job at hiding her tracks at least."

Taylor halted progression.

"Shit! You're looking through the wrong lenses. I forgot." He sounded slightly agitated with the ensuing small talk. "Copy me."

He showed each step of a spell slow enough for Collin to implement on his own. He made a mental note to devise an extensive hand-stretching regiment if they ever returned from tracking Alice and her shapeshifter. By the end of it, he had each thumb and index finger forming a box in front of his face like he was taking a mental picture, but what he saw through the invisible lens was spectacular.

Magic was everywhere. Its pervasive presence in the everyday world was shockingly astounding. Specks of luminescent green and blue floated in the air like dust particles while white veins traced the botanical abundance. The same bright pathways traced Taylor's and his own cardiovascular system with flecks of gold spread throughout. The mundane material was a background gray, making any traces of magical influence impossible to overlook. This was life on acid, and it was mesmerizing.

Snapchat filters, eat your heart out, he thought to himself.

"How have I never learned of this filter?"

"This is as close as we'll ever get to getting a glimpse of magic's entirety, but this is how a lot of theorizers developed their hypotheses on magic's origins in biology or in an entire magic realm on its own. It's also what adds to the difficulty of fighting some monsters, because they naturally see magic and can see the fingerprint of each spell getting ready to be cast."

"It's amazing," Collin gawked, mouth partially opened, temporarily forgetting his conflict with Taylor. "But how are you seeing everything without your hands up?"

"Contacts."

"Did you make them?"

"Yes."

Collin took the hint from Taylor's concise demeanor and bit his tongue. He wanted to know if it were possible to make this sight permanent. He turned around to examine what they'd already left behind, hoping he left nothing overlooked. Not that he fully understood the interpretation of the different shapes and colors he was seeing, but it felt best not to press the issue with Alice's whereabouts still undetermined.

"Shh!" Taylor held up a hand after another lengthy walk in silence.

He took a couple precautionary sidesteps before Collin noticed a short figure to the left of them ahead in the distance, concealed by brush. It would've been difficult to miss if Collin hadn't been searching in the other direction. Whatever it was blinded him like a bomb of yellow inferno. He lowered his hands to find what they were looking at was camouflaged well.

"Could just be a bramble fairy of no importance," Taylor whispered.

I think you'll find I'm of great importance, a feminine voice echoed in Collin's head.

He locked worrisome eyes with Taylor, who gave a stare that reassured him this was a normal occurrence with fairies. They stepped with careful unison. Collin raised his hands again in time to watch the creature move, possibly swim, through the wooden terrain toward them. A tail dragged behind.

"Definitely a bramble fairy."

"Is there any need for concern?" Collin whispered in hopes of not being overheard.

Taylor shook his head, saying nothing.

You have nothing to fear, human, the voice spoke telepathically once again.

Yet, despite the lack of concern in the atmosphere, he was understandably uneased. The creature inched to the edge of their path, but Collin still couldn't detect anything with regular eyes. It was deduced she wasn't simply camouflaged, but entirely invisible to the naked eye. The image of her was like staring at body heat with infrared, but was almost blinding. The magic radiating off her was immense.

First poking her head out, and then her torso, the fairy was watchful of onlookers. Not that she needed to be. There was no way of seeing the creature normally.

"Put your hands down," the female voice spoke aloud this time, and there she was, visible to Collin as Taylor was.

She wasn't entirely what he'd expected but, he also wasn't sure what to expect with his education lacking in supernatural beings. While roughly three feet tall, the fairy was a fully-grown woman in breasts and hips. Her posture was slightly arched under the weight of the vegetation sprouting around her body. She could've been mistaken for terrifying if Taylor hadn't alerted him sooner that everything was fine.

Vines and leaves covered her head like a helmet, twigs popping out as horns above the ears. Viny tendrils strived to cover the mythical beast's face from all directions to no avail. She had powerfully vibrant, baby blue eyes and an instinctively pouty face. Vegetation also sought to cover the entirety of her back. All throughout, bunches of two or three red berries clumped asymmetrically in different regions of her verdant raiment.

Short twigs stood from the messy spikes trailing her spine, protruding all the way to the thistle-like spear that made the fairy's tail an appendage to be feared for enemies and prey alike. Observing her front, the same vines hung from the back and wrapped around symbiotically.

There were straps fully ensnared around the neck and parts of her thighs, but most else remained revealed. Some did happen to cover her nipples, but even the soft pink of their color slipped through obtusely. Parts of her exposed skin were branded dark brown with tribal-like markings Collin didn't understand, and her forearms-to-hands and calves-to-feet appeared stuck in the process of transitioning between skin and wood, almost like gauntlets and boots.

"Sorry," said Collin, the second his hands clapped his sides.

The fairy's gaze altered from Collin to Taylor. Her eyes wandered from top to bottom, analyzing meticulously. A long and low *hmm* reverberated from her throat before she spoke.

"She overestimated you by a day, unfortunately."

"Alice?" Collin leapt enthusiastically without a second's notice.

The fairy confirmed this, but with the similar mannerisms of Taylor when he wants people to know they're being annoying. Collin almost dove straight into requesting details, but enough time around his combat mentor taught him to straighten up and be quiet with the sort of look this intelligible creature was giving.

"My name is Shaylee. Young Alice has been in these woods time and time again as refuge from the boisterous world, as you clearly already know, or else you wouldn't be here," Shaylee said, now with a smile and glossy reminiscence in her searing blue eyes. "She has shown our forest nothing but kindness with nothing asked in return, save one request."

Taylor nodded in understanding.

"May we ask where she is?" his voice mellowed with a smear of submissiveness.

Her dreamy expression faltered slightly when her attention swayed to the speaker.

Shaylee spent half a minute considering. "You may. That is what she wanted, but you'll need to act fast. I imagine the poor girl will discover the beast by twilight."

16

Alice, Where Art Thou?

Clark, Oscar, and Olivia cut through the brush and came sprinting alarmingly fast as soon as Taylor summoned the most basic finger-tingling spell and pressed that same appendage to the magicked scar he and Olivia shared. It required a short-lived game of Marco Polo in which Taylor barked at the trio to follow his fucking voice and stop horsing around.

Shaylee had been alerted beforehand of their arrival. Fairies were apparently skittish at initial exposure, but expected unwavering respect afterwards. Luckily, Alice already warned her days ago how five people may pay the Losco Trails a visit if she didn't return home soon.

"She said she was aware a timora plagued this city," said Shaylee. "She said she wanted to purge it, but its movements were too unpredictable. So, we assisted. Timoras are insatiable beasts that feed on the mundane and the gifted alike."

Collin assumed the context of mundane to mean them,

Overture

the humans, and gifted to either be exclusive to fairies or generalized to all magical creatures.

"If Veil has a hard enough time tracking something like a timora, do you mind me asking how fairies would go about it?" asked Olivia, her sass transformed into a similar submission as Taylor's had so as not to offend Shaylee.

It proved efficient enough.

"We have a network, young human. Even those of impure intent wish to see the monster felled. Timoras are archaic. They are the common ancestors of shapeshifters and pure embodiments of dark magic. They are the result of those who were once accepted by Magik's gifts, yet did not possess hearts pure enough to harness it. They protrude a powerful aura, but only when it's too late. The fact one even exists, after so long a peaceful era in their absence, is most peculiar these days.

"Most creatures with half a brain will remain in packs for safety or will have already vacated this region, but it does not mean we do not hear word. It lurks mostly in sewers, where it remains hidden and stays in control of easy access to and fro its prey above ground. It's convenient."

Mighty convenient, Collin's thoughts paralleling their predicament back to King's *IT*.

"They're unnatural and a source of something unbalancing, but it is a pawn, "said Shaylee."

To hell with the riddles, Collin said to himself.

"A pawn to what?" he asked plainly, but not politely.

Silence ensued as all eyes turned to him. He'd clearly

overstepped his boundaries, and there would be reckoning for his insolence.

"Please, don't mind him," Clark swooped in in a hair's breadth of the tick of the clock. "He's been newly inducted and is unfamiliar with common courtesies."

Collin bit his tongue for his mistake and peered with sudden nervousness. Was that a shallowly tilted bow the gang offered Shaylee? Unsure, he bent slightly forward and declared his apologies. For Clark and Oscar to take this matter without a crack of humor spoke volumes to the instant regret swelling inside Collin.

The fairy's lips grew thin and her eyes narrowed as she huffed impatiently. A debate raged in her head, apparent by the hardly noticeable shrug of her shoulders and the darting of her line of vision from person to person, always glaring at Collin. He made motion to apologize again, but was cut off by Shaylee's huff of air.

"You're all pawns of a bigger game." The fairy was acridly uninformative. "But it's your move on the board now."

She pulled out a piece of rolled parchment from behind her. The paper was handed sharply to Taylor, who took it in both hands with unyielding eye contact.

"If you want to find her, this is how."

The others bowed again and pledged their gratitude, and Collin made sure to do the same. Shaylee vanished from plain sight to retreat deep into the bush.

"Not that it's entirely your fault, but remind us to brush

you up on the different etiquettes of magical creatures," Oscar said, his tone more impartial than scornful.

"Sorry," Collin mumbled with his eyes glued to the gravel and twigs at his feet.

"What the hell was she trying to say?" asked Olivia. "Pawns?"

"One problem at a time," said Taylor.

"Fine, then what does the paper say?"

Taylor loosened the strings holding the roll together and unraveled it at an angle for all to see. A circular sigil, unrecognizable to Collin, was etched elaborately, along with two words: *Five Points*.

"Shit," Taylor breathed.

"You think she might've gone to Riverside instead?" Olivia asked.

"No way," Clark chimed in. "If she'd done that, I'm sure we'd recognize her doodle. God knows we've hung out there enough times."

"And *does* anyone recognize her doodle?" Oscar asked.

No one did. Collin barely even knew about the Five Points area. It had Riverside Park and Memorial Park, with a handful of breweries somewhere around there, but his typical adventures with past high school friends consisted of gallivanting at the Avenues Mall, Town Center, or going back and forth between the Avenues Theater and Steak 'n Shake off Philips Highway.

"It's still a lead," said Taylor. "We have a general area. The only question is whether or not her trail is still good."

"Only one way to find out," and Clark went into focus mode to summon a tear.

"Where're we going?" asked Oscar.

"The Cummer Museum, if no one's opposed?"

They all shook their heads in unison. With no definitive place to start, anywhere would do, and this was apparently another are Alice frequented. They stood back and observed Clark's work as he constructed an opening for them to a nearly empty lot behind a bank surrounded by trees.

Once regrouped, they stepped out onto the sidewalk nonchalantly and surveyed the area in the event of witnesses. There weren't any. They ambled over to the end of Riverside Park Place and crossed Riverside Avenue to the side of the street the museum was constructed, right along St. Johns River. No more roads stood between them and their destination except a couple businesses and another parking lot.

A few people were seen commencing their daily routine. It must've been inching close to ten or eleven o'clock. Taylor was comparing the sigil on Alice's parchment with any etchings on or around any of the facilities. They passed the Cummer Café first before reaching the entrance that read *Cummer Museum of Art & Gardens.*

"We're gonna have to split up again," Taylor pointed out.

"Some in the building, others in the courtyard and gardens?" Clark asked.

"Yes."

"Same teams?"

Overture

A sign of confirmation. The three were instructed to scope out the gardens while Taylor and Collin questioned the employees and searched for any marks matching Alice's.

"So, this is definitely another one of her common places?" Collin asked through magicked vision.

"It is," Taylor concisely replied, and it embarrassed Collin how little he knew of this girl.

He didn't see each and every one of the members of Mandarin Mansion in overly abundance, but for some reason it was difficult seeing them having personal days outside of work and studies. Maybe it was because he was so secluded in his own studies, or maybe it was because, not only were they his friends, but they were also his teachers, and nobody considered their teachers as having lives outside school.

If he ever wanted to explore a commitment with Alice, he recognized the desperate need to establish an in-depth and personal understanding of her. Finding her seemed like a great place to start this commitment.

The venture was unsuccessful for both parties. Nowhere inside nor out of the infrastructure showed any markings remotely similar to the symbol Alice left for them. Nothing on the paintings, sculptures, tablets, or pottery either.

They took their manhunt to the streets to burn the hours. They sucked it up and searched Memorial Park first, after grabbing a quick lunch at Einstein Bros. Bagels across the street. The park also resided on the north bank of the St. Johns River not far from the Cummer Museum, designed by the Olmsted Brothers shortly after World War One.

Several laps were conducted around the field as well as within it. Outside the circle, closer to the edge of the water, they inspected Charles Pillars's bronze sculpture *Life*. This sculpture depicted a bronze sphere composed of nude men and women, with a male angel standing atop, holding up a branch of some sort. The statue lay center of a penny fountain full of coins. They found nothing on it. There weren't any signs embedded on the two bronze eagle statues surrounding the piece of art either. Magical visors and all, there wasn't a trace of Alice to be found. Meanwhile, the clock ticked away their countdown to dusk.

They trekked stealthily through Riverside Park, hoping Ms. Glenda and her husband concluded their own investigation. Nothing. They checked the St. Vincent's Hospital, breweries, even though Alice was underage, book stores, even a comic shop on the outskirts of the area.

The air of the group grew grim. They'd hit a point in their efforts where nobody even spoke, partly in compiled agitation and partly so as not to let any of their words be the last straw on anyone else's nerves. As they headed back north and crossed over Post Street, Olivia made the suggestion to check out Bold Bean a block away.

"Of course," Clark said glumly, "So help me fucking god, if she left her mark at a coffee shop, I'll brand her as a goddamn basic white girl for life."

It was uncharacteristically crass of him to say, but it would later serve as a frequented joke.

Overture

"There's nothing wrong with enjoying a cup of cappuccino art," Olivia snapped.

"There's everything wrong with it. Just drink your damn drink. It's not for staring at."

They arrived shortly at their destination, wedged between a yoga studio and a tattoo shop. With summer over and school back in session, they were all secretly grateful the streets were minimally populated, although they doubted they looked any less befit traveling as a pack.

The biggest godsend to their task was that autumn was already upon them. In Florida, it didn't make too much a difference; the temperature still lingered at sweating peeks, but the choking humidity mercifully thinned out so the heat wasn't as sweltering as the summer months. They could still get away with shorts and a t-shirt, as most of them did. Collin and Taylor, however, were clad in pants.

"I could go for a coffee, if anyone's down," Oscar said with a look of bitter defeat scrawled on his face.

"Maybe an iced one," responded Olivia.

"Make it to-go," Taylor commanded.

The passing of time wore their leader thin, becoming increasingly apparent with each minute. There was no telling what he was thinking outside of his urgency to find Alice. It wasn't even a concern expressed openly, yet Collin could read it. The devil on his shoulder reignited, telling him it was possible Taylor possessed an affectionate investment with Alice.

"Obviously," Oscar retorted in a manner that said he wasn't

stupid enough to prolong their coffee break longer than necessary. "Collin, you want anything?"

"Just a regular coffee. Little cream, one sugar."

"Any preference of sugar?"

Taylor shot Oscar a livid glare.

"Surprise me," and Oscar and Olivia retreated indoors once Clark added his request.

The three of them loitered under the handicap parking sign before standing still made Collin too antsy. He diverged a few yards to the corner of the block and moved his fingers in the intricate motions necessary to establish a glimpse into the magical nervous system.

Nothing seemed any less out of the ordinary than before. Same neon specks floated through the air to be inhaled by passersby and in the veins. Concept of such commonality perplexed Collin with the knowledge not everyone would tap into such an invasive force of nature. However, his attention was caught by something rather peculiar.

At the crossroads of Stockton Street and Myra Street were two manhole covers. On one was engraved JEA, while the other bore no irregularity when looked at through normal vision. Through the square formed by his thumbs and index fingers, however, shone the same emblem sketched onto the paper Alice left Shaylee in charge of.

He reversed and flagged Clark and Taylor down, aiming not be too attention-seeking. When they were near, he instructed them to use the special lenses and directed them to the manhole cover closest to them. Taylor was already examining it with his enchanted contacts. Clark withdrew a chipped fragment of glass to gaze through.

"Shit," Taylor sighed.

"You think we have to go down there, or could it just be a coincidence she marked a manhole in this area?" Clark asked.

"No." There was zero hesitation. "You heard Shaylee about sewers being the perfect place for timoras."

"Well, fuck."

"How do we get down without being noticed?" Collin asked.

The other two considered his question, giving glances around the environment for any nearby alternative routes. Collin did the same, but no other entries to the sewer appeared within the proximity of sight.

"Alice could've marked any other cover, but she chose that one specifically. We'll need to work up some illusionment charms," Taylor said, the ghost of aggravation evaporating, leaving behind the true spark of leadership in its place.

It was a good look for him, and for one brief moment Collin understood what everyone else meant when they said Taylor was a good man at the core.

"Easy," Clark replied, flagging Oscar and Olivia as they exited with a cardboard tray of coffee cups. "Oscar and I can do that in no time."

As the others arrived, they read the vibes of the group and grew cautious. When Taylor pointed out their discovery, even giving full credit to Collin, Olivia looked as if she might be on the brink of tears.

"You expect us to trace through waist-high shit wearing shorts?" her voice heightened with displeasure.

"No," Taylor growled. "Chug your coffee, get under cover, get back home, and gear up. Now!"

"You can't chug freshly brewed coffee," Oscar lightly joked. "S'too hot."

The glint of leadership faded behind a resurfaced look of raw annoyance. Without making any performances, he placed a finger on Oscar's cup of coffee and chilled the entire beverage.

"Right then," Oscar half-grinned.

Nothing more needed saying. The drinks were passed around, and Collin managed to cool his own drink, albeit not as effortlessly as Taylor could. Afterwards, they powered forward behind the shops with hastened strides. Zero time was perverted in their transition from Bold Bean to Mandarin Mansion. The process was so swift that barely half of Collin's drink was consumed before he returned to the familiar sight and scent of walls and walls of books. An unusual calm swept over him in spite of the calamity.

"Five minutes," Taylor barked. "Collin, stay here."

"What?"

"You're still new. Plus, you swore an oath to not take part in any missions until you were properly educated. It would be on all of us to let you tag along and allow something to happen."

Clark, Oscar, and Olivia were already passing through the doorway, but turned to watch this exchange. Collin stole glances from Taylor to them. The sympathy in their eyes told him the trio wouldn't be providing any support in this matter. He was defeated before he could even get a second word out.

Taylor bustled past him, and Collin could hear them faintly debating sending word to Glenda, Oz, and the other safe houses. A single "no" was the last he heard before everyone stepped out of earshot and left him standing there wondering how his helpfulness turned to uselessness so quickly. If it hadn't been for him, they wouldn't have even known the extent of the urgency in finding Alice. Although, if he hadn't said anything, the lack of urgency could've led to her death, so he chalked it up to being more detrimentally his fault, but he did find her sigil on the sewer entrance.

They probably would've found it without you before long, he argued with himself.

Regardless, if they weren't going to get the adults involved, ignoring the fact they were all technically adults, they'd need all hands on deck, right?

They're practically master magicians already.

Oh, fuck you.

No, this was not how it was going to end. Inexperienced or not, Alice was his…what? Friend? Girlfriend? Minor love interest? It didn't matter. He joined Veil to be a hero and he wasn't going to let his rookie status impede his stoking flair to be where others are in need. It might take him longer than five minutes, but goddamn it he was going whether they approved or not!

He dashed over to William Wrights' five volume set of

Elementary Spells, Intermediate Spells, and *Advanced Spells.* There was no way constructing tears would be an amateur spell, but that didn't make it any easier to narrow it in the other four books. Slinging the second volume off the shelf, he flipped through the table of contents, hoping for some guidance.

He barely made it three-quarters of the way through before he heard a rushed pair of footsteps echoing in the hallway. It was an effort to shove the book back in place before Clark and Oscar turned the corner, but there wasn't any time to establish a nonchalant composure.

They were adorned in darker, more sleek garments, with long sleeves and pants fitted snugly enough to not permit any flappy fabric impeding even the slightest movement. Collin additionally knew the material of their battle raiment was bewitched to be significantly less penetrable from bites, scratches, charms, jinxes, curses, and most other arrays of magic. The pair eyed him and eyed the section he stood in before eyeing each other with shared smirks.

"Volume Three, page two hundred twenty-seven," they said in unison.

"Wait 'til we're gone," said Clark.

"And maybe stand away from the books," added Oscar.

Collin obeyed hastily and tried to return to his original spot before the remaining returned, which they did right away. Their clothes all matched in a cult-ish fashion, and in Taylor's left hand was a duffle bag. He tossed it on the ground and ferociously ripped it open. Collin attempted to step forward to get a better look, but Taylor was on high alert for him with a furtive stare at the slightest motion. That was all Collin needed to take a defeated step back and observe.

Weapon after weapon was brandished, from wooden stakes dipped in blood, silver daggers, a handful of unknown vials, what looked to be actual wands, and…

Holy hell, a colt revolver?

One-by-one, everyone picked something and dematerialized it, fashioning its inexistence around a waist or an arm or a leg. The colt stayed with Taylor.

They utilized a well-established system for storing and summoning with magic. One couldn't simply create physical objects out of thin air. In order to call upon an object, one had to be familiar with its composition or location in order to relocate items. Even when doing something as easy as producing a flame at the fingertip, oxygen in the atmosphere needed to be pulled and forcefully ignited. There was a lot they could do with magic to break many laws of physics, but even the law of conservation of mass was off limits to them. They were spellcasters, not gods.

So, as they vanished their weapons, Collin knew they were preparing themselves with instruments of death for a moment of need. Once finished, Taylor went to work creating a tear to return them to Bold Bean. The eagerness to go must've shown on Collin's face, because he was spooked by a chair taking him out by his knees and binding him for the second time that day.

"I'm sorry," Taylor said with the slightest tone of genuine sympathy.

Struggling did nothing, and he was unfamiliar with any spell strong enough to break the bond. Nobody said a word, only slipped through to the other side of the portal. Collin was freed only after the cracks resealed. A twinge of anger surfed his veins, but he managed to swallow it, knowing what was done truly was done for his own safety.

But fuck that.

He dashed back to the textbooks and flung Volume Three off the shelf, flipping to page two hundred twenty-seven. A grin spread with divine gratefulness for Clark's and Oscar's penchant for mischief. Before him was the same spell they used to exit.

He skimmed and skimmed for particular circumstances involving the specific hourly, daily, weekly, monthly, yearly cycles, gender, weather, and other requirements. Once satisfied, he laid the book flat on one of the desks. He stepped back, loosening his fingers with a couple shakes of the hands. The biggest requirement was to have a steely focus on where he was going, but it wasn't enough. Try as hard as he might, it took Collin a stressful twenty minutes to get the hand gestures accurate enough to obtain the results he hoped for.

The abnormalities of the spellwork were prominent compared to what he was accustomed to. The amount of energy needed alone saw to that, but when the tear was conjured successfully it evoked a suctioning effect on Collin. For a split second, after his fingers were dug into the sliver of altered reality, it became a battle of will to open and stabilize the window to another area. Otherwise, it might've taken him to god knows where.

Everyone else made it look so much easier. Skepticism paired with his adrenaline. He wanted to be sure his product was safe. Sure enough, reviewing *Intermediate Spells,* the warning label was placed after the instructions to not perform the spell without the supervision of a trained spellcaster as a precaution against indefinite death. Otherwise, everything seemed right.

One big drawback on his plan steadied on him possessing neither the weapons nor the education to prove a challenge for whatever lay before him. More likely than not he'd serve more as a liability than an aid to his friends. He knew this, but still didn't care. In the event these were their final moments, at least he'd see her face before Death knocked on his door with a sardonic fist and that Cheshire grin.

He stuck one leg through before dipping his whole body in. He found himself safely concealed beneath the shade of a tree in a back parking lot, no civilians. Jogging to the street corner, he found the designated manhole and checked it with the enchanted lens to ensure he was in the same place. He was.

The biggest issue would be lifting it to crawl in without drawing attention, but he didn't have time to orchestrate a proper plan. If he was an amateur, then an amateur plan would have to do. All he would have to do is cast a little levitation charm and move with the trickster movement to appear to be lifting the manhole cover. Best case scenario, any witnesses would believe him to be some delinquent teen. He would slip through, cover it back up, and the citizens of Jacksonville would curse openly about the decline of behavior from the younger generations.

So, that's what he did. Once the area seemed clear to move, and no one was there to shout at him, he lifted the lid. He noticed there weren't any stairs leading downward into the abyss, but he could shimmy his way down with his back pressed against one side of the tube and his legs on the other.

The daunting part was the descent into darkness. Blackness enshrouded the sewers without a hint of a bottom. The scent of shit and rot singed away his nose hairs. The manhole cover shut with little resistance and he was truly engulfed. A single second after, his balance wasn't lost, it was stolen, and Collin Quinn plunged into nothingness.

17

A Taste

Bursts of pain shocked Collin from his tailbone to the base of his neck as he collided on stone ground with a shallow splash. Stars circled around his vision. First attempts of establishing balance failed with further soaking of his regular, non-spell-woven cotton, but equilibrium eventually returned to the semicircular canals of his inner ear after a slow rising.

While he wasn't waterproof, he decided to experiment with the ability to warm himself dry. He managed to get warm, but not dry. Squinting through the barren nothingness of his shadowy surroundings, he was in trouble, but he still had time to find the others. He'd have to be quick without lingering too closely. If Taylor found out he trailed behind them too early he'd force him back. Wiggling his fingers choreographically, Collin proceeded to implement the spell necessary to further warm his hands in order to keep them nimble. Before completion, he fused it with the theoretical gestures from his courses in status magic with the almost-twins to hasten the process.

Spellwork wasn't as complicatedly unique as one might

think. It was painful, but it all relied on memorization, handcraft, and understanding the reason for each movement. Alice had been correct on how it would eventually feel like second nature. He wasn't quite *that* accomplished, but at least he was protected by the limited experience he had. Specific motions were needed for specific attributes. A particular twist of the hands here for heat, or opposite for cold. Sometimes one would steal the portion of another spell meant to shroud one in a widely protective shell from assaults and copy and paste the expansion portion into a ball of light to enlighten an entire area. It took a lot of studying over the last few months to recognize the similarities and differences of spells following particular patterns, and, ever since his inauguration and contact with the divine stone, he'd discovered his aptitude for magic was escalating.

His clothes eventually did dry, all except his footwear. Waterproofing still being above his pay grade, he abandoned the notion entirely and examined the silence around him.

No trickling of feet dragged through the water. No voices, no general signs of anyone hinted for him to follow or run from. Furthermore, there was nothing to discern any direction to start in. All angles were possible, and this invoked an overwhelming sense of regret in his decision to go solo. Here, not even magic could provide him with directions, nor could a glimpse through the other-worldly specs help. The whole expanse of darkness bombarded his sight like a flash bomb to the point of needing three solid minutes to readjust his eyes.

Why take time to agonize then?

Collin strode forward one fateful step at a time. His pace hastened more out of quickening palpitations than assured decisiveness. Left. Right. Left. Right. Left, right. Left, right.

Nothing changed. Producing light was a likely mistake. The likelihood of it giving away his location to friend or foe was too great a compromise, despite his waded steps. He swallowed deeply and pushed forward blindly.

He couldn't recall being this scared since his confrontation with the wendigo. His heart lodged in his throat as he labored for thinned intakes of breath. Cold sweats welled and trickled down his back while his warmed palms grew slick. He was lost in a world he was ill-equipped for, undoubtedly already engulfed by the monster's den.

The possibility of that being true made him adamant at keeping his head straight and his mind attentive. He mentally recited a checklist of spells and even used a handful as he trudged his soaked feet aimlessly. He quickened his natural speed, heightened his senses, occasionally conjured temporary barriers since he wasn't seasoned enough to create sustainable ones. Everything an amateur could do, he did. Was it enough? Absolutely not! And certainly not enough to take on something as detrimental as a timora. He doubted any of them were. The longer he wandered aimlessly through the darkness, Collin's doubt even trespassed on Alice's capabilities. She said it herself how literature was ridiculously limited on the demon, so what chance did the others have if she spent months studying it and they only pursued off rumors.

A distant *splash*. A diminished echo. Collin almost ran toward the sound on an instinct bred from anticipation, but planted his feet in methodical fear. He was Collin fucking Quinn. Terrified as he was, he wasn't about to let his mental faculties be overwritten by the early stages of trepidation. He bent low and dragged his feet silently through the water. Had the echo been any louder it may have given the illusion of protruding from all directions. However, it had been distinct enough to pinpoint ahead of him.

Convenient, he pondered skeptically, but as he approached, he caught a glimpse of a dark silhouette.

Nothing big. The vague adjustment of his night eyes made it look human-esque. It cost him pace, but Collin enchanted each step to be as quiet as the breezeless wind, so the only audible noises were the rippling water from foreign splashes and the heavy *thud thud* of blood pumping persistently in his ears.

Even when the object before him lay a couple feet away, he still kept a comfortable space to react as necessary. When nothing happened minutes later, he made the choice to respond.

Light. Faint light. He made just enough to illuminate the tip of his pinky, like a skyward ember destined to exhale its final breath on the canvas of a starry night.

Collin flickered his hand outward and made out a leg.

Overture

He inched forward. A waist. His warmth evaporated with consecutive chills rolling through every appendage. The torso. Whatever or whoever this was lay face-down based on the ridges of the back muscles. An arm and shoulder. Chills morphed in shakes as he discovered the coward behind his bravado. A neck. Clark.

His face was sculpted for eternity to relive the shock he'd endured before his head twisted one hundred eighty degrees before the ultimate *crick* of his snapped spinal cord. The urge to vomit was unbearable as a hand shot to his mouth to stifle an inescapable gasp. Collin's balance faltered and he tripped into the oddly viscous, murky flood.

The splash he made rendered hiding futile. He shot out an illuminating orb and rushed to Clark's side with a gape of horror and misunderstanding. They couldn't have been apart more than thirty minutes! A more ominous collision with water forced him to act quickly. He stood vigilant, but his vision was becoming obscured. The orb he'd summoned was already fading.

A bundle of huffed curses sailed their way through the narrowing trail of his esophagus. No more sounds were heard in the distance. He sent two more semi-sustainable beacons of light higher in the air and found a trail of bodies coaxing him into the unknown. Too frozen, the reality of his situation offered the temptation to turn tail and run, but what was the point of being a member of Veil and willingly facing evil if cowardice was too easy an option.

But was it better than certain death? If four advanced spellcasters couldn't stop whatever killed Clark, what chance do I have?

Yet he stayed. If this was as far as they got, he was undoubtedly close to falling victim as well. One step. Another. It was harder than when he started. The spell gifting him speed either wasn't working or it was the only thing giving him the ability to move. The spell heightening his senses backfired to heightening his fears. Nerves were shot so sensitively, his own imagination of the infinite darkness and all its offspring sent more recurring shivers throughout the entire surface of his skin, so violently they could drive a man insane from prolonged vibration.

This was happening too fast to comprehend. Not long ago, Collin was outside, basking in the setting sun. Now, minutes lingered like hours as he crept up to the second figure, this time face-down and drowned. It was Oscar no doubt. The build was too similar to Clark's. He maintained distance.

He grew confused as to how his life ended up here. He sees a mangled cat and a woman get killed by a wendigo and thinks…

No big deal. TV's desensitized me enough. If that's as horrific as Oz and Ms. Glenda make it out to be, it should be manageable.

Now, he couldn't stop himself from whispering "This is real. This is real. Oh, fuck, God, this is real," as a means to choke back his nausea. Nothing and no one could've truly prepared him.

The third person discovered was Olivia. Patches of her hair were ripped out by the roots and floating around. A deep gash ran diagonally from her right jawline to her stomach, bathing her in her own blood.

The dimming lights were restored as a fourth body struggled to move. Collin lost all sense of self-preservation when he lifted his feet and broke water with each step to get to his only remaining companion. Taylor managed to lift himself to his hands and knees, but slipped and expelled his fading supply of air in the form of thickly bubbles popping the surface of their surroundings.

Collin rolled him over and flinched at the ghastly white hue of his previously tanned skin. Circular teeth marks traced the side of his neck with puncture wounds resembling wide-gauged needles. On his lower arm, stringy sinew and muscle fibers forfeited his life's blood to the chunk of gnawed off flesh. Claw marks pierced his black clothing in five straight lines, not jaggedly as the single cut on Olivia.

"Dead. Why…would you?" Taylor sputtered weakly. "I knew…should've said…"

He coughed and trickles of blood streamed from his mouth.

"Deceive…us."

Taylor went limp. Collin fiercely shook his hands a few times and tried a couple minor healing charms, but the wounds refused to patch themselves. There simply wasn't enough life to restore.

All around, more bodies were strewn in the darkness. New lights revealed the faces of Osmond Pyhrral, Glenda Goodall, Paul Ganley, other members he'd come in brief contact with from the other Jacksonville safe houses. He even caught a glimpse of his ex-girlfriend Shannon and his bloated father. A heap of undifferentiated corpses became visible all around them.

In his attempt to make out the people, the orbs burnt out. With practiced hands, he set two new lamps overhead, but the instant he invoked light someone stood a few short inches from his face, shrieking. Hands dug into each of Collin's shoulders and shoved him onto his back. Demented laughter emanated.

"Look at what you've done," Collin's attacker spoke familiarly, a guy's voice. "You fucked up. Yes, you did."

He released a hand from one of Collin's shoulders and withdrew a blade from a sheath on his waist. The metal glinted in the magical illumination, reflecting the still-moist ruby red of blood. The weapon was dropped with a sickening *thuk* as it was swallowed by something now undeniably thicker than water. The free hand resumed its grasp on Collin.

"Why'd you have to kill them?" the voice demanded maniacally through such a sinisterly bright grin.

Through the glum darkness, Collin could barely make out how he wasn't being throttled by a stranger, but himself. He'd gazed narcissistically at his teenage self enough times to know his own features in the ever dimming of his environment. The shrill screams and moaning of his doppelganger terrified his throat shut from making any noises. This imposter's hands fastened themselves around his neck and splashed his head up and down, occasionally scraping the ground beneath. Collin couldn't think straight enough to devise any action plans, and he wasn't skilled enough as his friends to use magic without hand motions.

Viscous fluid flooded down his face into trickles, obscuring his vision. Not that it mattered; his orbs of light had vanquished entirely at this point.

"This isn't real. You're not real," Collin muttered on a loop through sheer shock.

His words ignited demented glee in the copycat. His throttling of his victim came to an abrupt halt and the voice ringing out wasn't Collins, but a more affronted high-pitch.

"I'm not real? This will be real enough for you."

Collin couldn't make out the unhinging of the monster's mouth, revealing a second and third row of jagged teeth behind its perfect impersonation of his teeth. He couldn't make out the supernaturally swift descent of its head. Oh, but he could feel it!

Innumerous razors clamped over his left hand. Bone and tendon severed with a traumatic *crunch*. The boisterousness of cracking bone haunted Collin with mute terror for a few drawn out seconds before the impact of what happened droned everything out in white-hot tinnitus. The agony in his wrist lay buried beneath an overdose of adrenaline as he cocked his head to the side and vomited all over his right shoulder and bicep.

Chuckles echoed softly on the outskirts of Collin's ringing ears. Somewhere in the mistaken difference he could hear the creature chuckling "It was real enough for them. You're off limits, but I know you'll live."

In a flash and a loud *bang*, the weight upon Collin lifted away in smoke. The smoke wasn't entirely dissipating, as it wafted a comfortable distance and rematerialized out of Collin's muddied sight.

"Get up! Now!" Taylor's muffled voice commanded.

He was prepared to believe Taylor's materialization was the result of pain and terror cooperating past the threshold of hallucinating. Collin continued to lay limp and stare dazedly at his combat instructor even after he nudged him with his feet. There was no telling how long it took Taylor's bellowed commands to pierce the haze, but being physically assaulted by this corporeal figure eventually got through to him.

Collin blinked hard, eyelids pleading desperately to close and let drift into unconsciousness as a sheet of agony gradually enveloped him past the shock. He was yanked by his right forearm and dragged to his feet, sucking in air like a vacuum.

"Goddamn it! Move!" Taylor started tugging on him

Collin was slow to regaining control of his bodily functions. His muscles were reduced to semi-cooked noodles. He had to wipe his vision clean with his upper arm and still managed to smear a little of his own blood on his cheek. Seeing the messy cut from the timora's bite paled him further as it spewed profusely. Taylor must've noticed too as Collin fought for independence, but did nothing. Every second was precious in their escape, and if that meant sacrificing half a gallon of blood or more, so fucking be it. He shouldn't have been there in the first place.

From stumbling, to jogging, to running, they found a cooperative pace, but his elevating heart rate made Collin a ticking time bomb for tragedy if they didn't get the hell out of dodge soon. As they traced their way through the bodies, he deduced the ground to be covered in a few inches of blood based on the drench of Collin's matted clothes. Taylor appeared untouched by the drag. At one point, Collin could swear he saw him pass through a corpse or two.

"This isn't real. This isn't real." He ingrained his new mantra.

"It *isn't* real!" Taylor snapped. "Whatever you're seeing *isn't* real!"

Collin couldn't help glimpse his missing hand and feel troubled by the potential flaw in his words. It sure as hell seemed real! Taylor must've caught a side view of Collin's train of thought.

"We can mend it, but we need. To. Get. Out!"

They made oddly precise twists and turns in such a spacious trap. It bewildered Collin why they didn't make a straight route instead. Eventually, all their leeway narrowed into a scabrous mess of dungeon-like hallways lit with torches.

People were impaled to the wall by their hands, feet, arms, and legs. Some were dead with their heads bent low. Collin made an obvious assumption that the cause of death was the result of bleeding out, based on the streaks of blood pooling down into the flood. Others were still alive, but only on the cusp of their finale with each raspy plea for freedom.

Laughter clomped off the walls and ceiling like a pale horse approaching. Collin urged to help them, but Taylor insisted there was nobody there to help.

"Taylor!" Olivia's voice rang hesitantly.

"I got him!" Taylor shouted back.

A softer "Oh, thank God" was faintly heard. A left and a right turn later, Taylor gripped Collin harder as they passed through the bubble of a protective charm. Olivia was knelt over an unconscious Oscar, stroking his mysteriously ghost-white hair. The sight was disturbing, the striking resemblance of the almost-twins from a distance now their antithesis. Tear marks streaked her cheeks. Clark was sitting cross-legged staring into nothingness.

"Is he...?" Collin trailed off in his inquiry about Oscar.

"Just to be sure, you do see him, Liv?" Taylor spoke over him.

She nodded, and on the dime, Taylor pressed the barrel of the colt revolver between Collin's eyes.

"You have one chance to prove you're the real Collin," he offered maliciously.

Collin threw his hand and stump in the air to signal surrender, blood still draining at an alarming rate. Was this a joke?

Couldn't be.

Taylor was such an amalgam of leader and tyrant, it was

head-spinning. From their perspective, however, he must've figured Collin was safely at home. So how could he be here?

"W-what am I s-s-supposed to say?"

Taylor cocked the hammer. Collin floundered for a response, but locked eyes and blurted the first thing to come to his mouth more fiercely than anticipated.

"There's other ways to prove this! You're such an asshole!"

They all staggered in their reactions. Olivia appeared too shaken to grin, but gave Taylor a look of acceptance when he looked over his shoulder to gauge her thoughts at this outburst. He lowered the gun.

"How did you get here?" he demanded.

"I created a tear to Bold Bean shortly after y'all left."

"And how did *you* create a tear?"

He could tell by the accusatory intonation of Taylor's voice that Collin's uncanny ability to learn from a textbook was the same reason he recently held the colt pinned to his forehead.

"I found it in *Intermediate Spells* and followed the instructions."

The adrenaline in his system was tapering and the throbbing in his phantom hand pulsated strongly enough to procure a growing headache and shallowing respiration. His wan complexion transitioned further to a shade of pasty white. A second round of vomiting wasn't out of the question just yet.

"You learned how to create portals in a *that* short amount of time?" Taylor asked in agitated disbelief.

"Yes."

Collin caught the shared look of shock and awe in his conscious companions' expressions but, ultimately, they accepted his word.

"You're a fucking idiot for following us after I told you no." Taylor cast a spell to stave, but not discontinue, the bleeding out of Collin's stump, "But you may have more promise than I gave you credit for. Hurry, we need to figure out how we're gonna find Alice and get out of here, and we've only got about a minute before –"

Before what wasn't hard to comprehend. The timora was already standing at the edge of their spellwork, waving a hand in greetings in the mockery form of Stephen King's Pennywise the Dancing Clown.

18

A Taste of Fear

It held an uncanny accurate resemblance to Bill Skarsgård's rendition of Pennywise from the reboot films, from the puffy, silver clown costume with three red balls lining the center, to the receding red hairline, to the same dip of the lower lip with that drooling, demonic smile. It was everything Collin recalled from his movie-watching days. Even the cracked forehead was detailed and a red balloon floated from the hand that wasn't waving.

"Hiya, Collin!" it said in that same alluring voice.

Yet it didn't recognize its mistake until the transformation was already completed. The timora had given them a familiar face to temporarily allay their fears. Pennywise was fixed in a timeless classic of fictitious horror. For a slightest moment, Collin couldn't take the monster serious. So long as they were protected within the bubble, his attention was more focused on the well-being of Clark and Oscar.

"What happened to him?" Collin asked in regards to Oscar.

"I don't know," Olivia spoke quickly. "That *thing* affects us all differently. We see and *don't see* different things. As soon as we landed, we were all separated."

"Knock, knooooock," it sang.

It traced a white-gloved finger along the barrier between them. The timora took a curious sniff of the air and grinned atrociously. That same finger extended until the fabric ripped, revealing a long spider-like leg blanketed in barbed spurs. The appendage penetrated their safety and began corrupting their spellwork. The dim transparency of the enchantment began hardening into a wall of black stone, spreading like a disease.

"Collin, get Clark. Olivia, we're carrying Oscar. Move!" Taylor commanded.

Sharing the knowledge of being trapped and dead if they didn't escape their calcifying bubble, nobody questioned their orders. Collin dashed to his semi-comatose friend in two steps. Calling his name twice received nothing. A slap as hard as he could delivery warranted eye contact. He was able to drag Clark to his feet under the support of Collin's right shoulder. Unquestioning, even Clark could read the situation in such a short span of attention.

Taylor and Olivia labored forward more dangerously. They did what they could to magic Oscar lighter, but they couldn't diminish the bulkiness of lugging him through the winding lair. They all managed to surpass the threshold of their miniature sanctuary as the cancerous counterspell enveloped it. Now all that stood between them and the shapeshifting demon were two brittle walls of decay.

"Taylor, can you still see through the illusion?" Olivia shouted frantically.

"Yes. C'mon!"

At first, Collin didn't comprehend the question, but he surmised that the monster's magic forced them all to experience different nightmares. This is it what Taylor meant when he said nothing was real. Nobody else could see the blood on the ground or the bodies pinned up, drooping, or moaning on the black and red-stained walls. His hypothesis was put to the test when they all, Clark now recovered enough to sustain himself, traversed a wall. There was hesitation on his behalf. The possibility of his friends being illusions also transpired. However, when the situation of life or death was cut short to the length of a single breath, he put his faith in them and was rewarded with barely missing a shadowy hand extending from above.

The laughter down the halls approached quicker and quicker with frequent tremors at their backs. At times, they relied on Clark to conjure consecutive shield charms to impede the trickster's path, but his wards were paltry attempts. Whatever effect the timora's trap had on him wasn't easily sloughed, and while Collin wasn't properly trained to withstand field work at this magnitude, he still threw his own feeble shield charms in hopes of adding some sort of stability.

Their trek seemed immortal. Before long, Taylor and Olivia started shouting out Alice's name, knowing there was no chance in remaining hidden in the timora's own home. The constant upkeep of taunting giggles frequently reminded them so. Several more walls were passed through and, at one point, a portion of the ceiling fooled Collin for a second when it appeared to collapse and crush his friends.

This power is goddamn brilliant. Collin couldn't help but spare a fleeting moment of admiration.

Observing Clark, even he had moments of almost coming to complete stops or splitting off from the group. The hardest part of it was putting his utmost faith in his comrades when they guided him full-sprint over the mirage of a waterfall draining into a bottomless abyss. However, discovering each fault in the façades chipped away at the mask of fear. The blood meekly adhering Collin to the ground eventually thinned and dried. The bodies of familiar and unfamiliar faces screamed out "Failure!" and "Disappointment!" before they were silenced. Eventually, the confined people were fewer and fewer apart until none appeared.

Fortuitous perseverance granted cracks in the foundation, revealing veins of purple and black before the true path they strode unveiled itself altogether. Unfortunately, the devouring of his left hand and its current excruciating throb were not part of the game. The only other consistencies of it all were the roars and screams and hoots and hollers of the beast teasing them on their tails.

The room they stalled in was shaped like a dome. Wriggling black and purple, elephant truck-thick tendrils snaked along the walls and ceiling. Five paths encompassed them with their foreboding archways. The only few feet not swamped with whatever plant-like organism this was was the onyx flooring. Chilly air crept through the illusion of warm, liquid iron humidifying their atmosphere.

"What are these things?" Collin huffed, bent over trying to heave as much air as possible before their next run.

"You can see them now?" Taylor asked bewilderedly.

Collin explained what he saw as proof, and even Olivia scoffed in disbelief at her own inability to see through the façade. What world she was living in she wouldn't say, but she was aware of its false reality with emphasis on needing to escape it.

"Do you know which way?" Collin asked, waving an exhausted, dismissive hand at the paths before them.

Taylor shook his head defeatedly, but, before he could verbally answer, a taunting whisper fluttered through the cold air like a puff of frozen mid-January breath from the archway they'd entered. A sheet of silence fell upon them with anticipation. Single muscle fibers refused to twitch. Once the small cloud evaporated, a single second ticked away until the room blacked out. The only illumination now was regal purple revealing their ghostly silhouettes to one another.

Before anything could be done about it, one of the tendrils firmly wrapped itself around Taylor's neck like a whip and dragged him against the wall. Oscar toppled from his grasp. His upper body collided on the stone ground with a disheartening *thunk*. The imbalance of the load, and the swiftness of the need to act, left Olivia at a disadvantage.

She dropped Oscar's legs and lunged forward to help as the tendrils now tangled around Taylor's arms and legs.

Another creepy limb snagged Clark by the ankle and dangled him. This was Collin's chance to contribute.

Olivia withdrew a knife from her invisible utility belt and went to stabbing the thing to rescue Taylor. The animated room shrank back in shock of having its flesh sliced open, but it quickly composed itself and tackled Olivia for her weapon. It eventually won and flung its attacker a couple feet back, the blade now buried within the walls.

Meanwhile, Collin was doing the best he could. He managed to evade a few swings with a shield charm Alice taught him. It thankfully only required one hand to conjure. His aim granted him safe passage through the barrage, save for one lash across the chest. A chilled contact with the air alerted him to his shirt having been ripped, and the sensation of wet on his remaining fingertips told him blood was drawn. He tucked and rolled away from further whips, altering his defensive stance to an offensive one. Quick and concise as one could be in the dark, darts of flame ignited in the air and zoomed toward this mysterious organism. Two out of five found their intended target. Two missed entirely and the last missed Clark by a few singed hairs.

"Watch it!" Clark shouted, the immediate danger having seemingly sobered him.

Collin bellowed his apology and took note on the unyielding behavior of the Clark's captor. Even Clark's attempts failed. The only real effect any of them had happened as Collin took the time to shoot up minuscule orbs of light to illuminate their surroundings.

"Light!" he shouted. "Use light!"

Olivia was the only one currently able to implement his advice. The thing holding Clark wiggled and waved too ferociously to grant proper form in casting. He could've used magic by will, but his mind remained still too foggy to concentrate effectively. In addition, Taylor was becoming increasingly devoured by the sentient roots. He couldn't hear a thing at this point, except the thrumming of the tentacles.

Not an orb, but a literal beam of light shot from Olivia's upraised hand. It bleached the room so thoroughly, Collin found himself filled with instant regret for not shutting his eyes. Taylor was freed from his confines and Clark struck the ground discomfortingly. In its retreat, the dark arms coiled around Oscar's limp shoulder and dragged him. Taylor freed him with an arrow of pure light.

"Move, goddamn it!" Taylor shouted.

He and Collin went for the still unconscious Oscar, grateful to no ends that the enchantment keeping him nearly weightless was sustained. It forced Collin to bite his lip all the more when he had to endure the agony of even the slightest pressure placed on his wound. He had to tuck Oscar's legs under his left armpit.

They ran and ran. With no sense of directions, they maneuvered blindly. They each had to summon a trailing source of light to stay safe as the demon's den grew more aggressive and narrow in its attempts to consume them.

"ALICE!" everyone screamed at the top of their lungs, save for Oscar and Collin.

The black liquid his chewed wrist now oozed was concerning, but they couldn't afford to stop. Things may have been different had Oscar remained conscious. His Variant abilities to heal could've been of use, but, until then, it was a part of Collin's responsibility to keep his ghostly friend alive.

Alice's name reverberated off the walls in torrents of desperation to find her. The best they could hope for was to keep running in this labyrinth and hope she showed. It didn't help that the monster's illusionary abilities were creeping back over reality. Body after body of Alice appeared, pinned to the walls, hanging from the ceiling, severed on the ground. Shrieks of terror and agony echoed, heard by everyone. The only sliver of hope to see past the trickery rested on the fact they could all see the *multiple* bodies of their friend.

A roar quaked the air. Intent unknown, it sounded either frustrated or giddy, depending on one's interpretation. The pep in their step had already begun to fizzle out. They were jogging on fumes. At this point, they were merely delaying the inevitable confrontation. The fact it hadn't caught them yet suggested it was playing with its food.

They had no knowledge of their location save for the path they'd taken, and even that was limited to tumultuous memory. As a result, it came as a disheartening loss, but as no surprise, when they hit a dead end. It was too late to turn back.

The flailing tendrils around them stiffened as two pale eyes approached them from along the wall. The new shape of the beast could be unveiled. There were no pupils or irises. There wasn't even a blink. Only the steady rhythm of arms and legs lifting and falling gained volume on the students of Veil. Seeing such a thing blanketed Collin in a fresh wave of fear.

"Put him down," Taylor practically whispered without breaking eye contact with the thing.

Collin recognized the do-or-die tone. Together they lowered Oscar to the ground, with more struggle on Collin's part.

In Taylor's palms alit sapphire fire that consumed his hands. He balled them as if preparing for a fistfight with the demon. Olivia and Clark stepped forward with orders to protect Oscar and Collin. Collin didn't argue. Mentally, he was rotating a list of spells potentially useful, but remembered he was handless. At least he could still use minor lights, fires, and shields. They stalled in hopes of it making the first move.

No lunges came. Not even a hiss, chuckle, or taunt. The timora crawled and crawled until it clung a few short yards in front of them. It slumped over before it rose, and it rose and rose. The figure was still a shadow as far as detail was concerned, but it towered them with its head nearly scraping the top of the cave. Arms extended lankily to its knobby knees, and suddenly Collin relived the horror of his confrontation with the wendigo.

Does it have the same effect on the others? He gauged the upward tilt of their heads and figured it did.

Its glowing eyes elevated hypnotically on contact. Try as he may, Collin couldn't break free of the unblinking eyes captivating him so fatally.

"I can't...look away," he sighed.

A foot moved forward. *His* foot moved forward.

I didn't say you could move! he screamed in his head.

The others said nothing. They hadn't moved yet, but the dimming of Taylor's flames told him the boiling blood of battle in their veins was simmering down.

The timora stepped forward for them, slowly raising an outstretched arm as if to savor its victory. Feet away, then inches. A low growl could be heard emanating from deep within its throat. Wisps of black smoke danced and sang the tune of its approach. It was going to reach Taylor first, knowing the one with the most spunk would be strategically wiser to eliminate first, but Collin wanted to go first.

A spark of infuriation brewed in his amygdala that the timora didn't consider him worthy to be the first victim, while his frontal lobe fought to keep level-headedness. Manufacturing such foreign thoughts must've been part of its allure.

If defeat was this easy, why didn't it open with this tactic, instead of toying with them like some sadistic asshole?

If absence of light had a smell, Collin was getting a bountiful whiff. It reeked beyond rotted flesh or the fermentation of a couple week's stock of garbage in the direct

Florida sun, and yet he couldn't turn away from this repulsion.

The timora's claws spread and were seconds from claiming its first victim when something steely sliced through it like smoke. Its figure didn't evaporate, but the assault distracted it enough to splinter the trance they were bound to.

Taylor's dimming sapphire flames reignited and soared for its face. Olivia and Clark summoned dirks enchanted celestially bright. Two unison slashes proved ineffective, but it did show signs of irritation to the point of dissipation. Behind where the timora stood was a disheveled Alice.

All members stood ready to attack. The only two who didn't were the unconscious Oscar and the crippled Collin.

"Prove you're real!" Alice desperately demanded.

Her eyes were darting over the trio before her. She'd evidently been through her own ordeal and was about as likely to believe they were an illusion as the others were of her.

"When you first moved in with us," Clark said weakly, "we had to pull your arm for a solid hour to get your first drink to be our experimental Blueberry Bamboozle."

"We're here to help you kill it with as little interference to your project as possible," added Taylor.

The others looked at him with annoyed disbelief.

"How do you know about that?" Alice asked. Something about her posture and projected voice seemed different.

"You told me," Collin croaked, and Taylor, Clark, and Olivia parted. His condition must've worsened in his appearance, but his fear of their situation still kept him from passing out. "Sorry," he added weakly.

"Oh, God." She moved past the three to reach him.

She withdrew a vial and forced him to drink. Her eyes caught of glimpse of Oscar at their feet but ensured Collin got the immediate attention. A new wind fluttered through him. The paleness in his complexion darkened a little with a restock of fresh blood pumping through his body, but, when he glanced down, the opening on his wrist still seeped black liquid. The veins around the injury shared the same hue as they crisscrossed up his arm, almost to the elbow. The edges around his vision were starting to blur.

"What happened to you two?" Alice asked, gazing in Oscar's direction.

"Now's not the time, Alice," said Taylor. "Do you know how to kill it?"

"I have an idea, but we need to leave. Now!"

She grabbed Collin and Oscar by the shoulder and asked the others to hold on to her. Without spinning a tear, or even using her hands at all, she relocated them all topside, somewhere off McCoy Creek Boulevard, north of the Bold Bean they'd started from, but the city they left wasn't the city they stood in.

19

What Was and Is

The sun shone through a cloudless blue sky upon a deteriorating community, rotting and crumbling from the inside out. Urban health decayed into a shell still being emptied into piles of ash and debris for as far as the eye could see. Buildings and even downtown skyscrapers showed evidence of the same plague poisoning Collin. Few appeared still unscathed by the disaster, or at least in the early stages of development. Same went for surrounding life.

Plantation was sucked fruitless and blackened. The citizens of the area walked among them shriveled and graying as the life slowly drained from their ignorant bodies. They were beyond the veil of whatever curse they participated in. The only one who still couldn't make heads or tails of their confusion was Olivia. Alice remedied her conundrum effortlessly, although not without a twinge of sorrow for the awestruck horror sculpting Olivia's face thereafter.

"Alice, what the fuck?" Olivia shrieked simultaneously as Taylor inquired what they were looking at.

"This is the condition Jacksonville has been in for several months."

"Months?!" Olivia shouted.

A few heads turned in their direction to reveal sets of sallow and sunken, curious eyes. Collin was in observatory shock. To the onlookers, he must've looked like a tourist, awed by the city life, but they didn't know.

"Not everything or everyone is affected equally. I believe we just left the focal point of it all."

"That you found how?" asked Taylor. "How did you move us without a tear? How did you uncover this illusion?"

That was easy, thought Collin regrettably. *She's Alice. She's been working on this far more thoroughly than I gave credit.*

The look in her eyes spoke a sorrowfully wishful desire to answer all questions. Even Collin could tell she was dying to strike a prideful ramble, but she kept her composure.

"I'll tell you everything, I promise, but we need to move. It's not enough to kill a timora where it stands. To be strong enough to infect a city means it's as good *as* the city, but it hasn't infected *all* of Jacksonville, which means it might still be containable. If it's containable, *then* it's killable, but we have to cut it off at its core first."

Nobody spoke. Nobody wanted to consider the beast to be uncontainable. Even Taylor was confounded, yet Alice appeared annoyed at the hesitation.

"We need more help," Clark groaned.

"No!" she replied with hastened steel in her voice.

"No?" Olivia shot back. "I'm not dying for the sake of your greedy ambition."

"I've got the juice to kill it, okay? And I'll do it with or without you."

The steel sharpened to an implicit threat, revealing a side Collin wasn't too sure he was pleased to see, coming from the quiet, infallible girl he knew. In fact, he was growing more sure he wasn't even staring at the same person. Her aura thrummed familiarly, but uncertainty never crossed his mind. Was she making this energy radiate to give them an idea of what the past few days had made her capable of? Or was it her power as a spellcaster peaking exponentially with an unnatural innateness?

The juice *reference seemed a little strange.*

A lack of confidence from the remainder of the crowd bogged down Alice's own. It was clear they weren't giving up without a fight for answers when hunting something as seriously underestimated as a timora. Reading the air for the imminently losing battle, Alice sighed in agitation, hoping to shave a few minutes off whatever questions they may have. The sooner they resumed their attempts of ridding their city of such a prominent monster the better. What couldn't they grasp about such a simple concept?

"Start. Now," she said curtly.

As Taylor and Olivia took the lead, Alice bent over Oscar to reinstate his consciousness. She then gave a firm grip around Collin's wounded arm and produced a soft, warm glow to belay the inky tendrils trailing through his veins.

"*How* did you move us without a creating a tear?" Taylor insisted with choppy pauses in his speech.

Terror flickered in his eyes at the sight of the miracles she was performing, but he refused to be swayed. Even as the uncertain determination quavered temporarily in his question, he stood his ground with caution. Olivia appeared only marginally more frightened with her eyes bugged wider. It would've been denial in its rawest form for Collin to claim he wasn't a little wary of this new Alice himself.

Oscar stirred with excessive blinking as his gears whirled to recollect and understand. Clark gave him a summarized version of their dilemma in a few short sentences, ending with the six of them concealed behind a number of trees from the deadened civilians. All eyes returned to an impatient Alice.

"On the night I left, I found an exceptional source of magic I tapped into today. It has enough power in it to let me utilize magic in undiscovered ways, and it's what's given me the ability to kill the timora."

"What source?" Taylor asked suspiciously.

"How do you kill it?" Clark asked simultaneously.

Alice's eyes trailed the ground piercingly. Her actions gave the impression of listening keenly for something.

Was this magic source able to amp her senses beyond regular buffing spells?

She overlooked Taylor's question and favored Clark's instead. "I can't determine how long it's been in the city. I originally thought it had been here only a few short months, but I'm starting to wonder if it hasn't been here for nearly a year. Maybe more."

"*Maybe* more?" Olivia blurted.

"Judging by the progression of its disease, it's been affecting the city for quite some time."

"Will killing it reverse the disease?" Oscar asked.

"I don't know."

"Will killing it even *stop* the disease?" Taylor demanded.

"I don't know."

"What *do* you know?" Olivia charged. She was prominently teetering on the edge of hysteria with each glance around the decaying foundation of her city.

"I know these creatures were created, twisted and warped by powerful sources of magic, like the orb in possession of the Council, purposefully intending to do so. There's more to it than saying a spellcaster is accepted or rejected by embodiments of raw magic. That's too black and white. A person who is accepted is accepted to be a representative of either light or darkness, but there always tends to be a balance between the two. Good and evil. Creation, destruction. Gain and loss."

Terrifying though as it may be, to be caught in the center of such a world-shattering revelation, Collin couldn't help but pause to indulge in the idea of having fallen into some fictitious novel or movie. Dozens of references flashed across his mind about the balancing of light and dark: *Star Wars, Kingdom Hearts,* superhero comics, and so on.

"I also know timoras aren't typically mindless brutes either.

They're beyond clever. While we've been thinking them to be most likely extinct, they've been laying strategically dormant, or in plain sight. It took me a couple days to look past the illusion-work it embedded to conceal its disease. If it hadn't been for Shaylee, who I'm assuming you've visited, since you found me, I may have remained as ignorant as the rest of the world. She opened my eyes and helped point me in the right direction, but I know more things. Terrible things." At this her tone leveled out monotonously as if professing prophecy. "A past and a future concealed behind a wall I can't see past, yet I can feel. We are on one strand of a spider's web, and we are on all components of this greater plan. What happens tonight is but a stepping stone in the fate that binds us."

"Your source told you all that, huh?" Taylor inquired flatly, but his bravado stirred minutely.

Alice hesitated with another entranced stare at the ground before finally saying "We officially have three minutes before it finds us, and also yes, this source of magic informed me so."

"And where did this source of power come from?" Taylor spoke more quickly, hoping to wring out as many answers as possible in such a limited amount of time.

The rest of the crew grew uneasy knowing the exact time before the timora would be upon them, but what may have upset them further was the mention of this *greater plan*. It wasn't the first time this had been teased under their noses, but it was the first time it'd been brought as forthright, blanketing them in mysticism and inadvertently swelling them with tremors of undetermined emotions.

The strange reality of everything began its divide on Collin. Observation could only get him so far before the unsettling sinking sensation of this situation seemed less and less like his story, less like his destiny. He played his role in something larger by finding the manhole, although it was possible they could've found it without him.

No, judging by the climax of her efforts to become a respectable member of Veil, this was Alice's tale. However, that didn't mean he couldn't tag along for the ride. Swallowing his self-made, dawning comprehension, he fought to stay atop what everyone said and merely expressed the appropriate reactions. It was a fool's feat. After all, he'd only been a part of their world barely more than three months. Even to more experienced eyes and ears, this must have been one frustrating day to wrap one's mind around.

"I suspect you already know where the source comes from," Alice answered Taylor, still in a deep monotone.

Taylor didn't need to pause to contemplate. "You're the thief," he said with plain finality, shooting a sideways look of guilt in Collin's direction.

A ghost of a smile curled at the edges of Alice's lips, but her eyes didn't portray any joy. "There's more to the story, but we don't have time."

"What do we need to do?" Taylor asked in calm acceptance.

Her slender smile grew eerily wider as she informed them

that they'd need to return to the nightmarish maze they'd left. She didn't have time to say why, except that she'd pulled them out in the first place to make an attempt at making them understand. Collin only partially comprehended.

They must've already lost a minute, maybe more. Alice gathered them around and made sure each of them were in contact.

"You don't have to go," she suggested to Collin with a glimmer of concern behind her otherwise vacantly power-inebriated expression.

Collin shook her words off. His hand was already gone, and something about the demon's words... *You're off limits, but I know you'll live* rang conclusively in his ears about any danger he may be in. The others made motion to object, but, in a blink of an eye, they were plunged back into the nightmarish hellhole they'd all suffered in to some degree or another.

20

Under Threat of Determinism

The instantaneous transition left a queasy feeling in Collin's stomach. The desire to vomit eventually caught up with him, though fleetingly so. The rapid onset of blindness was a lesser feat to accustom to. Lights all around him glowed from the others. He even managed to summon his own guiding light, albeit a weaker form of the spell gifting illumination of a single fingertip. There wasn't enough strength to produce more.

The severity of their situation was emphasized when not even a snigger emanated from Clark or Oscar at the otherwise hilarity of Collin's meager attempt. He'd be grateful for their lack of input on his handicap later.

"How do you know where to go?" Clark inquired with comforting severance from the silence foreboding impending doom.

For a second, Alice didn't answer. They wondered if she even heard. "I can feel it. The heart *and* the body. Both separated by the evolutionary desire to grow, reproduce, and preserve," she finally replied.

"You say it like the heart and body separate," said Oscar.

"They are."

"How can it survive separately?" Collin jumped in.

"It's a natural part of its growth. Once its body becomes strong enough to endure it, it will split into two. The heart will serve as a hive mind for what we're standing in, as well as an additional method of staying alive. If the body dies, the heart may continue to grow strong with the roots it's ingrained into the earth to suck the life out of anything it touches."

"And that's what it's done to the city," Taylor stated.

The tunnels were too dark for anyone to see Alice nod. "In addition, if the heart dies, the body may still function until it's strong enough to split off another heart, but it's the heart that produces the level of magic needed to conceal the disease it spreads from the public eye. Without it, the beast will continue to lurk in secret to conceal its habitation."

"So, what happens if we kill the heart, but not the body, and the entire city becomes aware of the state of things?"

Their pace hastened to the beat of the question. The midnight tendrils were dormant to their presence, yet pulsated in defiance. Was Alice keeping them at bay? Did her new magical high extended an influence *that* powerful?

"Regardless, whether we kill the heart or kill both entities, it will be up to Veil to keep things contained."

"Veil should've been contacted from the beginning!" Olivia piped in irritably.

The absence of objection from the crowd conceded in a

unanimous agreement. Even Collin considered the loss of his limb warranted a dose of spite, but a small part still lingered on the hope she'd achieve all she sought to.

"Not yet," Alice said, "but they will. It's all part of the plan."

"Fuck your plan, you selfish bitch!" Olivia escalated. "Do we look like we give two shits about your class project?"

Alice remained unperturbed. Whatever unearthly high she was on, it was becoming increasingly concerning and, quite frankly, appalling.

Alice?

"You know what? No." Olivia halted abruptly when nobody spoke. "I'm leaving."

She developed the stance to create a tear in sync with Clark's, Oscar's, and Taylor's reflexive objection. Olivia would hear none of it. Collin found himself in the position not to argue with someone he'd never formed a genuine connection with. Alice stood unfazed. Collin studied her curiously, but she never returned his gaze.

The others merely attempted to persuade their companion to stay, not resolving to any physical or spellbinding means, which only allowed the schism in their fellowship to fracture deep enough for Olivia to construct her portal and leave.

"It's okay," Alice's voice stole through the settling silence of the pervasively forlorn air making everyone question their safety in lessened numbers. "I told you, there's a plan. It's likely Olivia will fulfill her purpose in raising the alarm. The Council *will* be notified, like I said, just not yet. Come."

She tilted her head in the direction they resumed. The boys

were hesitant to follow, but obeyed all the same. Their only other option was to abandon ship with their absent friend, but they held an obligation as members of Veil.

Collin could devise no pattern to Alice's knowledgeable directions through the fleshy tunnels. The lights they bore blinded him from the majority of detail they strode through, save for the mildly sinking steps into the ground and the progressive thickening of the air the deeper they trekked. Temperature escalated from chilly to stifling ends, growing as thick as the awkward silence that predominated. Gratefully, Oscar was the one who eventually ended it.

"So, if all this is preordained, why didn't you just tell Olivia to go warn the others?"

"I didn't know she would be the one to warn anyone, but at the same time, I knew she wouldn't be around for our part in it all. Besides, even if I did know what role Olivia was meant to play, her leaving on request is not the way it's supposed to go."

"Explain," Taylor replied.

"I can feel the path beneath my feet, but I cannot see the material constructing it nor where it leads. There's a sort of…foresight…that the details of each scenario must align as perfect as possible to follow a common theme. If I suggested Olivia go warn the Council, then she might not have out of defiance. I needed her to be with us as long as I could manage and for her to enter a state as angry as she left us in."

"So, you're toying with us," Clark said in solemn

disbelief. Her riddles were starting to rub them the wrong way.

"I am not."

"Then what else is going to happen?" he demanded, his tone growing opposed, fueled by frantic. "Was Oscar supposed to change the way he did. Did Collin *need* to lose his hand? Are we even going to *live*?"

Alice paused to consider her answer. Everyone else stopped moving with her.

"I don't know, to your first question," she said finally. "Yes to the second, and yes to the third. Don't ask me how or why. I am…guided…in the direction things are supposed to be. I am not shown the outcome, only the constants and variables needed to be kept in check."

"And the orb is what's *guiding* you?" Taylor asked bitterly.

"Yes."

Collin was following along as best he could, but the agony he was in stole his focus and his lingering doubt left him feeling disconnected. He cared about the outcome of their predicament, and yet, despite the thundering of his evermore beating heart inside his throat, a flutter of disinterest randomly reminded him of the day he stepped off that plane.

But why? And why now? Was living in a plot where severed limbs was mandatory too real? And what is this orb?

He was worried about this disconnected sensation. He had magic now. He could literally defy the laws of his remnant life. Hell, with enough education and practice, he could probably play fucking God one day. What was this sliver of existentialism doing creeping into him? Was it bred from a sense of hopelessness? Was the adrenaline tapering off, and the sight of emptiness where a hand recently lay attached not even an hour ago making connections with the frenetically chaotic pangs of indeterminism?

Collin shook the idea from his head. That couldn't be it. His thoughts were bordering into the field of pandemonium and randomness. Alice was speaking predetermined causes and effects. "Constants and variables" in her words.

Fate and destiny were fleeting concepts in his teenage mind, stemmed as a result of literature from AP Language back in high school tangoing with his Eriksonian confliction of identity versus role confusion. It made him feel important, made him feel as though he had a place in the universe. Freud might've said he was in denial, but based on Alice's words he was staring the damn concept of determinism in the face! Collin literally stood where he needed to be, and *now* he was taking the time to feel disconnected?

Could it be the theft of mystery and the unknown that place them under threat of determinism? More beings than just the timora alluded to this foresight. Shaylee so recently said they were pawns of a bigger game. Shaylee said whatever is happening is *unbalancing*. The wendigo acted so out of behavior in how it didn't savagely shred Collin on contact. Collin's mind raced from thread to thread until it stuck on one image…and then it clicked.

"And the person in the skull mask," he thrust his idea forwardly.

Overture

All eyes directed on him, Alice last of all. He set his sights on her for confirmation, but the shine of their spells distorted her expression. He could only make out a sadly misplaced forelonging.

"The who?" Clark asked.

"Yes," Alice assured.

One word was all it took before Collin felt reminiscent terror of his first encounter. Terror of being seen by the stranger in his cult-ish mask, whom Collin firmly believed murdered the cat in the road flooded over him. They weren't just in the lair of a timora, they were in the lair of his first true fear.

"We could leave," he suggested.

"Leave?" Taylor tested.

Clark and Oscar seemed intrigued by this notion, but they couldn't meet anyone's eyes except each other's. Collin interpreted so as to not seem cowardly, and, in truth, he worried perhaps his sudden panic attack may have made him seem so, but no.

"No one can leave," droned Alice. "I already offered you the chance to stay behind and you refused, that feels right." She turned around and portrayed someone having an internal dialogue and outward debate with only herself. "It adds up. It's a sign of your bravery, but was there anything else?"

Any other pointers she made, they were muffled by her quiet voice and conflicting body language. The boys strained to hear more, but even enchanted ears couldn't translate.

"Let us go," Collin suggested again. "You said it yourself

you have the power to stop the thing. So, what if we stop it tomorrow?"

"No, it *has* to be today!" Alice whirled around vehemently.

"And if we decline and leave anyways?" He was finding a fresh leaf of courage.

"I won't let you," Her tone turned coolly, almost precariously. "Everything is already set in motion. We've broken its illusionment spell between ourselves and the Council is due to be informed of the situation momentarily. Before they are, I *have* to ensure the beast is killed. If anyone tries to leave or interfere, I will keep you here with force."

Is she absolutely insane?

Collin, and even Clark, were getting ready to respond angrily, maybe even test Alice's challenge, but before they could, Taylor interjected.

"Enough! Just take us where we need to be so we can end this."

Alice bowed her head and reassumed their venture. "If it helps, we'll see how it ends within the hour," she said over her shoulder, but no one was eager to respond.

21

The Overture

The best part of knowing they were within the eleventh hour was two-part. The first being they hadn't been aware of this truth to fall victim to the effects of anticipation. Secondly, the walk to the inner sanctum spent another ten minutes, minimizing the time they'd spend in horrific turmoil.

Entering the domain of the monstrous heart nearly mimicked exactly what Collin's imagination managed to muster. A vivid purple hue flushed throughout, leaving no use for spellwork to illuminate their way. The sentient tendrils now lining the ground, walls, and ceiling progressively engorged until they arrived at the epicenter.

The only detail lacking from Collin's mind was symmetry. Where its heart was concealed wasn't in a perfectly circumferential room. There was no special pattern to it all. The shape of its most vulnerable hideout was more crudely cut out, like the beast buried its way beneath the earth and split itself the second it was distanced enough from peeping eyes. Surmising as much, Collin felt burdened with the suspicion the tunnels they ventured were the product of biological growth, consuming the earth rather than actively burrowing.

Discontenting comfort radiated from the slow flickering organ that lay strung from the top and bottom by blackened, fleshy sinew. An outer layer of thick skin transparently encased the radiating purple, its final efforts of survival being to entrance predators with its softly beautiful glow.

"That's it?" Oscar asked.

His two simple syllables transpired skepticism like oxygen forced from the lungs. A similar wave of doubt flooded the other two clueless members of their minuscule congregation. Alice, however, stood more circumspect as they'd ever seen her. Her eyes weren't on the heart, but scanned every other inch of the area. She ignored Oscar's question.

"How do we kill it?" Taylor asked.

Still no response, and by the fifteenth second of furtive silence, Clark stepped in with one of Shrapnel's Spear spells. Collin couldn't decipher the gauge size of the needle-like tip, but Clark's fingers conjured a translucent javelin that he proceeded to hurl with all the finesse of a professional thrower. Nobody had protested, so why not?

To their dismay, it struck a barrier and shattered before evaporating into the wisps of nothingness it'd been born from. No apparent damage was taken from the invisible wall standing between them and their target.

"Now would be a great time for some input," Taylor spoke agitatedly, almost degradingly, to Alice.

She still didn't speak, but strode over to the line the javelin couldn't cross. She raised a hand, but was cautious not to place it directly on the barrier. Instead, tiny streams of electricity ejected from her palm and fingertips through sheer will, instead of finger-work. Once her examination was done, a single finger was pressed to the wall. Ripples flowed from their point of origin, until, much like the outcome of a pebble in a pond, the waves died out. In their place, white cracks spread into a monochrome mosaic burning through the protective spell.

When they had initially entered the room, the air lay sediment with layers of negative emotions. As soon as Alice degraded the barrier encasing the timora's heart the air became impregnated with something much worse. What filled every nook and cranny were air particles of some acrid jinx. They were spore-like in their flight, near-microscopic black particles bursting out like smoke and debris in an explosion. Soon, the tunnels they'd been wandering would become toxic for anyone to enter unguarded.

Naturally, Alice was unscathed. Collin and the boys were taken aback at once. There was an immediate burning in their lungs. Whatever they inhaled bonded with blood in a similar manner as oxygen molecules and rapidly spread throughout the body, except it wouldn't exhale. The longer this dark magic resided within each of them, the more detrimental the effects became. That burning sensation evolved into itching, which evolved into cramps, which began to feel like tiny razors scratching and clawing their way from the inside out. Fifteen seconds. Twenty seconds. Worse and worse it got. By the time their agony was noticed, Collin could already taste the iron in the droplets of blood he coughed up.

Alice raced over to Collin first. She was unclear with what she was dealing with at first. A second cough, spewing more blood this time, was used as a sample as she dipped a finger into a drop of crimson. After heavy examination, she did something he hadn't anticipated. She put her mouth to his. Not in a romantic way. There was a forceful exhalation on her end as she breathed new life into his lungs. Taylor, Clark, and Oscar received the same treatment, but it wasn't enough to rid the painful exhaustion from any of them.

"Sorry," Alice spoke while the others gasped desperately. "I should've known there'd be more than the one defensive measure. I imagine the entire underground will be tainted now. The immediate blast would've been concentrated enough to kill anyone able to demolish the barrier. Afterwards, anyone who discovers these tunnels will become diseased and deceased before ever having a chance to locate the heart. It's brilliant."

"That's one opinion," Clark said weakly, wobbling up straight.

"I'll finish the heart." Alice resumed her absentminded demeanor. "Its body will have felt the breaking of its spell."

Sure enough, as if her words were an evocation to its insurmountable subsistence, a wide, mischievous grin carved through the wall as its vessel bulged out of the wall like the product of asexual budding.

"Do it now then!" Collin hollered hoarsely.

The others followed his gaze and swore in an equally sore voice. It was a strenuous task for them to sustain the will to stand, let alone fight. Alice's exorcism of the spores hadn't healed them entirely from the damage they endured. Whatever otherworldly curse it came from, it might've even overpowered Alice's magic. That didn't mean the boys couldn't imbue themselves in protective and enhancing spells. Collin could see shield charms, added agility, strength, and keenness performed, but they were all two-handed spells. He was as good as bait, yet he was strangely calm, like a one-man audience staring at the forthcoming transgressions from the rafters.

The eyes of the beast met his and its creepy smile widened. Its height was adjusted to match theirs this time, but its figure was still as shadowy and featureless as their most recent exposure to the beast. It scanned the others who staggered marginally firmer in their defiance.

"Breathe it iiin," it hissed in a shivering high-pitched voice. "Her protection won't last very long."

It caught sight of Alice as she cocked her throwing arm back, a spear similar to Clark's in her grip, but with a radiant glimmer in its semi-transparency. It needn't move. Its left arm whipped up and stretched several yards to steal her weapon mid-flight.

Taylor attempted to take advantage of the distraction, but failed to complete whichever spell he was putting together. Its right arm acted as similarly as its left and flung forward elastically to pin Taylor to the ground. Flat on his back, Taylor became bound by fingers stretching into rope. As it wrung the air out of his lungs, Clark and Oscar rained fire and ice ineffectually upon their foe.

In the timora's left hand, Alice's javelin dematerialized into black smoke. Alice reacted reflexively to take hold of its outstretched arm and burn it with white light. It recoiled instinctually back to its normal length before striking at her snakelike. She parried the blow with her own shield charm, but it broke through to leave a gash across her face. If she hadn't moved so quickly, Collin gathered the momentum would've initially sliced right through her. A thin line of blood welled up and spilled into a trickle before the cut on her cheek could seal itself whole.

Meanwhile, the timora retreated both appendages before Alice could counter, its attention only a fraction divided for the others. Not a single glance was spared for Collin, who was using all his might to remain levelheaded enough to recollect any one-handed spells to assist his friends. Elementary light, fires, and shields seemed pretty useless in this situation.

"What form will you use this time?" Alice taunted familiarly.

The creature didn't retort, but exposed a row of razors for teeth before its human figure expanded and warped. It grew to be over ten feet tall and gathered enough mass to occupy one-third of its inner sanctum. It looked like a slug bent upward in the middle, strengthened by three sprouting stocky, shovel-like appendages on each side similar to the legs of a mole cricket. A tail thinned out as it expanded outward. A total of four arms germinated out from the upper-half of the body and touched the ground as they manifested themselves into the same shape as a praying mantis'. Out of its back protruded a pair of dragon wings, each as long as its body and divided by four phalanges to stabilize the thickly muscular areas in-between. The wing thumb at its highest point grew as menacingly lethal as the sharp tips of its arms. A short beak formed where its mouth should be. Above them was a pair of red, soul-gazing eyes. They became nearly eclipsed by a semi-circular plate that armored its seemingly most sensitive spot. Once its shape finalized, an adapted layer of impenetrable scales enveloped its skin.

Alice seemed impressed. Everyone else was mortified by such a rapid and treacherous transformation. No amount of education could've prepared them for something so unpredictable. Was there a book out there, somewhere, that might've informed Alice of such behavior, or was her fierce demeanor merely the product of her…whatever she was?

I need to help, he supplicated his own thoughts. *Something. Something useful. What can I do? Do something!*

Even his wounded companions were at a loss. They attempted every spell they could to weaken its mobility, senses, strength, but their jets of lights ricocheted off its thick scales. One of Oscar's spells even rebounded and struck Taylor square in the chest. The monster paid no mind. It only had sights for Alice, who was studying it through a rectangular, invisible lens created with her thumbs and forefingers.

"Not bad," she commented.

The demon growled at her as midnight billows of smoke surrounded them. Its tail swung around to grab her, but she fought it off with a flick of her wrist releasing a jet of yellow light. It was fruitless discerning which spells she was using. Not only could she summon her power without lectured form, but she was dabbling in spellwork outside the scope of Veil's knowledge.

The rest of them redirected their aim at the creature's eyes. Collin too. With his remaining hand, he was able to recreate the basic format of a stunning jinx, Flander's Fledgling Fireball, and a spell typically used to close objects like doors or windows, but in hopes this figure gave itself eyelids. Taylor fired as many rounds from the revolver as possible, but this new monstrosity didn't bat an eye.

It maneuvered with unforeseen speed and flexibility. It charged Alice with its swift feet. Each time it moved, its lethal arms pierced the ground, granting it the ability to heave its entire body forward. Despite the quick blur Collin was watching, he noticed their movements were a graceful dance beyond all the grunts and groans. The timora spared no precaution to avoid scuffing its own heart or give its opponent a second's moment to destroy it.

In Alice's attempts to duck and dodge, it was on her agenda to come in direct contact with the beast itself. The intent was obvious. The monster's tail whipped too fast even for her to catch, and the beast was wise enough to keep a constant distance between them.

She webbed the right side of its hind legs and the left side of its front, stalling it long enough to barrage it with more yellow and white spells. As it broke free seconds later, she moved so fast she practically teleported underneath the colossal thing and went to stab it with an unknown object, but was wrenched back when its tail finally wrapped itself around her forearm and flung her against the cavern wall. There was a gruesome *thud* that followed, but the padding of its lair's surface protected her. Not to say she was protected. Tendrils unfurled from the wall to arrest her, but she simultaneously glowed a faint white that burned whatever touched her. As she broke free, the aura surrounding her vanished to conserve her strength. It was a duel of wit, power, and precision. Until…at last!

They fought for what might've been an eternity as Collin, Taylor, Clark, and Oscar continued to fall short of adequate assistance, but near the finality of it all, Alice faked a falter. She fought to free a chunk of the ceiling in order to collapse it atop the monster, but its vascular roots refused to give way. The creature took that moment to lash at her as it charged with four bladed arms breaking ground beneath them. Under the weight and ferocity of its actions, a fissure trailed ahead of her, below the surface of fleshy tentacles, unbalancing the field. As Alice permitted the circumstance to trip her, she twisted her body and leapt atop the timora as it dove in for a peck. Beak open, two thin rows of serrated teeth chomped on nothing. Alice lunged at the neck, and, as her enemy raised itself, she created another glimmering weapon she dug into the base of the neck and slid down the spine. A roar of pain echoed throughout the inner sanctum. The engorged beast deflated to its featureless, human form.

"Interesssting," it hissed.

Alice charged with a fist of light, but it broke into a cloud of smoke and rematerialized a couple yards back. She bolted forward again and the damned thing retreated in response. She doubled back and Collin watched her devise a second javelin meant for stabbing the heart, but the same elastic arms stole the pointed rod from its direct course.

"Fight, you coward!" she screamed.

The tone of her voice was agony. She appeared both fiercely determined and tormented at the same time.

Is she growing tired?

Surely possessing so much energy was taxing on the body, but what was the source? Taylor said the orb, but what orb? Like the one the Council uses for inaugurations? Were there more, because that object *definitely* contained more power in it than he'd ever seen. Alice and her opposition were worthily giving their display a run for its money before the beast backed away and sunk into the wall, vanishing from sight.

"Where'd it go?!" Taylor shouted, a hint of panic in his voice.

Alice seemed worried too. Her eyes darted in every possible direction, but she noticed it a moment too late. It crawled eerily on the ceiling. As it was detected, one arm outstretched and laced itself around Collin's neck.

"No!" Alice yelled, twirling her arm to wind up a momentous spell.

Upon its launch, the demon leapt down to evade. Its free arm swung around and knocked Clark and Oscar with enough force to raise them at a high enough angle for them to crash into the ceiling, collide with the wall, and thump stilly to the ground. The grip around Collin's throat denied the passage of air in or out, but why was he being attacked in the first place? Hadn't the thing told him he would survive? Alice quickened her pace, but its retaliations were canceling.

"Let. Him. Go!" she demanded between throws.

The timora laughed its high-pitched laugh. "What'sss one loss if it meansss one victory?"

In an instant, it was knocked forward by Taylor abandoning all hopes of using any useful magic and using brute force to ram the being from behind. Collin was caught off guard by such an action and was dragged to his knees. One second was all it took.

Alice willed her body to burst and rematerialize as the timora had, however, instead of retreating, they stood noses apart. Her fist gutted the shadow, forcing it from escaping. It struggled and fought to tug itself free from her invasive power. The fingers around Collin's throat relinquished their grip, leaving only red imprints behind.

For a brief second, Collin saw a flicker of fear reshape Alice's tenacious expression. During that period, the light within the timora dimmed. Her strength dwindled, but she held her ground. Taylor was shouting her name and pleading with her to stop.

The last thing Collin could recall was the terrorizing creature bursting into light and ashes with enough force to jolt the three of them back and into the air. His head made a critical impact with the wall and knocked him out cold before his body hit the ground.

22

An Aftermath to Remember

Four days elapsed before Collin woke. It was a slow wake, unknowingly similar to that of coming off anesthesia, minus the loopy behavior. What stimulated his consciousness were the whispers at his bedside. Inaudible in his daze, he could still tell the voices belonged to Ms. Glenda and Clark. He shifted in his soft bed before he realized he was actually in a bed.

Jolting up, both hands made a natural lunge for something to grip, like he'd dreamed he was falling and awoke with a start. There was no immediate shock of *both* hands gripping metal railings around his bed. He'd temporarily forgotten his left hand had been messily chewed off. His sudden motion startled his two visitors, who each smiled afterwards.

"Oh, thank God!" Ms. Glenda sighed with relief. "How are you, dear?"

Collin was lost for words. Last he could remember was being flung by the sheer annihilation of the timora. She gave him a pityingly look in response to the look he gave her, Clark, and the hospital room they were in. On his second scan of the room, he caught a glimpse of a head full of white hair two beds over from his.

"He'll be all right," Ms. Glenda explained soothingly. "They're only keeping him for further examination of any lasting damage other than his altered appearance."

"But he's otherwise okay?"

"He's fine," Clark chimed in. "That bump on the head knocked us out, but did no worse damage than it did to you."

"There isn't a spell to turn his hair back to black?"

"Apparently not. Whatever happened to him in the sewers was extremely dark magic." Mrs. Goodall was getting to her feet to try to push Collin back down into his bed to rest. "Nothing we do will reverse the effects. It's not like your hand—"

Collin immediately glanced at his left hand with confused apprehension. It was really, truly there.

"—where it was physically removed."

A tear could be seen welling in the corner of Ms. Glenda's eye at the mere concept of one of her makeshift children coming to such harm. "Something was cast on Oscar. That's not to say your injuries weren't awful either. You could've been released yesterday, possibly even two days ago, but whatever venom was in the timora's saliva made it difficult to regrow."

"Oscar's been unconscious this whole time too?"

"No, no." Mrs. Goodall spared a glance at the head of white hair. "He's just finished a round of testing. He's resting."

Whatever changed Oscar, Collin was willing to bet it

involved a *very* close call with his demise. There was a moment of silence as the *tap tap* of shoes echoed on the tile floor from one of the nurses checking on a patient at the opposite side of the generously large room. Either this was a ward where the sick were left to finish their recovery or the number of patients in this hospital was so large that there wasn't much room for private practice.

Despite the all-natural lighting, it was no doubt a magical hospital. The typical machinery he would've expected to see, the heart monitors, IV drips, blood-filters, defibrillators, were nowhere in sight. Come to think of it, he couldn't spot a single outlet, let alone a cord. Instead, beside nightstands, and in a few tall cabinets six or seven beds over, were racks and racks of small and large vials, beakers, flasks, and mortars and pestles. There were liquids of of every color, but a curiously wider variety of thick reds looking suspiciously like different types of blood. Others held a monumental array of botanical options, which he suspected to constitute a combination of herbs of the mundane and the extraordinary. There were pockets of powders, metals, teeth, claws, hairs, and...

Snake skin? Maybe it's best to wait until potions lessons, he thought.

Flexing his new hand, he noticed it had a strained tightness to it, like new shoes needing an adjustment, but there were more pressing matters at present. "The timora..."

"Dead," Clark assured.

"But...what happened?"

Clark opened his mouth and proactively extended a breath.

"Well, according to Taylor, we weren't revived until after we were brought here, but he said Alice overdid herself with tapping into whatever gave her all her abilities. She didn't just kill it. She blew the damn thing up."

Collin nodded in remembrance.

"Apparently, before she passed out, she managed to also kill the heart, but in doing so all the tentacle wall things shriveled up. Then, just like your typical cliché, Olivia showed up with Oz and Ms. Glenda and half the Council in the nick of time. They got us out and got us here."

"Where's here?"

He didn't mean to interrupt, but he was uncertain if Jacksonville remained in its decaying state after the defeat of the timora. He had a sneaking suspicion that the look they gave him told him all he needed to know.

"Saint Augustine," Mrs. Goodall answered. "They have one of the best medical and educational facilities in the state of Florida."

"Jacksonville is quarantined for God knows how long. Forever, probably. I was released first, but you, Oscar, and Alice stayed here. Alice made her recovery pretty quickly and is back to normal. She's got a few gaps in her memory, conveniently enough, but she's functional. Her, me, and Taylor have been getting interrogated left and right about our participation in the whole matter. We'll all be facing a hearing about it soon, yourself included."

"What?!" Collin bellowed in disbelief. "For stopping that...that...*thing*?"

Overture

"For not informing anyone sooner. Alice is actually under twenty-four-hour surveillance. She's known about it for months, but she kept it to herself for the sake of a school project."

Clark's tongue grew slyly caustic with each word. His stab got him a sharp look from Ms. Glenda, informing him he needed to keep his temper under control. He took a pause to prevent his tone from becoming increasingly bitter.

"Her argument is that there isn't enough literature on timoras to warrant any action on behalf of Article Thirteen, Section Seven of some law on hunting and safety stating something about requiring a notice to the Department of Surveillance of Dark Beasts when suspecting an exceptionally powerful creature in one's area. She holds a pretty fair argument. What doesn't hold is that whatever gave her all her power is allegedly missing, buuut her practically single-handedly taking down a timora has anyone who's heard about the situation in an uproar for her release."

"Do you think she'll get it?"

"Of course, she will!" Ms. Glenda interjected. "We wouldn't let anything happen to her. She's still just a kid, and still considered new to Veil's norms, and yet still managed to prove herself above most fully qualified Veil members."

She had a point there, but it didn't stop Collin's palms from growing clammy with a budding fear. He too knew about the timora and Alice's intentions. Pleading ignorance on the extent of the timora's threat and the policies otherwise known among other spellcasters might not be enough to save him.

Would I be more likely to be given a slap on the wrist or be seen as too great a liability and simply returned to conventional society?

His concern must've etched itself superficially, because Ms. Glenda assured him on the dime she wouldn't allow anything to happen to him either.

"You've barely been with us a season, there's no way they'd disregard your lack of education in our laws."

This failed to sooth his worries.

"When you say only the three of you have been interrogated," he started, quick to try to change his own thoughts, "what about Olivia?"

Clark shifted in his seat uncomfortably. "She's not...*entirely* angry with us for seeing the thing through with Alice," he paused to uncover a delicate way to approach the matter, "but she isn't exactly on speaking terms with anyone other than Ms. Glenda and Oz, nor is she facing any charges."

Collin's affect went from one of worry to incredulous disbelief. If it hadn't been for the hurt in Clark's voice, he might've even indulged in an instantaneous outburst.

"She did do what anyone else *should've* done, I'm sure, and exactly what Alice said she'd do, and raised the alarm. She never conspired with anything or anyone. She saw a threat beyond her control, and she went to people higher up than us."

Collin opened his mouth to respond in a rudely manner, but Clark made it apparent it would be wise to remain silent on the topic in present company.

"We don't want to get you flustered, dear." Mrs. Goodall

stood and leaned over to kiss him endearingly atop his head. "There are more things you best be informed of, but all that matters at the moment is that you're safe, everyone is safe, and you all managed to bring down that demon before it could cause any more harm. Legal implications aside, you're all heroes."

Collin blushed a little at this. A hero was what he wanted to be more than anything. Yet, now that the title was bestowed upon him, it didn't feel earned.

How many more people could we have saved had we acted sooner, or had I acted sooner? How many died just because I let my hormones get the better of me?

Ms. Glenda sent Clark to inform the remaining household Collin would be coming home with them, while she sought out a physician to clear him into her custody. Once his vitals were confirmed healthy and the functionality of his regrown hand were cleared, they trotted out to the lobby where they found a wall of doors lined a dozen long. Glenda Goodall explained how creating a portal in and out of hospitals was restricted to avoid overcrowding, stealing, stealthy patient visits, and the occasional vulnerable murder. The only way to enter was by linking a doorway with a door leading to the lobby, rather than a tear. This way, most hospitals were able to rule in their own plane of existence. There was no main facility to enter or exit generally. The isolation made it easier for practicing healthcare and for patients to be left alone to rest.

Once a doorway was conjured, Collin crossed the

threshold onto the linoleum floor of an unfamiliar front entrance brightened by an almost agitating orange glow. Sustained in midair with a rippling effect was a *Welcome Home* banner. Underneath it were Osmond Pyrrhal, Clark, and Taylor, whom was the only one not overly beaming at him.

"I thought it's only been four days." Collin grinned, concealing a sense of mild hurt at the fact Alice and Olivia weren't present.

"It has," Clark assured," but they've been very tense four days."

"No, no," Mr. Pyrrhal cut in. "Only *in*tense. We've much to celebrate."

For a flicker, Collin could've sworn he'd seen the topmost corners of his caretaker's smile falter. His eyes bore a nervous glaze if nothing else, but he did his best to let Collin know he was still immensely grateful to have another of his boys home and safe.

Ms. Glenda surely did the same. In the later hours of the afternoon, the five of them sat around a significantly smaller, less ornate dining room table to one of her masterpieces of a meal. Similar to his birthday was an over-abundant taco buffet. The amount wasn't as massive as he recalled, but given they were three members short, it still proved too much to complete. She'd apparently prepared glorified dinners for all the survivors of the ordeal.

For the duration, nobody made mention of the three empty seats. Oscar clearly couldn't come home yet, and Alice was least likely to show if she was under another's supervision, but it burned away at Collin to not at least ask about Olivia's whereabouts. Only topics everyone seemed focused on were ones meant to get Collin up to speed, *except* anything related to their fractured family.

According to Oz, the decayed state of the northern and western sides of Jacksonville became a public matter for all of the city's inhabitants. The riotous pandemonium became a nationwide emergency for all departments of Veil's government employees, relative to their line of work or not. Every eye witness, every recording device, and even as many migratory animals as possible were in the process of being rounded up. That last one seemed less possible than finding anyone who's stepped within Jacksonville city limits, given the duration of the infection.

The majority of the masses letting news slip was staved-off in time. Occasionally, a tabloid was printed covering the mess, but anyone with any form of access to digital media saw nothing wrong with Jacksonville. Every now and again a YouTube video tried to manifest onto the Internet, but proactive spellwork managed to erase the files before surfacing.

Around the clock management was necessary to sustain Jacksonville's quarantine. Maintaining an illusionment charm as powerful as the timora's, while simultaneously trying to repair all the infrastructural and environmental damage and citizens' health, was proving to be a tough job even for magic.

"And it doesn't help that this new rabies virus is mutating and spreading at an alarming rate along the west coast, and even some in Canada," Oz informed. "Glenda and I tried to volunteer to help out any way we could, but the Council's forbidden us from stepping outside Saint Augustine until the hearing is said and done with."

A sweltering wave of guilt flooded over Collin with each heart-thundering breath. Why didn't he tell them all about Alice's project? This could've all been avoided, and his two guardians, who've been nothing but kind and caring to him since the first day, wouldn't have to deal with the stress and sadness lingering over their heads.

Jacksonville wouldn't have gotten in such a bad condition either, and Oscar would be here, unscathed, joking around with Clark and annoying Taylor.

He swallowed bitterly and was glad when dinner concluded. Clark and Taylor never attempted to make contact with him that night or the next several nights. He spent the span wallowing in his barren new bedroom. The Council set them up in a temporary home while awaiting the outcome of their hearing.

It took six more days for Oscar to finally be released into their custody. His official reuniting with Clark alleviated some of the tension weighing them, but it panged Collin's heart to see the two side-by-side and accept that he could no longer mentally consider them the almost-twins. Clark's dark hair and Oscar's white contrasted them as clear as night and day.

Overture

Only glimpses of Olivia were made throughout it all. Since his return, Collin saw her a total of four times: once stealthily sneaking back into her bedroom, once entering and exiting the kitchen, and twice leaving their newly appointed home altogether. The one time they met each other's gaze, he saw how the ostentatious flirt he previously knew had died in the black abyss of the timora's dwelling. Bags formed around the red glaze of her dilated eyes. Her hair remained disheveled and her standard artistic makeup was blotchy. She looked at him in passing with anhedonic eyes, but never paused to say anything. Everyone else made their own attempts to reach her, but even Clark and Oscar came to no avail.

Aside from their hospital visits leading up to Oscar's release, Collin's house arrest had been spent practicing his spellwork and studying. His education was placed on hiatus until further notice, so the best he could do was contortion his new hand back into shape and skim through the few educational texts he could find lying around.

He learned that on the Flagler College campus was the Proctor Library, which allegedly held the largest collection of spellbooks, from historical, to practical, to the dark arts, in all the southern states.

"Only if you know how to find them," Clark informed.

However, he wasn't allowed to leave to check any of them out, and he couldn't ask Ms. Glenda or Oz to check any out for him. The whole process led to a magical contract making the books only utilizable by the borrower, for liability purposes.

No matter. By the two-week mark of Collin's return, and after enduring a brief moment of oncoming cabin fever, they were visited by an official member of the Board of Magical Maxims and Regulations to escort them to where all matters would finally be decided. Olivia intended to be at the meeting, but she hung back to arrive separately.

Once inside, the ambiance of the courtroom was nothing like the dungeon he was initiated in. First of all, the copious number of observers in the right and left rafters of the centered podium was overwhelming. Twelve towering pillars lined together but differed in heights of six to ten feet tall for each member of the Council of Spell.

There was no hearth or blue lighting. Instead, the stained glass behind the Council patterned the room in every color of the spectrum. In any other situation, Collin imagined himself experiencing more euphoric emotions. He even considered it a relaxing place to get studying done in.

Oz, Glenda, Taylor, Clark, Oscar, and Collin were guided to the front row on the right-hand side of the room. Every row behind them and every seat in the opposite rafters, save for the front, were packed shoulder-to-shoulder with eager onlookers. Collin couldn't remember seeing this many people crammed together in one area since his last high school pep rally back in May. Moments later, Collin saw Olivia enter and sit opposite of them.

Chatter enveloped them intimidatingly as eyes bore into

their being. His chest cavity shrunk with embarrassment of what people may be saying of their family and in fear of whatever may happen. Oz, however, was shaking hands with a couple men seated behind them and giving thanks to a comment Collin didn't hear.

None of the rest of their party spoke. Eternity fit into the span of ten minutes before the massive double doors slammed shut to announce their hearing was in session. From nowhere, the council members' seats filled, Eleanor Merriweather dead center.

23

The Parting of Ways

"Settle down, everyone," her voice echoed derisively as her eyes glimpsed up from the papers before her to the massive crowd there to support the family that killed the diabolical timora. All chattering ceased. "Today, we are here to discuss the disciplinary actions of the occupants of the Mandarin Division of Jacksonville, Florida. Despite the dire need for such a creature to be disposed of, the calamity left in its absence requires a need for immediate attention. Let's make this quick. Osmond Pyrrhal."

Her summon pierced the air sharply. Oz stood and marched to the podium before the Council. A woman in an official black uniform bearing Veil's double scythed emblem over her left breast handed him a plastic shot glass consumed in a single sip.

"Your name is Osmond Connolly Pyrrhal, is that correct?"

"It is." Oz's telltale boom of a voice reverberated off the chamber walls deeper than ever heard.

"Husband of Glenda Gillian Goodall? Master of the Mandarin Division of Jacksonville, Florida? Guardian of

Overture

Taylor DeWitt, Olivia Koch, Clark McLachlan, Oscar Blair, Alice Pottle, and Collin Quinn, brought here today to question their involvement with a timora that even *now* threatens the safety of our nation and the secrecy of our world?"

"I am."

"And were you aware that, in your city, lurked a beast as archaic as a timora?"

"No."

"Did you suspect your protégés were plotting against something as powerful as a timora?"

"No, Head Councilwoman."

Collin sighed deeply, not realizing he'd been holding his breath. He suspected half the room must've been doing the same given the level of stilled attentiveness disseminating through the air.

"And what were you doing the day you found out what was happening in your own city?" The bitterness in Merriweather's words held an oddly formal posture rather than a humiliating cruelness.

It was tallied that she might've been frustrated by the lack of regulations in law and the local oversight, but at the same time held no contempt for oversight of such an unsuspecting, ancient evil. Collin could also deduce that timoras were a far more serious matter than he ever would've imagined when Alice first informed him. Given the lack of literature about them, he wondered if other spellcasters underestimated the matter as well.

Oz went into his account of his and Glenda's interpretation of Alice's abnormally isolated behavior as being studious ambition. He explained how they always believed she would climb to great heights with how actively she sought to master spell after spell and, better yet, how naturally it came to her already. According to Oz, he and the rest of the household accurately translated her absence as working on her solo field project.

"We wanted to give Alice her privacy, but when we found out she wasn't home, and possibly hadn't been home for a few days, we started a search party to try and find her. When it became obvious she warded herself against locator spells is when we really worried.

"Other divisions agreed to help us, and our own agreed to split into groups. Glenda and I suspected the kids would have a more intimate knowledge of where to find her, so we agreed. Riverside Park was a favorite of hers, so we went there. Once we had no luck there, Glenda and I started looking into other places we've been to with Alice: Town Center, museums, the beaches, some of her favorite coffee shops and bookstores.

"It was hours later before Olivia found us and told us how they'd found Alice and how she'd dragged the boys with her to find a timora."

Merriweather and the rest of the Council proceeded to be inquisitive about Oz's knowledge about timoras, his familiarity with Veil law, whether or not their law was in his and Glenda's curriculum, if he was aware of the punishment for conscious disobedience, and what he considered a fair punishment for their particular circumstance. Before long, the inquiry stretched and bordered on repetitive. When the Council was satisfied with Oz's testimony, they called Glenda to the stand, followed by Clark, Taylor, and then Oscar.

"Would you please state your name for the record?" the handsome Nephilim requested after Oscar had finished taking his sip of what was guessed to be a truth potion.

"Oscar Leobald Blair."

"And what is your status?"

Collin was confused for a moment before Oscar replied "I'm a registered Variant at the Mandarin Division of Jacksonville, Florida."

The onlookers shifted interestedly. Something about the word *Variant* swallowed everyone's attention until the room was left in an uncomfortably still state. Collin pondered why. He knew Variants were special, and a *very* rare breed of people, but everyone's demeanor was borderline unnerving. He also had no idea Variants of Veil needed to register with their government.

"And what ability do you possess?" Merriweather asked.

"I can effortlessly heal myself quickly and help heal others."

"Any limitations?"

"I can treat, but not cure, lethal diseases. My ability won't allow me to alter the body chemistry or physique outside of mending cuts, tears, and fractures, and I can't prolong longevity if one is to die from natural aging."

"However, these abilities proved ineffective against the timora, is that correct?"

"Yes, Head Councilwoman. I was unconscious for the first half of our exposure to the monster. That's when I got my new appearance." He waved a finger at his white hair and eyebrows. The facial hair would've been white as well, but he'd shaved his two-day-old stubble that morning.

"Do you mind if we ask how you came to look how you do now?" a man on the far right of the Council spoke.

"No. The second my friends and I went into its nest we were separated, minus Collin, who we'd left behind at the house, because we didn't want him getting hurt after only *just* getting inducted."

"We recall," said Merriweather. "Continue."

It was Collin's turn to shift, uncomfortably, not interestedly.

"There was an illusion for each of us. Something terrifying. On the surface, it can take on the shape of whatever fears someone the most, but in its own territory, it can make the surroundings themselves take on something terrifying. Its magic was on a whole other level."

An image of black emptiness flooded with blood and bodies crept its way into Collin's memory. A spike of anxiety shorted him a breath as he recounted razor teeth sinking into his flesh and chomping through bone with that sickening *crunch*. Ms. Glenda placed a comforting hand on his arm, startling him back into focus with his current environment.

Overture

"It took me back to school, when I first learned I had my powers, before Veil found me. There was a school shooter harming more than just the kid I'd saved on that occasion. He was killing everyone, and then killing me, and he kept killing me. It just kept grinning and grinning, and then it would let me live long enough to try and save everyone who was screaming and writhing, but my abilities wouldn't work. The students turned into friends and family. I must've watched them die a dozen times. All I could do was accumulate their sprays of blood and…"

Oscar's voice shook and ultimately choked. He cleared his throat a couple times before regaining his composure.

"Sorry, uh, anyways, the shooter was changing with each murder. I was caught in a cycle. It became faceless and rotten. Its skin and flesh were peeling and melting, and underneath it was this mesmerizing, white light. It blinded me and put me in some trance after bleaching my features. Next thing I remember, I'm on the ground with Alice standing over me getting ready to take us out of that pit." Oscar cleared his throat again as a finality.

"Thank you, Mr. Blair," Merriweather said.

She proceeded to make a few more inquiries, but they were muted out from Collin's ears by the resonating impression Oscar left on him. A light snivel to his right came from Ms. Glenda as he noticed her wipe her eyes out of his peripheral vision. Olivia, across from them, appeared in worse condition, and who happened to be called to the podium next.

Her name and position were stated shakily for everyone. She could aptly provide answers to general questions asked of her, but as the conversation skirted gradually to the topic of what happened throughout the day, she became progressively incoherent through the quavering of her voice and the tears that trickled. By the time the Council inquired about what she uniquely experienced under the timora's trickeries, she ceased making any sense entirely.

She was given time to pull herself together, but the efforts proved fruitless. Collin couldn't believe his eyes, that this was the same easygoing and playful girl who stood in his prison cell in a pair of booty shorts and a sassy attitude during his first stay in Mandarin Mansion was almost appalling. Whatever the timora did to her ultimately broke her. Olivia was dismissed. Collin was called to the stand.

With nervous shakes and clammy palms, Collin swallowed the lump in his throat again and again, hoping for a bit of extra air. The accumulation of eyes bearing upon him made his skin crawl. He rose slowly and shuffled his way off the mahogany bleacher.

"You'll be OK. Promise," he heard Oz whisper to him.

At the podium, the routine followed what he was now familiar with. A Veil officer approached him with a plastic shot glass of clear liquid, which he took in a single small gulp. As odorless and colorless as water, it left a strange tingle as it coated Collin's insides.

"Can you state your name for us?" Merriweather asked.

Collin was still choking on his stage fright, but there was

something more at play. He opened his mouth to speak and could feel his tongue and lips moving toward the pronunciation of his name for him. He paused for the briefest second to try to say anything else, any other name, but his mouth became inoperable at the slightest attempt.

"Collin Seguin Quinn."

"And Mr. Quinn, how long have you been an honorary member of Veil?"

"Uh," he shut his eyes to recollect, "Since somewhere in the second week of July, I believe."

Again, his lips and tongues didn't necessarily work against him, but they guided him forcefully to speak the truth.

"And how long have you been granted the official title of Spellcaster?"

His face flushed as he did the math in his head. "Twenty-two days?"

"And of these twenty-two days, how many days was it from your induction into Veil before you disregarded our disclaimer that you were not permitted to partake in any hunts?"

"T-three days. After my eighteenth birthday." The reddening of his face spread to his ears as the heat made his eyes tremble with potential tears. "My friends were in danger," he mumbled.

"I'm sorry?" a few of the council members didn't hear.

"My friends were in danger," Collin spoke more loudly, but still slightly gargled. "I couldn't stay behind."

"It appears they were able to leave *you* behind."

Merriweather's words stung. "So how is it you were able to get back to them?"

"I created a tear."

Mutterings were passed back and forth on each side of the rafters, subtle at first, but grew louder as more people spoke. Still, the Head Councilwoman's voice rang louder than any of them, and blanketed the onlookers with silence.

"Are you aware that creating tears is a spell deemed complex enough to be taught no earlier than as a second-semester Intermediate Spellcaster? Without a swig of our Candor it would be difficult to believe you, so we must ask how you came by this knowledge."

It was safely assumed the swig of Candor she referred to was the clear liquid he recently drank. His knowledge of creating tears to be considered so complex was less easily assumed.

"I found it in Intermediate Spells and followed the instructions," he repeated the same response he gave Taylor that fateful day.

"I see. Mr. Quinn, would you mind telling the Council your involvement in the ridding of the timora, from the start?"

***

All members, except Alice, were tucked away in a recess room, waiting for the Council's final judgement. Collin's heart stood guard for a precipitous plunge back into mundane society, back to his life of college preparations, high school gossip, and his lazy sack of shit of a father. Altering his memory or not, how was he supposed to survive in a world of no spells?

Putting his faith in a world valuing hard work and higher education when the universal motto of "It's not what you know, it's who you know" ruled supreme was enough to drive any over-anxious teen into the arms of heavily-medicated America. No, he needed this. Forget whatever disconnected feeling he felt down in the tunnels. He needed magic. It took the fear of their consequences to reintroduce him to this revelation.

Overwhelming noiselessness informed him everybody else held a similarly disparaging outlook. Olivia continued her vow of isolation, but beneath it all were worrisome side glances. Clark and Oscar were on their feet, pacing in opposite directions, while Oz and Ms. Glenda sat together at the provided conference table holding hands. They offered anyone who shared their glances an encouraging smile, but their efforts were feeble.

Nobody wanted to talk. After all the testimony on the horrors now plaguing each of them, on top of everything else, the constant ticking away of the anticipatory clock only deepened the moroseness. This pursued for a half hour, an hour, and finally two hours before the lock on the door clicked open. A representative informed them it was time to return to the courtroom to hear the decisions made.

The crowd hadn't thinned out the least. Quite the opposite, in fact. While the front row on the left and right side of the rafters remained empty for them, there were now people cluttering the aisles all the way to the doorway. The entire Council was already present and awaiting their return. Once seated, the final words were given.

"Members of the Mandarin Division of Jacksonville, Florida, this is not a trial of guilty and not guilty. This is simply a hearing to observe a potential breach in the policies meant to keep our world concealed and safe from the non-magical community, as well as keep all who reside within this nation protected from harm. On that note, the Council of Spell wishes to give you our gratitude for whichever role you may have played in ridding this world of an utmost evil."

There was a thunderous applause from all around. The entire room erupted in cheers of congratulations and handshakes so unexpected it made Collin uncomfortable and shy to well-wishers.

"Yes, yes, quiet, please!" Merriweather half-shouted. "That being said, given a number of oversights on your behalf, deliberate and undeliberate, and given the state your city now stands in, there are still disciplines to be dealt with.

"First, the seven of you will be assigned your own facility in Saint Augustine. *No one* is to step outside city limits without permission of the Council for the duration of one year. Taylor, Clark, and Oscar, as you are now official graduates, this probationary period will equally apply to you as it does Osmond and Glenda. You are all revoked of your rights as huntsmen and huntresses and will find a new route to contribute to Veil. The exception in this case is Ms. Olivia, who did as was expected by warning others about the circumstances, and who has agreed to reside with her colleagues.

"And Collin Quinn, you have acknowledged our conditions as a new inductee that you were forbidden to partake as a hunter, yet chose to engage anyways, despite being too immature in your repertoire of spellwork and ignorant of our laws."

Collin offered a disheartened nod but said nothing. He wiped his sweaty palms on his pants and saw the disgusting dab of moisture they left behind.

"However, you display resounding promise as a spellcaster with your preternatural abilities, and so we will give you one, *and only one*, warning. Here, we will have a verbal accord showing that you agree that if you break this rule again you will be ostracized from our world and placed back into conventional society. Do you consent?"

"Y-yes, Head Councilwoman, thank you," he said meekly, actively remembering the politeness displayed by his cohort.

"Good, then from this point forward, you will also be enrolled as a student of Flagler's College. Underneath its exterior as a college for a more traditional education, we have our own facilities, including one of the best education systems in the nation. We do not want your skills going to waste. In addition, your exam will be changed to the fifth of January. I suggest you study a little harder moving forward, but we're sure you'll be able to pull it off.

"Finally, in regards to Alice Pottle." Everyone from their household straightened at the mention of her name. No one had seen or heard from Alice in two weeks and were inexpressibly desperate for any scrap of news. "She has made her statements with us privately, and her penances owning up to her negligence in the name of ambition. It appears her testimony and the testimony of all who were involved align: that, with the assistance of a relic now gone, she was able to track the beast herself and see it through to the end, killing not only its body, but its heart, all in the intent of completing her coursework.

"As I'm sure you all know, the completion of this assignment is a regular expectation in order to graduate and must be completed solo. It is the advanced student's decision to spend his or her first six months undergoing the educational curriculum or six months composing an operation without assistance.

"Alice opted to conduct her hunt first, in hopes of defeating the timora before anyone else, showing an active disobedience for our laws, but nonetheless following the expectations of our curriculum. In addition, our literature on timoras *has* proven limited and disgracefully underwhelming to its nature and abilities and, as a consequence to these events, Alice will be providing all the information she has in updating our texts. Furthermore, we will be enrolling Alice into Asterope's Academy in New York, where we will be able to keep a closer eye on her own natural gifts and ensure her probationary requirements are met."

In a rushed manner, Merriweather adjourned the meeting. Feet scraped quickly along the floor as onlookers stood, allowing for Oz and his family to depart first. From the door, to their designated tear, to their new home, everything moved nearly too quickly to comprehend. In the span of roughly ten minutes was their sentencing, a loud buzz of chatter, followed by gapped quiet.

Oz and Glenda went to prepare food together with whatever ingredients they had. They're stock wasn't nearly as elegant as what they had in Jacksonville, but that could be remedied easily with a grocery trip now they knew where they were confined. Olivia was the first to wander away from them without a word.

"Clever," Clark said, coming up beside Collin.

"She'll get the next best bedroom, after the master bedroom, of course," said Oscar.

"Pity."

"If only we cared enough at a time like this."

Collin couldn't help but congratulate their sarcasm with a sigh of weak laughter. The quality of the rooms weren't a priority. With magic, anything was possible, and he figured one way or another Clark's and Oscar's rooms would be rejoined again. The three of them watched Taylor take off as well. His stomps on the beautifully polished wooden floors filled the space between Olivia's as he evaded the entryway stairway and hung a right.

The house truly was beautiful with its historically ornate woodwork along the floorboards, doorways, and even around the marbled fireplace in the living room. It might not have been Mandarin Mansion's garden of zen, but it held an aura capable of soothing his confusions and sadness.

"Pretty sure I saw a second-floor deck, if y'all are interested," Oscar suggested.

They were. There wasn't much to be opposed to after their swift reprimanding by the Council. In passing, they were impressed to see even the second floor had its own fireplace. They found Olivia peeking around the layout and offered her to join them, but she declined.

"You think she'll be okay?" Collin asked.

"I don't think any of us will be okay," Clark answered truthfully.

"And this whole mess isn't over, is it?

"Doubtful."

Oscar found the room with the door leading outside and swung it open. "You heard Alice. The timora was just a stepping stone to something else."

"Not just Alice," Clark replied. "Shaylee might've alluded to something else."

"And no one told the Council about this fact?"

Clark and Oscar both shook their heads.

"Should we have? Didn't we just get in trouble for not confiding in them?"

"Look, if it's something so big and mysterious not even Alice or Olivia told them, then I'm keeping my damn mouth shut and being grateful we got off as easy as we did," Oscar said. Clark agreed, and Collin couldn't think of a counterargument.

Overture

The view from the deck revealed a white privacy fence stooping eight feet tall around the backyard. A floral garden of mainly sunflowers and blue anemones greeted the new occupants of Carrera Street. A garage stood in the back, nearly large enough to be considered a second house on the property.

"What're y'all gonna do then?" Collin asked.

"Sit and wait, I suppose," Clark sighed.

"We can't do any hunting, but Flagler's has a good research facility," Oscar chimed in.

"If all this is only the beginning, I'm sure whatever *this* is will find us in its own time. Might as well be prepared for it when it does."

Their answers were no comfort. In fact, they created a twinge of unease in Collin's mind, but he was able to shove it down with a scan of the peaceful environment. It was nothing like the hustle and bustle of Jacksonville. One could hear the rustle of leaves and the screams and laughter of children in the distance without the sound of a siren polluting their eardrums every half hour or so. A chilly gust of Floridian autumn air gave him goosebumps as he caught a whiff.

He thought back to his family and old friends, and growing up on Losco Road, and suddenly the last few months felt much longer than a year. Nothing felt the same in that moment of finality. He stood on the cusp of a new chapter after the mess they left behind. He almost didn't even recognize himself when revisiting how he'd been and how life was before stepping off that plane. So much had happened, it would be foolish to regret his decisions now. Nearly an hour ago he was terrified of going back to his old life, but he doubted he even could with no Jacksonville to return to.

His mind lulled onto Alice and his nostalgia ran full circle. He missed her more than ever in that moment, but he supposed he couldn't be too surprised. She was an ambitious girl. She'd be happy at that New York school. She deserved it.

If that wasn't proof enough that they were components of Alice's accomplished story what was? According to Oz, it was the most elite school of spellcasters the nation had to offer, and it wasn't like they wouldn't see her again. She could always visit. Maybe. He was unsure of the limitations of her own probation, but at least she'd be receiving a top-tier education.

The sound of skateboard wheels on cobblestone jutted him away from his daydream. There was no denying his new group of friends was already withering. Taylor was back in his personal isolation, Olivia wanted absolutely nothing to do with them, Alice now resided in an entirely different state, and Clark and Oscar, while still attempting their humorous ways, hadn't smiled the same since they'd survived. Their eyes revealed a minor chip of their souls.

Surely Oz and Ms. Glenda would come around, but he supposed they needed to endure their own pain and suffering by the outcome of their adopted children. If his current companions had a quote for their situation, they would've said "The fellowship is breaking."

But it's not over until the person in the skull mask is confronted, and perhaps that was the solution.

If Flagler's was as great a place to conduct research, would the others be willing to help him? The no-longer-almost-twins would at least lend a hand, he hoped, but that also meant he would have to put everything he had into his studies on top of everything else. He was admirable for his rank, but nowhere near ready for his exam in less than two months.

But what a challenge!

A wave of conviction rocked him at the idea of becoming skilled enough to pass and win the adoration of Alice. Besides, the winds of change were perfect for uncovering one's potential, and the Fall breeze was certainly blowing. Collin bid the two a day and reentered the house to claim his bedroom.

Lightning Source UK Ltd.
Milton Keynes UK
UKHW011952200521
384081UK00003B/14/J